Chronicles of Faith: Book One

A Season of Change

Lori Redula

To my Heavenly Father--
the source of my inspiration.

PROLOGUE

United States Military Academy
West Point, New York
June 1860

Lieutenant Eric Ramsey stood marveling at the pristine
blue sky above him as he waited for his trunk to be
loaded onto the back of the carriage that would be taking
him to the train station. He couldn't have asked for a more
perfect day to begin his journey home, doubly special for it
also marked his graduation from the United States Military
Academy.

The twenty-one-year old still got chills every time he
thought back to the ceremony that had taken place earlier
that morning. He had been longing for career in the military
ever since he could remember and now it was finally his to
claim.

His only regret was that his family had been unable to
attend. They'd wanted to come, his pa had assured him in a
recent letter from home, but "money is tight and train tickets
aren't cheap". Eric understood. He couldn't recall a time
growing up when money *hadn't* been tight. As a country
doctor, his father was paid "in kind" for his services more
often than cash money, and with five other children to clothe
and feed besides himself, there never seemed to be enough.

Eric refocused his attention on the carriage as the driver finished with the loading. "All set here, Lieutenant."

"Lieutenant." The young man smiled to himself as he stepped on board. It was going to take some time to get use to hearing himself referred to as such.

As soon as he was settled, Eric signaled the driver by rapping on the inside of the door. The carriage pulled away slowly, allowing him time for one final glimpse of the imposing looking structure where he had spent the last four years of his life. He had arrived here as green as the unripened wheat fields that dotted the countryside of his native Pennsylvania, but he was leaving as an officer in the United States Army. One chapter in his life complete; another just beginning.

Eric slid to his knees on floor of the carriage, turning to bow his head against the edge of the seat. Only two words seemed anywhere near adequate enough to express to his Heavenly Father the content of his heart at that moment. "Thank you."

CHAPTER ONE

SONS AND DAUGHTERS

Baxter, Pennsylvania

"Stephen Michael Ramsey, you come back here with my ribbon!"

Three-year-old Stephen giggled as he ran through the upstairs hallway of the Ramsey home, his seven-year-old sister, Kaitlin, in close pursuit behind him.

"I mean it, Stephen!" she squawked, fighting to keep the unbound tresses of her golden-brown hair at bay. "Give it back!"

Stephen squealed and ran even faster, tightening his grip more possessively around the ribbon.

"If you don't give it back before I count to three, I'm going to tell Papa on you!"

Stephen ignored his sister's threat and kept running.

Kaitlin began her count. "One…two…!"

"What is all the ruckus up here?"

Stephen skidded to a stop as his father appeared at the top of the stairs, blocking his only means of escape.

Kaitlin sailed right on past him, eager to plead her case. "He took my ribbon, Papa!" she clamored, glaring back at her brother. "And now he won't give it back!"

Alec Ramsey locked eyes with his youngest son. "Is that true, Stephen?"

9

Stephen squirmed beneath his father's gaze, like Adam in the Garden of Eden caught holding the forbidden fruit. "Yes, Papa," he confessed.

"I told you he took it!" Kaitlin screeched. Her glare turned to a sneer as she leveled her gaze back on her brother. "You're gonna get it now!"

"Kaitlin, that's quite enough," Alec scolded.

"But he—"

"Kaitlin," he said more sternly.

Kaitlin silenced herself by chomping down on her bottom lip.

Alec turned his attention back to Stephen. "Give her back the ribbon, son," he instructed, giving the youngster's backside a gentle swat of encouragement.

Stephen reluctantly did as he was asked. "I'm sorry."

"You better be," Kaitlin lashed right back. "'Cause if I ever catch you taking anything of mine again—"

Alec cleared his throat, bringing a quick halt to her chiding remarks. "Hadn't you better finish getting ready? We don't want to be late to meet your brother's train."

"I'll hurry, Papa," she promised, dashing back down the hall to her room.

"And as for you, young man…." Alec scooped Stephen up into his arms. "Why did you take your sister's ribbon in the first place?"

"For my frog," he stated plainly.

Alec tried not to laugh as he envisioned Stephen's pet bullfrog with Kaitlin's hair ribbon tied around its neck. "Son, what does your frog need with a ribbon?"

"I want him to look pretty for the contest."

"Of course." Alec smacked the palm of his hand against his forehead. "The frog jumping contest at the Founder's Day picnic today. How could I have forgotten something as important as that?"

Stephen patted him on the shoulder. "That's okay, Papa."

"But it wasn't okay for you to take your sister's ribbon without asking, was it?"

Stephen ducked his head. "No, Papa."

"I'll tell you what." Alec lowered him back to the floor. "Why don't you go downstairs and take a peek in your mama's sewing basket. I bet you can find something in there for your frog that's even better than Kaitlin's ribbon."

Stephen's long lashed brown eyes blinked expectantly. "Do you really think so, Papa?"

"I'm sure of it. Now you run along while I find your brother, Colin."

"Okay, Papa." Stephen sped off down the stairs, nearly colliding with his eleven-year-old brother, Nathan.

Alec took note of the makeshift net that was slung over the older boys' shoulder as he trudged his way up the last few steps. "Did you have any luck?" he asked needlessly. The aroma of frog permeated the young mans' clothing like a cheap smelling perfume.

"I only caught two," Nathan replied dejectedly, "and neither of them can jump very high. I might as well not even enter that contest today. I'll never win."

"With an attitude like that you can count on it."

"But I want to win so bad, Pa."

"Haven't your mother and I always taught you that as long as you do your best you're always a winner?"

"Yes, sir."

"Then I'll expect you to do no less. Whether you win or not isn't what's important."

"It is when you've got ten cents bet on it."

"What was that?"

"Nothing, Pa," Nathan answered hurriedly. "I just came up to ask you if my friend David can come to the picnic with us after we pick up Eric. He's staying with his aunt while his folks are out of town and she doesn't want to come. She already said it was all right."

"Well, I don't see why we can't make David an honorary member of the Ramsey clan for one day."

Nathan pondered his father's offer. "I don't think there's any need for that. He just wants to come to the picnic with us."

Alec smiled, giving the young man's head of dark brown hair a tousle. "You tell him he's more than welcome to join us."

"Thanks, Pa."

"And, Nate?"

Nathan detected an unwelcome change in his father's tone. The smile was gone from his face, as well. "Yes, Pa?"

"If I see or so much as hear of any money changing hands after that contest this afternoon, you can expect extra chores for the next two months. Is that understood?"

"Yes, sir."

"Now go get cleaned up."

Nathan had taken only a few steps when the sound of barking stopped him cold in his tracks. "My frogs!" he wailed.

"What's the matter?" Alec asked as he went flying back towards the stairs.

"I left them on the back porch and the Franklin's dog is out!"

"Hey, wait up a second! Do you happen to know where your brother Colin is?"

Nathan pointed to the door at the top of the stairs. "He's up there!"

Alec turned to the door Nathan had indicated. "The attic?"

* * * * *

"Hold still, frog, or I'll bop you!"

Kathleen Ramsey stood watching with a baffled look on her face as her youngest son struggled to tie a scrap of material around the neck of his croaking bullfrog. She had thought she'd seen everything in her twenty plus years of raising children, but every so often one of them did something to cause her to think otherwise. This was one of those times. "Stephen Michael, you keep a tight hold on that creature," she warned. "I don't want to find it loose in the house again." Just the mention of yesterday's incident sent a squeamish shudder up her spine. "I mean it, Stephen," she warned again.

"I will, Mama," he promised.

Satisfied that she had gotten her point across, Kathleen retook her seat on the sofa beneath the living room window and resumed work on her knitting. It wasn't long, though, before her attention wandered back to the strange scene across the room. "Just where did you get such an idea, anyway?" she asked the youngster.

Stephen smiled up at her from his perch on her overturned sewing basket. "From, Papa!" he declared proudly.

Kathleen frowned. "I should have known. Alec James Ramsey, you had better have a good explanation for this."

Kathleen's frown didn't remain a frown for long. After all the years they'd been married, she still found it impossible to stay mad at him. She'd certainly had cause to often enough, but it was proving more and more difficult with each passing year.

Twenty-three years, to be exact, Kathleen thought to herself. It was hard to believe they had been together that long. She remembered their first meeting as if it had been yesterday....

When Kathleen Jordan fled her home in Charleston, South Carolina at the age of fourteen and headed north, she had no way of knowing how closely entwined her life would become with that of a handsome, young medical student from Harvard named Alec Ramsey. They met in the summer of 1837 at a picnic sponsored by the local Methodist church in Cambridge, Massachusetts. For Kathleen it had been love at first sight. Just a few moments in the presence of the tall, dark-haired Scotsman and she was convinced that she would one day be Mrs. Alec Ramsey. Fortunately for her, Alec needed little convincing of this fact himself. They were married just three weeks later, at which time they settled into a boardinghouse in downtown Cambridge while Alec continued his studies at Harvard. Eighteen months later, they celebrated the birth of their first child, Eric Lee.

Following Alec's graduation from medical school in 1840, he offered his services to the army with the commissioned rank of captain. When war broke out with Mexico in 1846, his skills as a surgeon were sorely put to the test on the front lines of battle, causing him to have second thoughts about his chosen field of practice. As the war drew to a close in 1848, Alec resigned his commission and moved Kathleen and Eric, along with new additions Colin and Kirsten, to Baxter, Pennsylvania, where he set up a medical practice out of their home. It was here, in that very same house, that three more additions to the Ramsey clan had made their entrances into the world: sons Nathan and Stephen, and daughter Kaitlin. From all appearances, theirs was a union that many might have thought doomed from the start. She was the daughter of a prominent politician; he the son of a Scottish shepherd. She was a Baptist; he a Methodist. She from the South; he from the North. Yet throughout the years, they had discovered their differences to often be their greatest strengths. It hadn't always been an easy life, but Kathleen had never once regretted her decision to become Alec's wife.

An unexpected knock at the front door forced Kathleen to set her memories aside. She glanced up just as fourteen-year-old Kirsten entered the foyer area adjoining the living room and positioned herself at the foot of the stairs in direct line with the door. Kathleen stifled a chuckle as she rose to perform her motherly duty, knowing full well that Kirsten had no intention of answering the door herself.

As she crossed from the living room into the foyer, she cast her eldest daughter a knowing smile. "I wonder who that could be?"

"Oh, Mama," Kirsten chided, her cheeks blushing to match the color of her dress. "You know very well who it is." The young woman's hands flew quickly up to the bow that was securing her long brown tresses and then back down to her dress. "Do I look all right?" she asked uncertainly.

"You look as lovely as always, sweetheart." Kathleen continued on to the door where she stood poised with her hand on the knob far longer than was necessary. She could feel her daughter's impatience mounting with each second that she delayed its opening.

"Mama!" Kirsten finally urged, stamping her foot in a most unladylike fashion on the hardwood floor. "Open the door!"

"Is there someone out here?" Kathleen swung the door open to reveal a very prim and proper looking young gentleman waiting on the porch. "Well, good afternoon, Jesse," she exclaimed in mock surprise. "What a pleasure to see you."

Seventeen-year-old Jesse Cameron swept off the cap that was nestled on his head, unleashing a well-kept mop of curly brown hair. "Good afternoon, Mrs. Ramsey," he said nervously, wringing the brim of his cap. "Is Kirsten ready?"

"Yes, I do believe she is." Kathleen turned to summon her daughter. "Kirs—"

Kirsten popped out from behind her mother, eagerly taking her appointed place beside her at the door. "Hello, Jesse," she said quietly.

"Hi," he replied, smiling shyly in return.

A long moment of silence ensued as the smitten young couple stood gazing tenderly at one another, brown eyes into brown.

"So, Jesse," Kathleen finally said. "What are your plans for this afternoon?"

"Huh?" he uttered, transferring his gaze from daughter to mother.

"Your plans?" Kathleen prompted him. "With my daughter?"

"Oh." Jesse shuffled his feet as he collected his response. "I'm going to take Kirsten over to see the new colt at the Hanson farm before we go to the station to meet Eric. And then on to the Founder's Day picnic, of course."

Kathleen nodded. "That sounds just fine. You two enjoy yourselves."

"Thank you, ma'am." Jesse offered Kirsten his hand. "Shall we?"

Kirsten smiled back at her mother as she clung closely to Jesse's side. "Good-bye, Mama."

"Good-bye, sweetheart."

As Kathleen watched the young couple walk hand-in-hand down the porch steps, she realized that saying "good-bye" to her daughter might soon take on a whole new meaning. She was more than prepared for that to happen, but had just always assumed that Eric, being the eldest, would be the first to marry. Life at West Point, however, had left him little time for proper courting. But she intended to remedy that while he was home on leave. And she knew of just the young woman who would be more than willing to assist her in her efforts.

"Yes," Kathleen said with a satisfied smile. "Alicia Randall will do quite nicely."

* * * * *

Alec reached the top of the attic staircase and stood for a moment looking about him. The space was cluttered with old boxes and crates, most of which had remained unused since their move to Baxter some twelve years earlier. "I'd say it's about time we clean this place out," he suggested. "What do you think?" His question had been directed toward his sixteen-year-old son, Colin. The young man was sitting on a crate in front of one of the small dormer windows that overlooked the backside of the house.

"I don't care," Colin replied with a noncommittal shrug.

Alec was not in a position to see the look of dejection in his son's eyes but he could hear it plainly enough in his voice.

He had first noticed a change in Colin's behavior earlier that morning at breakfast. The young man had appeared distant and sullen, not at all his usual jovial self. Then after hardly touching his food, he had up and disappeared without a trace. Alec couldn't be absolutely sure without asking him straight out, but he had a pretty good notion of what was troubling him and why.

Several weeks ago Colin had received word that he failed to pass the entrance exam to get into West Point. He had been hoping to follow in the footsteps of his older brother, so when he reacted to the news as if he didn't care, Alec had begun to suspect that he wasn't being completely honest about his feelings. His behavior today confirmed those suspicions.

Alec dragged another crate over to the window and sat down next to him. "What are you watching?" he asked, noting how intently Colin was looking out the window.

"Nothing," Colin said with another shrug.

"Well, something's got your attention." Alec followed Colin's gaze out the window, chuckling when he saw the tug-of war that Nathan was engaged in to rescue one of his frogs from the mouth of the neighbor's St. Bernard. "Looks like you brother has quite a fight on his hands. Though I dare say that frog's not going to be in any condition to enter any contest today even if Nathan does get it back."

Colin turned his back on the window, losing interest now that he was no longer the only spectator.

"We'll be leaving soon to go pick up Eric," Alec said after a lengthy pause, watching closely to see how Colin would react.

The young man glanced up at his father then quickly slid his gaze back to the floor. "I don't feel much like going, Pa."

Alec pressed the back of his hand to Colin's forehead, checking for the presence of a fever. "You're not ill, are you?" he asked needlessly, aware that Colin's reasons for wanting to avoid Eric's homecoming were not of a physical nature.

"No, sir," he replied with a wag of his head. "I just don't feel like going, is all."

"I'm sure that Eric will be disappointed if you don't. I know he's really looking forward to seeing you."

Colin couldn't say the same. Seeing Eric now would only be a painful reminder of his own failure. "Do I have to go, Pa?"

Colin obviously wasn't ready to talk about the exam and Alec didn't see any sense in adding further to his discomfort. He was hurting enough as it was. "Not if you really don't want to."

The tension in Colin's face drained away almost immediately. "Thanks, Pa."

"Sure." Alec rose from the crate. "You know where we'll be if you need anything…or if you change your mind about going," he tossed in.

Colin nodded that he understood.

Alec slipped back down the stairs, leaving Colin alone with his thoughts. He hoped that he had done the right thing by not insisting that he accompany them today. Eric would understand. He was sure of that. But Kathleen was another matter entirely. How was he going to explain it to her?

"Hey, handsome."

Alec started as Kathleen came up beside him in the hallway. "Did you find—" Before she could utter another word, Alec grabbed her hand and steered her back down the stairs. Kathleen looked at him curiously. "What's wrong?"

"Nothing."

"Nothing? You're acting as if you don't want me upstairs."

Alec offered no response to her claims, causing Kathleen's suspicions to rise. "Well, would you at least tell me if you found Colin?" she implored him.

"He's in the attic," Alec replied hesitantly.

"The attic?" Kathleen strained against the hand that was holding hers, looking back over her shoulder at the attic door. "What is he doing up there?"

"Sulking." Alec released her hand, moving his arm up around her waist. "He doesn't want to go with us today to meet Eric."

Kathleen's attention came forward again. "Why on earth not?"

"He's still smarting over not getting into West Point."

"Oh, for goodness sakes. That was weeks ago. It's not the end of the world."

"To a sixteen-year-old boy that's exactly what it feels like."

"Well, I certainly hope you set him straight," Kathleen informed him, making her feelings about the matter quite clear. "This is a very special day for Eric and I don't want anything to spoil it."

Alec turned her around to face him as they reached the bottom of the stairs, his hands sliding up to rest on her shoulders. "I told him he didn't have to go."

Kathleen's eyes widened in disbelief. "Whatever possessed you to tell him that?"

"We can't force him to go if he doesn't want to, Kathleen."

"We most certainly can," she insisted. "And he will go. I'll see to that."

Alec tightened his grip on her shoulders as she made a move toward the stairs. "Alec, let go of me."

"No. I already told him that he didn't have to go. If he changes his mind it will be of his own choosing."

"But, Alec—" Alec pressed a finger to her lips, halting any further protests. Kathleen's shoulders slumped beneath his grasp. "Eric is going to be so disappointed."

Alec cupped her chin in his hand, drawing her gaze up level with his. "Eric is going to be so excited to be home that he probably won't even notice whether Colin is there or not. It's you who's disappointed."

Kathleen tried to restrain the smile that she felt coming on but failed miserably in her attempt. She knew he was right. "How come you know me so well?" she demanded, pretending to be annoyed.

"After twenty-three years of marriage there aren't many secrets left."

"Oh, you'd be surprised how many more I have," she told him with a teasing smile. "But you're going to have to stay married to me for another twenty-three years to find them all out."

Alec leaned down and pressed a kiss to her lips. "It will be my pleasure."

"Mama, look!" Stephen proudly held up his frog for her approval. "Isn't he pretty?"

"Oh, Stephen!" Kathleen gasped, backing up against the staircase banister. "Get that thing away from me!"

Alec bit back a chuckle. "You really don't like frogs, do you?"

"No, I don't like frogs!" she snapped back. "I don't know what ever possessed me to let Nathan catch that horrid creature for him in the first place. It's smelly and slimy and—" Kathleen closed her eyes with a shudder. "Oh, Stephen, please!"

Alec quickly ushered Stephen back into the living room. "He looks real fine, son. But I think you best keep him away from your mama for awhile."

"Okay, Papa."

Alec returned to Kathleen's side. "How about some fresh air?" he suggested. "We should be leaving for the station now anyway."

"I think that would be a good idea."

"I'll go round up the kids. Where's Kirsten?" Alec glanced at the door that led into his study. "Is she reading again?" Kirsten had expressed an interest in pursuing a career in medicine almost from the time she could walk and often spent her spare time pouring over the musty, yellowed pages of his old medical texts. Alec couldn't have been prouder. "Is she?" he asked again.

Kathleen smiled, recalling the last time she had seen their daughter. "Not anymore, she's not."

"What's that supposed to mean?"

"Jesse came by a few minutes ago and took her to—"

"Jesse?" Alec said with a hard edge to his voice. "Again? That's the third time this week. Doesn't he ever go fishing or anything?"

"He's sure enough caught our daughter."

"Well, let him go fishing for someone else's daughter," Alec grumbled. "How's she supposed to get any studying done with him always coming around here dragging her off somewhere?"

"Now, Alec, surely you can remember what it was like when we were courting."

"Courting," he scoffed. "She's only fourteen."

"She'll be fifteen in two months," Kathleen reminded him, "and I wasn't any older than her when we met."

"Well, that's different."

"How is it different?"

"Because she's my daughter."

21

"Well, she's my daughter, too, and I happen to like the young man she's been keeping company with." Kathleen slid her hands up behind his head, intertwining her fingers in the thick, dark brown locks at the nape of his neck. "You know, Mr. Ramsey," she said matter-of-factly, "I wouldn't be at all surprised if young Jesse Cameron comes calling on you one of these afternoons."

"Well, I hope he won't be too disappointed when he finds out that I'm already married."

Kathleen chuckled, giving him a sound whack across the chest. "Alec Ramsey, you are impossible!"

"Frog, you come back here!"

Kathleen gaped in horror as Stephen went scrambling by on all fours in pursuit of his errant frog. "Stephen, you catch that thing or the next place it's going to be hopping is into a frying pan for supper!"

"Pa!" Nathan came bursting through the front door, gasping to catch his breath. His clothes were muddied and torn from his scuffle with the neighbor's dog.

"Nathan Thomas, just look at you!" Kathleen shrieked. "You're filthy!"

"Pa, it's the train!" Nathan blurted.

"Easy, son, slow down. What about the train?"

"It's coming!"

"Are you sure?"

Nathan bobbed his head. "I heard the whistle. Couldn't have been more than a few miles off."

"Okay, Ramsey's, let's get a move on," Alec ordered. "Your brother's train is going to be early."

"Nathan, quick!" Kathleen implored him. "Run upstairs and change."

"There's no time for that now, Kathleen."

"But, Alec, he can't go looking like that."

"He's going to have to. He can come back and change before we go on to the picnic."

"Frog, where are you!" Stephen bellowed.

"Stephen, me boy, let's go!" Alec walked into the living room and pulled him out from behind the sofa.

"No, Papa!" he protested, squirming and kicking as he was flung up over his father's shoulder. "Put me down! I gotta find my frog! Mama wants to eat him!"

"No time for that now, son. Your big brother's train is coming." Alec smiled at Kathleen as he offered her his arm at the door. "Shall we go get our son, Mrs. Ramsey?"

CHAPTER TWO

HOMECOMING

"**N**ext stop, Baxter!"
The booming voice of the conductor rumbled down the aisle like a clap of thunder, startling Eric from a sound sleep. After taking a few moments to gather his senses, he turned to gaze out the window next to him. The familiar sights of rolling hills and farmlands caused a warm sensation to steal all through him. He was finally home.

Eric's heart beat a little faster as his thoughts turned to the upcoming reunion with his family. He had only seen them once in the past four years, eighteen months ago at Christmas. His fondest memory of that visit had been meeting his brother, Stephen, for the very first time. Eric still felt bad about not having been there when he was born, but no worse than he did about all of the other special moments he had missed in the lives of his siblings. First days of school, loose teeth, graduations.... If he were to enumerate them all, the list would be endless.

A long, piercing whistle blast echoed through the Pennsylvania countryside as the giant steam-powered leviathan began swallowing up the final few miles of track on its' approach into Baxter. It was a sound that up until several months ago had been unfamiliar to the inhabitants of these parts. Before then, travelers had been forced to begin and end their journeys from the capital city of Harrisburg ten miles to the north. They never seemed to mind this inconvenience until a representative with the Baltimore and Ohio Railroad came to town with a proposed plan to run a line straight through the heart of Baxter. Suddenly, its' citizens couldn't imagine how they had ever managed so long without it. Just to think of all the time and money they would save in being able to ship their crops off to market not more than a stone's throw from where they had been harvested. It was an opportunity too good to pass up.

But not everyone had seen the proposal in such a favorable light. Eric recalled the letter that his father had sent him detailing just such concerns. "Many folks," he'd written, "fear that the train's coming will bring all sorts of 'undesirables' into our midst, forever changing the face of the town." He tended to agree, he went on to admit, but he was also excited about the impact that the train would have on his practice, allowing him to gain access to valuable medical literature and supplies that much faster.

Eric had yet to form an opinion one-way or the other. But considering the alternative would have been a long, dusty stage ride from Harrisburg, he was glad that the railroad had come to Baxter.

The train broke out from beneath a canopy of trees, giving Eric his first glimpse of the new station house up ahead. The small brick structure had been erected on a wooden platform that extended out from the front of the building to within a few feet of the tracks. Even from a distance, Eric was able to pick out several familiar faces from among the crowd of onlookers that had gathered to welcome the incoming train. But to his dismay, not one of them belonged to a member of his family. Was it possible they had forgotten he would be arriving today? Eric decided to not even entertain such a thought. He was sure there was a logical explanation for their absence.

After grabbing his satchel off the seat beside him, he made his way down the aisle to the exit. As he stepped out onto the platform, his gaze came to rest upon the couple that was seated on a bench outside the station house door. The young woman rose at the sight of him, beaming a smile in his direction. "Eric!" she cried, flapping her arms wildly about as if she were trying to take flight.

Eric's first thought was that she had him confused with someone else. He neither recognized her or her companion. Or did he?

Eric squinted, bringing the woman's face into clearer focus. "Kirsten?" he said in disbelief.

Eric tossed his bag down as Kirsten rushed up and threw herself into his arms. "Look at you!" he exclaimed. "You're all grown up!" Eric released her back to her feet. "I almost didn't recognize you."

"It's only been eighteen months," Kirsten reminded him.

"But what an eighteen months." Eric's gaze traveled from her head down to her feet and then back again. "Wow!"

"Oh, Eric, really," Kirsten chided him.

"Yes, really. But if you don't believe me...." Eric inclined his head towards Jesse. "Why not ask the young gentleman there? You know, Kirsten, it really isn't polite to keep a man waiting."

Kirsten turned with a gasp to find Jesse still sitting on the bench. She quickly rushed back to get him, ignoring the smirk on her brother's face as they rejoined him, hand-in-hand. "Eric, I'd like for you to meet Jesse Cameron...a friend," she added hesitantly.

Jesse released his right hand from Kirsten's and extended it to Eric. "It's a pleasure to finally meet you. Kirsten has been talking about little else since we heard you were coming home."

Eric exchanged an amused look with his sister as he pumped Jesse's hand. "Well, that's funny. Kirsten hasn't mentioned a thing about you."

"Eric, please," Kirsten implored him. "You're embarrassing me."

"Then maybe next time you won't keep your *friends* such a secret." Eric shifted his gaze back to Jesse. "Are you fairly new to the area, Jesse?"

"My father and I moved here from Gettysburg three months ago."

"Jesse's father bought the smithy from Mr. Patterson," Kirsten told him.

Eric nodded. "Well, I hope you've found our town to your liking."

Jesse glanced at Kirsten, his lips quivering with the beginnings of a smile. "Yes, very much."

Eric grinned. "I guess that was a stupid question, wasn't it?"

Kirsten glared back at him, gritting her teeth. "Eric."

"So...." Eric cleared his throat, looking about him. "Where's everybody else?" he wondered.

"Your train got in a little early," Kirsten explained. "But I'm sure they're on their way."

"Excuse me. Could you tell me where I can find Crowley's General Store?"

Eric turned toward the voice behind him to find himself gazing at the most beautiful woman he had ever seen. She was tall and willowy, with a crown of raven-black hair that cascaded down into a gathering of soft curls about her shoulders. But her eyes were by far her most arresting feature. They were a stunning shade of violet, quite unlike anything that Eric had ever seen before. *A man could get lost in those eyes.*

"If you don't know," the woman continued politely, "then perhaps you could direct me to someone who does."

Eric blinked, wresting himself free from her gaze. "Did you say Crowley's?"

"Yes. I'm supposed to meet my—" The woman left the remainder of her thought suspended as her lips blossomed into a smile. "Uncle Josiah!"

"Uncle?" Eric watched as the woman swept past him into the arms of Josiah Crowley, the elderly proprietor of Baxter's general store.

"That must be Amber Lloyd," Kirsten said from behind Eric. "I'd forgotten that she was arriving today."

Eric spun around to face his sister. "You know her?"

"Only from what Mr. Crowley has told us. She's his niece, from Boston. She's going to be taking over for Mrs. Pritchard as Baxter's new school teacher this fall." Kirsten nudged him in the side. "Kind of pretty, don't you think? And unmarried from what I hear."

Eric responded to Kirsten's observation with a shrug of indifference. "She's all right, I guess."

Kirsten smiled to herself. Eric wasn't fooling anybody, least of all her. "Why don't you go over and introduce yourself?" she suggested. "It would be the gentlemanly thing to do, seeing as how she's new in town and all."

Eric met his sister's baiting smile with a look of defiance. He knew a dare when he heard one. "Maybe I'll just do that."

"Well, good," Kirsten retorted.

Eric turned before he lost his nerve and walked over to where Amber and her uncle stood talking. "Mr. Crowley?"

"Eric!" The elderly man's eyes brightened at the sight of him. "Welcome home to you, young man. How are you?"

"Fine, sir." Eric could feel Amber's gaze on him but didn't turn to acknowledge her presence. It wouldn't do to appear too anxious. "How's business?"

"Couldn't be better. You'll have to come by the store as soon as you get settled. The missus would love to see you."

"I'll do that."

Amber cleared her throat, inviting her uncle's attention back on her. "Oh, goodness, where are my manners?" he scolded himself. "Eric, this is my niece, Amber Lloyd. Amber, this is Eric Ramsey. He's just returned to us from West Point."

"The military academy?" Amber's eyes widened, making them appear even more attractive. "How exciting."

"You'll be attending the picnic this afternoon, won't you, Eric?" Josiah asked him.

Eric tore his gaze away from Amber. "The picnic, sir?"

"The Founder's Day picnic. I thought it would be a good chance for Amber to get to know some of the other young people in town. Perhaps you could act as her escort."

The proposal took Eric completely by surprise but he wasn't about to refuse. It would be the perfect opportunity to get to know Amber better. "I would be honored to, sir. With Miss Lloyd's permission, of course."

"I'd like that," she answered readily.

"Good." Josiah smiled, seemingly quite pleased with the arrangement. "We'll see you at the picnic then, Eric?"

"I'll be there."

Kirsten rushed to Eric's side as soon as Mr. Crowley and his niece were well out of hearing. "Well?" she pried.

"Well, what?"

"What did you say to her?"

"That, little sister, is none of your affair."

Kirsten grinned at him smugly. "I knew you liked her."

"There he is!"

"Where?"

"Right there!"

Eric chuckled as Nathan and Kaitlin came barreling towards him across the platform. "You two better slow down before someone gets—" The air left Eric's lungs in a rush as he went sprawling onto his back with Nathan atop him. "Hurt," he groaned.

"Oops." Nathan quickly scrambled back to his feet. "Sorry about that, Eric."

"Are you hurt bad?" Kaitlin asked, peering down at him with concern.

"If I were hurt bad, do you think I would be able to do this?" Kaitlin burst out giggling as Eric pulled her down beside him and began smothering her with kisses. "Don't go anywhere, Nate. You're next."

"No, way," Nathan balked, taking a step backwards. "Not me."

Eric sat up, cradling Kaitlin on his lap. "What happened to you, anyway?" he asked, taking note of his brother's disheveled appearance.

Nathan poked a finger through one of the many holes in his shirtsleeve. "I kind of got into a fight with the Franklin's dog."

Eric wrinkled up his nose as he caught a whiff of Nathan's clothing. "That's not all you got into. I'm surprised Ma let you out of the house smelling like that."

Kathleen stepped up behind him. "Well, if your train had gotten in when it was supposed to, he would have had plenty of time to change."

"Ma." Eric rose quickly and gathered her into his arms. "Oh, Ma, I have missed you."

Kathleen stepped back with a gasp as her hands dropped down to his waist. "Alec, look! He's practically skin and bones!" Eric winced as she poked him repeatedly in the stomach. "I can almost go right through to the other side."

"Kathleen, let the boy alone before you crack a rib. He looks the picture of health to me." Alec rescued Eric from his mother's probing fingers and enfolded him in a warm embrace. "It's good to have you home, son. How long can you stay?"

"I have three months leave. And you'll never guess. I've been assigned to staff headquarters at the engineering department in Washington."

"Is that safe?" Kathleen asked naively.

"Couldn't be safer, Kathleen," Alec assured her. He then fired a grin in Eric's direction. "Unless he cuts himself on all that paper he's going to be pushing. Congratulations, son. We're very proud of you."

"Thanks, Pa." Eric felt something brush against his leg and looked down to find Stephen staring up at him. "Well, who do we have here?" Eric knelt down in front of him. "This couldn't be my little brother Stephen, could it? Why, the last time I saw you— "

Stephen backed up and latched himself onto Alec's leg, his eyes registering his alarm.

"It's okay, son," Alec assured him. "This is your big brother, Eric. There's no need to be afraid."

Stephen tightened his grasp as Alec tried to pry him loose. "No, Papa, no!"

Alec looked to Eric with an apologetic shrug. "I guess he doesn't remember you."

"I have an idea," Eric whispered. He proceeded to reach into his satchel and take out a miniature replica of a cannon. "What am I going to do now?" he said with a dramatic sigh, holding the toy up where Stephen would be sure to see it. "I was going to give this to my little brother, Stephen, but he doesn't seem to be here. Oh, well...." He started to put the toy back into his bag, aware that Stephen's big brown eyes were following his every move.

"Here I am!" the youngster announced suddenly.

Eric clapped a hand to his cheek. "Stephen! Where did you come from?"

"Behind Papa!"

"Well, I am so glad you're here." Eric held the cannon out to him. "Would you like to have this?"

Stephen eagerly grabbed it out of his hand. "Thanks!"

"You're welcome."

Nathan gave Eric's bag a nudge with his foot. "You wouldn't happen to have anything in there for me, would you, Eric?"

"As a matter of fact, I brought something for everyone. But first...." Eric paused when he realized that Colin was absent from the gathering. "Didn't Colin come with you? I wanted to congratulate him on getting into West Point."

"Well, he, uh...." Alec hesitated, unsure what to tell him.

"He's in the attic," Nathan blurted. "Don't you remember, Pa?"

Eric stared at him. "He's where?"

Alec chuckled, clamping a hand over Nathan's mouth before he could repeat himself. "What your brother meant was—"

"There's Colin!"

All eyes turned in the direction that Kaitlin was pointing.

"You're tardy, Cadet Ramsey," Eric teased him. "That'll be ten demerits."

Colin slowed his already snail-like pace, grappling to make sense of what Eric was saying. *Cadet? But doesn't he know that I....*" Colin turned questioning eyes on his father. *Didn't you tell him?*

"I'm real proud of you, Col."

Colin snapped his attention back to Eric. "What?"

"I said, I'm proud of you."

"Oh." Colin averted his gaze, painfully aware of how unworthy he was of such praise. "Thanks," he uttered quietly.

"Well, you don't have to be so humble about it. It's not everyday you get accepted into West Point."

Alec cleared his throat. "Eric, if you're not too tired from your trip, we were all about to head over to the church for the Founder's Day picnic."

The mention of the picnic brought a welcome image of Amber to mind. "That sounds like fun. I'm really looking forward to seeing everyone again."

"Alicia Randall sure is looking forward to seeing you," Nathan said with a smirk. "You should have seen her in church last Sunday when Reverend Thompson announced that you were coming home. She just about—"

"That will be quite enough, Nathan," Alec warned him. "Now is not the time or the place to be discussing such matters."

"But all I was going to say was—"

Nathan once again found his father's hand clamped over his mouth. "Shouldn't you be on your way back to the house to change your clothes?"

"Yes, he should," Kathleen interjected.

"Aw, Ma," he whined. "David's probably already at the church waiting for me."

"And he will continue to wait until you change your clothes, young man. Now march."

"Yes, ma'am."

"Why don't the rest of you go on ahead," Kathleen suggested. "Nathan and I will be along shortly."

"I still have to get my trunk," Eric remembered.

"Colin and I can take it back to the house for you," Alec offered. "You take Stephen and Kaitlin on to the church."

"Thanks, Pa." Eric swung Stephen up behind his shoulders and then grasped Kaitlin's hand. "Ready, you two?"

"Ready!" they chorused.

Alec stepped over beside Colin as the trio headed down off the platform, followed closely by Kirsten and Jesse. "I'm real proud of you for coming today, Col. I know it wasn't easy for you."

Colin turned to face his father. "Why didn't you tell him, Pa? He thinks I got in."

"I just thought you might want to do that yourself."

Colin shook his head. "He's just going to make fun of me."

"He's not going to do anything of the kind and you know it. That's just your pride talking." Alec took him by the shoulders. "I'm sure you're not the only applicant who didn't pass the entrance exam on the first try. The hard part's over now. When you take it again—"

"I'm not going to take it again," Colin said with a look of defiance.

Alec was stunned by his admission. "But I thought for sure you'd—"

"Well, you thought wrong!" Colin shrugged his father's hands off his shoulders. "I never wanted to go to West Point anyway!" The sound of the lie coming from his own tongue brought a stinging rush of tears to the young man's eyes. "I never— " Colin's voice failed him as he turned and took off running up the street.

CHAPTER THREE

UNWELCOME GUEST

The churchyard was already swarming with picnickers by the time Eric arrived with Stephen and Kaitlin. Kirsten and Jesse had gone on ahead to save them a place to sit and it proved to be a good decision on their part. The small community of Baxter had grown considerably since his last visit. Eric counted no fewer than ten new families among the gathering and there were still more wagons and buggies arriving.

"Do you see your sister anywhere?" Eric asked his two young charges.

"There she is!" Kaitlin sang out, directing his attention up the grassy slope to their right. Kirsten and Jesse were sitting at the top beneath the shade of a large oak tree.

"Well, you two, looks like we're going on a little hike."

"No!" Stephen protested, pointing in the direction of the playground behind the church. "Seesaw!"

Eric chuckled. "All right, you can go play on the seesaw." He lifted Stephen down off his shoulders. "Kaitlin, you go with him."

"But I wanted to go down to the pond. Wouldn't you like to go to the pond, Stephen?"

"No," he protested again, folding his arms across his chest. "Seesaw."

Eric got down on one knee in front of Kaitlin. "Just keep an eye on him for me for a few minutes, would you, Kaitlin? There's someone I need to find."

"All right," she conceded. "But just for a few minutes. Come on, Stephen."

Eric watched as they disappeared around the side of the church and then began his ascent up the slope to join Kirsten and Jesse. Sweat was trickling down his face by the time he reached the top. "Either that hill has gotten steeper," he declared breathlessly, "or my legs have gotten shorter. Alan Thompson and I use to race to the top every Sunday after services. I could make it in less than thirty seconds without even breaking a sweat."

"You were also twelve at the time," Kirsten reminded him.

Eric smiled wryly. "Oh, yeah. I guess that was a few years ago. Funny how you forget things like that."

Eric sat down beside her, relishing in the feel of the cool grass beneath his palms as he reclined with his hands behind his back. "At least one thing hasn't changed. This is still the prettiest view for miles around." Eric trailed his gaze around the surrounding hills and then dropped it back in on the festivities below. "There sure are a lot of people here."

Kirsten nudged him with her elbow. "Any particular person you're looking for? Amber, perhaps?"

Eric rose stiffly to a sitting position, brushing his hands off on the sides of his trousers. "If you must know, yes. I told Mr. Crowley that I'd introduce her around at the picnic today."

"Does that include introducing her to Alicia, too?"

Just the mention of Alicia Randall produced a sour taste in Eric's mouth. She was the last person he wanted to see today. "She's here?"

"She's here, and looking for you," Kirsten warned. "I told her I didn't know where you were but you know how she is. I don't think she's going to give up that easy."

Eric knew all too well how persistent Alicia Randall could be. He had been the target of her unsolicited affections ever since her family moved to Baxter ten years ago. He had no more intention of returning those affections now than he did then but Alicia just didn't want to accept that he wasn't interested in her and never would be. What was it gong to take to convince her?

Eric smiled as an idea began to take shape. Maybe if Alicia saw him with Amber.... "Where's Alicia now?" he asked Kirsten.

"Colin might know. I saw her talking with him a few minutes ago. He's down there sitting on the church steps. What are you going to do?" she asked, sensing the wheels of thought spinning furiously in her brother's head.

"I'll let you know if it works. Wish me luck." Eric stood and began making his way back down the slope.

"If what works?" Kirsten called after him. "Hey, wait a minute! What do you want me to tell Alicia if I see her again?"

"Just stall her!"

"How am I supposed to do that!"

"You'll think of something!"

Eric ran the remainder of the way down the hill, keeping an eye out for both Amber and Alicia. If his plan worked, he would be rid of Alicia Randall once and for all. But he was going to need Colin's help to do it.

Eric slowed to a fast walk as he approached the church steps. "Just the man I was looking for."

Colin turned at the sound of his brother's voice, looking as if he'd just been startled from a bad dream. He knew the time had come for him to tell Eric the truth about his failure to get into West Point.

"Got room there for one more?"

Colin slid over to make room for Eric beside him, wishing now that he had stayed in the attic. "Eric," he began hesitantly, "there's something I have to tell you...."

"Can it wait, Col? I've got a big favor to ask of you." Eric dropped an arm around the younger man's shoulders. "I need you to keep Alicia occupied for me this afternoon. I know it's asking a lot," he hurried to add, "but it's really important."

Colin felt an enormous sense of relief, even though he knew it would only be temporary. Sooner or later he was going to have to tell Eric the truth. But at the moment, spending the afternoon with Alicia Randall seemed the less painful of the two tasks. "I'd be glad to."

Eric smiled. "You mean you'll do it? Oh, thanks, Col. I'll make it up to you somehow. I promise."

"Eric Ramsey." Reverend Clive Thompson stepped out the door of the church with a wide smile splayed across his face. "I thought that was your voice I heard out here. Welcome home."

"Thank you, sir." Eric reached up to clasp the hand that was being extended down to him. "It's good to be home. Though I must say I wasn't expecting all this." Eric's reference was to the size of the gathering.

"Yes," Clive agreed with a nod of his balding head. "Baxter has really grown since the railroad came to town. New families moving in all the time. Most of them God-fearing folk, I'm pleased to report. Still, I can't help but wonder what old Sam would think if he could see the town now. So many changes."

Eric knew that Thompson was referring to Samuel Baxter, the man who had founded the town back in 1833. It was in honor of his memory that they had gathered today, just as they had every year since his untimely passing thirteen years earlier. Eric had been only eight at the time, but he would never forget that chilly Sunday morning, the last Sunday he was ever to hear the sound of the elderly man's beautiful tenor voice lifted in joyful praise to their Creator. Less than an hour after the service ended, Samuel Baxter had passed on to sing in the presence of the Creator Himself.

"One thing is for certain," Clive continued. "Miss Lloyd is going to have quite a brood on her hands this year."

His reference to Amber brought an excited flush to Eric's cheeks. "You mean the new school teacher?"

"Yes. Lovely gal. Have you two met?"

"Just briefly, sir. At the station earlier." Eric cleared his throat, then swallowed, trying to dislodge the lump that had formed there. "You wouldn't happen to know where she is, would you?"

A grin split the elder man's face from ear to ear. "I think you'll find her down at the pond. She volunteered to help organize some games for the younger children later."

"Thank you, sir. Maybe I'll go and see if she needs any help."

Eric waited until Thompson had gone back inside the church and then headed towards the dirt path that led down to the pond. He was intercepted by Kaitlin as she came running from the direction of the playground, dragging a reluctant Stephen along behind her.

"Can I go to the pond now?" she pleaded, coming to a breathless stop in front of him. "It's been a few minutes."

"No!" Stephen balked, pointing back toward the playground. "I want to swing now!"

Eric crouched down, taking Kaitlin by the shoulders. "Can you watch him for just a few more minutes? I'll make it up to you later."

"But you said—"

"Mama!" Stephen broke free from Kaitlin's grasp and ran to greet the arriving wagon.

"Hey, wait for me!" Kaitlin squawked, taking off after him.

Eric grinned as he suddenly found himself alone once again. There was now nothing to stop him from going to look for Amber.

"Eric, can you give me a hand with one of these baskets?" Alec implored him. "Your mother has packed enough food to feed a small army."

Kathleen turned with a ready protest on her lips as she climbed down over the side of the wagon. "I packed just as much as I always do, and I can guarantee you that there won't be a scrap of it left by day's end. Not with your appetite."

Eric approached his father at the back of the wagon, fighting the urge to smile.

"What are you looking so smug about?" Alec asked him. "Your appetite is bigger than mine."

"It's not that, Pa." Eric stepped around him and hefted one of the wicker baskets down from the back of the wagon. "I was just thinking how impeccable your timing is."

Kathleen joined them, placing several blankets on top of the basket that Eric was holding. "Were you able to save us a place to sit?"

"Kirsten and Jesse are up on the hill," he said with a nod in their direction, "but I'm sure we can find someplace down here."

"Nonsense. I'd love to sit up on the hill."

"Me, too!" Stephen cheered, bobbing up and down at her feet.

Kathleen deferred the final decision to Alec. He shrugged as he lifted the second basket from the wagon. "It's fine with me."

Nathan eagerly led the way, setting a pace that was too blistering for anyone but Kaitlin and Stephen to match.

"Look at them go," Alec mused, momentarily grieving the loss of his youth. "Remember when we use to have energy like that?"

"What do you mean *use* to?" Kathleen said with a playful glint in her eyes.

"Kathleen, you wouldn't."

"Oh, wouldn't I?" Kathleen swiped the hat off his head with a girlish giggle and took off running. "See you at the top!"

"Kathleen Elizabeth Ramsey, you come back here!" Alec dropped the basket he was carrying and dashed after her.

Eric smiled as he stood witnessing his parents' flirtatious game of cat and mouse. It was obvious that they were still very much in love with one another, even after twenty-three years of marriage. He secretly longed for such a relationship of his own but up until now life at West Point had left little time for romantic pursuits. Nevertheless, it remained foremost in his mind, especially now that many of his childhood friends were married and had families of their own. The time had come for him to seriously consider doing the same. "Whenever you're ready, Lord," he hinted, "you know where to find me."

Kathleen was only a few yards from the top of the hill when she lost her footing and went sprawling onto her back in a fit of laughter. Alec collapsed beside her, gasping to catch his breath.

"Do you surrender?" Kathleen asked him as soon as she had stopped laughing.

"I was just about to ask you the same thing."

Kathleen handed him back his hat. "Truce?"

"Truce." Alec got to his feet and then helped her up.

"Who won?" Kirsten asked the exhausted couple as they staggered up to join the others beneath the tree.

"Your mother," Alec replied graciously. "She always wins."

"Why, thank you, Alec." Kathleen treated him to a smile that set his heart to racing. "Now, don't you think you should go help Eric with those baskets?"

"What baskets? Oh, right, the baskets. I'll do that."

"Mama, are we going to eat now?" Kaitlin asked.

"Not just yet, sweetheart. I've invited someone to join us and it wouldn't be polite to start without them."

"And David," Nathan reminded her. "We have to wait for David. Can I go find him, Ma?"

"All right. But don't be too long."

Alec and Eric returned with the baskets a few minutes after Nathan's departure. Kathleen directed their placement beneath the tree and then enlisted Kirsten's help in spreading out the blankets she had brought along for them to sit on.

"Is that apple pie I smell?"

Kathleen turned with a gasp to find Alec unbuckling the leather straps on one of the baskets. "Alec Ramsey, don't you dare!" She rushed over and planted her hand atop the basket, barring its opening. "I just got through explaining to the children that I've invited someone to join us. We can't start until she—until they get here."

"Who?" Alec asked, completely in the dark about the guest list.

"Oh, no one in particular," Kathleen said with a shrug.

Alec frowned. "Great. I'm going to starve while waiting for *no one in particular.*"

"Oh, stop that," Kathleen shooed him. "I'm sure she'll— I mean, I'm sure they'll be along shortly." She shifted her gaze over to Eric, noting the faraway look in his eyes. "Eric, are you all right?"

"Yeah, Ma," he assured her. "I just remembered something I need to do."

"Right now?" Kathleen seemed reluctant to let him go.

"It will only take a minute."

44

"Well...all right," she finally agreed. "But be sure to come right back."

Eric hurried down the hill and headed straight for the pond. After listening to his mother talk about the "someone" she had invited to join them, he had decided to invite Amber as well. He was certain that his mother wouldn't mind. She was always playing matchmaker for one unfortunate bachelor or another. And though she might not openly admit it, she was as eager to see him happily settled down with the right woman as he was. And who was to say that Amber wasn't that woman.

"Eric, wait up!"

Eric slowed his pace just enough to allow Colin to catch up with him. "Remember that little favor you asked me to help you with? I don't think it's going to work."

"Can this wait until later, Col? I'm kind of in a hurry."

"But, Eric—"

"Hello there, Eric." Alicia stepped out from behind a nearby tree, stopping Eric cold in his tracks. She feigned a pout when he didn't respond in kind. "Eric, didn't you hear me? I said, hello."

Eric met her gaze with all the enthusiasm of a man about to face a firing squad. It took considerable effort, but he managed to coax his mouth into a smile. "Hello, Alicia."

Alicia glided towards him, her deep-set, sea green eyes devouring him like a hungry feline. "I've been looking everywhere for you," she purred, twirling her finger in the golden-blonde curl dangling below her right ear. "You haven't been trying to avoid me, have you?"

Eric swallowed nervously. "No, of course not."

"Well, just to be sure...." Alicia drew a step closer, narrowing the gap between them to only a few inches. "I'm not going to let you out of my sight for a second." She latched onto his arm, further emphasizing her intentions.

Eric looked imploringly at his brother but he knew there was nothing that Colin could do to help. He was no match for the feminine wiles of someone as experienced as Alicia. What Alicia wanted, Alicia usually got.

"My father says that the moon will be nearly full tonight," Alicia told him eagerly. "I can't think of anything that would be more romantic than a moonlit walk down by the creek."

Eric knew exactly what she was up to but it wasn't going to work on him. She could wield her feminine wiles all she wanted but she was presuming an awful lot if she thought he was going to be roped into being her escort for a walk by the creek, moonlight or no moonlight. Who did she think she was to make such a presumption, anyway? There had never been any formal understanding between them. Any notions of courtship were solely figments of Alicia's imagination, and that's exactly where Eric wanted them to stay.

He was just about to tell her so when he caught sight of Amber coming up the path from the pond. The smile on her face quickly turned to a frown when she saw him at Alicia's side.

Eric followed her with his gaze as she walked off in the direction of the playground, aching to go after her and explain. It was bad enough that she had seen him with Alicia, but he didn't want her thinking there was more going on between them than there was.

Alicia burned with jealousy when she noticed where his attentions had strayed. She gave his arm a sharp tug, reminding him of her presence. "Don't you think we should go and join your family now? I wouldn't want to keep them waiting after your mother so graciously invited me to share your picnic."

Eric mentally kicked himself for not realizing sooner that Alicia was the mysterious "someone" his mother had invited. Now he would be forced to endure her company the entire afternoon or risk hurting his mother's feelings.

"Are you pleased?" Alicia asked, straining towards him on her tiptoes.

Eric opened his mouth to reply but nothing came out.

Alicia clapped her hands together with a gleeful giggle. "Your mother told me you'd be speechless. Now come along," she urged sternly as if addressing an errant child. "We've kept them waiting long enough."

CHAPTER FOUR

THE GAME OF LOVE

"**O**h, Mrs. Ramsey." Alicia rolled her eyes as her tongue made a circuitous licking motion around her lips. "I can't recall as I've ever tasted such—" She paused, grasping for just the right word to describe it. "Such succulent apple pie. It absolutely melts in your mouth. You simply must give me the recipe."

"I'll do better than that. You come by the house sometime this week and I'll show you how to make it. And then you can stay to supper afterwards."

Alicia responded to the offer as if it were an invitation to dine at the White House issued by President Buchanan himself. "Oh, Mrs. Ramsey, I couldn't possibly," she said breathlessly. "That's far too generous an offer."

"Oh, but you must," Kathleen insisted. "I won't take no for an answer."

"Well…." Alicia bit her lip, putting on a convincing show. "If you insist."

"I do." Kathleen slid her gaze over to Eric. "Won't that be nice, Eric? And then after supper you can walk Alicia home."

"Sure, Ma," Eric replied with a tight-lipped smile. He felt as spineless as a jellyfish for giving in so readily to her plans but he didn't want to hurt her feelings. He would endure Alicia's company for her sake just this one last time. But then he was telling her the truth, no matter what.

The smile vanished from Kathleen's face when she noticed the unsampled slice of pie on Eric's plate. "Eric, you haven't even touched your pie. And apple is your favorite. Aren't you feeling well?"

"Just not very hungry, I guess."

Kathleen reached for his plate. "Well, perhaps Alicia would like to eat it for you."

"Oh, no, I mustn't," Alicia replied with a disconcerted giggle. "I'm fairly busting out of this dress as it is. It's new, you know," she was quick to point out, fingering the delicate white lace that trimmed the collar. "Mother sent all the way to New York for it."

"Yes, I didn't think I had seen that one before." The dress was a striking shade of green that accentuated perfectly the color of Alicia's eyes. "It looks lovely on you, dear. And so flattering to your figure."

"I know," the young woman replied with an air of conceit, running her hands down the sides of the form-fitting bodice. She turned her full attention to Eric. "You do like it, don't you, Eric? I wore it just for you."

"It's fine," he replied curtly, casting her hardly more than a glance.

"Ma, can we go now?" Nathan pleaded, fidgeting anxiously beside her.

"What's the hurry?"

"They're going to start the games soon. I don't want to miss anything."

Kathleen glanced towards the open field behind the church where preparations were underway for the remainder of the afternoon's festivities. A crowd of spectators was already beginning to gather off to one side. "I suppose so. But stay out of mischief. That goes for you, too," she said with a wink directed at Nathan's friend, David. The gesture brought a flush to the timid boys' cheeks.

"I'm going to enter everything," Nathan boasted.

"Even the rope-jumping contest?" Kaitlin teased him.

"That's for girls," Nathan scoffed back. "You are coming down to watch, aren't you, Ma?"

"Just as soon as we get things packed up."

"Eric and I can take care of that," Alec offered. "You and Alicia go on with the others and save us a place to sit."

Kathleen smiled back at him. "With an invitation like that, I don't see how we can refuse. Shall we, Alicia?"

Alicia didn't like the idea of leaving Eric's side, especially not with that new schoolteacher lurking about. She had seen the way that Amber Lloyd had been looking at him earlier, and as naive as Eric was when it came to women, he was liable to be drawn right in by her deceptive charms. Just the thought of Amber Lloyd getting her claws into him brought a seething scowl to Alicia's face.

Kathleen laid a hand on the young woman's shoulder. "Are you coming, Alicia?"

Alicia quickly traded in her scowl for a demure looking smile. "Oh, Mrs. Ramsey, I just wouldn't feel right about putting all that work off onto Eric and your husband after you were so gracious to invite me. I think I should stay behind and help."

"Don't be silly. You're our guest. Now come along," Kathleen urged her. "It will give us a chance to talk—woman to woman."

Alicia rose reluctantly from beside Eric. "Don't be long," she implored him, though to Eric it sounded more like a threat. A shudder of relief ran through him when she finally disappeared down the hill. "Did you know that Ma was going to invite her today?" he asked his father.

"Not a clue," Alec admitted. "Your ma usually doesn't confide in me about such things. Even if she did, I don't think there's much I could do. You know how she is when she gets her mind made up about something."

"That's what I'm afraid of. I don't want to hurt her feelings, Pa, but Alicia...." Eric pressed his lips together, lowering his gaze with a frown.

"She's not your idea of the kind of woman you want to get serious about," Alec supplied for him.

"No, sir. She's not at all like—" Eric swallowed back the remainder of his reply.

Alec grinned. "Like who?"

"No one," Eric answered quickly. "We should get these baskets loaded back in the wagon."

"Son...." Alec waited for Eric to face him before he continued. "I wouldn't wait too long to tell your ma how you feel about Alicia. The two of them were in Crowley's yesterday afternoon looking at china patterns. I just thought you should know."

The news caused Eric's skin to crawl. Apparently he had been underestimating just how passionate his mother was about altering his matrimonial status. But with Alicia? How could she even think that he would be interested in someone like her? She was arrogant, spoiled and conceited. Not to mention deceptive, scheming and manipulative. Somehow he had to get his mother to see her for who she really was. Or better yet, give her a reason to stop looking altogether. But what reason?

Eric smiled as Amber's face suddenly came to mind. Maybe if his mother knew that he was interested in her she would abandon all of her crazy notions of trying to get him together with Alicia. It was certainly worth a try. But first he would have to rid himself of Alicia and that wasn't going to be easy. She had been clinging to him like a blood-sucking leech all afternoon. But even leeches had to let go sometime.

* * * * *

"Everyone, can I please have your attention!" The baritone voice of Baxter's sheriff, Zack Samuels, rose above the excited chatter of the crowd as he mounted the makeshift platform that had been erected behind the church for the days' festivities. "Our final event of the afternoon will be Baxter's second annual Founder's Day baseball game!"

Nathan exchanged a smile with David as the two boys pressed closer to the front of the platform.

"All men and boys eleven years and older wishing to play, please make you way to the schoolyard at this time!"

"Did you hear that?" Nathan whooped excitedly, exchanging another smile with David. "Eleven years and older. That means we can play."

"But what if your ma won't let us?"

"Of course she will," Nathan said confidently, giving his friend a clap on the shoulder. "You'll see. I'll go ask her right now."

Nathan took off running with David beside him and didn't stop until he reached the tree that his mother was sitting under. "Ma, can David and I play in the baseball game?"

"Baseball!" Kathleen gasped as if he had just uttered a blasphemy.

"Yeah," Nathan said nervously, his overconfidence catching up with him. "It's about to start over at the schoolyard. Sheriff Samuels just made the announcement."

"Baseball," Kathleen muttered again. "Don't you think you've played enough games for one day? You entered practically every contest there was."

"And won most of them," Alec added, noting with pride the collection of blue ribbons pinned to the front of the young man's shirt. "Even the frog jumping contest."

Nathan basked for a moment in his father's praise and then returned to pleading has case before his mother. "Can we, Ma?" he asked again, dropping to his knees beside her in the grass.

"I don't think so, Nathan. It could be dangerous. Besides, I'm sure you're much too young to play."

"Sheriff Samuels said boys eleven years and older." Nathan swung his gaze over to his father, in desperate need of reinforcements. "You heard him, didn't you, Pa?"

Alec nodded. "Yes, he did say that."

Kathleen scowled at him. "Alec, you're hardly helping matters."

"Why not just let the boy play, Kathleen? I don't see what harm could come of it."

"Harm? Have you forgotten what happened to the Hanson boy in last year's game? Or am I just imagining that broken arm of his you had to set?"

"He tripped over his own feet, Kathleen. That could have happened whether he was playing in the game or not."

"Well, I don't want to take that chance." Kathleen turned back to Nathan. "Why don't you go down to the pond and play?" she suggested, hoping to divert his attention away from the game. "I hear that Miss Lloyd has some fun things planned. Colin already took Kaitlin and Stephen down."

"Those are games for the little kids."

"Well, I'm sorry, but you're not playing baseball and that's final."

"Yes, ma'am." Nathan started to get to his feet and then thought to try one last thing. "Can we at least go and watch?" he pleaded.

"Well...I suppose so," she agreed. "But don't get too close."

"We won't. Come on, David."

Alicia watched as the two boys ran off in the direction of the schoolyard. "You wouldn't have any objections to Eric playing in the game, would you, Mrs. Ramsey?"

"Of course not, dear."

Alicia fastened her gaze on Eric. "You are going to play, aren't you?"

Eric had no desire whatsoever to play in the game and was about to tell her so when it occurred to him that this might be just the opportunity he had been waiting for to get rid of her. "I don't feel much like it," he told her honestly. "But if you want to go and watch, don't let me stop you."

Alicia made a sour face. "Oh, good heavens, no. I would if you were going to play, but personally I find the whole game rather absurd."

"I couldn't agree with you more," Kathleen interjected. "I'll never understand why any sensible woman would want to give up her good dinnerware."

Alec looked at her cockeyed. "What are you talking about?"

"The home plate."

Alec bit back a chuckle. "They don't use a real plate, Kathleen."

"Then why do they call it that?" she argued. "See, that just proves my point. It is an absurd game. I doubt if it will catch on anyway. Probably just another silly fad."

Alec reclined back in the grass with a smirk across his face. "You're probably right, dear."

"Oh, I almost forgot!" Alicia reached inside the small drawstring bag that was draped over her forearm and withdrew a slip of paper.

"What's that you have there, dear?" Kathleen asked curiously.

"It's a list of all the things that Eric and I are going to do while he's home." Alicia unfolded the paper, clearing her throat as she began. "The hayride next Saturday at the Miller farm, Susan Thatcher's birthday party a week from Thursday...."

Eric stole a fleeting glance at the list as Alicia continued her recitation, noting with disdain that "moonlit" walks ranked well near the top.

"I think those are all wonderful ideas," Kathleen told her. "In fact, why don't you give me a copy of the list? That way I can be sure that Eric doesn't miss a single engagement."

"Thank you, Mrs. Ramsey. That's so thoughtful of you."

"It's my pleasure, dear."

Alicia dangled the list in front of Eric like a piece of cheese in front of a hungry mouse. "Is there anything you want to add?" she asked suggestively. "A few more moonlit walks, perhaps?"

Eric backhanded the list aside as he rose to his knees, straining to see over his mother's head.

"Eric, what's wrong?" Kathleen asked, picking up on the urgency in his gaze.

"Someone's heading this way in an awful hurry."

Alicia followed Eric's gaze to the man that was running towards them. Recognition spawned a tempest in the depths of her sea green eyes. "That's Papa!" she exclaimed.

"Doc Ramsey!" Seth Randall's frantic cry sent chills plunging down the spines of all those within its' hearing.

Alicia jumped to her feet, scurrying to her father's side. "Papa, what is it? What's wrong?"

"It's your brother, Alicia. He's hurting real bad, Doc," he explained further, hastening to Alec's side. "It's his stomach. One minute he was fine, and then…." The words died in his throat, replaced by an anguished sob.

Alec got quickly to his feet. "Where is he?"

"With the missus over at the schoolyard."

"Okay, let's go."

Alicia hurried along behind her father as he led the way back to the schoolyard.

"I hope it's nothing serious," Kathleen remarked to Eric as she watched their departure.

"Yeah, me, too." It was then that Eric noticed Alicia's list fluttering in the grass beside him. Unfortunately, so did his mother. Before he could even blink twice it was in her hand.

"I'd best hold on to this for Alicia until she comes back," she explained in answer to the questioning look in his eyes. "We wouldn't want it to get misplaced, would we?"

"No, Ma," he fibbed.

Kathleen smiled as she looked over the list before slipping it safely into her skirt pocket. "You two are going to have such fun together. And Alicia is such a delightful—"

"I really like Kirsten's friend," Eric interrupted, hoping to divert the conversation away from Alicia.

"Her friend?"

"At least that's what she called him. I believe his Christian name is Jesse?"

"Oh, yes," Kathleen said with a telling smile. "I've grown quite fond of him myself."

"Is it serious?"

"Well, they haven't said as much, but I think it's only a matter of time. That is, of course, if your father will agree to the match."

"Why wouldn't he?" Eric wanted to know. "Jesse seems like a fine young man."

"It's not Jesse in particular that your father disapproves of," she hastened to explain. "It's...well, young men in general. As you can imagine, your sister has had quite a few suitors. 'The bane of his existence' is what your father calls them. Jesse is the only one who has survived this long."

Eric was shocked by her confession. "Excuse me?"

"Figuratively speaking, of course," Kathleen assured him. "You didn't think that I meant...." She chuckled. "Your father has a tad more restraint than that."

"I still don't understand," Eric admitted.

Kathleen grinned. "You will when you have a daughter of your own. And believe me, if she looks anything like Alicia, you'll be fighting the young men off in droves."

"Ma, I'm not going to marry Alicia!" Eric regretted the harshness of his tone as soon as the words left his tongue, but at least the truth was finally out. "I don't even like her."

Kathleen's mouth gaped open. "You never said anything before."

"I know, and I'm sorry. I didn't want to hurt your feelings. I know how set you were on getting us together."

An army of guilt pangs assaulted Kathleen's heart. Had she really been that unyielding? "I guess I did get a little carried away," she conceded upon further consideration. "It's just that Alicia is the only unmarried woman in town your age."

Not anymore, Eric thought to himself.

"Except for the new schoolteacher," Kathleen rambled on, barely halting long enough to draw her next breath. "Oh, I do wish I could remember her name."

"Amber." Eric didn't realize that he had spoken out loud until he saw the surprised look on his mother's face. "Well, that's just what I heard. Somewhere."

The corners of Kathleen's mouth drew up with a smile. "Then perhaps its Amber we should be inviting to supper this week."

Eric's cheeks turned bright red. "I'm sure she'll be too busy, getting settled in and all."

"You'll never know unless you ask."

"Ask who what?"

"Alec." Kathleen greeted him with a warm smile as he settled down beside her. "I didn't expect you back so soon. How's the Randall boy?"

"Nothing a generous dose of castor oil won't cure. Seems young Tad ate a few too many of his mother's candied apples. He'll be spending the remainder of the day in bed."

"Well, thank goodness it wasn't serious."

"Didn't Alicia come back with you?" Eric asked him.

"She decided to go on home with her family. But she did send you her apologies. She knew how much you were looking forward to tonight. Something to do with the moon, I believe it was?"

"Oh, that's all right. She should be with her family at a time like this." Eric cleared his throat as he got to his feet. "If you two will excuse me, I think I'll take a walk down to the pond."

Kathleen smiled secretly to herself as she watched him hurry away. Alec, in turn, was watching her. "I'm almost afraid to ask, but what's that look all about?"

"Oh, Alec, are you really that blind? Can't you see that Eric is going down to the pond?"

CHAPTER FIVE

MISUNDERSTANDINGS

"Amber, I'm really sorry that I wasn't able to introduce you around at the picnic today. You see, what happened was...." Eric let his voice trail off, not at all satisfied with the course that his explanation was taking. He didn't want Amber to think that he was trying to make excuses for his whereabouts and that's exactly what it sounded like. He needed to be more direct.

Eric pivoted away from the tree that he was using as a stand-in for her, took several deep breaths, then pivoted back. "Amber," he began again, "about that woman you saw me with earlier...." Eric balled up his fists with a frustrated sigh. "Maybe that's too direct. You should just be honest with her." He stepped closer to the tree, his hands outstretched imploringly. "Amber, I really like you a lot and I want for you to have supper with me tomorrow night."

Kirsten appeared beside him, the sound of muffled laughter escaping from behind the hand that she held clamped over her mouth. "I'm sorry," she apologized between outbursts. "I couldn't help it."

"How long have you been standing there?" Eric demanded.

"Long enough to hear you ask that tree to have supper with you tomorrow night. Really, Eric, do you think she's your type? She seems a little rough around the edges to me."

"That's very funny," Eric sneered back. "Don't you have anything better to do than go around spying on people?"

"I wasn't spying. Colin asked me to come and tell him when the baseball game was going to start. Is it my fault that this is the only path down to the pond?"

Eric felt about an inch tall beneath her rebuke. "I'm sorry. I shouldn't have jumped to conclusions."

"And I shouldn't have snuck up on you," Kirsten conceded, taking her share of the blame. "Are you really going to ask Amber to supper tomorrow night?"

"I am if I can get my nerve up. I just don't know what to say to her. Nothing comes out right."

"That's because you're trying too hard. Just be yourself. Like when you met her at the station earlier," Kirsten cited as an example. "You didn't seem to have any trouble talking to her then."

"That's because Mr. Crowley did most of the talking," Eric admitted.

"Then maybe you should invite Mr. Crowley to supper."

Eric looked at her wryly. "That's a big help, Kirsten."

"Eric...." Kirsten reached for his arm as he started to turn away. "Wouldn't you much rather have Amber like you for who you are than because your supper invitation sounds like a line from Romeo and Juliet?"

Eric smiled at her, quite impressed with the level of her maturity. "How did you get so wise?"

Kirsten shrugged. "Just repeating some advice my big brother once gave me."

"Well, he thanks you for the reminder." Eric leaned down and pressed a kiss to her forehead.

"You can thank me by taking your own advice." Kirsten steered him in the direction of the pond, giving him a subtle push. "Amber's waiting."

"Aren't you coming?"

"I think you're nervous enough without an audience. Just tell Colin about the game for me. And don't worry. You're going to do fine."

Eric stared after her as she started back up the path. "She's right you know," he told himself. "You can do this."

After steeling himself with a deep breath, Eric turned and headed towards the pond. He hadn't gone far when the excited shouts of children at play reached his ears. But it wasn't until he neared the end of the path that he discovered the reason for all the commotion. One end of the pond was teeming with paper boats, slowly bobbing their way across the murky waters to the throng of jubilant children waiting on the other side. Eric stopped to watch for a few moments and then continued further down the path, only to stop again when he heard a voice coming from behind the thicket of blackberry bushes off to his right. It was Amber's voice. And she wasn't alone.

"You've got to tell him as soon as possible," Eric heard her say to her unidentified companion. "The longer you wait, the harder it's going to be. Besides, how long do you think you can keep something like that a secret in a town this size?"

Keep what a secret? Eric wondered. *And from whom?*

"I know," replied a second voice. Eric recognized it immediately as Colin's. "He's just going to be so disappointed."

"You don't know that for sure," Amber offered encouragingly.

"You didn't see the look on his face at the station earlier. I haven't seen him that excited since...well, since he had a crush on Amy Milligan in the fifth grade."

Eric's curiosity continued to mount. They were talking about him.

"And then...." Colin fell silent.

"And then what?" Amber asked.

"And then he found out that I liked her, too." Colin moved out from behind the bushes, forcing Eric to retreat several steps back up the path to avoid being seen. "I know it's not exactly the same thing," he continued, "but I feel as if I'm betraying him all over again."

Eric felt as if he'd just been punched in the stomach. What did Colin mean it wasn't the same thing? He had just admitted to being interested in Amber. And she didn't sound as if she objected to his advances.

"Colin, you can't blame yourself. You couldn't have known this would happen." Amber joined him out from behind the bushes, her cupped hands brimming over with freshly picked blackberries. She quickly added them to the growing mound in the bowl that Colin was holding for her. "I'm sure Eric will understand that. But either way you have to tell him." Amber reached up and wiped her hands on the cloth that lay draped over her shoulder. "Promise me you will?"

Eric held his breath, waiting for Colin's response.

"I'll tell him," Colin agreed. "Today."

Somehow knowing what Colin wanted to talk to him about didn't make the knowing any easier. But self-pity was not something that Eric was going to allow himself to wallow in. Whatever disappointment he was feeling had been brought on by his own foolishness. He had no prior claim on Amber. She was free to like anyone she wanted, Colin included.

Eric wanted to walk away right then and forget the whole incident had ever happened, but he knew it wasn't going to be that easy. He would see the truth every time he looked in his brother's eyes…and Amber's. It would be better to get everything out in the open right now.

"Colin!" Eric's attention swerved to Stephen as he came running up from the pond. "My boat won!"

"Hey, congratulations, Captain Ramsey." Colin gave him a pat on the back. "That was mighty fine sailing."

"It sure was," Amber agreed. "Good enough to earn you a very special prize. Hold out your hands like this." Amber demonstrated by cupping her hands together.

Stephen did as she asked then watched with his mouth gaping as she selected five plump blackberries from the bowl and dropped them one by one into his outstretched hands. "Gol-ly! Berries!" The youngster proceeded to cram all five of them into his mouth at once, swiping away the stream of dark purple juice that trickled down his chin.

"What do you say to Miss Amber, Stephen?" Colin prompted him.

"Thank you!"

"You're very welcome. But the berries are only part of your prize." Amber reached into the pocket of her pinafore and withdrew a blue ribbon.

Stephen's mouth gaped open almost as wide as when he'd seen the berries. "Is that for me?"

"It sure is. Would you like for me to pin it on you?"

Stephen nodded, taking an eager step towards her.

A smile lit up Amber's face as she leaned down and fastened the ribbon to the front of his shirt. "There you are, young man. One first prize ribbon for the winner of the Founder's Day boat race."

"Did I hear someone mention something about a boat race?"

"Eric!" Stephen ran to meet him, his eyes beaming. "My boat won! Did you see?"

"I'm afraid not, sport. But let me have a look at that fine ribbon you have there." Eric crouched down so he could examine the ribbon more closely. "My, that's a fancy one."

"Miss Amber gave it to me," Stephen told him excitedly. "She's real nice."

"I'm sure she is," Eric said with an awkward smile, resisting the urge to look in Amber's direction. He stood back to his full height, cupping the back of Stephen's head. "Why don't we go show your ribbon to, Ma?" he suggested. "I'm sure she'll be proud to see it."

"Can I show her my boat, too?"

"Of course you can."

Stephen raced back to the pond, leaving Eric alone with Colin and Amber. He could tell from their flustered expressions that they were as uncomfortable as he was.

"If you'll excuse me," Amber remarked suddenly, "I really should be getting back to the children."

"Don't forget these." Colin handed her the bowl of blackberries.

"Thank you." Amber retrieved the cloth off her shoulder and draped it over the top of the bowl. "This should be enough for at least two pies."

Eric felt a pang of jealousy as her gaze continued to linger on Colin. "Remember what you promised," he heard her whisper.

Colin acknowledged her reminder with a nod, watching as she made her way back to the pond. He turned then to face Eric, a lump rising in his throat. "I suppose you're wondering what that was all about."

"You don't need to tell me. I already know," Eric confessed.

The left side of Colin's mouth twitched nervously. "You do?"

"I overheard you and Amber talking." Eric slid his gaze to the ground. "I'm sorry. I shouldn't have been eavesdropping."

"No, I'm the one who should be sorry," Colin argued, coming to his brother's defense. "I should have told you right off that I didn't get into West Point. I was just feeling sorry for myself."

"West Point?" Eric jerked his head up, staring hard at his brother. "You mean...that's what you and Amber were talking about?"

"Well, yeah. What did you think we were talking about?"

Eric's reply was drowned out by the sound of a loud splash, followed by a frantic plea from Amber. "Eric, Colin! Stephen just fell in the pond!"

* * * * *

"You mean he was actually talking to a tree?" Kathleen asked Kirsten.

Kirsten seesawed her head up and down, keeping her eyes trained on Jesse as he stepped up to bat.

Kathleen chuckled. "I had no idea he would be that nervous. Do you suppose he ever got around to inviting her to supper?"

Kirsten sprang to her feet with a loud cheer as Jesse drove the ball hard into left field with his first swing of the bat. "Run, Jesse, run!" she urged him.

Others in the crowd took up her chant as Jesse rounded first base and headed for second. A long throw from center field finally stopped him at third.

Kirsten squealed excitedly, drumming her hands together. "Oh, Mama, wasn't he just wonderful!"

"Just wonderful," she had to agree.

Kirsten sank back down into the grass, her applause continuing in earnest.

"You and Jesse have been seeing a lot of each other lately," Kathleen thought to mention, feeling the subject was long overdue.

Kirsten stopped mid-clap, a look of uncertainty marring her expression. She turned slowly to face her mother. "You do like him, don't you?"

"Oh, of course I do, sweetheart," Kathleen assured her. "I think Jesse is a fine man. In fact...." She turned her gaze upon the subject of their thoughts "I was just thinking about how much he reminds me of your father."

Kirsten lowered her gaze to her hands, knotting them together in the folds of her dress. "I don't know why you would think that. Pa doesn't even like Jesse."

"Now where did you get an idea like that? Of course he does."

"No he doesn't," Kirsten asserted more adamantly. "Every time Jesse comes by the house, Pa

won't even talk to him. He just pretends like he's not there." Her voice began to waver as her eyes welled with tears. "He won't even give him a chance. It's not fair."

"Now before you go judging your father too harshly," Kathleen implored her, "try putting yourself in his position. You use to give him all of your attention, and now he sees you giving it to another man. A man, I might add, who's known you for only three months. Your Pa's known you for almost fifteen years."

Kirsten smiled, suddenly seeing her relationship with Jesse through different eyes—those of her father. "I've never thought of it like that before," she admitted.

Kathleen reached up to stroke the back of her daughter's head. "It's not easy for pa's to watch their little girls grow up. Or ma's either, for that matter," she added with a smile.

"Just be patient with him, Kirsten. He loves you so much and he only wants what's best for you."

Kirsten considered her mother's appeal as she gazed towards the schoolhouse steps where her father sat talking with Sheriff Samuels. "Do you think he knows how much I love him?"

Kathleen nodded. "I'm sure he does. But that doesn't mean he doesn't need to hear it from time to time."

Kirsten smiled back at her mother. "I'm going to go tell him right now."

"That's my girl."

"Mama!" Kaitlin came running towards her through the crowd. "Stephen fell in the pond!"

"He did what!" Kathleen leapt to her feet, her eyes broadcasting her worst fears. "Kaitlin, you didn't leave him there, did you?"

"No, Mama," she panted as she came to a stop. "Eric and Colin are bringing him. They told me to run ahead."

Kathleen fidgeted nervously as she watched for the threesome to appear. She finally spotted them coming around the side of the church. Eric was carrying a sopping wet Stephen. "Kaitlin, run get your father," she instructed. "He's over at the schoolhouse talking with Sheriff Samuels."

Kirsten laid a hand on her mother's arm, redirecting her attention. "Here he comes now, Ma."

Kathleen turned with relief to find Alec hurrying towards them. She took a few anxious steps in his direction and then stopped and swung her attention back to Stephen.

"What happened?" Alec asked as he drew up beside her.

"Stephen fell in the pond, Papa," Kaitlin told him. "And Eric, too."

"Is he all right, Eric?" Kathleen asked as the trio approached.

"I think so, Ma. Just shaken up a bit."

Alec grinned at his eldest son. "I thought you outgrew swimming in the pond years ago."

"I lost my balance when I was pulling him out," Eric explained.

"Just as long as you're both all right." Kathleen watched anxiously as Alec began probing Stephen's arms and legs for injuries. "He is all right, isn't he, Alec?"

"He appears to be. Do you hurt anywhere, son?" Alec asked him.

"No, Papa," Stephen replied through chattering teeth. "I'm just wet."

"You can say that again. If you wanted to go swimming, why didn't you say so?"

"I lost my ribbon, Papa," Stephen sobbed, his tears mingling with the droplets of pond water that speckled his cheeks.

"Never you mind about that now," Kathleen crooned, sweeping back the damp tendrils of hair from his forehead. "Let's just get you home and into some dry clothes. And that goes for you, too," she said to Eric.

"You won't get any arguments from me, Ma," he said with a shiver.

"Why doesn't everyone go wait in front of the school-house," Alec suggested. "I'll bring the wagon around there."

"What about Nathan?" Kathleen asked. "He's not going to want to leave until the game is over."

"I'll stay with him, Ma," Kirsten volunteered. "I wanted to see the rest of the game, anyway. Jesse can walk us home later." Kirsten deferred her plans to her father. "But only if that's okay with you, Pa."

Alec didn't know what to make of her request. She had never sought his permission where Jesse was concerned before. Why the sudden change now?

"Well, Pa?" Kirsten prompted him.

Alec cleared his throat, breaking his own silence. "Just be sure you're home in time for supper."

"Yes, sir."

"And, Kirsten?"

Kirsten waited anxiously for him to continue. Was he going to change his mind?

"Why don't you see if Jesse would like to join us."

Kirsten's chin began to quiver with the onset of tears. "Do you really mean it, Pa?"

"Of course I mean it," he said with false gruffness, unnerved by her sudden show of emotion. "I said it, didn't I? Now go on before I change my mind. You don't want to miss the rest of the game."

Kirsten ran to him and threw her arms around his neck, her tears dampening the front of his shirt. "I love you, Pa," she whispered for only him to hear.

Alec turned to find Kathleen watching him as Kirsten ran back to the field. His shoulders lifted with a shrug. "All that fuss over a supper invitation."

Kathleen moved to stand before him, her mouth upturned with a smile. "It was much more than just a supper invitation, Alec Ramsey, and you know it." She moved a half step closer, her voice dropping to barely a whisper. "And by the way, I love you, too."

CHAPTER SIX

IN THE NAME OF PROGRESS

"**I** can't believe how much things have changed," Eric observed as the Ramsey's wagon rumbled its' way down the main street of Baxter. Everywhere he looked there were new businesses springing to life. "What's that brick building going up there on the corner?" he wondered aloud.

"A bank," Alec supplied.

"A bank?" Eric couldn't curb his surprise. "Baxter's never needed a bank before."

"Baxter's never been a railroad town before either, son," Alec reminded him. "With all of the strangers moving into the area, there are some folks who would just feel safer knowing that their money was in a bank rather than hidden behind the flour tin in their kitchen cupboard."

"Do we have any money to put in the bank, Papa?" Kaitlin asked.

Alec chuckled. "Not yet, sweetheart. But if my practice keeps growing the way it has been…."

"Do you have a lot of new patients, Pa?" Eric asked.

"More than I can handle at times," he admitted.

"And not nearly enough room," Kathleen interjected into their conversation. "Your father may have to move his office to a larger space in town."

Eric's mind reeled with all that he was hearing. "It's hard to imagine that things could change so quickly. I can remember back not so many years ago when there weren't more than two dozen families in this area and you got paid in apples and potatoes more often than cash money."

"That's still the case for the most part, but I think my days as a struggling country doctor will be fewer and farther between now that the railroad is here."

Eric hoped that his father's prediction would prove true. He had worked so hard all these years to clothe and feed their family, never once complaining or questioning God's provision. If anyone deserved to get ahead for once, it was his pa.

"Are you all right, Eric?"

Eric glanced up to find his mother's concerned gaze fastened upon him.

"You got so quiet all of a sudden," she continued, explaining the reason for her query. "I thought something might be wrong."

"I'm fine, Ma," Eric assured her. "Just anxious to get home, is all."

Kathleen smiled in understanding. "Not as anxious as we are to have you home. It's been too long."

Eric returned her smile as his father veered the wagon off the main street, following the steep rutted path that curved up and around behind the blacksmith shop before leveling off again.

"That's where Jesse lives!" Stephen announced, pointing at the clapboard structure.

"He doesn't live *in* the blacksmith shop, silly," Kaitlin chided him. "He lives in the house behind it."

Kathleen turned a scolding gaze upon her. "That'll do, Kaitlin."

"Yes, Mama."

Eric gave the dwelling in question only a brief glance as the wagon passed by. It was the house that stood waiting further up the road that interested him. He closed his eyes, trying to picture in his mind how it had looked the last time he'd been home. When he opened them again, he wasn't disappointed. Everything was just as he remembered.

"Notice any changes?" Kathleen asked above the rattle of the wagon.

"Changes?" Eric fixed his gaze back on the house. What could she be referring to?

Kathleen twisted to face him, grabbing hold of the back of the seat as the wagon hit a deep rut "You mean you don't notice anything...different?"

Eric was about to insist that he didn't when he noticed a couple of pipes running up the side of the house. "What are those pipes for?"

Kathleen smiled, advertising her delight. "You did notice. I knew you would."

Eric stared blankly at his mother and then again at the pipes as his father turned the wagon onto the graveled drive beside the house.

"Well, don't keep the boy in suspense, Kathleen," Alec urged her. "Tell him what they're for."

"I was getting to that." Kathleen faced Eric again. "Your father has installed facilities in the upstairs closet at the end of the hall," she announced proudly.

"We go inside now!" Stephen chimed in.

Eric studied the pipes more closely as the wagon passed by beneath them. "A water closet? I didn't know you knew how to install a water closet, Pa."

"He didn't," Kaitlin snickered. "Mama almost drowned the first time she tried it. Papa had the pipes hooked up wrong. She didn't talk to him for two whole days."

"Now it was hardly as dramatic as all that," Kathleen assured. "There were a few minor adjustments that needed to be made but I think your father did a marvelous job." She leaned over and gave him a peck on the cheek to show her appreciation.

Alec grinned back at her. "Maybe I should hook everything up wrong from now on. What do you say there, fellas?" he hollered to the horses. "Want this old wagon to pull you for a change?"

Kathleen gave him a playful slap on the arm as he brought the wagon to a halt behind the house. "Oh, don't be silly."

"Does anyone else in town have one?" Eric wondered.

"Just the Crowley's." Kathleen gathered up her skirt as she prepared to descend over the side of the wagon. "And I believe that the Randall's are thinking about getting one."

"Maybe I should volunteer my expertise to help them hook it up," Alec suggested.

"Not if I want to keep Caroline Randall as a friend, you won't. I'm sure that Seth will be able to handle things just fine."

Alec shrugged as he set to work unhitching the team. "It was only a suggestion."

"Well, put it out of your mind. Stephen Michael?" Kathleen turned to find him dangling by his fingertips over the side of the wagon. "I want you upstairs right now and out of those wet things."

"But I gotta find my frog," the youngster protested as he dropped to the ground.

"Out of those wet things right now, young man, or I heat up water for a bath."

Stephen lit out for the house without another word of protest, unbuttoning his shirt as he went.

"Colin, would you see that he does? I'll be up shortly."

"Sure, Ma." Colin hopped down off the back of the wagon.

"A hot bath," Eric mused as he followed Colin down. "You sure wouldn't have to twist my arm."

Kathleen chuckled. "All right, I'll heat up some water. You can try out the new tub."

"A new tub, too?" Eric joined her as she headed to the house. "Are there anymore surprises I should know about?"

Kathleen slowed her pace, turning to face him as they reached the back porch. "Now that you mention it...there is something."

Eric motioned for her to take a seat on the steps and then settled down beside her.

Kathleen folded her hands in her lap, taking a steadying breath. "Kirsten has been wanting to have a room all to herself for sometime now," she began. "Which is perfectly understandable. She is a young woman now and it isn't fair for her to have to be sharing with Kaitlin."

Eric nodded. "I agree."

"Well...we decided, that is, your father and I, to move Kaitlin into Colin's room and Colin in with you."

Eric assumed there had to be more to the story than that but she said nothing further. "That's it?"

Kathleen was surprised by his response. "You mean you don't mind?"

"Of course I don't mind," Eric told her honestly. "We've shared a room before."

"When you were seven and Colin was two," she reminded him.

"Then I'd say it's about time we shared one again."

Kathleen smiled in relief. "You really don't mind?"

"I really don't mind. Now tell me...." Eric helped her back to her feet. "Are there anymore surprises I should know about?"

Kathleen laid a finger against her pursed lips. "Now let me see...."

* * * * *

"Do you mind if I come in?"

Eric turned from the dresser beside his bed to find Colin standing in the doorway. "You don't have to ask, Col. This is your room, too."

"I know." Colin shoved his hands deep into his pockets, moving slowly through the door. "I just didn't want to disturb you if you were busy."

"Just unpacking a few things." Eric removed the remainder of his clothing from the trunk sitting on his bed and crammed it all into the top two drawers of the dresser. Colin's things were now occupying the bottom two drawers, greatly reducing the space available to him. "What's on your mind?"

Colin took a seat beside the trunk, watching as Eric struggled to close the tightly packed drawers. "I just wanted to tell you that I'm sorry we have to share a dresser. Ma left mine in the other room for Kaitlin."

Eric smiled as he turned to face him. "My socks and underwear appreciate your concern, Col. Now would you care to tell me what's really on your mind?"

Colin clammed up, absently drumming his fingers against the back of the trunk. "West Point," he finally admitted.

"That's what I thought." Eric pushed the trunk up to the head of the bed, making room for himself beside his brother. The bed springs groaned beneath their combined weight as he took a seat. "Is there anything in particular you want to talk about?"

Colin shook his head. "I just feel so ashamed. I couldn't even pass the entrance exam."

"A lot of guys don't pass on the first try, Col. It's nothing to be ashamed about. I'm just glad you finally told me."

"I probably wouldn't have if it hadn't been for Amber," the younger man confessed. "She talked me into it."

Eric could feel the laughter building up inside him until finally he had to let it go.

"What's so funny?" Colin wanted to know.

"When I heard you telling Amber about Amy Milligan, I thought...oh, never mind."

"Thought what?" Colin pressed him.

Eric hunched his shoulders. "Well, you know. I thought you liked her."

"Amber?" Colin said in disbelief.

Eric nodded sheepishly.

"Don't you think she's a little old for me?"

"So was Amy Milligan but that didn't stop you."

Colin chuckled. "No, it sure didn't."

"All right, enough about Amy Milligan. What are we going to do about getting you ready to take that exam again?"

Colin didn't have the heart to tell him that he wasn't going to take the exam again. It had been hard enough telling him that he'd failed it the first time.

"What areas did you have the most trouble in?" Eric asked him.

Colin lowered his gaze to the floor. "Well, you see...I haven't exactly decided if I'm going to take it again." Somehow that sounded better than telling him that his mind was already made up. "Besides, there's no guarantee that I'll pass even if I do."

"You will if you want it bad enough," Eric argued. "I thought you did. Was I wrong?"

Colin looked him straight in the eye. "I've never wanted anything more in my life."

"Then prove it," Eric urged him. "Take that exam again. Don't let fear rob you of your dreams."

Colin considered his brother's advice and actually found himself excited about the challenge before him. "All right, I will. Only...."

"Only what?"

"Well, I was just wondering…." Colin stalled, somewhat embarrassed about what he was going to ask. "Do you think you could tutor me?"

Eric clapped him on the shoulder. "I think that's a fine idea. That trunk of mine is full of books. We can get started anytime you like."

"There's no rush. I can't take the exam again until next year, anyway."

"Well, just remember that I only have three months leave and I'd like to spend some of that time fishing."

Colin grinned. "I'll remember."

"Eric?" Kathleen poked her head in the door. "Can I have a word with you? Alone?"

"Sure, Ma." Eric joined her out in the hallway, closing the bedroom door behind him. "Okay, what have I done now?" he jested.

Kathleen handed him the list of activities that Alicia had planned for them during his time home. "You might as well have this," she said with a momentary pang of regret.

Eric only then realized how disappointed she was by his lack of interest in Alicia. "You really wanted me to marry her, didn't you?"

"I was hoping," she admitted truthfully. "But now Alicia is no longer the only eligible young woman in town, is she?" Kathleen flashed him a triumphant smile before disappearing into the water closet.

Eric had to smile as well. His mother would never give up her matchmaking ventures. But at least this time he was in agreement with the young woman of her choosing.

"Eric?" Stephen came up beside him, his pudgy cheeks streaked with fresh tears. "I can't find my frog."

Kathleen let loose with a horrified shriek.

Eric grinned down at the distraught youngster. "I wouldn't fret about that if I were you, Stephen. I think Ma has."

* * * * *

"This is a wonderful supper, Mrs. Ramsey." Jesse helped himself to another biscuit as the basket made its way around the table for the second time. "My pa and I aren't very handy when it comes to meal fixin'. And since Ma passed on...." Jesse fell silent. The untimely death of his mother only a short six months ago was still a very painful topic for the young man to talk about.

Kathleen reached over and gave his hand an understanding squeeze. "I'm glad you're enjoying it, Jesse. You'll have to come again. And next time bring your father."

Jesse acknowledged her kindness with a faint smile. "Thank you, ma'am. He'd appreciate that."

Kirsten sensed the flow of conversation starting to drag as it had periodically throughout the course of the evening. She grappled for something to say. "Jesse hit two home runs today," she cast out for whoever might be listening. "Did I tell you?"

"Only a dozen times," Alec muttered under his breath.

Kathleen glared at him before offering Jesse her congratulations. "That's wonderful, Jesse. You're quite the ball player."

Jesse shrugged aside her compliment. "It was nothing, ma'am."

Silence settled in once again. This time it was Jesse who broke it. "I hear it's looking more and more likely that South Carolina will secede if Lincoln is elected in November. Do you think that will mean a war between the North and South, Mr. Ramsey?"

Alec paused with his fork midway to his mouth, flattered that Jesse was interested in his opinion. He laid the fork aside, giving the younger man his undivided attention. "I think there's a pretty good chance of it," he began by saying. "There are several forts in Charleston Harbor that I don't think Carolina is going to want to let fall into Northern hands if they do secede."

"I was thinking that myself, sir. The only question is to what lengths they'll go to get them back. I can't imagine them taking up arms against their own countrymen, but they've made it pretty clear how they feel about the North trying to tell then how to live their lives."

"And as long as they hold with the practice of slavery," Alec added, "the North is going to continue to do just that. Sooner or later, the kettle is going to boil over."

"Well, I for one wouldn't want to be within a mile of it when it does."

Kirsten's heart swelled with joy as she sat listening to the two men she loved more than anything in the world talking so freely with one another. It was the longest conversation they'd ever had. The *only* conversation, if truth be told. Perhaps her father was finally coming around. Perhaps. But Kirsten refused to get her hopes up until she heard such declarations from her father himself.

"Will you get to fight if there's a war, Eric?" Nathan asked.

Eric watched his mother's face pale at the implication of him going to war. "No, Nathan," Eric told him, hoping to alleviate some of her concern. "I'll be stationed in Washington D.C. That's a mighty long way from Carolina."

"That's right," Kathleen asserted, more for her own sake than Nathan's. "Your brother won't be anywhere near the fighting. That's to say there even is any."

"I'm sorry I brought the subject up, Mrs. Ramsey," Jesse apologized.

"Not at all, Jesse," Kathleen assured him, making light of her discomfort. She rose to her feet, forcing a smile past her lips, "Now who's for some dessert?"

CHAPTER SEVEN

THE INVITATION

Colin checked to make sure that Eric was still asleep and then knelt down in front of the trunk at the foot of his bed. A groan escaped his lips as he lifted the lid and saw how many books were inside. "I have to read all those?" There were at least a dozen different subjects represented, ranging from mathematics to rhetoric.

"Rhetoric." Colin pronounced the word with his mouth twisted wryly to one side. "I don't even know what rhetoric is. Or does."

Colin laid the book aside and continued to sort through the others until he found one that appealed more to his interests. It was a volume entitled *Rifle and Light Infantry Tactics*, written by a man named William J. Hardee. "Now this is more like it."

Colin lifted the book from the trunk and sank from his knees to sit cross-legged on the floor. After skimming quickly over the introduction, he plunged right into the first chapter. He was just beginning the second when Eric woke up.

"For someone who's not anxious to start studying, you've sure got you're nose buried pretty deep in that book."

"Eric!" Colin snapped the book shut, scrambling up to his feet. "I—I was just looking," he stammered.

Eric grinned. "So I see. Do you mind if I ask what changed your mind?"

Colin shrugged, cocking his head to one side. "Well, I've been thinking. Since you are going to be leaving in a few months...maybe it would be a good idea if you started tutoring me now."

"I'd say that's an excellent idea. Only I have to insist that you start with a different subject."

Colin looked down at the book that he had selected to begin his studies, unclear what was wrong with it. "How come?"

"Do you remember being asked to fire a rifle during the entrance exam?"

Colin's shoulders slumped. "Oh. I guess it would make more sense to study something that was actually going to be on the exam."

"Try mathematics or history," Eric suggested.

Colin was relieved that he hadn't suggested rhetoric. "I think I'll start with history." He returned his first selection to the trunk and picked out a text on American history. "When can we get started?"

Colin's sudden eagerness caused Eric to smile. "How about as soon as I get back from Crowley's. If you think you can wait that long."

"You're going to Crowley's?"

"Yeah. If there's anything you want me to pick up for you, just write it down. I was going to make a list, anyway."

"I don't need anything." Colin sat down at the foot of his bed and began thumbing through the volume he was holding. "But you might say hi to Amber for me."

"Amber?" Eric tried to sound disinterested but wasn't very successful in his attempt. "What makes you think I'll see her?"

"She mentioned that she was going to be helping her uncle out at the store for the next couple of months until school starts up."

"Oh," Eric replied casually. "That's nice."

Colin smiled, not at all fooled by Eric's attempt to belittle his interest in Amber. "You really like her, don't you?"

Eric pretended to take offense to hide his mounting discomfort. "I never said that."

"You didn't have to. It's as plain as the nose on your face. What I can't understand is why you thought *I* liked her."

Eric dropped onto the edge of his bed. "If you had overheard what you were saying to Amber yesterday, you would have thought you liked her, too."

"If I had overheard what I...huh?"

"Never mind."

Colin got to his feet, turning to look down at his brother. "For what it's worth, I think she likes you, too."

Eric quickly rose to stand beside him. "You do?"

"I can't be completely sure, but I think so. You coming down to breakfast?'

Eric ran a hand through his rumpled hair, then over the stubble on his chin. "I think I'll clean up a bit first. Tell the others not to wait."

"You don't have to clean up on my account," Colin teased. "I don't care what you look like."

Eric grabbed the pillow off his bed and hurled it at Colin as he scrambled out the door.

* * * * *

Eric arrived downstairs twenty minutes later, freshly combed and shaved. "Good morning, everybody. Sorry I'm late."

Kirsten whistled appreciatively as Eric took his seat beside her at the kitchen table. "My, don't you look handsome this morning. What's the occasion?"

"He's going to see—" Eric silenced Colin with a hard kick in the shin. "Ow!"

"Going to see who?" Kathleen asked as she passed Eric a stack of pancakes.

"No one, Ma," he replied, glaring sternly across the table at Colin. "I'm just going to Crowley's to get a few things."

Kathleen's face brightened with a smile. "Oh, good. I can have you check to see if that bolt of material I ordered has come in."

"Be glad to, Ma."

"I wanna go to!" Stephen sang out.

"Oh, Eric, would you?" Kathleen implored him as she rose to begin clearing the table. "I've got a ton of laundry to do today, not to mention all of these dishes. It would really help if he weren't underfoot."

Eric reached over and tousled Stephen's hair. "Why not. Maybe we'll even get in a little fishing later."

"Don't forget you promised to help me study," Colin reminded him.

"I won't forget."

Alec pushed his chair back from the table, downing the last of his coffee. "Well, I hate to eat and run, but I've got to get to my rounds. Eric, if you hurry I can drop you at the store on my way."

Eric considered the number of pancakes remaining on his plate. "Give me three minutes, Pa."

"Done. I'll go hitch up the buggy."

"And I'd best get started on these." Kathleen said with a sigh as she stood eyeing the stack of dishes before her on the table.

"I'll do that, Mama," Kirsten offered, rising quickly out of her chair. "You go ahead and start the laundry. I'll come help you when I'm finished."

"Thank you, Kirsten. It's liable to take me most of the day as it is."

Kathleen picked up the bundle of clothes lying by the back door and carried it out onto the porch. Alec followed her, closing the door behind them. "Okay, what are you up to?" he demanded to know.

Kathleen turned to face him with a cocky smile. "Laundry?"

"You know what I mean, Kathleen. When Eric mentioned that he was going to Crowley's this morning, your eyes lit up like a Forth of July fireworks display. And don't tell me it's because you're excited about getting a new bolt of material."

"Well, of course not."

"Then what?"

"Oh, Alec," she chided, dropping the bundle of laundry at his feet. "Do I have to spell it out for you? Amber is working at the store."

Alec frowned. "Who's Amber?"

* * * * *

"There's Jesse!" Stephen scrambled up to stand on the seat of the buggy as they passed by the blacksmith's shop on their way into town. "Hi, Jesse!" he hollered.

Jesse paused to return Stephen's wave before disappearing inside the clapboard structure leading a pair of geldings behind him.

"I like Jesse," Stephen declared as he scrunched himself back down onto the seat.

"So do I," Eric agreed.

Stephen turned large, inquiring eyes upon his father, waiting for him to declare his own words of praise on Jesse's behalf. He soon grew tired and turned back to Eric. "How does she tie him?"

"How does who tie what?"

"Mama says Jesse is Kirsten's bow. How does she tie him?"

Eric grinned. "Right around her little finger."

Stephen stared down at his hands, wiggling his fingers. "Mama says Kirsten and Jesse are gonna get married."

Alec stiffened as if he'd been stricken with a sudden case of tetanus.

"I wouldn't be a bit surprised," Eric told him, adding further to his father's discomfort. "They seem quite smitten with one another."

"Will Jesse come live at out house?" Stephen wondered.

"No, I expect Kirsten will go live with him."

"Will they have a baby?"

"I suppose so."

"Mama says—"

"Stephen?" Alec interrupted. "Do you have to listen to everything your mother says?"

Stephen bobbed his head.

"Well, now it's time to listen to what Papa says. And Papa says, let's not talk about Jesse anymore."

"Why?"

"Because."

"Mama says that's not a reason."

Eric snickered.

Alec scowled back at him. "Did you have something you wanted to add, Eric?"

"No, Pa."

"Good. Then we can consider the subject of Jesse closed."

"But I like Jes—" Eric clamped a hand over Stephen's mouth. "Not now, Stephen. Why don't we talk about something else?"

"Like what?" the youngster wanted to know.

"How about Amber?" Alec suggested as he brought the buggy to a stop in front of Crowley's.

Eric's face turned as pale as a sheet of parchment.

"I like Amber," Stephen announced.

"Well, you're in luck, then. A little bird told me that she was working here at the store." Alec cast a sidelong glance at Eric. "Isn't that right, Eric?"

Eric slouched down on the seat of the buggy, wanting to disappear. "How should I know?"

"Well, a man generally doesn't slick his hair all back and douse himself with cologne unless there's a woman in the picture somewhere."

Color rushed back into Eric's cheeks. "I didn't realize I was being that obvious."

"There are two things in this world that aren't hard to mistake. The look of a woman in love and a man who's got courtin' on his mind."

"Courting!" Eric sputtered. "But all I was going to do is invite her to supper."

"Supper, huh?" Alec considered Eric's appearance further. "Well, I'm afraid after one look at you she's liable to take an invitation like that to mean something more."

Eric couldn't allow that to happen. As much as he liked Amber, he wasn't ready for a commitment of the nature that his father was suggesting. They hardly knew one another. "You're right," he decided. "I wasn't thinking this through properly. It's probably best to just forget the whole thing."

"Now, hold on a second. I never said that."

"But you're right. I can't go in there looking like this. What if she gets the wrong idea?"

Alec shrugged. "Whether you go in or not is up to you. But I can guarantee that your Ma's going to have her fair share of questions if you show up back at the house without that bolt of material she's been wanting."

"The material," Eric said with a groan. "I forgot about that."

"What are you gong to do?" Alec asked.

"I'll have to go in and get. But that's all."

"Do you want me to wait for you?"

"We'll walk back." Eric stepped down from the buggy and then turned and lifted Stephen out. "Thanks for the ride."

"Anytime. Say, I'm planning on stopping by the Randall's to check up on Tad on my way home. Anything you want me to tell Alicia?"

"Nothing that Ma would want me to repeat in front of Stephen."

Alec chuckled. "Understood. See you both at lunch."

"Bye, Papa!" Stephen hollered after the departing buggy.

"Come on, Stephen." Eric reached down and took hold of his hand. "Let's go in before I lose my nerve."

"I'll help you find it if you do," the youngster offered.

"Thanks, kiddo."

Eric was relieved to find no one else in the store except for the elderly proprietress, Ida Crowley. The last thing he needed was an audience. If the true nature of his visit ever got out, the tongues would never stop wagging.

Ida turned from the row of shelves against the back wall of the store, clutching a can of peaches in either hand. Her plump, rosy-cheeked countenance brightened immediately with a warm smile of welcome. "Well, if this isn't a pleasant surprise this fine morning."

"Hello, Mrs. Crowley." Eric nudged Stephen in the back. "Say hello, Stephen."

"Hello."

"And a hello to you, too, Stephen. Just give me a moment to finish stacking these canned goods and I'll be right with you boys. We're a little shorthanded this morning with Josiah out making deliveries."

"You are? But I thought...." Eric breathed a sigh of relief. Colin must have been mistaken. Amber wasn't working at the store after all.

"You're not in a hurry, are you?" Ida asked, mistaking his sigh for impatience. "Or on your way somewhere special?" Her grayish-green eyes sparkled with curiosity as she took note of his appearance.

"Oh, no, ma'am," Eric answered hurriedly, managing to stave off a blush. "My ma just sent me in to see if—"

Stephen tugged at his pant leg.

"In a minute, Stephen. Can't you see I'm talking to Mrs. Crowley?"

"But I gotta go," he whispered back.

"You mean...." Eric frowned down at him. "Why didn't you go before we left home?"

"I didn't have to go then."

Eric turned back to face Ida. "Mrs. Crowley, can we use your—"

"Why don't you let me take him," she offered. "I baked some molasses cookies last night and I'm not sure I put enough brown sugar in. I could really use a second opinion."

Eric smiled at her thoughtfulness. "Thank you, Mrs. Crowley."

"It's no trouble at all. Amber can help you with whatever you need."

Eric's heart nearly stopped. "Amber?"

Ida turned towards the door that led into the storeroom. "Amber, dear?"

"Yes, Aunt Ida?"

"Could you come wait on Mr. Ramsey for me?" Ida smiled down at Stephen. "I have a small errand to attend to."

"I'll be right out," Amber called back.

Eric stood staring at the storeroom door with a panic-stricken look on his face. He couldn't let Amber see him. "On second thought, Mrs. Crowley, maybe I should take Stephen."

"There's no need for that. We won't be long."

"But, Mrs. Crowley, I—" Eric's shoulders sagged as he watched her disappear with Stephen through a door at the back of the store. "I don't want to be alone with your niece."

Eric refocused his gaze back on the storeroom, wiping his sweaty palms down the sides of his trousers. At any moment Amber was going to come walking through that door and he didn't have a clue what he was going to say to her. He couldn't lie, but he didn't dare tell her of his intentions to invite her to supper either, not while looking like a man who had "courtin' on his mind" as his father called it.

Eric stepped over to the full-length mirror that was fastened to the wall beside a display of women's hats and studied his appearance. He couldn't do anything about changing his clothing, but perhaps something could be done with his hair. He quickly mussed it up a bit and then took a step back, scrutinizing the new look he had given himself. A less than satisfied sigh passed between his lips. "I suppose that will have to do."

"Hello."

Eric started as Amber's reflection appeared beside him in the mirror. He turned slowly to face her, feeling suddenly weak in the knees. She was even more beautiful than he remembered.

"Eric, isn't it?"

Eric replied with a nod of his head, trying to detach his tongue from the roof of his mouth.

"What can I do for you?"

"Do?" he uttered.

"Well, I assume you didn't come in here just to fix your hair."

Eric responded with an embarrassed chuckle. "Of course not. I have a list of things I need right here." He quickly dug the list from his pocket, anxious to conduct his business and get out of the store while he still had some semblance of dignity left. "Here you are."

Amber brought a hand up to cover her mouth as she silently read through the list of items that Eric intended to purchase.

"Is something wrong?" he asked.

"I'm just not sure that I'll be able to fill your order." Amber studied the list again, suppressing a chuckle. "We may have a church social or two in the storeroom, but I'm fairly certain that we're all out of moon-lit walks. I could order you one from the catalog, though."

Alicia's list! Eric snatched the paper back, his face turning every shade of red in the color spectrum. "Wrong list," he said quickly, stuffing it back into his pocket.

"Not for some lucky young lady," Amber declared boldly.

Eric slid his gaze to the floor. "I guess I left the other list at home. I'm sorry to have bothered you."

"Oh, but it's no bother," Amber assured him. "I was just about finished in the storeroom, anyway. And besides...I was hoping I would see you again."

Eric's heart soared like an uncaged bird. "You were?"

"Wait here." Amber stepped over behind the store's main counter and retrieved something from a box on the bottom shelf. She returned to Eric's side holding a blue ribbon. "I felt so bad that Stephen lost the one I gave him yesterday when he fell in the pond," she explained. "Would you see that he gets this?"

Eric stared at the ribbon. That's it? That's the reason she had been hoping to see him again?

"You will, won't you?" Amber asked again.

Eric swallowed back his disappointment and took the ribbon. "I'll see that he gets it. Your aunt took him to the—" He caught himself before uttering the words "water closet". It just didn't seem proper. "But they should be back any minute."

Amber acknowledged his report with a faint smile, which she continued to hold fixed in place through the awkward moments of silence that followed. "Well, unless there's something else I can do for you, I should be finishing up in the storeroom."

"No!" Eric blurted as she turned to leave. "I mean, yes... there is something."

Amber walked back to where he was standing.

"You can accept my apology for not being able to introduce you around at the picnic yesterday. My mother had already made other plans for me with—" Eric waved aside what he was about to say. "But that's not important now."

"You don't have to explain," Amber said with a gracious smile. "Colin told me what happened. I respect the decision you made not to disappoint your mother."

"That's very understanding of you. I hope you were able to get acquainted with a few folks anyway."

"Oh, I did. The Reverend and Mrs. Thompson, Mr. and Mrs. Reynolds, and Anna Jenkins, the seamstress. Everyone in Baxter seems very nice. I think I'm going to like living here."

Eric was embarrassed to say that he didn't know either the Reynolds' *or* Anna Jenkins. They must have been among the influx of new arrivals that settled in Baxter during his absence.

"While on the subject of the picnic...." Amber took a half step toward him, her head cocked slightly to one side. "Did Colin mention anything to you about West Point?"

"He did. And I believe I have you to thank for that."

"I just told him that he should be honest with you. I'm sure you would have done the same."

Amber's assumption left Eric with a sour taste in his mouth. He was a fine one to be discussing honesty with. He hadn't been honest about a single thing since setting foot in the store. But that was about to change.

"I should be getting back to work." Amber started to turn away.

"Wait!" Eric implored her.

Amber halted in her tracks, her only movement the blinking of her eyes.

"I was wondering if you would...." Eric paused to clear his throat.

"Wondering if I would what?" Amber asked before he could continue.

"Wondering if you would like to have supper with my family tonight. I know it's kind of short notice...."

"Not at all," Amber assured him. "I would love to."

"You would?" Eric grinned through his surprise. "Great. Say around six o'clock?"

"That sounds fine. I'll have my uncle drive me over."

"Eric!" Stephen came bounding back into the store with a molasses cookie clutched in either hand. A grinning Ida followed along behind. "Mrs. Crowley goes inside like we do!"

Eric felt the heat of a blush coming on. "Stephen, it isn't proper to discuss such matters when there are ladies present. Now come see what Miss Amber has for you."

Stephen's eyes nearly tripled in size when he saw the ribbon that Eric was holding out to him. "Wow! Thanks, Miss Amber!"

"You're welcome, Stephen." Amber leaned down and helped him pin it on. "Now, no more falling in the pond. Deal?"

"Deal!"

"We should be getting home now." Eric began backing towards the door, drawing Stephen along with him. "Thanks for everything, Mrs. Crowley."

"You're welcome, dear. Tell your mother hello for me."

"I will."

"See you tonight!" Amber called out at the last moment. Eric turned back with a parting smile. "Tonight."

Ida descended upon her niece like hungry vulture as soon as Eric and Stephen had left the store. "Am I to understand that you'll be spending the evening at the Ramsey's?"

"That's right." Amber headed back to the storeroom with Ida close on her heels. "Eric invited me to supper."

"Did he."

Amber recognized a matchmaking tone when she heard one. "Now, Aunt Ida, don't go jumping to conclusions. It's just a supper invitation."

"That young man had more on his mind than just a supper invitation when he walked into this store."

Amber spun to face her aunt, shocked that she would suggest such a thing. "Surely you can't be serious."

"I've seen that look in many a young man's eye, including your Uncle Josiah's the day he asked my father for permission to court me."

"But he only set eyes on me yesterday," Amber reminded her. "We've hardly had time to get properly acquainted, let alone talk of such matters as you're suggesting."

"You've got to start somewhere. Why not tonight over supper?"

Amber stared after her aunt as she strolled to the other side of the store and began straightening up the shelves of yard goods. Could she be right? Could Eric Ramsey actually have designs on her? Amber restrained an excited giggle. It was going to be a most interesting evening.

CHAPTER EIGHT

MISMATCH

Eric was still reeling from Amber's acceptance of his supper invitation when he and Stephen arrived back home. "She said yes! She actually said yes!"

"What about Mama's material?" Stephen asked as he followed Eric in the front door.

"The material." Eric smacked the palm of his hand against his forehead. "I knew I forgot something."

"Is that you, Eric?" Kathleen called from the top of the stairs.

"Yeah, Ma," he answered hesitantly.

Kathleen made her way down with a basket of laundry propped on her left hip. "I didn't expect you home so soon. Did you have a nice time?"

Stephen ran to the foot of the stairs, nearly bowling her over in his excitement. "I got to use Mrs. Crowley's water closet and she gave me two masses cookies and Miss Amber gave me a ribbon!" Stephen pulled the ribbon from his shirt and waved it back and forth in front of her.

"Well, hold it still a moment so Mama can see," Kathleen implored him. "You say she gave it to you?"

"It's to replace the one he lost when he fell in the pond yesterday," Eric explained.

"Well, that was very thoughtful of her." Kathleen handed the ribbon back to Stephen. "I hope you told Miss Amber thank you."

"I did."

"Good. She seems like such a nice young woman. And I've been thinking…." Kathleen tapped a finger against her lips. "It might be a nice gesture if we invited her to take supper with us one of these evenings. She is going to be Nathan and Kaitlin's teacher this fall, and it would give them a chance to get to know her. What do you think about that idea, Eric?"

"Me?" Eric felt his pulse quicken its pace within the hollow of his neck. "Well…."

"Yes, I believe I will," Kathleen decided before he could respond. "I'll extend her an invitation the next time I see her."

"You're gonna see her tonight," Stephen told her.

"What?"

Eric quickly stepped in before Stephen could repeat himself. "Stephen, why don't you go get your fishing pole and I'll take you over to the pond."

"Oh, boy!"

Kathleen watched his hurried ascent up the stairs and then cast her gaze around to Eric. "Now where do you suppose he got the idea that I would be seeing Amber tonight?"

Eric hunched his shoulders. "I wouldn't know, Ma."

"Well, no matter. So tell me…." Kathleen hefted the basket of laundry back to her hip. "Did you find everything that you were looking for at the store?"

"Not exactly." Eric followed her down the hallway to the kitchen. "I forgot to get your material. But I can go back for it if you want."

Kathleen beamed him a smile over her shoulder as she headed for the back door. "There's no need for that. It's probably too soon for it to be in anyway. What about the other things you needed? Did you at least get those?"

"I forgot my list at home," Eric admitted.

"Oh, what a shame. Going all that way for nothing."

Eric grinned at the thought of seeing Amber again. *Not for nothing, Ma.*

"By the way…." Kathleen paused at the door, turning back to face him, "Alicia stopped by while you were out. I invited her to supper tonight."

Eric's grin petered out like a fire deprived of oxygen. "Tonight?"

"Well, I couldn't very well not invite her. I did offer to show her how to make an apple pie."

Eric began to sweat. Alicia couldn't come to supper tonight. Amber was coming.

"She already had other plans, though," Kathleen told him. "It's her aunt's birthday today and the family is throwing her a party. Alicia says you're welcome to come if you like."

Eric waved aside the invitation as if he were swatting at a fly. "I sort of already have other plans."

"Yes, I thought you might. Of course, I didn't say as much to Alicia." A hint of a smile appeared on Kathleen's lips. "So, what time will Amber be joining us?"

Eric's mouth dropped open like a well-oiled hinge. "How'd you know?"

"The look on your face when I told you that I'd invited Alicia for supper tonight as well."

"Oh." Eric slid his gaze to the floor then quickly brought it up again. "You don't mind that I invited her without asking you first, do you?"

"Of course not. I was hoping you—that is, I'm looking forward to getting to know her myself. And who knows? Maybe after tonight she'll be spending a lot more time around here."

"It's not what you're thinking, Ma. I only invited her to supper. Nothing more."

"Maybe so," she said, smiling as she slipped out the back door. "But you've got to start somewhere."

"Start somewhere with what?" Colin wondered, coming up beside Eric.

"With your studies. It's time we got started."

"I'm ready when you are."

"Good. Grab your fishing pole and meet me out front."

Colin scratched his head as Eric strode out of the kitchen. "My fishing pole? But I don't remember there being fishing on the exam."

* * * * *

"Thank you for the ride, Uncle Josiah." Amber placed her hand on his shoulder to steady herself as she stepped down from the wagon. "But it really wasn't necessary. If I had known they lived so close to town, I could've walked. I wouldn't have minded."

Josiah waved aside her objections. "Nonsense, gal. I was glad to bring you. Now, what time shall I come back for you?"

"Oh, dear." Amber clamped her bottom lip between her teeth. "I hadn't thought to ask that."

Josiah crossed his arms over his chest, gazing up at the evening sky. "Maybe Eric could walk you home," he suggested. "There's going to be a full moon tonight. Very romantic."

Amber blushed to the roots of her raven black hair. "Really, Uncle Josiah. A man your age making such a bold suggestion. What would Aunt Ida say?"

"Who do you think made the suggestion in the first place?" he said with a wink.

Amber laughed in spite of her discomfort. "Dear Aunt Ida. Always playing matchmaker."

"Yes, she does tend to get carried away at times. But for once I have to agree with her choice. Eric Ramsey is a fine young man. A woman couldn't hope to find any better. And he's handsome, to boot."

"Yes, he is rather—" Amber's blush returned in earnest as she realized what she was about to say. "I should be going in now. Why don't you just come for me around ten. If I decide to leave before then, I'll make other arrangements."

Josiah bobbed his head with a smile. "Ten it is."

* * * * *

"What's she doing now?" Eric asked as he worked furiously to straighten his tie.

"She just kissed her uncle good-bye...and now she's coming up to the door." Colin stepped away from the bedroom window, dropping the curtain back into place. "You almost ready?"

"Just about." Eric gave his tie one final tug before turning from the mirror atop his dresser to face Colin. "Give me your honest opinion. How do I look?"

Colin chuckled. "You're nervous, aren't you?"

"What makes you say that?"

"Well, for starters, you've got your pants on inside out."

"No, I—" Eric cut short his protest as he tried repeatedly to slip his hands into pockets that weren't there. "Well, maybe I am a little nervous. Will you tell Amber that I'll be down in a few minutes?"

"Sure. And don't worry. There are worse things that could happen tonight."

Eric frowned. "That's what I'm afraid of."

* * * * *

"More tea, Amber?"

"No thank you, Mrs. Ramsey." Amber placed her empty cup on the tray that Kathleen was holding out to her. "That was my third cup. I'm about to float away as it is."

Kathleen stole a glance at the stairway as she returned the tray to the table in front of the sofa. "I can't understand what's keeping Eric. Colin, he did say that he'd be right down."

"Yeah, Ma. He was having trouble putting on his— " Colin caught himself just before saying pants. "His tie."

"I'm hungry," Stephen complained, grasping at the sides of his stomach.

Nathan quickly joined him, groaning as if he were in pain. "Me, too."

"I know you are." Kathleen retook her seat next to Alec on the end of the sofa. "But we have to wait for your brother."

Alec leaned out around her, peering down to the other end where Amber was sitting. "So, Amber, I understand that you're from Boston."

"Cambridge, actually. Born and raised. But my last teaching position was in Boston."

"I know the Cambridge area well," Alec was pleased to tell her. "I attended medical school at Harvard."

"If you don't mind my asking," Kathleen piped in, "what prompted you to accept a teaching position here? Baxter seems a world away from Boston."

Amber refrained from answering as Eric entered the room. "Sorry to have kept everyone waiting."

"Eric, you're just in time." Kathleen patted the empty space between her and Amber on the sofa, indicating that he should occupy it. "Amber was about to tell us—" A knock at the front door interrupted the completion of her thought.

"I'll get it." Eric stepped back into the entryway, reaching the door in three lengthy strides.

"Hello, Eric," Alicia said giddily, as the door swung open before her. "Are you surprised?"

"That wasn't exactly the word I had in mind."

Alicia's smile slowly receded. "Didn't your mother tell you about the party that we're having for my Aunt Gertrude this evening?"

"Yes, she did, but—"

"Oh, Eric, you will come, won't you?" Alicia pressed towards him, her face upturned with a simpering pout. "For me?"

"I'm afraid I can't, Alicia," Eric told her plainly. "I already have other plans."

Alicia's gaze turned seething as Amber appeared beside him at the door. "So I see."

"Hello," Amber said politely, extending Alicia her hand. "I don't believe we've yet had the pleasure. I'm Amber Lloyd, the new schoolteacher. And you are...?"

"Not amused." Alicia turned abruptly on the heels of her pointy-toed shoes and marched down the porch steps in a huff.

Amber retracted her hand, puzzled by what could have prompted the young woman's brusqueness towards her. "You don't think it was something I said, do you?" she asked Eric. "Maybe I should go apologize."

"No!" Eric snapped back. "I mean...it would be best to just leave matters as they are."

Amber shrugged. "If that's what you think best."

"Anybody hungry?" Kathleen called from behind them.

"Famished," Eric answered heartily. He offered Amber his arm. "May I?"

Stephen crowded him aside. "I want to take her."

Amber swapped a smile with Eric. "My goodness. I've never been fought over by two such handsome gentlemen at the same time before. How ever am I going to decide?" Amber drummed her fingers against her cheek, considering the dilemma before her. "There seems to be only one solution. You're just going to have to share me."

Kathleen smiled as she watched the trio walk arm-in-arm down the hall. "I knew it," she said to herself. "I just knew it."

"Knew what?" Alec asked, coming up behind her.

"Shh." Kathleen pressed a finger against her lips. "They might hear you."

"Who?"

Kathleen clasped her hands to her chest with a contented sigh. "Oh, Alec, aren't they just perfect for one another?"

Alec followed her misty-eyed gaze down the hall. "Stephen and Amber?"

"No, silly. Amber and Eric."

Alec tossed her a look of caution. "Don't you think you might be putting the cart before the horse? Remember how wrong you were about Alicia."

"This is different," she insisted. "Anyone can see they're a perfect match. Trust me."

* * * * *

Amber gasped as she became conscious of the clock above the fireplace mantle. "It can't be that late already."

"Did you say something, dear?" Kathleen asked.

Amber snapped her mouth shut, fashioning it into a smile as she tore her gaze away from the clock. "No, Mrs. Ramsey. I was just thinking to myself how much I've enjoyed this evening."

"I'm so glad. And please call me Kathleen. I believe we know each other well enough now to be on a first name basis."

"All right," Amber agreed. "Kathleen."

The hum of conversation continued for another fifteen minutes without further interruption. Amber refrained from joining in unless spoken to, electing instead to keep her attention focused upon the clock. It was quickly approaching the time that she had told her uncle to return for her. Unless she made up an excuse to leave soon, she would be riding home with him in the wagon instead of walking beside Eric in the moonlight.

"If you need to leave, dear, we'll understand," Kathleen told her.

Amber turned to face her, a guilty flush settling upon her cheeks. Had Kathleen discerned her secret longings?

"I couldn't help but notice that you keep looking at the clock," she explained further.

"Do I? I'm sorry. I guess I am getting a little tired. It's been a long day."

"There's no need to apologize. I'm sure that Eric would be glad to take you home."

"Of course." Eric got at once to his feet. "I'll go hitch up the buggy."

"Eric, wait!" Amber's outburst came just as he was about to leave the room. Eric turned back, looking intently into her eyes as she continued. "It's such a beautiful night. I don't mind walking if you don't."

Eric was surprised and overjoyed at the same time. He had been thinking about suggesting that very thing but hadn't gotten up the courage to actually follow through and ask her. Thankfully, she had.

Amber waited anxiously for his reply, fearing that she may have overstepped the bounds of proper etiquette by making such as bold suggestion. But then Eric spoke the four words that her heart had been longing to hear. "I would love to."

Kathleen was positively beaming as the couple walked out the front door. "What did I tell you," she crowed, nudging Alec in the side. "The perfect match."

* * * * *

"Thanks again for walking me home, Eric. Good night." Amber scrambled quickly inside the store, shutting the door securely behind her. A shroud of disappointment settled in around her heart as she thought about what had just happened. Or rather, what *hadn't* happened. "How could I have been so wrong about him?"

"Amber, dear? Is that you?"

"Yes, Aunt Ida." Amber quickly put on a false smile as her aunt bustled through the door at the back of the store, bracing herself for the onslaught of questions that she knew was forthcoming. Ida didn't disappoint. "How was your evening? Did you have a good time?"

"Fine," Amber told her honestly. "The Ramsey's are a wonderful family."

"And Eric?" she asked, her eyes glowing with anticipation.

Amber touched a finger to her lips. She was no longer smiling. "He kissed me good night."

"Wonderful!" Ida sang out.

"No, horrible. Being kissed by Eric was like...like being kissed by Uncle Josiah."

Ida smiled coyly. "I happen to enjoy being kissed by your Uncle Josiah."

"Aunt Ida, you know what I mean."

"Yes, dear, I believe I do. There weren't any fireworks, were there?"

Amber shook her head. "Not even a spark. Only I'm afraid there were for him. I think he might be falling in love with me." Amber buried her face in the palms of her hands. "Oh, Aunt Ida, what am I going to do?"

"You're going to be honest with him, that's what you're going to do. And the sooner the better. You can't pretend feelings you don't have."

Amber knew wise counsel when she heard it. She couldn't allow Eric to go on thinking there was something between them when there wasn't, no matter how painful the truth might be for him to hear. "I'll go see him first thing in the morning."

"I think that would be wise. In the meantime...." Ida steered her through the door that led into their living quarters at the back of the store. "Try and get some sleep."

Amber kissed her cheek. "Good night, Aunt Ida."

"Good night, dear. Pleasant dreams."

As soon as Amber was comfortably settled in her room, Ida made her way to the kitchen for a much needed cup of coffee. Josiah was seated at the table reading a book when she entered. "Did Amber have a good time?" he asked.

"Not as good as I'd hoped," Ida confessed. "It turns out that she and Eric are all wrong for each other. I was really hoping that they...." A sigh punctuated the end of her thought. "But I guess it wasn't meant to be."

"Guess not."

Ida stared at her husband as she nestled her bulk onto the chair next to his. "Josiah, kiss me," she urged.

Josiah's gaze rose above the top of the book to meet hers. "Right now?"

"Oh, for Pete's sake." Ida leaned over and kissed him squarely on the mouth and then settled back in her chair to wait. It wasn't long before a smile appeared on her lips. "Well, what do you know about that. They're still there after all these years."

Josiah laid his book aside, looking at her curiously. "Are you feeling all right?"

"Fine, dear," she assured. "Just watching the fireworks."

* * * * *

Colin bounded out of bed as soon as he heard footsteps coming down the hall. He was waiting at the door of their room when Eric walked in. "It's about time you got home."

"What are you still doing up? It must be after eleven."

"Waiting for you. You didn't think I could go to sleep without finding out what happened, did you?"

"Colin, I'm really tired." Eric tossed his coat onto the chair inside the door. "Can we talk about this is the morning?"

Colin stepped in front of him, blocking his path. "Please?"

Eric realized that he wasn't going to get any rest until he had satisfied the younger man's curiosity. "All right." He motioned for Colin to take a seat on his bed and then settled down beside him. "What exactly is it that you want to know?"

"Oh, just the usual. Did you have a good time, did she have a good time...." Colin gave Eric a nudge in the ribs. "Did you kiss her good night?"

"Yes...yes...and none of your business." Eric got quickly to his feet.

"You did kiss her!" Colin slapped his hand down across his knee. "I knew it! What was it like?"

"Good night, Colin." Eric turned his back and began unbuttoning his shirt to prepare for bed.

"Oh, come on, Eric," Colin implored him. "I just want to know if you saw fireworks like my friend Chris says he does every time he kisses a girl."

"I didn't see any fireworks." Eric opened the top drawer of the dresser and took out a nightshirt. "Not even a spark."

Colin sat forward with an anxious gleam in his eyes. "What did you see?"

"Nothing."

Colin's shoulders slumped in disappointment. "Nothing?"

"Nothing. Kissing Amber was like...." Eric drew the nightshirt over his head, turning back towards Colin "Like kissing Kirsten. I care about her, but like I would a sister, or a friend. It will never be more than that."

"That's probably what Romeo said about Juliet at first, too."

"A friend, Colin," Eric told him sternly. "Just a friend."

Colin hopped up to his feet as Eric began turning down the bed. "But how can you know that for sure after only one kiss? Maybe you should kiss her again."

"I don't need to." Eric crawled beneath the sheets, drawing them up to his chest. "I know how I feel, Colin."

"But what if she doesn't feel the same way? What if she's madly in love with you?"

"Then I'll just have to be honest with her. I can't pretend something I don't feel. Now go to sleep." Eric reached over and dimmed the lamp beside his bed, plunging the room into darkness.

Colin turned with a scowl and stumbled blindly back to his own bed. "I waited up for that?"

CHAPTER NINE

JUST FRIENDS

Eric slept late the following morning, waking long after the sun had risen above the treetops. As he made his way downstairs, he was struck by how unusually quiet the house was considering the lateness of the hour. "Hello?" he called as he reached the bottom step. "Ma? Anybody?"

"In the kitchen, Eric!"

Kathleen was down on all fours giving the floor a thorough scrubbing when Eric found her. "Mind you don't slip," she cautioned him.

Eric spied a relatively dry patch over by the stove and went to stand there. "Where is everybody?" he wondered.

Kathleen sat back on her heels, pressing the back of her hand to her perspiring brow. "Colin went fishing with his friend Chris, Kirsten is with Jesse, your father's not yet back from his rounds, and I sent the younger three outside to play while I washed the floor."

"No wonder it's so quiet. For a moment I thought I was in the wrong house."

"It wasn't so quiet earlier," Kathleen recalled as she resumed her scrubbing. "I'm surprised you slept as soundly as you did. But then you did get in rather late last night. You and Amber must have had a lot to talk about."

"We weren't talking." Eric blushed as he realized the impression that his reply must have given her. "What I meant was, I took Amber straight home and then I went for a walk—*alone*," he emphasized.

Kathleen sat back again, fixing him with a sympathetic smile. "There's no need to explain. She's not the one, is she?"

Eric was impressed by the level of her insight but then realized that she may have had some assistance in arriving at her conclusion. "Colin said something to you, didn't he?"

"Just that there hadn't been any fireworks. Woman's intuition put two and two together from there. But don't be angry with him. I brought the subject up."

"I'm not angry," Eric assured her. "I just should've never told him that I kissed her."

Kathleen rose slowly to her feet, her eyes widening in proportion to her grin. "You did?"

Eric's jaw went slack. "Colin didn't mention that?"

"Colin didn't mention that."

Eric found himself blushing once again. "Well, it doesn't matter now, anyway. It's not going to happen again."

Kathleen took a step towards him, concerned that he might be dismissing the matter a bit prematurely. "Are you sure you're not overlooking something? Like how Amber feels?"

Eric hunched his shoulders. "I don't know how Amber feels," he admitted. "She disappeared inside the store last night before I had the chance to find out."

"Then perhaps you should ask her," Kathleen suggested. "You can't let her go on thinking you feel something for her when you don't."

Eric nodded in silent agreement. He knew all too well what needed to be done. "I guess there's no sense in putting it off. I'll go talk to her right now."

"Before you do...." Kathleen picked up the bucket of water that she'd been using to wash the floor "Would you mind emptying this for me?"

"Sure."

Eric carried the bucket out the back door, finding himself the unexpected guest at the tea party that Kaitlin was having with several of her dolls. "Well, now. What might you lovely ladies be up to this fine day?"

"We're having a tea party," Kaitlin told him excitedly. "Do you want to come?" She held up a miniature-sized cup filled with a mixture of dirt and water.

Eric took one look at the expectant gleam in her eyes and didn't have the heart to turn her down. His talk with Amber would just have to wait. "Don't mind if I do. It's been far too long since I've had a good cup of tea. Just let me empty this bucket for Ma first."

Eric tossed the contents over the porch railing and then tipped the bucket upside down against the side of the house to dry. "There, now. That didn't take long, did it?"

Kaitlin stood to her feet with a scowl, her arms folded snugly against her chest. "You shouldn't have done that."

Eric glanced back to where he'd placed the bucket, seeing nothing he'd done that warranted such a tongue-lashing. "Shouldn't have done what?" he asked.

"Throwed that water on Miss Amber. It wasn't very nice."

"I quite agree, Kaitlin. But I'm sure your brother must have a logical explanation."

Eric's heart stopped cold as Amber stepped up onto the porch, sopping wet from head to toe.

"Well, Eric?" Amber folded her arms across her chest, mirroring Kaitlin's stance. "Would you care to share it with us?"

* * * * *

113

Eric stood with his forehead pressed against the wall outside Kirsten's room. "How could I have been so stupid?" he chided himself.

"Are you sure you want me to answer that?"

Eric looked up as his mother stepped out, easing the door shut behind her. His gaze lingered for a moment on the bundle of Amber's damp clothing that she was carrying. "Ma, how is she?"

"Fine now that she's out of these wet things. I found her something of Kirsten's to put on."

Eric still wasn't breathing any easier. "Does she seem mad?" he was curious to know.

Kathleen adjusted the bundle in her arms, considering how best to describe Amber's current state of mind. "I suppose that would depend on how you define mad."

"Well, do you think she'll talk to me?"

"She might," came a gruff reply from behind the door.

Kathleen took that as her cue to make an exit and began backing her way down the hall. "I best go hang these things up to dry."

Eric stared after her, horrified at the thought of being left alone with Amber. "You're not staying?"

"Don't worry," she whispered back with a teasing smile. "She's not going to bite."

Eric could hardly blame her if she did. She had every right to be furious with him.

"I'm waiting," Amber called impatiently.

Eric would have preferred a few more minutes to collect his thoughts but Amber didn't sound as if she were going to comply with his wishes. She wanted her apology now.

"Well?" she urged again.

"I'm really sorry about what happened," Eric told her earnestly. "There was no excuse for it."

"And?"

Eric inched his way closer to the door. "And you have every right to be angry."

"True," Amber agreed.

"In fact...." Eric swallowed hard. "I wouldn't blame you if you never wanted to speak to me again...ever."

This time there was nothing but silence in return. "Like I said, I wouldn't blame you if—" Eric took a half step back as the door began to open, just a crack at first, then wide enough for Amber to poke her head out. "Apology accepted."

Eric smiled. "Then you're not mad?"

"I didn't say I wasn't mad," Amber was quick to point out. "But I figure it's not your fault that I was in the wrong place at the wrong time. I'll just have to be more careful where I walk from now on, won't I?"

"And I'll have to be more careful where I empty the buckets."

Amber returned his smile. "Would you mind if we continue this conversation after I finish getting dressed? There's something I need to discuss with you and I'd rather not do it with this door between us."

"Of course."

"Wait right there. I won't be long."

Eric had a hunch that what Amber wanted to discuss with him was the same matter he wanted to discuss with her. It would be good to finely get everything out in the open.

"There you are."

Eric did a double take as Alicia came scurrying towards him. "Alicia. What are you doing here?"

"Your mother told me I could come on up. As to why I'm here...." She sighed deeply. "I came to apologize for my behavior yesterday evening and to beg your forgiveness for not giving you a chance to explain. It was purely selfish on my part."

"Explain?"

"Yes. I'm sure there was a perfectly logical reason why that woman—" Alicia's voice faltered as the subject in question stepped out of Kirsten's room.

"Eric, would you mind helping me with this last button? I can't quite seem to reach—" Amber dropped her hands from behind her neck when she saw Alicia. "Oh, excuse me. I didn't realize you had a guest."

"A guest?" Alicia glared at Eric, her lips trembling with unrestrained fury. "Is that all I am to you, Eric Ramsey, a guest? Well, I—I never want to speak to you again!" She turned on her heel in a repeat of yesterday evening's performance and marched back down the hall.

Amber turned timidly to face Eric. "Wrong place again?"

"No," he assured her. "This time you were in the right place. Now what was it you wanted to talk to me about?"

Amber stared down at her clasped hands. "It's about what happened between us last night."

"You mean the kiss?" Eric asked needlessly.

Amber nodded, forcing herself to look him in the eye. "Eric, I'm very fond of you, but not in the way I think you want me to be. The way it is between two people who...."

"You don't have to explain. I was planning on coming by the store today to tell you the very same thing."

Amber blinked in surprise. "Honest?"

"Honest."

"When did you...?"

"As soon as we kissed."

"Me, too," Amber confessed. "Don't take this the wrong way, but kissing you was like kissing my uncle."

"Believe me, I understand."

Amber smiled in relief. "So what do we do now?"

"Well...." Eric paused to consider their options. "There seems to be only one thing *to* do—start over. Only this time as friends. Agreed?"

"Agreed."

Kathleen cleared her throat from the top of the stairs. "I hope I'm not interrupting."

"Not at all, Ma."

"Good." Kathleen shifted her attention to Amber. "I just came up to see if the dress fits all right. If it doesn't, I'm sure we can find you something else."

"It fits just fine, Kathleen. Will you be sure and tell Kirsten thank you for me?"

"You can tell her yourself, if you'd like. She and Jesse are downstairs now. Then perhaps after that I can persuade you to stay and have lunch with us? It's the least we can do, considering."

"I don't think any persuading will be necessary," Amber told her honestly. "I'd love to."

"Fine. We'll be eating just as soon as Mr. Ramsey returns from his rounds. It shouldn't be more than twenty minutes or so."

"Twenty minutes," Eric said to himself. "That should be enough time."

"Enough time for what?" Amber wondered.

"How would you like to come with me to a tea party?"

CHAPTER TEN

OUT OF THE FRYING PAN, INTO THE FIRE

July 1860

A s the summer wore on, tensions between the North and South continued to escalate. Extremists on both sides felt certain that the only way to avoid hostilities would be for Abraham Lincoln to falter in his upcoming bid for the presidency. But that didn't seem likely. His popularity was gaining momentum all throughout the North, especially among those ardently opposed to slavery. As far as they were concerned, the November election was just a mere formality. Lincoln would be the next president of the United States.

Eric tried not to allow the many speculations to overshadow his visit with his family, avoiding conversations on the subject whenever possible. Yet for all his good intentions, he often found himself wondering what role he might be called upon to play. He certainly wasn't naïve enough to believe that an assignment in Washington would shield him completely, but he was grateful all the same that he would be hundreds of miles away from the caldron of war when it began to boil.

"Eric, I'm finished with chapters nine and ten. What do you want me to do now?"

Eric glanced up from the letter he sat penning at his desk. "Nine *and* ten?" Colin had pursued his studies over the course of the last month at a pace that even Eric would have found challenging to keep up with, and he wasn't showing any signs of slowing.

"Should I start on the next one?"

Eric sat back in his chair with a chuckle. "Colin, you are entitled to a break once in awhile."

"I know, but—"

"Why don't you take your fishing pole down to the pond and catch supper. You've done more than enough studying for today."

"But you're only going to be here a couple more months, and I haven't even gotten through half of—"

"Colin, you're more than ready to take that exam again any time you want," Eric assured him. "I have to admit that you've even surprised me. I'm proud of you."

Colin basked in the shower of his older brothers' praise. It meant more to him than getting into West Point ever would.

"Now, get." Eric shooed him out of the room. "I don't want to see your nose buried in another book all day. Is that understood?"

Colin smiled slyly. "On one condition...."

* * * * *

"Ma, get the frying pan ready. I reckon we've caught enough fish for a month of Sunday suppers."

"Good heavens." Kathleen gaped at the string of fish that Eric was dangling before her. "Did you leave any in the pond?"

Colin pretended to take offense. "You dare to ask the two greatest fishermen in all of Baxter, Pennsylvania a question like that?"

Kathleen grinned back at him. "Well, pardon me. I didn't know who I was talking to." Her attention returned to the fish. "And I do thank you for these. Jesse and his father are coming for supper tonight and I didn't have a clue what I was going to serve."

"Say no more." Eric stepped around her and headed for the sink. "I'll have these cleaned and ready for the frying pan in twenty minutes."

"I'll take care of that." Kathleen relieved him of the fish, handing him a towel in their place. "There's a letter for you there on the table. Mrs. Hanson dropped it by on her way home for lunch. She thought it might be important."

Eric quickly wiped his hands and stepped back to the table. He silently thanked the postmistress for her thoughtful gesture as he took note of the postmark on the letter. Important, indeed. It was from Washington.

Eric carefully unsealed the envelope as he took a seat at the table. "I hope it's more details about my assignment. I'd like to know as much as possible before—" Eric caught his breath as the word *reassigned* leapt off the page at him.

"What's the matter?" Colin sat down beside him, grabbing an apple from the basket on the table. "Did they put you in charge of polishing all the doorknobs or something?"

If only it were that simple, Eric thought. It took him a few moments to once again find his voice. "I won't be going to Washington after all."

Kathleen was quick to offer her sympathies, knowing how much the assignment had meant to him. "I'm sorry, Eric. Do they give you any explanation why?"

Eric swallowed, finding what he was about to say most difficult. "I've been reassigned…to Fort Moultrie."

Kathleen's blood ran cold at the news. She didn't need to be told where Fort Moultrie was, or the danger that Eric would be in should war break out while he was there.

Colin was equally stunned. "No fooling, Eric? They're really sending you to South Carolina?"

"Yeah." Eric turned to gauge how his mother was handling the news. The grief-stricken look on her face was enough to make him wish that he'd never joined the army. He quickly crossed to where she was standing, placing his hands gently on her shoulders. "Ma, they're just sending me down there to help make some repairs to the fort. I'm sure I'll be gone long before—" Eric couldn't bring himself to speak the remainder of his thoughts out loud. It was wishful thinking, anyway. He knew that if war broke out every man in uniform would be indispensable, him included.

"I'm sure you're right, dear," she said with a spirited smile, trying her best to put forth a brave front. "I have to get supper started. Excuse me."

Colin watched in dismay as she disappeared into the pantry. "I didn't think she'd take it so well."

"Don't be too sure she has, Col."

* * * * *

Kathleen extinguished the sconce outside of Stephen and Nathan's room before slipping quietly into the room that she and Alec occupied across the hall.

Alec looked up from the chair beside their bed where he sat taking off his shoes. "Are the kids asleep?"

"All except for Colin and Eric. And if I know those two, they'll be up talking half the night."

Kathleen picked up the lamp that sat burning on the stand inside the door and carried it with her to the small dressing table in the far corner of the room. A smile warmed her face as she took a seat on the matching stool and began the nightly routine of brushing out her hair. "I had such a fun time tonight, didn't you?"

"Yeah. I think Mr. Cameron did, too. We'll have to invite him again real soon."

"I was thinking the same thing. How about after church on Sunday?"

Alec sat back in his chair, studying her reflection in the mirror that was mounted to the back of the dressing table.

Kathleen smiled at him as she caught his eye. "Are you going to say something or just sit there gawking at me like a lovesick schoolboy?"

Alec's gaze didn't waver.

"Alec, what on earth—"

"Are you sure that you're okay with Eric being sent to South Carolina?"

Kathleen ceased her brushing for a few seconds and then furiously resumed it again. "You already asked me that once this evening. I told you that I was."

"I know what you said, Kathleen." Alec came to stand behind her, resting his hands on her shoulders. "It's what you're not saying that has me concerned. Eric, too."

"Well, there's no need for either of you to be," she said quite self-assuredly. "I'm perfectly fine."

Alec wrested the brush from her grasp and laid it aside on the table. "Are you really?"

Kathleen pivoted on the stool to face him. "Well, how do you expect me to feel? If South Carolina secedes like everyone is saying it will, there's probably going to be a war. Eric will be right in the middle of it. Are you telling me that doesn't frighten you?"

"Of course it does. But we're not discussing me." Alec caught her arm as she started to turn away. "You're concerned about more than just the threat of war, Kathleen." She opened her mouth to protest but he didn't give her the chance. "You're thinking about your folks, aren't you?"

Kathleen felt the wall that she had been concealing her true emotions behind come tumbling down around her. She knew that it would be senseless to protest any further. "I'm worried about Mama," she finally admitted to him. "It's been so long since I've heard from her. I don't even know if she's been getting my letters."

"I'm sure she has."

"Then why doesn't she write back?" she begged to know. "Why?" A solitary tear trickled down her cheek.

Alec drew her up into his arms, cradling her head against his shoulder. "There is one way to find out."

Kathleen looked up at him, interested to know what he had in mind.

"Since Eric has to go through Charleston anyway—"

"No," she said before he could finish.

"Kathleen, we've been over this before. Don't you think it's time he knew the truth?"

"I said, no." She pulled away from him and plunked herself down on the edge of the bed. Her hands moved as with a mind of their own, kneading themselves together at a furious pace. "Alec, can't we talk about this another time? I'm very tired."

Alec moved to sit beside her, taking a firm grasp on her hands. "You can't ignore this forever, Kathleen. You've got to tell him. All of them. They have a right to know their grandparents."

"I know. But I'm just not ready yet. Please, Alec. I just…." Her tears began now in earnest.

Alec coaxed her head down against his shoulder. "All right. I won't say anything more for now. But you've got to promise me that you'll tell Eric before he leaves."

"I will," she agreed, fighting back a surge of fresh tears. "I promise."

* * * * *

"There's something she's not telling me, Col."

"Who?"

"Ma." Eric leaned forward in his chair, resting his arms in front of him on the kitchen table. "I know she's not handling my going to South Carolina as well as she's letting on."

Colin drained the last few drops of milk from his glass and then wiped his mouth on the edge of the tablecloth. "She's probably just worried about her folks. With all this talk about war, who could blame her? Are you going to eat your pie?"

Eric sat up straighter in his chair. "What did you say?"

Colin pointed to the untouched slice of pie on his plate. "Your pie."

"Not about the pie. About her folks. What did you mean?"

"They're from Charleston, aren't they?"

Eric mentally kicked himself. How could he have over-looked such an important piece of the puzzle? "I guess I forgot," he admitted to Colin.

"That doesn't surprise me. She never talks about them. Now...." Colin rubbed his hands together, once again eyeing Eric's plate. "About that pie." Eric pushed it over in front of him. "Thanks."

"Sure."

Colin forked a huge bite into his mouth and then refilled his glass with milk from the pitcher on the table. He paused with the glass halfway to his lips. "It is kind of strange now that I think about it."

"What is?"

"That she never talks about her family." Colin took a quick sip and then set his glass back on the table. "We don't even know if she has any brothers or sisters. Why would she want to keep something like that a secret?"

Eric had to agree with Colin. It was strange. All they really did know about their mother was that she had left home as a young woman, no older than Kirsten. The reason why had never been discussed.

Colin emitted a groan, grasping onto the sides of his stomach. "I think three pieces was enough. I can't eat another bite." He slid the unfinished slice of pie back over in front of Eric and rose groggily out of his chair. "I'm going up to bed. You coming?"

"In a little while. Good night, Col."

"Night."

Eric realized soon after Colin left just how tired he was, but he couldn't stop thinking about his mother long enough to drag himself up to bed. Something had happened in her past, something so painful that she had kept it locked away inside her all these years.

"But what?" Eric uttered into the stillness of the room. He slid his head down onto his arm, gazing into the soft light that was spilling forth from the lamp in the center of the table. "What are you hiding, Ma?"

* * * * *

Eric jerked his head up from the table, blinking as his eyes adjusted to the light streaming through the window across the room.

"Good morning, sleepyhead."

Eric swung his gaze around to meet his father's grinning face. "Have you been down here all night?" Alec asked him.

"I must have been. Colin and I were talking and I guess I fell asleep. What time is it?"

"Just after six. I made some coffee." Alec indicated the pot he was tending on the stove. "Would you like some?"

"Please."

Alec transferred the pot to the table and then took down two cups from the cabinet beside the sink. He filled both to within a half-inch from the brim, placing one in front of Eric. "I can't guarantee that it will be as good as your ma's."

"As long as it's strong." Eric gingerly raised the cup to his lips, taking a tentative first sip. "It's fine. Thanks."

Alec settled onto the chair beside him. "So what were you and Colin talking about until all hours of the night?"

Eric lowered his cup back to the table, absently tracing his finger around the rim. "Pa, why hasn't Ma ever told us about her family? Or why she left home when she was only fourteen?"

Alec was caught off guard by both the content and the timing of Eric's inquiry. "Why the sudden interest in your mother's family tree?"

"Colin reminded me last night that she was from Charleston and I was just wondering why she never talks about that part of her life. I figured you must know something. If anyone, she would have confided in you."

True enough. Alec did have the answers that Eric was seeking. But he had promised Kathleen right after they were married that he would keep her secret for as long as she asked him to. She had yet to release him from that vow. "Eric, I really don't think it's my place to—"

"Pa, please," Eric implored him. "At least tell me why she—" He swallowed back the remainder of his plea as the subject of their discussion entered the room. Except for a brief glance in her direction, Eric kept his gaze trained on his father.

"Well, you two are certainly up bright and early this morning," Kathleen said with a cheery smile as she moved past them to the stove. "And starving, no doubt. How about pancakes this morning?" She plucked her apron off of the rack that was mounted outside the pantry door. "Or would you rather have bacon and eggs?"

Alec spoke first. "Bacon and eggs will be fine."

"How about you, Eric?" Kathleen slipped the apron over her head, securing it around her waist. "Bacon and eggs all right?"

Eric continued to stare at his father, silently conveying to him that their conversation was far from over. He wanted answers to his questions just as soon as a more opportune time presented itself.

"Eric?" Kathleen prompted him again.

"Bacon and eggs for me, too, Ma."

CHAPTER ELEVEN

THE LETTER

Kathleen released a frustrated sigh as she set a plate of sandwiches on the kitchen table. "Late again."

Nathan scrambled onto his chair, quickly claiming two of the sandwiches for himself. "Did you say something, Ma?" he asked before chomping into one of them.

"No, Nate." Kathleen secured a towel around Stephen's neck and then placed a sandwich in front of him. "You children go on and eat."

"Aren't we going to wait for Papa?" Kaitlin wondered.

Kathleen stole one last hopeful glance at the back door. "It doesn't appear as if your father is going to be joining us."

It was the forth time in as many days that Alec had been unable to have lunch with her and the children. While the number of patients that he had to see each day kept increasing, the number of hours he had to do it in didn't. He was wearing himself out and she was becoming increasingly concerned for his physical well-being. Something had to be done.

As soon as they were through eating, Kathleen sent the children outside to play and started on the dishes. She was just finishing up the last of them when Alec walked in the back door. A smile tugged at her lips as he took the towel that was draped over her shoulder and waved it back and forth like a flag of truce.

"I'm sorry I'm late," he offered contritely. "Are you upset?"

Kathleen propped her hands on her hips, regarding him as if she'd never heard a more ridiculous question. "Alec James Ramsey, if I bothered getting upset every time you were a few minutes late I wouldn't have time to do anything else. Of course I'm not upset."

Alec handed her back the towel. "But?"

Kathleen sucked in her bottom lip, taking a tentative step towards him. "But I am concerned," she confessed. "You've been working such long hours lately. Between making your rounds and seeing patients here at the house…well, it's getting so that the children and I hardly see you anymore." She quickly reached for his hand, regretting the accusatory path that her words had taken. "I'm not blaming you, Alec," she assured him, "just stating a fact. I know that your responsibilities as a doctor have to come first sometimes. It's just that…." She tightened her grip on his hand. "Well, they're becoming more than one man can handle. And that's why I think it's time that you seriously consider hiring an assistant."

"I agree."

Kathleen was surprised by how readily he conceded to her wishes. She thought she was going to have a fight on her hands. "You mean it? You'll really think about it?"

"I'm way ahead of you." Alec pulled a slip of paper from his vest pocket. "I stopped by the telegraph office on my way home to send this notice to several newspapers in New York and Boston, as well as to Chicago. That's why I'm late."

Kathleen's voice rose excitedly as she read the advertisement he had prepared. "Ambitious young physician wanted to share medical practice in growing Pennsylvania community. Apply in care of Doctor Alec Ramsey, Baxter, Pennsylvania. Oh, Alec, it's wonderful."

"Well, I don't know how wonderful it is, but it should bring in a response or two."

"A response or two?" Kathleen echoed back. "Alec Ramsey, you are far too modest. You are going to have more applicants knocking down your door than you know what to do with. Just you wait and see."

"I'm sure you're right," Alec replied, smiling with a confidence he didn't feel. He knew that finding a qualified physician willing to work for the meager salary he could afford to pay wasn't going to be as easy as she proposed it to be.

Kathleen patted his stomach. "You must be starved. I'll get you something."

"Not just yet." Alec pulled out a chair at the table and backed her into it. "We haven't discussed the other reason as to why I'm late."

"What other reason?" Kathleen wondered.

"This other reason." Alec withdrew an envelope from his jacket pocket, holding it so she could see the postmark. "All the way from Charleston in only two weeks. Isn't the United States postal service a wonder?"

Kathleen let loose with an ear-piercing squeal, snatching the envelope out of his hand. "I can hardly believe it. After all this time." She crushed the envelope against her chest and then quickly pulled it back again, studying the familiar script used to pen her name. "It's Mama's handwriting, all right. I wonder why she took so long to write."

"There's one way to find out."

Kathleen broke the seal on the envelope with trembling fingers and withdrew the single sheet of stationary from inside. Her heart was pounding so loud as she began to read that she could hardly hear the sound of her own voice. "My Dearest Kathleen," the letter began. "By now you have probably given up all hope of ever hearing from me again, but I assure you that not a day has gone by in the past six months that I have not written to you." Kathleen sat a little straighter in her chair, frowning as she continued. "It has only recently come to my attention that your father...." She lapsed into silence, looking as if the wind had been knocked out of her.

Alec pulled another chair around beside her and sat down. "What is it?"

Kathleen handed him the letter, her voice shaking as she quoted from memory the remainder of the sentence. "Your father has been secretly destroying my letters to you before they could be mailed."

"What?" Alec skimmed over the letter, locating the portion she had just read.

"I knew that he was capable of some cruel things, but...." Kathleen pressed a hand to her mouth, fighting back the onset of tears. "He's never going to forgive me for marrying you."

"Would you rather we hadn't gotten married at all?" Alec asked without thinking.

Kathleen lifted her eyes to him. "Would you?"

Alec silently rebuked himself for his insensitive choice of words. "Kathleen, I was only joking. Of course I don't wish that."

"I wouldn't blame you if you did. This has all been so unfair to you."

"Unfair? What are you talking about?"

"The way he treated you that time we went to visit. Like you were one of his—" Kathleen bit her tongue before the word "slave" could materialize upon it.

"Kathleen, that was over twenty years ago. You can't keep living in the past." Alec took her hands, gazing at her affectionately. "And as for whether or not I'd rather we hadn't gotten married...I'd do it all over again in a heartbeat."

Kathleen blinked, unleashing a single tear down her cheek. "Do you really mean it?"

Alec slipped off his chair onto one knee, still clutching her hands. "Kathleen Elizabeth Ramsey, I love you with all my heart. And I would be honored if you'd once again consent to becoming my wife."

"Yes!" she exclaimed happily, getting caught up in the moment.

Alec gathered her into his arms as he rose to his feet, grinning like a first time bridegroom. "We'll have to set a date. How about August tenth?" he suggested. "It is our anniversary. Unless you have another date in mind."

Kathleen stepped out of his embrace. "A date for what?"

"For our wedding."

The word "wedding" erased all doubt about what he had in mind. "Alec, you're not seriously suggesting that we— that you and I...."

"That's exactly what I'm suggesting. I said I would marry you again and I meant it." Alec regarded her expectantly. "What do you say?"

Kathleen broke out in joyful laughter. "I say yes!"

Alec gathered her back into his arms just as Kirsten and Jesse stepped into the room. "What's all the excitement about?" Kirsten asked. "We could hear you clear in the living room."

"Your father and I are getting remarried," Kathleen announced

"What? Oh, Mama, that's wonderful! When?"

Kathleen deferred the decision to Alec. "August tenth?"

"August tenth."

"The tenth.... But that's only two weeks away," Kirsten realized. "We'll never be ready in time!"

Alec chuckled as she dashed out of the kitchen dragging a bewildered Jesse along behind her. "I don't know who's more excited about this wedding, you or Kirsten."

Kathleen nestled herself back into his arms. "Me," she assured him.

Alec leaned down and pressed a kiss to her lips. "Us."

Kathleen laid her head against his shoulder with a contented sigh. "I can't believe we're actually doing this—getting remarried."

"I think we should have done it years ago. What would you say if I asked my brother, Neal, to be my best man?"

Kathleen lifted her head, smiling up at him. "Oh, Alec, that's a wonderful idea. It would be so good to see him again, and Rachel and the children."

"It's settled then. I'll send a wire today."

"Oh, this is so exciting." Kathleen's gaze inadvertently came to rest upon her mother's letter. The happy glow drained from her eyes. "I wish that Mama could be here," she said wistfully. "She was so disappointed that she wasn't able to attend our first wedding."

"Then invite her. We can even move the date back if we have to."

"There's no need," Kathleen said dejectedly. "My father would never allow her to come."

"You don't know that for sure. Why don't you write and ask her? I'll post the letter when I go back into town."

Kathleen appeared on the verge of accepting his offer but fear quickly snuffed out her resolve. "No. It's probably best for all concerned if I just leave matters as they are."

"Why? Because if she came you'd have to explain to the children why they suddenly have a grandmother they never knew about?"

Kathleen wrenched free of his grasp, turning her back. "Alec, please. Now's not the time."

"I think it is. Those children have a right to know their grandparents, Kathleen. Eric has already been asking me questions."

Kathleen spun back to face him. "You haven't told him anything, have you?"

"No. I promised you years ago that I wouldn't. But you should. It's time, Kathleen. It's time to let go of the past. To turn it over to the Lord. He can heal your heart if you just give Him the chance."

Kathleen retook her seat at the table, reaching for her mother's letter with a trembling hand. "I need to finish reading Mama's letter. Would you mind getting your own lunch?"

"I lost my appetite." Alec stalked out the back door, slamming it shut behind him.

* * * * *

Chicago Police Department

"Robbery?" Detective Neal Ramsey leaned forward in his chair, his attention riveted upon the elderly gentleman seated across from him at his desk. "Are you sure it was him, Charlie?"

Charlie Cavanaugh bobbed his head, though with considerable hesitancy. "As sure as I can be. As I told ya before, I only saw him for a moment, just before he was arrested. He was staying in the same boardinghouse where me daughter is living." A look of regret clouded his grayish-green eyes. "I'm sorry, Neal. I wish I could be of more help to ya than that."

"Charlie, whatever you do, don't apologize. You've just given us the first solid lead we've had in thirteen years." Neal plucked a pencil from the tin cup on his desk and began jotting down the information.

"Truth is...." Cavanaugh appeared on the verge of tears. "I'm hoping I'm wrong. I don't want to believe the lad is mixed up in something like this."

Neal ceased his note taking, sharing for a moment in the elder gentleman's concern. "Neither do I, Charlie. But if all you've told me is true...."

"How can we know for sure?"

"I have a good friend on the police department in Philadelphia. I'll wire him Sean's description. If there's even the remotest possibility that he's the man they have in custody, I'll be on the next train. In the meantime…." Neal rose from his chair to take a seat on the edge of his desk, facing Cavanaugh. "I'll have to ask you not to say anything about this until I've had a chance to talk with Sean myself. It was hard enough on Rachel when her brother disappeared thirteen years ago. If he has no intention of being a part of her life now, I'd just as soon she never knew that we found him, especially under the circumstances. I don't think I could bare to watch her go through the pain of losing him all over again."

Cavanaugh inclined his head in understanding. "Ya have me word on it."

"Thanks, Charlie." Neal clapped him lightly on the shoulder before returning to the chair behind his desk. "I'll get that wire out straight away."

"Will you let me know when ya hear something?" Cavanaugh asked.

Neal was not at all surprised to hear him make such a request. Charlie Cavanaugh had never been one to keep his fondness for Sean Donnelly a secret. "You know I will, Charlie."

Cavanaugh inclined his head again, this time as a gesture of thanks. "I've known that boy ever since his family moved into this area some twenty years ago. He and the youngest one, Ned, used to stop by me bakery every day on their way home from school."

Neal was well aware of this fact but sat listening respectfully as the elder man continued to pay homage to his memories.

"They were both such fine boys, but I took a special liking to Sean," Cavanaugh admitted without shame. "He was always so polite and well-mannered. Accept for that one incident a few years after his folks had passed on." He squinted as if to bring a certain portion of his memory into sharper focus. "Do ya remember the day ya caught him throwing that brick through the window of Mr. Hanson's dry goods store next door?"

"How could I forget? If it hadn't been for that broken window I would have never met Rachel." Neal smiled at the thought of the beautiful, auburn-haired woman who had shown up at the station to bail out her younger brother after Zachariah Hanson had insisted on pressing charges. Four months later he had taken her to be his wife. "It's hard to believe that was almost fifteen years ago."

Cavanaugh's face took on a wistful expression that made him appear far older than his sixty-two years. "Sean would be close to thirty now. No longer a boy." He locked eyes with Neal's across the desk. "Why did he do it?"

Neal realized that it wasn't the incident with the brick to which Cavanaugh was referring, but rather to Sean's unexplained disappearance two years later. "I've been asking myself that same question for the last thirteen years, Charlie." Neal wagged his head, admitting that he was no closer to unearthing the truth than before. "I'm afraid that Sean is the only one who can answer that."

* * * * *

Baxter

Kathleen tried to concentrate on the plans that Kirsten was sharing with her for the wedding but her thoughts kept straying to the conversation she'd had with Alec right before his abrupt departure two hours earlier. Was it true what he'd said? Was she so afraid of telling the children about her past that she'd deny herself the chance of seeing her own mother again? As disturbing as it was to consider, she feared that he might be right.

"Mama, are you listening?" Kirsten implored her.

"What was that, dear?"

"I asked what kind of flowers you want for your bouquet."

"Oh. How about...." Kathleen made one last effort to focus her attention on the plans but her heart just wasn't in it. "I'm sorry, sweetheart. I guess I'm not much in the mood for wedding planning at the moment. Would you mind if we discussed it later? After supper, perhaps?"

Kirsten concealed her disappointment behind a tight-lipped smile. "All right. I need to start making out the guest list, anyway." She picked up a paper tablet and a pencil from off the table. "Is there anyone special that you want to invite?"

Kathleen naturally thought of her mother. But as much as she would like for her to be present at the wedding, she was even more fearful of what might happen if she were. "No, dear," she told Kirsten with obvious difficulty. "There's no one special." Kathleen rose from the table, her face drawn taut in an effort to conceal her pain. "I need to get supper started."

"I can help if you'd like." Kirsten laid the tablet back on the table, dismissing her other plans. "The list can wait."

Kathleen declined her offer, suddenly wanting to be alone. "You go ahead with your planning. I'll let you know if I need any help."

Kathleen waited until Kirsten had left the room and then slipped her mother's letter out of her apron pocket. Tears began to pool in her eyes as she stood holding it against her chest, overwhelmed by the thought that this might be as close as she ever got to her mother again. "Forgive me, Mama," she whispered in a prayer-like fashion. "I just couldn't—"

Kathleen started as Alec walked in the back door, taking an involuntary step away from him.

"I'm sorry if I startled you," he apologized.

"No harm done." Kathleen moved quickly over to the stove, dashing the tears from her eyes. "I was just about to get supper started."

"Supper can wait. We need to talk."

Kathleen sensed from the tone of his voice that any objection on her part would be met with stern resistance. She walked back to the table and settled onto the chair that he was holding out for her, still clutching onto her mother's letter.

Alec took note of it as he sat down beside her. "Did you finish reading the letter?"

"Yes," she replied before tucking it back into her pocket. "Mama's fine. Considering."

"I'm glad to hear it. But it's her daughter that I'm concerned about."

Kathleen turned to him with a ready protest on her tongue, intending to deny that there was any need for concern, but the look in his eyes convinced her that she would only be wasting her breath. It was her turn to listen for a change.

"I'm sorry if the things I said earlier upset you," Alec began, choosing his words cautiously, "but I love you too much to sit by and watch you continue to hold on to the pain of something that happened over twenty years ago." He paused just long enough to take a breath. "I know now that I should have said something a long time ago. It took that letter from your mother for me to finally realize that."

Kathleen swallowed around the lump in her throat, coming to terms with a few disturbing realizations of her own. She had never surrendered the hurts of her past to the Lord as Alec had suggested, trusting Him to heal her heart. She had continued to cling to her pain like a security blanket, fearing that if she let go she would be forced to forgive those who had hurt her. But in refusing to let go, she had also denied her children the chance of knowing their grandparents.

"Regardless of whether you decide to invite your mother to the wedding or not," Alec went on to say, "the children have a right to know her, and your father. And I'm asking that you would allow them that much." He gave her a few moments to formulate a response to his request if she should choose to do so and then pushed his chair back from the table. "That's all I wanted to say."

Kathleen took hold of his arm as he stood to his feet. "You're right," she admitted humbly. "The children do have a right to know their grandparents. It's been wrong of me to deny them that."

Alec settled back onto his chair, noticing a look of peace in her eyes that hadn't been there before.

"I've been fooling myself all this time into believing that it was the children I've been trying to protect by keeping silent about the past. But it wasn't," she now realized. "I've been protecting myself." Kathleen took a deep breath before she continued, bracing herself for what lie ahead. "If you don't have any plans later...I'd like to talk to the children right after supper tonight."

Alec reached out and took her hands, conveying his support for her decision with a smile. "I'll be here."

* * * * *

Chicago

Neal turned up the collar of his overcoat, sinking deeper into its warmth as he stepped out of Cavanaugh's buggy in front of the two-story brick town house where he lived with Rachel and their four children. "Thanks for the ride, Charlie." Neal opened his hand to the chilling rain that was pelting down. "Another half hour of this and I would have been swimming home."

"It was me pleasure, Neal."

"Can I persuade you to stay and take supper with us? I know that Rachel and the children would love to see you."

"Another time perhaps," the elder man declined graciously. "But do give them me best."

"I will." Neal lifted his hand in a parting gesture as the buggy pulled away and then hurried to get in out of the rain. A welcome rush of warmth from the living room hearth greeted him as he stepped in the front door. "I'm home!" he announced for all interested parties.

"Papa!" Eight-year-old Emily came bounding out of the kitchen at the sound of her father's voice. "Papa, can you smell it!" she clamored excitedly.

Neal bent over his daughter, sniffing first behind her left ear and then her right. "New perfume?"

"No," Emily giggled. "It's gingerbread. I helped Mama bake it for supper."

"So I see." Neal wiped a smudge of flour from the tip of her nose, sending Emily into another fit of giggles.

Rachel stepped out of the kitchen into the dining area that adjoined the living room and set a stack of plates on the table where the family took their meals. She beamed Neal a smile before shifting her attention to Emily. "Emily, why don't you go and get washed up. And tell your brothers to do the same. Supper's almost ready."

"All right, Mama."

Rachel cut her gaze over to Neal as Emily ran upstairs. "And that goes for you, too."

"Yes, ma'am," he grinned back.

Rachel gathered up a handful of forks and spoons off the table and began arranging them appropriately beside each plate. She shuddered as a loud clap of thunder rattled the window at her back. "That's quite a storm brewing out there. I hope you didn't walk home."

"No." Neal shrugged off his coat and hung it up to dry on the rack inside the door. "Charlie Cavanaugh gave me a ride."

Rachel looked up from the table, following him intently with her gaze as he entered the living room. "Old Charlie from the bakery? I thought he was in Philadelphia visiting his daughter."

"He just got back today." Neal squatted in front of the fireplace, stretching the palms of his hands toward the crackling blaze. "I invited him to supper but he said maybe another time."

"I'm sorry to hear that. I always enjoy talking with him. The stories he tells about Sean—" Rachel became uncomfortable with the direction the conversation was taking. She snapped her gaze back to the table, straightening things that didn't need to be straightened. "You didn't say how you happened to run into him."

"He came by the station this afternoon." Neal rose back to his full height. "But enough about Charlie Cavanaugh." He moved up behind her at the table, slipping his arms around her waist. "I want to hear about your day."

Rachel pivoted in his arms, unleashing a mischievous grin intended to pique his curiosity. "You'll never guess who we got a telegram from today."

Neal dropped his arms from around her waist. "Who?" he asked, electing not to play the guessing game she had initiated.

"Your brother."

"Alec?"

"Unless you have another brother you haven't told me about."

"Is everything all right?"

Rachel rolled her eyes towards the ceiling. "Why does everyone always assume that a telegram is going to contain bad news?"

"Because they usually do."

"Well, not this time." Rachel pulled the telegram out of her skirt pocket, smiling in anticipation of the news that she was about to share with him. "Alec and Kathleen are getting remarried and Alec has asked you to be his best man."

Neal's mouth twisted wryly to one side. "You're kidding."

"Read it for yourself." Rachel handed him the telegram. "Oh, Neal, just imagine it," she said with a dreamy smile. "Getting married again after all these years. Isn't it romantic?"

Neal's attention remained riveted upon the telegram.

"Neal?" Rachel waved a hand in front of his face. "Did you hear me?"

"It says here that the wedding is August tenth. That's only two weeks away."

Rachel anxiously bit the corner of her lip, sensing the door of opportunity about to close. "I know it's kind of short notice," she admitted, reemphasizing what he had already pointed out. "But we were planning on taking a vacation sometime this summer anyway. And I already talked to your sister, Christine. She said she'd be more than willing to stay with the children while we're gone."

Neal finally tore his attention away from the telegram. "But the invitation is for the children, too."

"I'm aware of that. But I thought it might be nice if just the two of us went." Rachel slipped her hands up behind his neck, smiling at him coyly. "It's been so long since we've had any time alone together. It would be kind of like a second honeymoon."

Neal couldn't deny that her idea had a certain appeal to it, but the situation with Sean had to take precedence. Getting her to understand that without actually bringing her brother's name into the conversation wasn't going to be easy.

Rachel dropped her hands from behind his neck, frowning at his apparent lack of interest. "You don't seem too excited about the idea. If you don't want to go, just say so."

"Rach, I would love to spend a few romantic days alone with you," he assured her. "Not to mention the chance to see Alec and Kathleen again. But now's just not a good time for me to be taking a vacation. I started working on a new case today that may require me to go out of town for a few days."

"Well, couldn't I come with you?" she suggested with a subtle note of pleading. "I won't get in the way while you're working, I promise."

"Rach, it's not as simple as that. I wish I knew what more I could say to get you to understand."

"Oh, I understand perfectly. You just don't want to take me."

"That's not it at all."

"Then what?" she demanded.

Neal admired her tenacity for trying to get at the truth, but it wasn't making his resolve to keep it from her any easier. He had to buy himself some time until he heard back from his friend in Philadelphia, a couple of days at the most. Then he would decide what to do. "I'll think about it," he told her plainly, offering nothing in the way of a promise.

Rachel once again slipped her hands up behind his neck as her frown turned back into a smile. "I guess I can't ask for any more than that."

CHAPTER TWELVE

THE TRUTH SHALL SET YOU FREE

Baxter

Kathleen looked on quietly from the end of the sofa as Alec ushered the children into the living room. She was much more relaxed than she thought she'd be now that the moment to talk to them had finally arrived. All that remained was deciding what to say. Alec agreed with her that it would be best to withhold certain things from Stephen and Kaitlin, particularly her reason for leaving home, but she was determined to hold nothing back from the others, Nathan included. Only when she was able to be completely honest with them about her past would she truly be free from it herself.

"I'm sure that you're all wondering why I called you together this evening," she began once they were all seated.

"Couldn't be anything good," said Nathan. "The last time my friend David had a family meeting at his house it was to tell him that his dog died."

"That shows what you know, Nathan Ramsey," Kaitlin sneered back. "We don't even have a dog."

"All right, you two, that's enough," Alec told them sternly. "Your mother has something important to talk to you about and I expect you to sit quietly and listen. That goes for the rest of you as well."

Nathan and Kaitlin exchanged one final scathing look with one another before turning their attention to their mother as instructed.

"Your father's right," Kathleen began again. "I do have something important to tell you." Her gaze briefly came to rest on each of the children in turn, youngest to the oldest. "It's about your grandparents."

"Grandma and Grandpa Ramsey?" Kaitlin asked.

"No, sweetheart. Your Grandma and Grandpa Jordan... my parents."

Eric was stunned. After his unsuccessful attempt to solicit information from his father on that very subject, he had felt certain that the door to his mother's past would remain locked to him forever. Now here she was voluntarily handing over the key. What had prompted her to finally break her silence after all these years?

"I'm sorry that I haven't told you about them before," she continued, looking directly at Eric. "There have been some...well, some differences between my father and I that I felt were better left unspoken. But I realize now that I shouldn't allow that to keep you from knowing them if you wish to, or them from knowing you." Her gaze left Eric and circulated among the others. "As a matter of fact, I received a letter from your grandmother just today, and she asked me to give each and every one of you a very special hug just from her."

"How come she can't hug us herself?" Stephen asked.

"Because she doesn't live here, Stephen. She and your grandfather live in South Carolina. That's a very long way from here. But not too far away that you can't write to them. I know they would love to hear from you."

"How come you don't live in South Carolina?" Stephen asked.

Kathleen had been anticipating such a question but not from Stephen. She looked to Alec for any suggestions that he might have for how to answer but he appeared to be as stumped as she. "I use to live there, Stephen," she finally told him. "When I was a little girl."

"How come no more?" he persisted.

"Well...." Kathleen thought carefully about how to frame her response in such a way that would satisfy his curiosity while not revealing more than she desired for him to know. "I decided that I wanted to move to Massachusetts for awhile," she explained, emitting all reference to the reason why.

"That's where you met, Papa!" Kaitlin exclaimed.

"That's right, Kaitlin, it is."

"And you fell in love and got married and had all of us." Kaitlin flung her arms out, nearly swatting Nathan in the head.

Stephen turned questioning eyes from Kaitlin back to his mother. "Don't you miss your mama and papa?" he wondered.

"Of course I do, Stephen. I'll always miss them." Kathleen lifted him up to sit on her lap. "But my home is here now, with you and your brothers and sisters."

"And Papa," Stephen reminded her.

"Yes." Kathleen met Alec's gaze over the top of Stephen's head, experiencing a sense of peace that she hadn't known in twenty years. "And your Papa."

* * * * *

Chicago

Neal settled the children in their beds and then headed downstairs to join Rachael for their nightly cup of coffee in front of the fire. Aside from a few brief moments in the morning before he left for work, it was really the only chance they had to spend any time alone together. Rachel had been the one to suggest that they start such a practice shortly after they were married, and over the years Neal had come to appreciate her wisdom in doing so, especially now with the added responsibilities of raising four active children.

"I'm sorry that it took me so long," he apologized as he came into the living room. "Michael decided at the last minute that he had to have a glass of water, and Emily insisted on no fewer than three bedtime stories. I know I shouldn't have given in to her, but she turned those big brown eyes of hers on me and I just couldn't resist. I'm afraid one day she's going to ask me for the moon and I'm just liable to—" Neal felt Rachel shrink back from him as he took a seat beside her on the sofa. He didn't need to enlist his keen powers of perception to know that something was terribly wrong. "Rach?"

"How long have you known that he's in Philadelphia?"

Neal stared back at her, startled by the obvious reference she had made to Sean. He was sure that he had let nothing slip to even suggest to her that her brother might be in Philadelphia, and he had Charlie Cavanaugh's word that he would say nothing. That left only one other way that she could have found out.

"In case you're wondering...." Rachel withdrew what appeared to be a telegram from beneath the cushions of the sofa, confirming Neal's worst fear. "This arrived while you were upstairs with the children. It's from a Detective Daniel Collins with the Philadelphia Police Department. But I can see from the look on your face that you're not at all surprised."

"Rach—"

"Of course, my first thought was that there has to be some mistake," she continued with an airy smile that belied her true feelings. "The Neal Ramsey I know would never keep the whereabouts of my brother a secret if he knew."

"Rachel, I can explain."

"How long?" she asked, raking him with a smoldering gaze. "Months? Years? Were you ever going to tell me?"

"I just found out today."

Rachel thrust the telegram out in front of him. "You expect me to believe that after seeing this?"

"Yes."

Rachel's eyes lost some of their defensive fire. The least she could do was hear him out. "Okay, I'm listening."

Neal proceeded to relate for her the information that Charlie Cavanaugh had shared with him that afternoon about Sean's arrest and his own decision to contact his friend in Philadelphia. "I didn't expect to hear anything back this soon," he said in reference to the telegram that she had intercepted. "Or that you would see it."

Rachel hadn't heard a single word he'd said past the retelling of Sean's arrest. "Arrested for what?" she wanted to know.

"Attempted robbery."

Rachel shook her head in denial. The man they had in custody in Philadelphia couldn't be Sean. She didn't care that the telegram said differently. She knew her brother. "There has to be some mistake. Sean would never do something like that."

"I pray you're right, Rach."

Rachel regarded him suspiciously, recalling snatches of their earlier conversation. "This is the case you were talking about, isn't it? The one you said that might take you out of town."

"Yes," Neal admitted.

The word betrayal echoed around and around in Rachel's head. "You weren't going to tell me, were you?"

"I didn't want you to get your hopes up. What if I had told you and then it turned out not to be Sean? Or it was him but he wanted nothing to do with you?"

Rachel recoiled from his accusation as if it were a slap in the face. "How dare you even suggest such a thing!" she flailed back at him.

"Rach, he's been gone for thirteen years. Not once in all that time has he tried to contact us or even let us know where he is." Neal reached over and laid his hands atop hers, urging her to consider the facts for herself. "You have to accept that he might not want to be found."

"No," she declared adamantly, jerking her hands out from beneath his. "Sean would never do that to me. You're wrong. He would never...." A strangling sob prevented her from continuing.

Neal gathered her into his arms as she surrendered to her tears, vowing to himself right then and there that he wasn't going to rest until he had uncovered the truth behind her brother's disappearance, no matter how long it took. "I'll find him, Rach," he whispered just loud enough for her to hear. "I promise you."

Rachel lifted her head off his shoulder, her tears already beginning to dry on her cheeks. "I want to go with you to Philadelphia. Please, Neal," she implored, sensing that he was about to object. "If Sean wants nothing to do with me... I need to hear it from him myself."

Neal nodded in agreement, realizing the futility of trying to talk her out of it. "I'll make the necessary arrangements first thing in the morning."

* * * * *

Baxter

"Time for bed, Kaitlin."

"Ah, Papa," she whined. "I want to hear more about Grandma and Grandpa Jordan."

"Me, too," Stephen said groggily, fighting to keep his eyes open.

"You can both ask your mother all the questions you want some other time. You should have been in bed a half hour ago." Alec scooped Stephen off Kathleen's lap and settled him against his shoulder. He was asleep almost immediately. "Nathan?"

"Coming, Pa."

"Not so fast." Alec planted a hand on his shoulder as he started to rise. "I was just about to tell you that you can stay up for awhile longer if you'd like."

Nathan sank back to the floor, staring up at his father. "I can?"

"Your Ma's not through talking with you yet." Alec turned to smile down at her. "Do you want me to come back after I get these two settled?"

"I think I can handle things from here."

Alec winked at her. "Never doubted that for a second."

Kathleen waited until he had taken Stephen and Kaitlin upstairs before addressing the other children. "There are some things about my past, particularly the reason I left home, that your father and I felt Stephen and Kaitlin were too young to understand. But I want for the rest of you to know the whole story."

Eric strained forward in his chair, anxious to catch every word that she was about to say. This was what he'd been waiting to hear.

"When I was about Kirsten's age," she began, "my father arranged for me to marry the son of a prominent politician in the South Carolina government. It didn't matter to him whether I wanted the marriage or not. All he cared about was furthering his own political ambitions and he was willing to go to any lengths to do so, even if it meant sacrificing the happiness of his own daughter." Bitter feelings that Kathleen hadn't been in touch with for years began to reassert themselves, making it extremely difficult for her to continue. "My mother did everything that she could to persuade him to call off the wedding but his mind was made up."

"Did you marry him?" Nathan asked.

"Of course she didn't," Kirsten told him. But after taking one look at the pained expression on her mother's face she wasn't so sure. "You didn't, did you, Ma?"

"No, sweetheart," Kathleen assured her. "The day before the wedding was to take place my mother took me into town under the pretense of doing some last minute shopping for the ceremony. The next thing I knew I was on a train heading north."

"Weren't you afraid?" Nathan asked.

"Yes, Nathan, I was. But I was even more afraid of what would happen if I didn't go. And I knew it wouldn't be forever. My mother and I agreed that I would stay away just long enough for my father to calm down and accept the fact that I was not marrying Chandler Fredrickson the third under any circumstances. Of course by the time he did, I had already met your father and we'd made our own plans to marry." The first trace of a smile appeared on her lips. "I wasn't about to go back then."

"Was your Pa mad?" Nathan wondered.

"Very. In his eyes I had turned my back on our family and everything he had brought me up to believe in. I was nothing but a disgrace to him."

"Did you ever go back?" Eric asked.

"Only once, a few months after you were born. I was hoping that when he saw he had a grandchild...." Kathleen bit her lip to keep it from trembling. "But he wanted nothing to do with me. As far as he was concerned I had ceased to be his daughter the day I married your father."

Kirsten shuddered. "I can't believe your own father would do that to you."

"Neither could I," Kathleen admitted, finding the thought just as hard to accept now as it had been twenty years ago. "I was very bitter towards him for a long time after that. I suppose a part of me still is. But it's time to put all of that in the past. Telling you was the first step in doing that."

"Are you going to invite him to the wedding?" Colin asked.

Everything in her wanted to dismiss Colin's suggestion without giving it a second thought, but she couldn't very well invite her mother without extending the invitation to her father as well. "I think that's a fine idea, Colin."

* * * * *

Alec stopped in the kitchen doorway, staring for a moment at the figure seated at the table. "Kathleen?"

Kathleen turned to look up at him.

"I got worried when I woke up and you weren't in bed." Alec took a few steps towards her. "Are you all right?"

"Fine," she assured, stealing a quick glance at the envelope that was lying beside her on the table. "I just had something I needed to do."

"And that something couldn't wait until morning, I suppose."

Kathleen smiled, picking up the coffee pot in front of her. "Join me?"

"Why not. I can't get any more awake than I am right now." Alec shuffled his way over to the table and took a seat beside her. "What's all this?" he asked, noting the papers strewn about.

"Wedding plans." Kathleen pushed them aside to make room for his coffee. "I promised Kirsten that I would make a least one decision of my own before the day arrives."

Alec detected a considerable amount of tension in her voice. "Problems?"

"In a manner of speaking. I'm beginning to that think Kirsten may have had a point. Two weeks is hardly enough time to plan a wedding. There's just so much to do."

"Like what?" he asked.

"Like my wedding dress, for one thing. It's been locked away in that trunk at the foot of our bed all these years. It will need to be washed and pressed…. And then there's the flowers to arrange and the cake to bake and the invitations to mail." Kathleen gripped the sides of her head, resting her elbows on the table in front of her. "I just don't know how we're going to get it all done in time."

Alec took a sip of his coffee and then set his cup back on the table. "There wouldn't be any need for all of those things if we eloped."

Kathleen grinned at his suggestion. "And I suppose you intend on climbing up a ladder to our bedroom window, as well?"

Alec shrugged. "Why not? It sure would be romantic."

Kathleen found his solution to their dilemma more than a little tempting but her wiser head prevailed. "It wouldn't be fair to Kirsten. She was so excited when we told her that we were getting remarried. I don't want to spoil it for her."

"She'll understand. You said yourself that she thinks two weeks isn't enough time to plan a wedding."

"It's not just Kirsten, Alec. I want all of our family and friends to be there. It's not everyday we get remarried. I want it to be special."

"It will be," he assured her. "Whether we have two weeks to prepare or only two days. And as for all this…." Alec swept his hand across the table. "You just let me know what I can do to help."

"Well, now that you mention it…." Kathleen picked up the envelope beside her and placed in front of him. "You can post this letter for me to Charleston. I've decided to invite both Mama and Papa to the wedding. That's the something that couldn't wait until morning."

Alec laid a hand atop the envelope. "Are you sure you're ready for this?"

"No," she admitted. "But it's the right thing to do."

Alec smiled at her. "I'm proud of you."

"Don't be. There's still a part of me that's hoping he won't come."

Alec turned to face her more squarely, still smiling. "Like I said…I'm proud of you."

CHAPTER THIRTEEN

AN ENTERPRISING PROPOSAL

August 1860

Nathan crouched forward at the edge of the circle he had drawn in the dirt, every muscle in his body tense with concentration as he decided which marble to make his next target.

"You're taking too long," Stephen complained. "I want a turn."

"Hush," Nathan snapped back. "I'm almost ready."

"Can I play?" Kaitlin asked, dropping to her knees beside Stephen

"No," Nathan told her.

"How come?"

"'Cause girls don't know how to shoot marbles," Stephen sneered.

Kaitlin reared back her shoulders in protest. "We do so."

"Do not."

"Do so." Kaitlin pried one of Stephen's marbles out of his hand and fired it into the center of the circle, sending all but two of the remaining marbles careening out.

157

Stephen gasped in surprise. "Golly! Did you see that, Nate?"

Nathan dismissed Kaitlin's effort with a wave of his hand, suffering the discomfort of a slightly bruised ego. "Beginners' luck," he scoffed. "That's all it was. Bet you couldn't do it again."

"Oh, yeah?" Kaitlin reclaimed her marble, plenty eager to prove him wrong. "Bet you I could."

"Could not."

"Could so."

"Could not."

"Papa's home!" Stephen cried out.

Nathan and Kaitlin put a quick halt to their bickering as their father's buggy came around the side of the house.

Stephen began clamoring to get his attention as soon as he stepped down. "Papa, we're playing marbles!"

"So I see." Alec walked over to where the trio was sitting, looking with sincere interest upon the game in progress. "Who's winning?"

"I am," Kaitlin bragged, displaying a bulging fist full of marbles.

"Beginners' luck," Nathan muttered under his breath.

Kaitlin scowled at him. "You're just sore 'cause you got beaten by a girl," she taunted.

"Yeah," Stephen agreed, coming to Kaitlin's defense. "You're just sore."

"What do you know about it?" Nathan flung back. "She beat you, too."

Alec cleared his throat, advising a quick end to their dispute. "Is your ma about?"

"She's inside," Nathan told him. "But you might not wanna to go in there just now."

"Why's that?"

"There's wedding talk going on. You know, women stuff."

Alec fought to keep a straight face. "Well, I appreciate the warning, Nate, but I think I'll take my chances."

Kathleen and Kirsten were engaged in a lively discussion when Alec stepped in the back door. His presence would have gone undetected had he not taken the initiative to announce himself. "How goes the planning, ladies?"

"Fine, Pa," Kirsten told him. "But I never realized how much work is involved in planning a wedding."

"Do you think this might be of some help?"

Kirsten squealed in delight as her father withdrew the latest copy of *Godey's Lady's Book* magazine from behind his back. "Oh, Pa, thank you! But how did you know I—Mrs. Crowley," she realized. "She told you I wanted a copy, didn't she? I was looking through hers the other day when we were in the store and I saw the perfect hairstyle for Ma to wear in the wedding. Wait until you—" Kirsten halted her furious page flipping as she came upon the picture she was seeking. "There," she said breathlessly. "Isn't it the most exquisite thing you've ever seen?"

Alec studied the picture in question. "Quite," he agreed. "But I don't see anything wrong with the way your ma's hair is right now. I happen to be quite partial to it."

"There's nothing wrong with it," Kirsten assured him. "But sometimes a woman likes to—" She sighed with a wave of her hand. "Oh, never mind. You wouldn't understand."

Alec turned to find the bride-to-be watching him with a look of restrained laughter in her eyes. "I take it you agree with her?"

"I have to, Alec," she confessed. "She's right."

Alec grinned. "Say no more. I'll just get me a quick bite to eat and then I'll be out of your way." He rubbed his hands together with a ravenous look in his eyes. "What's for lunch?"

Kathleen shot to her feet with a gasp. "Is it that time already?"

Alec was no longer grinning. "No lunch?"

"Oh, Alec, I'm so sorry. I got so caught up with all the plans for the wedding that I...I kind of forgot. But it will only take me a minute to fix you something."

Alec halted her as she started to move past him. "Never mind about that now. I have something for you."

Kathleen swallowed nervously at the sight of the telegram that he pulled from his pocket.

"I know how anxious you've been to hear something so I've been stopping by the telegraph office every day just to check," he explained. "This came over the wire just a few hours ago."

"Who's it from, Pa?" Kirsten asked.

"Your Ma's folks."

Kirsten bolted around the table to her mother's side. "They must be responding to the invitation you sent them to the wedding. Oh, won't it be wonderful if they can come?"

Kathleen didn't agree. For the past week she had been second-guessing her decision in even sending that invitation to her folks. It had seemed the appropriate thing to do at the time, but now when faced with the possibility of actually seeing her father again, propriety seemed of little importance.

"Are you going to keep us in suspense all day?" Alec teased.

Kathleen braced herself for whatever the telegram might contain and proceeded to open it.

Kirsten inched closer to her side, shifting anxiously on the balls of her feet. "Well, Ma?"

Kathleen looked up with a dazed expression on her face and then quickly read through the telegram again, hoping that she hadn't misunderstood its contents.

"Is something wrong?" Alec asked her.

"No. I was just afraid that...." Kathleen handed him the telegram, fighting to keep her relief from becoming too obvious. "Read it for yourself. They're not coming."

Kirsten mistook her reaction for disappointment. "I'm sorry, Ma. I know how much you wanted them to come."

Kathleen felt a pang of guilt at the thought of how easily she had deceived everyone. "It's all right, sweetheart. There'll be another time."

Alec handed her back the telegram with a sympathetic smile. "Of course there will."

Kirsten sulked her way back to her chair. "Well, it still would have been nice if they could've come. But at least Aunt Rachel and Uncle Neal will be here."

"*Might* be here," Alec reminded her. "Neal doesn't know how long they'll be in Philadelphia."

"But they've just got to be, Pa. Ma's going to ask Rachel to be her matron of honor and Uncle Neal's your best man."

"I'm sure they'll be here if they can," Alec said in the couples' defense. "But finding Sean is their first priority. Now, if we can put the wedding plans on hold for a moment, I have some important news of my own."

Kathleen retook her seat at the table, curious to hear what news he was referring to.

"I have received a response to my ad for an assistant," he announced.

"Really, Pa?" Kirsten rose back to her feet. "Who from?"

"I have all the particulars right here." Alec took a second telegram from his pocket. "His name is Carter Buchanan, he's twenty-two years old, graduated first in his class from Harvard Medical School...." Alec suppressed a chuckle before he continued. "And he's excited about taking on the challenges of practicing medicine, and I quote, 'on the frontier.'"

"The frontier?" Kirsten scoffed. "Just where does he think Baxter is? In Indian Territory?"

"Now, now," Alec cautioned her. "Let's give the lad some credit, shall we? After all, he did spell frontier right."

Kirsten giggled despite her best efforts not to.

Kathleen was appalled by the way they were carrying on. "You two are terrible," she scolded. "I'm sure Dr. Buchanan has many fine qualities that would make him a valuable addition to our community." She regarded Alec expectantly. "Are you going to invite him to come?"

"I haven't decided that yet. It's only been a week since I placed the ad...." Alec paused to consider the telegram in his hand, mentally reviewing its' contents. "But on the other hand, I do need an assistant and this is the only response I've received."

"I think you should wait another week, Pa," Kirsten advised him. "Nothing against Dr. Buchanan, but I'm sure you'll get some more responses. And even if you don't, you can always run the ad again."

Alec considered her suggestion at some length. "I suppose that would be best. This isn't a decision to be taken lightly." He refolded the telegram and tucked it back in his pocket. "In the meantime, I'll start looking around town for someplace to move the practice to. When I do get around to hiring someone I'm going to be needing a great deal more space."

Kirsten smiled as an idea came to her. "Pa, what about Samuel Baxter's old house?"

Kathleen turned to her with an excited gleam in her eyes. "The Baxter house. Kirsten, that's a wonderful idea. It's a little run down but nothing that can't be fixed. And it certainly would be big enough. There are plenty of rooms. And the location is perfect," she emphasized, as if that alone settled everything. "I don't know why we didn't think of it sooner."

Alec moved closer to the table, looking back and forth between them. "I think you're both overlooking something. Samuel Baxter willed the deed to that property to the church. And even if it were for sale, we could never afford the mortgage payments and still be able to hire an assistant."

Kathleen hunched her shoulders. "I don't remember saying anything about buying it."

Alec cocked his head at her. "You mean rent?"

"Well, why not?" Kathleen rose out of her chair and stepped towards him. "That house has just been sitting there empty ever since old man Baxter died. And I'm sure the church could use the extra money."

Alec still wasn't ready to fully embrace the idea and the expression on his face told her so.

"At least talk to Reverend Thompson, Alec," she urged him. "What could it hurt?"

Alec smiled as he brought his hands up to rest on her shoulders. "Nothing, I suppose. I'll go talk to him right after lunch."

* * * * *

Clive Thompson listened attentively as Alec outlined his proposal to turn the Baxter house into a medical clinic.

"To be frank with you, Reverend," Alec was saying, "there's just no way that I can continue to treat the growing number of patients I have in the office I'm working out of now. A clinic such as I'm proposing would allow for not only a much bigger exam room but recovery rooms as well. Not to mention all of the space for new equipment. And I'm even making plans to hire an assistant...." Alec ground his plea to a halt, sensing that he had rambled on long enough. "Well, that's about it, sir," he said in conclusion.

Thompson rose from the bench where the two men were sitting and walked to the front of the church, carefully considering all that he had heard. The decision before him seemed clear. "As much as I'd like to, Alec," he said as he started back up he aisle, "I'm afraid that I can't allow you to rent the house."

Alec took the rejection of his proposal all in stride. "I understand, Reverend. The property does belong to the church. I reminded Kathleen of that but she still insisted that I come talk to you."

"Now hold on a second." Thompson retook his seat. "I said that I couldn't allow you to rent it...but I can give it to you."

Alec's jaw would have dropped clean off his face had it not been attached. "Excuse me?"

"Well, as you pointed out, the property does belong to the church. And therefore it's up to the church to decide what should be done with it." A smile appeared on the elder man's lips. "I personally can't think of a worthier use than a medical clinic. And I'm sure once the congregation hears your proposal, the decision will be unanimous. We'll put it to a vote this Sunday."

"Reverend, I...." Thompson's generous offer left Alec speechless. "I don't know what to say."

"Then don't say anything." Thompson regained his feet, drawing Alec up beside him. "Let's go have a look at Baxter's new medical clinic."

* * * * *

Kathleen's reaction was much the same as Alec's had been. "He gave it to you? Oh, Alec...do you realize what this will mean? For us? For the town?"

"It's not set in stone yet," he reminded her. "The congregation still has to agree."

"They will," Kathleen said confidently, refusing to be denied one ounce of her optimism. "Now we have to make a list of everything that needs to be done. We'll need to sew all new curtains and linens for the beds, scrub the floors, wash the windows—"

Alec silenced her with a lingering kiss. "Do you think maybe we can hold off on some of that until after the wedding? And the honeymoon?"

Kathleen had no difficulty shifting the focus of her excitement. "Maybe you're right," she consented, leaning forward to return his kiss.

CHAPTER FOURTEEN

LOST AND FOUND

Chicago, 1847

"*R*achel. Rachel, honey, wake up."
Rachel rolled onto her back with a groan, every muscle in her body protesting the earliness of the hour. "Neal?"

"Sorry I had to wake you."

"What's the matter?" Rachel pushed herself up to a sitting position, straining her ears for the hungry squall of their infant son in the next room. "Is it the baby?"

"No, the baby's fine," he assured, settling onto the edge of the bed beside her. "It's Sean."

"He's not ill, is he?"

"No." Neal reached to take her hand. "I think he might have run away."

"Run away?" Rachel faced him with a blank stare. "What do you mean he's run away?"

"He told Ned that he was going to get a drink of water but he never came back to bed. I just checked their room. All of Sean's things are gone."

"But why?" she demanded to know. "Why would he run away?" Hot tears began streaming down her face as

the magnitude of what he was telling her finally sank in. Her brother was gone. "Why, Sean?" she demanded again, sobbing uncontrollably. "Why...."

Near Philadelphia

"Sean...." Rachel rolled her head from side to side, her eyes pinched tightly shut against the disturbing images encroaching upon her dreams. "Why, Sean?" she cried out. "Why?"

"Rachel." Neal gently tried to rouse her amid curious stares from several passengers seated across the aisle from them. "Rachel, wake up."

Rachel bolted upright in her seat, gasping to catch her breath. The panic-stricken look on her face subsided as soon as she realized where she was. "Neal?"

"I'm right here." Neal reached to grasp her hand. "Was it another nightmare?"

"Yes," she said with a shudder. "Same as the one last night." Rachel shook her head as she buried her face in the palms of her hands. "Why did they have to come back now?"

Neal realized that she was referring to the nightmares she had experienced after her brother's disappearance thirteen years ago. Every night she would awaken from a sound sleep, shaking and perspiring from head-to-toe. This continued for three straight months. And then just as mysteriously as they had started, the nightmares were gone. Until last night. Neal suspected that it was the news of finding Sean that had triggered their unwelcome return.

"Where are we?" Rachel turned to the window beside her, straining to see through the descending darkness.

"About an hour outside of Philadelphia. I'm afraid it will be too late to go and see Sean by the time we get there."

Rachel acknowledged this fact with a nod. She had waited thirteen long years to be reunited with her brother.

What difference could one more day make? Besides, she didn't know what she was going to say to him when they finally did meet. He had been a boy when he left. He was a man now, with a life of his own that didn't include her. Rachel found this thought disturbing. What if he wanted to keep it that way? What if he wanted nothing to do with her as Neal had suggested?

Neal slid his arm around her shoulders, sensing the path her thoughts had taken. "Are you okay?"

Rachel nodded again, leaning over to snuggle her head into the crook of his arm. She felt her eyes beginning to grow heavy but fought against her body's desire for more sleep. "How long has it been since you've seen your friend?" she asked drowsily.

"Daniel? Let's see…." Neal quickly thought back over the years, trying to place the day he had last seen his college classmate, Daniel Collins. "It must be going on sixteen years," he realized. "Daniel moved to Philadelphia right after we graduated and we never kept in touch." Neal's tone of voice suggested that he regretted this fact very much. "Boy, did we have some good times together." He chuckled as one amusing thought in particular came to mind. "Did I ever tell you about the time that we put a dozen frogs in the faculty lounge? You should have seen the look on the Professor Ryland's face when—" Neal smiled as he glanced down to find his audience fast asleep. "Well, maybe it wasn't that funny after all."

* * * * *

Sixteen years. Daniel Collins could hardly believe it had been that long since he'd seen his good friend, Neal Ramsey. He regretted this fact very much, as well as the fact that he hadn't taken it upon himself to stay in touch after his move to Philadelphia. But what he regretted most of all is that it had taken such tragic circumstances to finally bring them together again.

Daniel turned his thoughts to the disturbing telegram he had received from Neal just one week ago as he stood watching the arrival of their train. He was still reeling from the fact that the man he had arrested for armed robbery was Neal's brother-in-law. And as if that weren't tragic enough, he now had to tell them they had made the long trip from Chicago for nothing. Sean had been released from custody yesterday and Daniel didn't have a clue where he was. Rachel's agonizing wait to be reunited with her brother was far from over.

As soon as the train had come to a complete stop, Daniel moved to the area where the passengers were beginning to file off. Neal was among the first to step down, accompanied closely by a petite, auburn-haired woman. Even without the benefit of an introduction, Daniel knew this had to be Rachel. The resemblance she bore to her brother was striking.

"Neal!" Daniel raised a hand to catch his attention.

Neal swerved his gaze towards the sound of his name, smiling as it settled upon Daniel. He reached his side in three lengthy strides.

Daniel thumped him on the back as they embraced. "Gosh, it's good to see you."

"You too, friend." Neal stepped back, eager to complete the introductions. "Daniel," he said, beaming proudly at the woman beside him, "I'd like for you to meet my wife, Rachel."

"Rachel." Daniel affectionately clasped the hand she was holding out to him. "So you're the woman who stole Neal's heart. Believe it or not, ma'am, but there was a time when I was convinced that your husband was a confirmed bachelor."

"I use to think the same about you," Neal confessed. He had only just learned of Daniel's recent trip down the aisle in their latest correspondence. "Congratulations. I wish I could have been here."

"Thanks. Sarah was well worth the wait," Daniel bragged on behalf of his new bride. "I can't wait for you to meet her."

"Excuse me, Mr. Collins, but how's my brother?"

Daniel found it difficult to look Rachel in the eye. He was no stranger to being the bearer of bad news. It was an all too common practice in his line of work. But most of the people he dealt with were total strangers. This was different. This was the wife of the man he considered to be his best friend. What hurt her, hurt him.

Rachel began to fear the worst when there was no immediate response to her question. "Something's wrong, isn't it?"

Daniel forced a smile to his lips. "You two must be starved. There's a little café right around the corner. Why don't we go get a bite to eat? We can talk there."

* * * * *

Neal was beside himself as he sat listening to Daniel relate the details of Sean's release.

"Nobody came forward who could positively identify him as one of the men involved in the hold up," Daniel explained. "We had no choice but to release him."

"Which means he could be anywhere by now." Neal heaved a sigh, wearied by just the thought of the enormous task now before them. "I can't believe this is happening."

"I'm sorry you had to come all this way for nothing, Neal. I did everything I could to get him held longer but my hands were tied."

"It's not your fault, Daniel." Neal drained the last few drops of coffee from his cup and then set it down in front of him on the table. "We'll just have to try and pick up his trail again before it gets any colder."

"I'll give you all the help I can," Daniel offered.

Neal considered the facts already presented to him, trying to decide where would be the most logical place for them to start their search. "What about the boardinghouse where he was staying?" he suggested. "It's doubtful that he would have gone back there, but right now we don't have much else to go on. I'd like to at least talk to the landlady."

"I can take you over there right now if you'd like."

Neal would have jumped at the opportunity had he not been so concerned about Rachel. She hadn't said a word since learning of Sean's release and he was beginning to fear for her mental well-being. "Tomorrow will be soon enough. What we need right now is sleep. Can you recommend a good hotel?"

"The Chateau Collins awaits your arrival. Sarah and I want you to stay with us."

"I appreciate the offer, Daniel, but we don't know how long we're going to be here. It wouldn't be fair to you and Sarah. You're still on your honeymoon."

Daniel waved aside any further protests. "The last thing Sarah said to me before I left for the station was to not come back without you. Now you wouldn't want to get me in trouble with my beautiful bride, would you?"

Neal smiled over at Rachel. "We can't let that happen, can we, Rach?"

Rachel managed a weak smile in return. "I suppose not."

* * * * *

Neal remained at Rachel's side until she had fallen asleep and then quietly slipped from the room that Daniel's wife had so graciously prepared for their arrival. The pleasing aroma of freshly made coffee lured him down the hallway to the small kitchen at the back of the house. Daniel's concerned gaze met him as he entered the room. "How is she?"

"Sleeping, thank God." Neal joined him at the makeshift table in the center of the room, smiling his thanks to Sarah as she set a steaming cup of coffee in front of him. "I'm really worried about her. I've never seen her so exhausted."

"That's understandable considering everything she's been through." Sarah Collins took a seat beside her husband, intertwining her arm with his. "But I wouldn't be too concerned. A good night's sleep will do her wonders."

Neal didn't dispute Rachel's need for sleep, but nothing short of finding Sean alive and well was going to bring about the healing that her fragile emotional state was so in desperate need of. The prospect of that not happening was too disturbing to even consider.

Neal leveled his gaze on Daniel with a renewed sense of urgency. "Is that offer to go to the boardinghouse still good?"

"Of course it is."

Neal turned to Sarah next. "Would you mind looking in on her once in awhile? She's been having these nightmares lately...."

"Don't worry about a thing," Sarah told him with a reassuring smile. "You two go on. The sooner you find her brother the better."

* * * * *

It was approaching ten thirty by the time Neal and Daniel arrived at the boardinghouse where Sean had been staying up until the time of his arrest. They were greeted at the front door by the landlady, Esther Tyler. "Detective Collins," the elderly woman said with an engaging smile. "What a pleasure to see you again."

"I hope we didn't wake you, ma'am."

"Not at all. I was up doing some baking for tomorrow. Won't you come in?"

Neal followed Daniel inside, taking a leisurely glance around the modestly furnished sitting room.

"Can I offer you gentlemen some coffee? Or perhaps a piece of blueberry pie. It's fresh out of the oven."

"Perhaps another time, ma'am. We'd like to speak with you about Sean if we may." Daniel turned to introduce Neal. "This is Detective Neal Ramsey with the Chicago Police Department, Sean's brother-in-law."

"Neal," she exclaimed, reaching with both hands to clasp the one that Neal was extending to her. "I should have recognized you right off. Sean speaks of you and Rachel often. It's so refreshing to encounter a young man with such devotion to his family."

Neal was confused by the picture that the elderly woman was painting of his brother-in-law. It didn't resemble that of a man who had not bothered to contact his family in over thirteen years.

"I was so disturbed by his arrest," she continued. "I still refuse to believe that he had anything to do with that robbery."

"Yes, ma'am," Daniel nodded. "That's what we're all hoping for."

"Oh, I do so wish that you gentlemen had come by earlier. Sean will be so disappointed that he missed you."

"You mean he's still staying here?" Neal asked.

"Why, yes. He left not more than ten minutes ago."

Neal mentally kicked himself for not coming sooner. "Do you know where he went?"

"To work. He was starting a new job tonight."

"And where might that be?" Daniel asked, pulling a small notebook from his coat pocket.

"At a warehouse down on Fifth Street, I believe he said."

Daniel quickly jotted down the information. "Thank you, Mrs. Tyler. You've been most helpful. Excuse me." Daniel stepped aside, drawing Neal along with him. "It might be best if you wait here," he suggested. "We don't know what frame of mind Sean might be in. If he sees you...." Daniel's implication was clear.

"I was thinking the same thing," Neal agreed. He turned back to a waiting Mrs. Tyler. "With your permission, ma'am, I'd like to have a look around Sean's room. I realize that it was already searched after his arrest, but perhaps there's something they missed."

"Oh, I do hope so. As I said before, I don't believe for a moment that Sean had anything to do with that robbery. I'm sure there's a perfectly logical explanation ...."

Neal followed Mrs. Tyler down a narrow hallway as she continued to expound upon her convictions of Sean's inno-cence. As much as he wanted to prove her right, finding clues as to the young man's whereabouts for the past thirteen years was his primary concern.

Neal waited in the hallway as Mrs. Tyler lit a lamp for *him inside the door of* Sean's room. "If there's anything else you need, just give a holler. I'll be in the kitchen."

"Thank you, ma'am." Neal stepped through the door, turning to survey the layout of the room. The first thing that caught his eye was the Bible that he saw lying on the small stand beside the bed. He recognized it as the one they had given Sean on his sixteenth birthday, exactly one week before his disappearance. Neal opened it to the front cover, recalling the inscription that Rachel had penned before they had each signed their name. He was startled by what he found. His name had been completely scratched out, leaving only Rachel's and Ned's visible. Neal wondered what could have prompted such an action on Sean's part. Was he to blame for the young man's decision to run away?

"Mr. Ramsey?"

Neal started at the voice behind him. He turned to find the silhouette of a young woman in the doorway. "Yes?"

"I'm sorry if I startled you." The woman took a tentative step forward into the lamplight. "I'm not sure if you remember me. Hannah Cavanaugh?"

She has her father's eyes, Neal thought to himself. "Hannah, of course. It's been awhile."

"Yes, it has." Hannah moved slowly towards him, clearly troubled about something. "Mrs. Tyler told me that you were here. I'd like to speak with you if I may...about Sean."

"Certainly." Neal escorted her to the only chair in the room.

"I've had the chance to get to know Sean during the few months that he's been living here. Mr.

Ramsey," Hannah leaned forward in the chair, her eyes pleading with him, "Sean isn't capable of what they're saying about him. You've got to believe me."

Neal had always considered himself a pretty good judge of character, and as he stood listening to the young woman's ardent pleas on Sean's behalf, it was obvious to him that her feelings for Sean went far beyond that of a casual acquaintance. But at the same time, Hannah Cavanaugh did not strike him as someone who would allow her feelings to cloud her judgment. She truly believed that Sean was innocent of any involvement in the robbery.

"Please, Mr. Ramsey," she implored him. "If you would just give him a chance to explain, I know this whole matter could be cleared up."

"There's nothing I want more," Neal assured her, "but I have to find him first to do that. Do you know where he went tonight?"

"He said to work...but I didn't believe him." Hannah seemed embarrassed by her admission, as if she were in some way betraying Sean's trust. "I'm afraid for him, Mr. Ramsey," she continued on the verge of tears. "Afraid he's going to—" That's where she stopped.

"Going to what?" Neal asked, beginning to suspect the young woman knew far more than she was letting on.

"That's just it. I don't know." Hannah shook her head as if trying to jar something loose from her memory that might help. "I started noticing a change in him a few days before the robbery. He was nervous...scared, you might even say. It was right after he met—" Her eyes brightened as if a candle had been lit behind them. "Liam."

"Liam who?"

Hannah bit her bottom lip, trying to remember his last name. "I don't know. I only met him once. He came by the boardinghouse looking for Sean." But once had been enough. Hannah shuddered, recalling how uncomfortable she had been in the man's presence. "They left together and Sean didn't come back for hours. He wouldn't tell me anything. That's when I started getting worried." Hannah's face paled as the unthinkable came to mind. "Mr. Ramsey, you don't think that Sean—"

"Now let's not go jumping to conclusions," Neal cautioned her. "You said yourself that he wasn't capable. Do you still believe that?"

Hannah only hesitated a moment before nodding her head.

"Okay, then. Until we know differently, we hold on to that hope. Remember, things aren't always what they seem." Neal laid a hand on her shoulder, offering a smile to go along with it. "We'll get to the bottom of this. I promise you."

Hannah rose to her feet, feeling much lighter in spirit than when she'd first entered the room. "Thank you, Mr. Ramsey."

Neal walked with her to the door. "If you happen to remember anything else, you can leave a message for me at the police department."

Hannah paused in the doorway, that familiar light returning to her eyes. "There is something. I just remem-

bered that Sean started keeping a journal right around the
time of the robbery. I don't know if it will help, but maybe
there's something...."

"I'll keep an eye out for it." It was then that Neal remembered Sean's Bible and the disturbing thought that he might
have played a role in the younger man's decision to run away
thirteen years ago. He wavered for only a moment before
deciding to ask Hannah if she knew anything. "Did Sean
ever tell you why he ran away?"

"Yes," she said with a sympathetic smile. "But I think
that's something you should ask him yourself."

Neal knew better than to press the issue. "I hope I'll get
that chance."

As soon as Hannah had left the room, Neal continued
his search. He turned up nothing to aid his investigation into
Sean's disappearance...and no journal. "So much for wishful
thinking."

He was about to leave the room when a gap between two
of the floorboards beside the bed caught his eye. Neal knelt
down and felt along the gap for a finger hold. Finding none,
he took out the small knife that he carried in his pocket and
managed to work one of the boards loose. He was rewarded
for his effort. Underneath was the journal that Hannah had
alluded to, along with twenty dollars concealed in a small
drawstring bag. Neal opened the journal to the first entry,
dated just two days before the robbery. It detailed Sean's
encounter with a man named Liam O'Brien, whose claims of
being a special security agent with the railroad already had
Neal's suspicions on the rise.

*O'Brien has offered me five hundred dollars to help guard
a shipment of gold that will be passing through Philadelphia
on its' way to the Federal Treasury in Washington,* Sean
wrote. *Five hundred dollars! That's twice as much as I can
make working down at the warehouse in a whole year. I plan*

on contacting him tonight to let him know that I'll do it. This could be the start of a whole new life.

He's being set up, Neal thought to himself as he looked ahead to the next entry. It was dated the night of the robbery.

Tonight's the night. I've been having second thoughts but I already gave O'Brien my word. Besides, what could go wrong? In a few hours I'll be five hundred dollars richer. Then I'll finally be able to provide for Hannah in the manner she deserves.

There was one final entry, dated that very night. It was here that Neal's suspicions were confirmed.

Liam O'Brien is not who he claims to be. How could I have been so naïve not to see the truth? I still shudder when I think about what I've done. God forgive me! O'Brien is planning another job but I don't want any part of it. I will tell him so tonight and that will be the end of it.

Neal shuddered at the thought of Sean confronting O'Brien on his own. He knew too much. O'Brien was never going to let him walk away alive. "Sean...where are you?"

"Neal?"

Neal quickly put the floorboard back in place and got to his feet. He slid the journal into his coat pocket just moments before Daniel entered the room.

"There you are."

Neal took a few steps away from the bed, trying not to draw attention to the gap in the floorboards. "Did you find out anything?"

"Well, I talked with the foreman down at the warehouse, a Mr...." Daniel flipped through the pages of his notebook.

"Carlson. He confirms that Sean was scheduled to start work tonight but he never showed up."

Neal had been expecting as much.

"How about you?" Daniel glanced around the room. "Anything turn up in here?"

Neal became uncomfortably aware of the journal concealed in his pocket. The right thing to do would be to share his discovery with Daniel, but something held him back from doing so. Maybe it was Hannah's unwavering faith in Sean's innocence, or Sean's own pleas for forgiveness. Whatever the reason, he just couldn't bring himself to hand Sean over to be tried and convicted without first giving him the chance to explain. If he ever got that chance.

"Neal?"

Neal snapped his attention back to Daniel. "Uh, no. Just a Bible and a few other personal items."

"I guess we're back to square one, then."

"Yeah, I guess."

Daniel studied him for a moment, sensing something was wrong. "Are you all right, partner?"

"Just worried about Rachel." Neal clapped him on the back on his way out the door. "Let's get out of here."

CHAPTER FIFTEEN

DAY OF RECKONING

Rachel was furious when she awoke the following morning to learn of Neal's late night visit to the boardinghouse. "How could you? How could you go without telling me?"

"Rachel, you were exhausted. You needed to rest."

"I don't want to hear it." Rachel paced away from him with her arms crossed firmly against her chest.

"Rach, please try to calm down. Sarah has a nice breakfast prepared for us. Why don't we go get something to eat?"

"I'm not hungry."

Neal sank down onto the end of the bed, watching her restless pacing. He had been expecting her to be upset, but it was nothing compared to how she was going to react when she heard the rest of the story. Up to that point he had told her nothing about his conversation with Hannah Cavanaugh or the discovery of Sean's journal. All she knew was that her brother had been out when he and Daniel had paid their visit to the boardinghouse last night.

Rachel turned and walked over to where he was sitting. "I want you to take me over to the boardinghouse right now," she demanded.

"Rach, I don't think—" A knock at the door prevented Neal from completing his thought. He rose to answer it, finding Daniel and Sarah waiting on the other side.

Daniel started to say something but quickly held back as Rachel came over to stand beside Neal. "Neal, can I have a word with you? Down the hall?"

"Whatever needs to be said will be done right here," Rachel insisted. She refused to be left out of anything else.

Daniel waited for an "okay" nod from Neal before proceeding. "I just came back from the station. I'm afraid the news isn't good."

Rachel balled up her fists, bracing herself as best she could. "Say it."

"Another train was held up last night…"

Neal slid an arm around Rachel's waist as she began to sway on her feet.

"Sean was one of the men involved," Daniel continued. "He got away…but witnesses say that he was shot during the escape."

"No!" Rachel went limp in Neal's embrace, sobbing uncontrollably. "Sean!"

Neal picked her up in his arms and carried her over to the bed. Sarah was quickly at his side. "Let me," she offered, sensing Rachel's need for a woman's touch right now.

Neal backed away from the bed, watching helplessly as Sarah cradled Rachel in her arms like a newborn babe. He feared that this latest news about Sean had finally pushed her over the edge. What if she never recovered?

Neal felt a strong hand on his shoulder and turned to find Daniel beside him. "Come on. She's in good hands."

Neal followed him out of the room and down the hall to the kitchen where he took a seat at the table. Daniel poured them both a cup of coffee before sitting down across from him. "So what now?" he wondered. "It's a safe bet that Sean won't be going back to the boardinghouse any time soon."

Neal realized that he couldn't keep what he knew to himself any longer. Sean was going to need all the help he could get. "That's exactly where he'll go."

Daniel paused with his coffee cup halfway to his lips. "Why would he do that? He's got to know that's the first place we'll look."

"To get this." Neal reached beneath one of his pant legs and pulled the journal out of his sock. "It Sean's. It details his involvement in the hold up last week."

Daniel leaned forward in his chair, staring at the small black book that Neal was holding. "Where did you get that?"

"I found it last night under a loose floorboard in his room."

Neal's confession left Daniel's head spinning. "I can't believe I'm hearing this. Do you realize that I could arrest you for obstructing justice?"

"I know. But I didn't have any choice." Neal quickly told him about Sean's encounter with Liam O'Brien. "He was set up, Daniel, can't you see that? But by the time he knew the truth about O'Brien it was too late."

"Then how do you explain last night?"

Neal flung the journal down on the table. "I can't. Maybe he was threatened if he didn't go along. I don't know." Neal realized that he was grasping at straws, but until he heard the whole story from Sean directly, speculations were all he had to go on. "Please, Daniel. I'm asking you as a friend. Just give me the chance to find Sean before you go to the authorities."

Daniel picked up the journal, blindly thumbing through its pages. He knew it could cost him his job if he heeded to Neal's request, yet something told him he should take that chance. "I'm probably going to regret this...." He slid the journal back over in front of Neal. "You have twenty-four hours."

* * * * *

Neal had been anticipating a fight on his hands when he suggested to Rachel that she go on and attend Alec and Kathleen's wedding without him, but to his relief she didn't object. His only concern was that she shouldn't be traveling alone in her present state of mind and readily accepted Sarah's gracious offer to accompany her. Rachel, however, assured everyone that she would be just fine on her own

After seeing her safely off on the evening train, Neal went straight to the boardinghouse and filled Hannah and Mrs. Tyler in on the latest news about Sean. Both women were quite eager to help in whatever way they could.

"You're sure he'll come back here?" Hannah asked.

"I don't think he has much choice. That journal can implicate him in both of the robberies. He can't take the chance of it falling into the wrong hands."

Hannah paled at his mention of the journal. She had been disturbed to learn that Sean's desire to provide for her had played a role in his decision to accept Liam O'Brien's offer.

"I know what you're thinking, Hannah. But no one is to blame for Sean's decision except for Sean."

"But if I had said something...."

"Do you really think you could have changed his mind?"

No, Hannah's inner voice told her. The quest for wealth was a powerful lure. It had sent more than a few well-intentioned young men down the road of wrack and ruin. Sean had made an unwise decision and now he would have to suffer the consequences. "What will happen to him, Mr. Ramsey?"

"A lot of that is going to depend on him," Neal told her. "I won't lie to you, though. The charges against him are serious. But if he's willing to cooperate with the authorities, I think there's a good chance that he can avoid prison time. I promise you. I'm going to do everything I can to make that happen."

The thought of Sean spending time in prison was far less frightening to Hannah than the alternative. What if he hadn't survived his escape last night?

Hannah shook her head, not wanting to even consider a life without him. "I love him so much," she whispered tearfully. "I don't know what I would do if...."

"There, there, child." Mrs. Tyler coaxed Hannah's head down onto her shoulder. "The Good Lord purposed you two should be together. He's not going to forsake Sean now."

Neal tried to think of something comforting of his own to add but nothing came to mind. He decided he would do better to concern himself with preparing for Sean's arrival and excused himself to do just that. The twenty-four hour deadline that Daniel had given him was fast approaching.

* * * * *

Sean Donnelly watched from across the street as one by one the windows of the boardinghouse grew dark. To be safe, he would wait another hour before attempting to retrieve his things.

But then what? As much as he wanted to, Sean knew that staying in Philadelphia was out of the question. By now his description had probably been circulated throughout the entire city. He had no choice but to move on.

Sean winced as the bullet wound in his left shoulder began to throb. It was yet another unpleasant reminder of what a nightmare the past twenty-four hours had been. He had gone to tell O'Brien that he didn't want to take part in any more robberies and found himself staring down the barrel of a gun. He was lucky to have escaped with his life. If only he had just taken what he knew about the man to the authorities in the first place. At least then he would have had cause to hold his head up again. But now it was too late. After last night no one was going to believe that he hadn't gone along with O'Brien willingly. He had lost everything.

And everyone, Sean realized, thinking about Hannah. Losing her was the most painful of all. But how could he ever expect her to forgive him when he couldn't even forgive himself? The sooner he was out of her life the better.

After waiting for what he felt was a safe enough length of time, Sean darted across the street and around the side of the house. He was prepared to break a window if need be but found the backdoor unlocked. The smell of freshly baked bread assaulted his senses as soon as he stepped inside, reminding him that he hadn't eaten since yesterday morning, but he ignored his growling stomach and proceeded down the hall to his room. Deciding not to waste time lighting a lamp, he set straight to gathering his things. His first stop was the loose floorboard beside the bed. After prying it up, he reached blindly inside, feeling around for what he expected to be there. His heart nearly stopped cold when he realized that the journal was not among its contents.

"Looking for this?"

Sean bolted to his feet as the lamp by the door flared to life. Neal stepped forward holding the journal up in front of him.

The sight of his brother-in-law sent a wave of emotions through Sean that he had denied himself access to for the past thirteen years. It had been easy to do when there were so many miles separating them. But now he was here, standing not more than five feet away. It was only by a sheer force of will that Sean kept himself from running into his arms. That, and an even stronger instinct for survival. If Neal had read his journal, he could be here for only one purpose.

Sean made a sudden lunge for the door which Neal was quick to block. "Out of my way, Neal!"

"Not until we talk."

"I got nothin' to say to you!"

Neal drew his attention back to the journal. "I think you do."

Sean swallowed nervously, glancing around for a way to escape. "What do you want?"

"Just to talk," Neal told him honestly. "I'm here to help you, Sean."

"You're lying!" Sean pulled a knife in a final act of desperation. "Out of my way!"

Neal stood his ground. "I know you don't want to hurt me," he said calmly, hoping to diffuse the situation before Sean forced him to take more drastic measures. "Just put the knife down."

Sean backed up to the edge of the bed as Neal came towards him, the hand that he held the knife in shaking as if he had palsy. "Stay where you are!"

"It's over, Sean." Neal reached out and took hold of the young man's wrist, gently forcing his arm back to his side. "No more running."

"He's right, Sean." Hannah stepped into the room, choosing that precise moment to make her presence known. "It's time to go home."

The sight of her drained Sean of every last ounce of fight he had left in him. He released his grip on the knife, bursting into tears as it clattered to the floor. "Forgive me," he sobbed, dropping to his knees beside the bed. "Oh, God...forgive me."

Hannah knelt down beside him, resting her head against his shoulder as tears of thanksgiving rolled down her cheeks. "He does, Sean," she assured him. "He does...and so do I."

* * * * *

Sean stared aimlessly into the dying embers in the fireplace as Hannah tended to his wounded shoulder. As hard as he tried, he couldn't shake from his mind the vision of her kneeling beside him, or her accompanying offer of forgiveness. How could she still care so deeply for him after everything he'd done? It didn't make sense, and it didn't make what he had to do any easier. He knew that she'd be better off without him. The sooner he convinced her of that the better.

"There." Hannah put the finishing touches on her handiwork, tying one last knot in the bandage she had applied to his shoulder. "Is it too tight?"

Sean slipped his arm back into his shirtsleeve. "No, it's fine."

"I can loosen it if—"

"I said its fine!" he snapped back.

Hannah withdrew from him as if she'd been slapped, confusion in the form of tears burning behind her eyes. He had never been harsh with her before. What could she have done to prompt such an intense burst of anger from him? "I—I'm sorry," she stammered nervously. "I didn't mean to upset you."

Sean closed his eyes against the pain that he heard in her voice. It was breaking his heart to treat her in such a fashion, but it was the only way he could think of to drive her affections from him.

"Sean...." Hannah knelt in front of him, placing her hands atop his. "Whatever it is that I've done, if you would just tell me—"

Neal stepped in the front door, cutting short Hannah's impassioned plea. "I'm not interrupting anything, am I?"

"No." Hannah rose to her feet and began gathering up the unused bandages. "We're through here."

Neal detected a hidden meaning in her choice of words but he couldn't grasp what. He got no further clues from Sean. The young man's expression was as hard as stone. "We should be going now. Daniel is waiting for us down at the station."

Sean got quickly to his feet. "I'm ready."

Hannah tossed the bandages back on the sofa and strode purposefully to the rack by the door to retrieve her shawl. "I'm coming, too."

"No," Sean railed at her. "I don't want you there."

Hannah stared after him as he stalked out the door, the hurt in her eyes unmistakable.

Neal struggled for something to say. "I'm sure he didn't mean it," was all he could think of.

Hannah smiled as she reached up to fasten the shawl around her neck, recalling Mrs. Tyler's declaration that she and Sean "were purposed to be together". "He meant it, Mr. Ramsey," she told him bravely. "But I'm coming anyway."

* * * * *

Philadelphia Police Department

Sean was not pleased with Hannah's decision to accompany them but said nothing further to discourage her. He would have suffered his brother-in-law's wrath if he had. Neal thought it was inexcusable the way he had been treating her, though not entirely without explanation. He was clearly trying to sabotage her affections, hoping to drive her away from him once and for all. But Neal sensed he had sorely underestimated the magnitude of the young woman's love for him. Ridding himself of Hannah Cavanaugh was not going to be as easy as Sean Donnelly might have first thought.

"What's taking so long?" Hannah stopped her pacing just long enough to stare down the hallway where Sean's interrogation was taking place. "They've been in there for hours."

"I'm sure that Daniel just wants to make sure everything's done by the book," Neal told her. "Sean's testimony will be very important in putting O'Brien behind bars."

Hannah shuddered at the mention of Liam O'Brien. She drew her shawl more snugly about her shoulders as she joined Neal on the bench where he was sitting. "That horrible man," she seethed. "I wish that Sean had never met him."

Neal was inclined to agree with her except for one reason. He was a firm believer that God worked all things together for good, and that included Sean's brief encounter with one Liam O'Brien. If the two men had not met when they had, Sean may have been lost to them forever.

Hannah leapt back to her feet when she saw Daniel coming down the hall, hungry for any news that he might have. "Detective Collins, how's Sean?"

"Well, if one of you can convince him to testify against O'Brien, he can walk out of here right now a free man."

"And if he won't?" Hannah asked.

"If he won't...." Daniel looked her directly in the eye, wishing he could offer her more hope. "Then I'm afraid there's not a court in the land that's going to believe he wasn't a willing party to those robberies."

Neal wasn't surprised by Sean's refusal to defend himself. The young man was wallowing in self-pity, and until he was able to forgive himself, accepting pardon from anyone else was not even an option he was willing to entertain.

"I tried reasoning with him," Daniel assured them both, "but his mind is made up. He's guilty and he deserves what's coming to him. His exact words."

Hannah looked from Daniel to Neal. "We have to do something. We can't just let him be sent to prison."

"We won't," Neal promised her. "Not if I can help it." His gaze went quickly back to Daniel. "Has a date been set for the trial?"

"Nothing definite. The courts are backlogged for at least another week."

Neal smiled at this fortunate turn of events. A week would buy him just the amount of time that he needed. He was fairly certain that if he could get Sean alone for a few days, away from Philadelphia and any reminders of Liam O'Brien, he could talk some sense into the young man. And if he couldn't, surely Rachel could. *All things work together for good....* "I know I may be going out on a limb here, Daniel, but what are the chances of getting Sean released into my custody until the trial?"

"You'll have to talk to the man in charge."

"I thought I was."

"Not anymore. I just got word that the investigation has been turned over to Allan Pinkerton."

"By whose request?" Neal was curious to know.

"The president of the railroad, Jonathan Hammond. Apparently he and Pinkerton are old friends and he wants him to handle the investigation personally from here on out."

"Old friends, is it? Well, Mr. Hammond is not the only *old friend* that Pinkerton has."

It took Daniel a moment to realize that Neal was talking about himself. "You?"

"We worked together for almost three years before he left the department to start his own agency."

Hannah turned imploring eyes in his direction, feeling optimistic for the first time since learning of Sean's impending fate. "Do you think that he'd be willing to help Sean, Mr. Ramsey?"

Neal smiled down at her. "There's no harm in asking."

* * * * *

Thirty years. That was how long Detective Collins had said that he could expect to spend behind bars if he didn't testify against Liam O'Brien.

A lifetime, Sean thought as he lay staring up at the ceiling of his cell. *His* lifetime. He would turn thirty next week. Thirty years on the face of God's green earth and what did he have to show for it? He had willfully turned his back on everyone and everything that had ever meant anything to him. Now he was alone and deservedly so. He had no right to accept the gift of freedom that Detective Collins was offering him. He had transgressed far beyond even God's ability to forgive. Besides, what was thirty more years on top of the thirteen he had already spent in the prison of his own making?

Sean silenced his thoughts as the door to the cell area opened. He watched curiously as Daniel walked in and proceeded to unlock his cell. "You have a visitor."

Sean sat up on his cot as Neal stepped in.

"Grab your stuff and come on. You're being released into my custody."

Sean stared back at his brother-in-law as if he had never seen him before. "What?"

"You heard me."

Sean continued to stare, unable to fathom why Neal would even bother. What could there possibly be in it for him?

"Well, come on," Neal barked impatiently. "The next train leaves in an hour and I don't want to miss it."

Sean was more confused than ever. "Train to where?"

"Baxter, Pennsylvania. It's beautiful this time of year. You'll love it."

* * * * *

Baxter, Pennsylvania

"Alec Ramsey!" Kathleen rushed into the waiting room of the new medical clinic and made a grab for the curtain that he was holding up to one of the front windows. "Give me that!"

Alec stood with a dumbfounded look on his face, his now empty hands still raised towards the window. "What did I do?"

"Well, for one thing, this is a curtain for one of the recovery rooms upstairs. And secondly, hanging curtains is woman's work. Rachel and I will get to this right after we finish scrubbing the exam room floor."

Alec watched as she returned the curtain to the pile on the back of the sofa. "There must be something that I can do."

Kathleen considered his request for a moment. "Maybe you could...." She shook her head after thinking twice about what she was going to propose. "No, you'd better leave that to us, too. Don't you have any patients to see?"

"I cancelled all of my appointments for this afternoon so I could help out here."

Kathleen realized that could prove a problem. If she didn't find something for him to do he was going to be under foot all afternoon. "Why don't you go and sweep the front steps?" She said it in a way that suggested he'd be doing her a great favor. "The broom is by the door."

Alec raised his hand to his forehead in a mock salute. "At your service, ma'am."

Kathleen breathed a sigh of relief as he disappeared out the front door. "Thank goodness."

Alec was completely engrossed in his appointed task when he saw Reverend Thompson coming up the front walk. "Afternoon, Reverend."

"Alec." Thompson stopped with one foot poised on the bottom step. "I hope I'm not interrupting your work."

"Not at all. What's brings you to this part of town?"

"Just thought I'd check in and see how the transformation is taking place." Thompson paused to gaze up at the front of the house. "I must say you've got the place fairly shining. It's hardly recognizable as the same house."

Alec joined him in evaluating their progress. "Yeah, it's really shaping up. Jesse's father is working on the sign for us and I figure I should be able to start seeing patients here in a week or so."

Thompson cast him a look of concern. "Don't you think you're over doing things a bit? You are getting married in two days, remember? And then there's the honeymoon to consider."

Alec smiled. "I remember. Truth is, we weren't planning on starting on the clinic until after the wedding but Kathleen thought it would be good for Rachel to keep busy."

"No word yet from Neal?"

"Not yet. But I'm sure we'll hear something soon."

"Excuse me, gentleman."

Alec turned towards the voice behind him, as did Thompson. Neither one recognized the man that was coming up the walk. He was dressed as if he had just walked out of the pages of a fashion magazine.

"I'm looking for one Reverend Thompson," the stranger announced.

Thompson stepped forward with a smile. "I'm Reverend Thompson. What can I do for you?"

The man swept off his hat, tucking it securely under his left arm. "I'm Isaac P. Jameson, the third." His self-introduction was followed by a lengthy pause, as if his name alone should have been explanation enough as to why he was there. "I'm the town's new banker," he added for further clarification.

"Mr. Jameson, yes. The whole town has been eagerly awaiting your arrival."

"Yes, I'm sure." He cleared his throat. "I'll get right to the point of my visit, Reverend. I was told that you are the man with whom I need to converse about purchasing this fine establishment." He made a sweeping motion towards the house.

Thompson exchanged an awkward glance with Alec before addressing Jameson's request. "I'm afraid you're a little late, Mr. Jameson. The house is already being occupied by the town's new medical clinic. This is Alec Ramsey, the town's doctor."

Jameson locked eyes with Alec and then quickly dismissed him as no one of consequence. "Yes, I was told that, as well. But I'm sure we can come to some mutual agreement. I'm prepared to offer a handsome sum." He slid his hand beneath his suit coat on the pretense of reaching for his billfold.

"I'm sorry, Mr. Jameson, but as I said before—"

"Uh, Reverend? Might I have a word with you?"

"Certainly, Alec." Thompson excused himself and followed Alec inside, waiting patiently for him to begin.

"This isn't easy for me to say," Alec admitted, "but I'll understand if you want to accept his offer. The church could really use the—"

Thompson halted him with an upraised hand. "Alec, I gave this house to you. The congregation agreed unanimously. That's the end of it."

Alec smiled. He knew better than to argue with Clive Thompson once his mind was made up. "Do you want to do the honors or should I?"

"Oh, by all means. Allow me."

Jameson stood smugly at attention as the two men returned, presuming that all obstacles to his purchase of the house had been resolved. "I trust that we can now come to some agreement, Reverend?"

"I'm sorry, Mr. Jameson," Thomson had the express pleasure of telling him. "But as I stated once before, the house is already occupied."

Isaac Jameson was not a man accustomed to being denied what he wanted and his expression said exactly what he thought about the outcome of the negotiations. "It seems I've underestimated the importance of this clinic." He turned to Alec with a scowl. "Not to mention the influence of the good doctor, here." Jameson placed his hat firmly back on his head, shifting his gaze back to Thompson. "I kindly thank you for your time, Reverend. I won't be troubling you further."

Alec was unaware that he had been holding his breath until he opened his mouth to make a comment after Jameson's departure. "Why do I get the feeling he doesn't like me very much?"

"Pa!" Kirsten came tearing up the walkway. "A telegram, Pa! From Uncle Neal!"

A smile spread quickly across Alec's face as he read the telegram that Kirsten handed him.

"Good news, Alec?" Thompson asked.

"The best, Reverend." Alec rushed back inside the clinic. "Rachel!"

Kathleen stepped out of the exam room, followed closely by Rachel. "Alec, what's wrong? Did something happen to one of the children?"

Alec moved towards Rachel, holding the telegram up in front of him. "From Neal." Rachel caught her breath in anticipation of what he was going to say next. "He's bringing Sean home."

Rachel turned to bury her face against Kathleen's shoulder as thirteen years of emotions came spilling forth in that one moment. Her brother was coming home.

CHAPTER SIXTEEN

THE PRODIGAL'S RETURN

"**S**andwich?"

Sean stared for a moment at the offering of food and then fixed his gaze back out the train window. "I'm not hungry."

Neal extended the invitation a second time. "Are you sure? There's still plenty of food left." He indicated the basket beside him on the seat. "Sarah packed enough for us to take a trip around the world."

But we're not taking a trip around the world, Sean wanted to scream at him. *We're going to Baxter, Pennsylvania.* Why of all places had Neal decided to take him there? That question had been gnawing at him ever since they'd left Philadelphia two days ago. Of course, Sean figured he was partly to blame for that. He had never asked Neal for an explanation.

Neal closed the lid on the basket and settled back in his seat, taking a chomp out of an apple. "We should be there in a few hours."

Sean decided he had waited long enough. "You still haven't told me why you're taking me to Baxter."

Neal withdrew the apple from his mouth, turning to face the younger man. He had been hoping to avoid any discussion as to the reason for their visit until after they had arrived but Sean's curiosity wasn't going to wait. "There are three reasons, actually," Neal told him. "First of all, my older brother and his wife are getting remarried today and I've been asked to be the best man. Secondly, your case is being turned over to Allan Pinkerton. He's agreed to meet us in Baxter the day after tomorrow. He says he has a proposition for you."

Sean frowned. "What kind of proposition?"

"I don't know the details." Neal went back to munching on his apple.

Sean continued to frown. "You said there were three reasons."

Neal turned to face him again. "I'm taking you to see your sister."

Sean reacted in much the way that Neal had been expecting. He looked like a frightened child in the midst of a thunderstorm. "Rachel's there?"

"Yeah."

"Does she...?" Sean swallowed nervously. "Does she know about the robberies?"

"She knows."

Sean ducked his head, any joy he felt at the thought of seeing his sister again snuffed out by his shame. How could he face her after everything he'd done? What was she going to think of him?

"She loves you, Sean," Neal assured him. "Nothing you've done is going to change that."

Sean shook his head. "I don't deserve her love."

"Just like you don't deserve Hannah's?" Neal decided not to pull any punches. "That's why you've been so hard on her, isn't it?"

Sean pressed his lips together to keep them from trembling. Hannah still remained a very sensitive topic with him. "She deserves better than me."

"Maybe so. But it's you she wants."

Neal said it with such conviction that Sean almost believed him. "But why?" he still wanted to know. "Why can't she just forget about me and go on with her life?"

"Because maybe she believes the Good Lord intended for the two of you to be together. And you know something? I'm just crazy enough to believe she might be right."

Sean turned to stare at the back of the seat in front of them, trying to decide whether to believe it for himself.

"Sean, listen to me." Neal waited until he was sure that he had the younger man's complete attention before continuing. "There isn't a one of us who hasn't done something that we regret in this life. Good Lord knows I've done more than my share. But He's forgiving. Give Him a chance. And us. We want you to come home."

Easy for him to say now, Sean thought. But what about six months from now? Or a year? Would they still want him then? "You don't even know why I left in the first place."

Sean's voice barely rose above a whisper but Neal was still able to understand

what he had said. "As far as I'm concerned the reasons why aren't important. All that

matters is having you home."

As Sean sat considering Neal's invitation, he was reminded of the parable that Jesus had taught about the prodigal son. After squandering his inheritance in wild living, the young man in the story had found himself alone and destitute, with nothing but guilt and shame to show for his selfish reveling. Sean felt sick to his stomach as he realized how closely the story mirrored his own life. But he also remembered how it ended. He wanted his own story to end the same and knew in his heart what he needed to do to make that happen, just as surely as the prodigal must have known it then. He had been away long enough. It was time to return to his Father.

"Will you pray with me?"

Neal smiled as he reached over to lay a hand on the younger man's shoulder. "I've just been waiting for you to ask."

Sean once again bowed his head, this time as an act of surrender instead of in shame. He had given his heart to the Lord as a young boy. Now it was time to offer his life as well. Tears streamed down his face as years of pride and selfishness were washed away in a single moment of repentance. And all the while the Father's gentle voice was whispering...*Welcome home.*

* * * * *

Baxter, Pennsylvania

"Oh, Mama." Kirsten joined her in gazing into the full-length mirror they had borrowed from the Crowley's to assist her in her wedding preparations. "You look absolutely beautiful. You're going to take Pa's breath away."

"I quite agree," Rachel chimed in.

Kathleen took a step closer to the mirror, fixated on the waistline of her dress. "I don't know," she said with a deepening frown. "It doesn't seem to fit quite right." She tried to pinch some of the material between her fingers but there was none to spare. "It tighter than when I tried it on just a week ago."

"Well, there's nothing we can do about that now." Rachel joined the twosome in front of the mirror. "You are getting married in less than two hours, Kathleen Ramsey, dress or no dress."

"Either way," Kirsten said with a telling smile, "I don't think Pa's going to mind."

Kathleen sighed. "I suppose you're right." She paid her reflection one final visit and then turned away from the mirror. "It's probably just— "

"Mama!" Kirsten's quick grab for her mother's arm was all that prevented her from plummeting to the floor in a dead faint. "Mama, are you all right?"

"Yes, sweetheart." Kathleen continued to sway unsteadily on her feet, prompting Rachel to take hold of her other arm. "Just a tad dizzy, is all."

"Here, come sit down." Rachel guided her over to the bed. "Where's your father, Kirsten?"

"Eric said that he was going over to the clinic to get ready. I'll go see if he's left yet."

"No, sweetheart," Kathleen objected. "I'm fine. It's probably just nerves."

"You're sure?"

Kathleen pressed a hand against her thickening midsection, curbing the smile that so wanted to reveal what she now suspected was reason for her dizzy spell. "Quite sure," she murmured contentedly.

Despite her repeated assurances, Kirsten and Rachel continued to flock around her like a couple of doting hens. "Now really, you two. I said I was fine." Kathleen rose to her feet without assistance and paraded across the room to prove her point. "Are you satisfied?"

"Knock, knock." Eric poked his head in the door. "Everyone decent?"

"As decent as can be," Kathleen called back. "Come in, dear."

Rachel's gaze went immediately to the telegram that Eric was holding. "Is that from Neal?"

"Sure is. He says that if their train stays on schedule, they should be getting in around two-thirty. Colin will bring them right over to the church."

Rachel's stomach flip-flopped nervously. Now that the moment to be reunited with her brother was finally at hand, she found herself wrestling once again with many of the fears that had plagued her at the start of their search just one week ago. *What will I say to him? Will he be glad to see me? What if he doesn't want to see me at all?* That was the fear that tormented Rachel most of all. Sean wasn't coming here of his own free will. He was in Neal's custody and had no say in the matter. What if he was angry about being tricked into a meeting with her? That's the last thing that Rachel wanted to overshadow what was supposed to be a happy reunion with her brother, but it remained a very real possibility that she had to prepare herself for.

Kathleen mistook the look on her face for disappointment. "Rachel, why don't you go with Colin to the station to meet Sean? I don't know why we didn't plan on that in the first place."

Rachel quickly repelled the idea from her mind. Meeting her brother at the station was the last thing she wanted to do. "I think I'd better just wait at the church with everyone else. We might not get back in time."

"Kirsten can stand up with me if you're not back in time. You should be there to welcome your brother home. I'm sure he can hardly wait to see you."

Rachel silently prayed she was right. "Whatever you think best."

Kathleen looked up at Eric. "Are you sure you still want to walk your mother down the aisle?"

"Honored beyond words," he told her.

"Oh, wait." Kathleen made a grab for his arm. "Your father's not still downstairs, is he?"

"He left for the clinic a few minutes ago," Eric assured her. "Took Nathan and Stephen with him."

Kathleen relaxed, extending him her hand. "Then shall we?"

Eric placed it securely atop his arm, smiling as they headed for the door. "Ready or not, here comes the bride."

* * * * *

"Neal?"

Neal's left eye opened halfway, followed slowly by the right. "What?" he asked
groggily.

"Sorry to wake you, but my shoulder is bleeding again."

Neal sat up on the seat, turning his attention to the small patch of red staining the front of Sean's shirt. "When did it start?"

"I don't know." Sean winced as Neal unbuttoned his shirt and began peeling back the old bandages. "Twenty minutes ago, I guess."

"You should've woken me sooner."

"I thought it would stop on its own."

Neal made a quick assessment of the wound. "Well, I'm no doctor, but I'd say you need more than a few stitches."

Sean's apprehension at the prospect of Neal putting a needle to him was visible all over his face. "You're not thinking of…?"

"Relax. I'm just going to try and stop the bleeding. I'll leave the fancy sewing to Alec."

"Might I be of some assistance?"

Neal turned to find a stylishly dressed young man standing in the aisle beside their seat. The fingers of his right hand were wrapped securely around the handle of a small black bag. "Are you a doctor?"

"Yes," he replied enthusiastically, clearly delighted by the fact. "Doctor Carter Buchanan."

Neal's relief was slow in manifesting itself. He didn't like the thought of having to explain the nature of
Sean's wound to a total stranger, doctor or not. How did he know if he could trust this young man?

"I'm sorry if I was out of line," Carter apologized.

"No, not at all." Neal decided not to err on the side of caution this time. Sean needed help. "Truth is, you couldn't have come along at a more perfect time." He quickly stepped out into the aisle, allowing the young man his seat beside Sean.

Carter set his bag down by his feet and then turned to make his own assessment of the wound. "This doesn't appear too bad," he pronounced. "But stitches will be in order. When did it happen?"

"A few days ago." Neal braced himself in anticipation of additional questions but the barrage never came. If the young doctor knew that it was a gunshot wound he was tending to, he didn't let on. "Is there anything I can do to help?" Neal offered, looking on as Carter readied a needle and thread.

"Thanks, but this shouldn't take long."

Neal watched as the young man confidently set about the task before him. His hands remained rock steady, moving with the skill of someone far beyond his years, every stitch administered with expert precision. "If you don't mind me asking, how long have you been practicing medicine?"

"Actually, this is my first patient," Carter admitted. "Live one, that is." He paused to tie off a small knot before continuing. "I graduated from Harvard Medical School just a few weeks ago."

"No fooling. What brings you out this way?"

"I've accepted a position as the assistant to the doctor in Baxter. That's where I'm heading."

Neal grinned. "Alec Ramsey?"

"Yes. Do you know him?"

"Only all my life. He's my older brother."

Carter stopped mid-stitch, turning his head just enough to meet Neal's gaze. "You're not kidding, are you?"

"Nope. Small world, isn't it?"

"I couldn't agree more."

Carter finished closing up the wound in Sean's shoulder and then put a fresh dressing over it. "He should be fine now. Just change the bandages at least once a day."

"Will do." Neal fished around in his pocket for some loose change. "What do I owe you?"

Carter rose to his feet, waving aside any offer of payment. "No charge."

"Are you sure?" Neal reluctantly dropped the coins back into his pocket. "It may be the last cash money you see in a long time. Most of my brother's patients pay him in apples and potatoes."

Carter wasn't at all put off by the bleak financial prospects ahead of him. If Alec Ramsey was anything like his brother, it was going to be a pleasure to work alongside him. That was compensation enough. "I'm sure. It's the least I can do for the brother of my future employer."

Neal offered the young man his hand along with a grateful smile. "Thanks for everything. Especially for not asking a lot of questions."

Carter shrugged. "It's none of my business, is it?"

Neal's respect for the young man soared. "How would you like to attend a wedding with me this afternoon? I'd like to personally introduce you to the groom."

* * * * *

Baxter, Pennsylvania

"Stephen, would you please stop jumping on the bed." Alec heard him land one last time on his knees before sliding off onto the floor with a thud. "Where is that brother of yours? I thought he was supposed to be keeping an eye on you."

"Which one?" Stephen giggled. "The right or the left?"

Alec turned from the mirror where he was frantically engaged in trying to straighten his tie. "I'm talking about Nathan."

Nathan ducked in the door. "Did you call me, Pa?"

"Where have you been?" Alec demanded to know.

"I'm sorry, Pa. I had to go to the outhouse. I tried to hold it as long as I—"

Alec waved aside his apology. "Never mind. Did you happen to see Sheriff Samuels while you were down there? Or your Uncle Neal?"

"In the outhouse?"

"Downstairs," Alec clarified for him.

"Nope."

"Great. I'm getting married in twenty minutes, I can't get my tie tied and I don't have a best man." Alec pivoted back to the mirror. "Nathan, take Stephen downstairs and watch for him."

"Which one?"

"Either one. And make sure Stephen stays out of the exam room."

"Yes, Pa." Nathan led Stephen out into the hallway, closing the door behind them. His eyes lit up at the sight of his uncle coming up the stairs.

Neal pressed a finger to his lips before Nathan could sound the alarm and spoil his surprise. The young man nodded that he understood and continued down the hall with Stephen in tow.

Alec breathed a sigh of relief when he heard the door open and close behind him. "Zack, am I glad you're here. I can't seem to get this stupid tie—" He fell silent as his brother's reflection appeared beside him in the mirror instead of Zack's. "Neal." Alec turned to face him.

Neal held out his arms. "You're not disappointed it's me, are you?"

"Don't be silly." Alec gathered him close, landing a solid thump on his back. "When did you get in?"

"About twenty minutes ago." Neal stepped back, his gaze going directly to Alec's lopsided tie. "Colin told us you were here."

Alec assumed that *us* meant Sean and Rachel. "Are they downstairs?"

Neal realized too late the impression that he had given. "No. I took Sean over to the jail. Rachel stayed with him."

A frown appeared on Alec's face. "Would you mind explaining to me why?"

"Because that's my job, Alec. I don't like it anymore than you do but Sean is still under arrest. I'm afraid he'll have to stay locked up at least until Pinkerton gets here."

"And when will that be?" Alec asked, trying not to sound too critical of his brother's decision.

"The day after tomorrow at the latest. But let's not concern ourselves with that now." Neal yanked Alec's tie undone and retied it perfectly on his first try. "There is a beautiful woman waiting over at the church to become your bride."

Alec smiled. "How could I forget?"

Neal followed him out of the room, resting a hand on his shoulder. "Oh, by the way. I met your new assistant on the train. He's waiting for us downstairs."

Alec backhanded him across the chest. "What new assistant?"

"Carter Buchanan."

Alec recalled the name from the response he had received to his ad last week, but what had given the young man the impression that he had been hired? "There must be some mistake. I never—"

"Pa!" Nathan came tearing up the stairs, scrambling his way up the last few steps on his hands and knees. "Stephen fell and hit his head! There's blood everywhere!"

* * * * *

Sean saw Rachel comfortably settled onto a chair in his cell before turning his attention to Sheriff Samuels. "Can we have a few moments alone?"

Zack smiled at the young man's request. "You're not going to try and escape on me, are you?"

"He'll have to answer to me if he does, sheriff," Rachel warned, smiling up at her brother.

Sean grinned back. "No escape attempt today, sheriff. My sister and I have thirteen years of catching up to do."

"Fine, then." Zack closed the cell door but purposely left it unlocked so that Rachel could let herself out when they were through. He then strode to the office door, retrieving his hat off his desk as he passed by. "If you two will excuse me, I have a wedding to attend."

Sean waited until they were alone and then walked over to the cot against the back wall of the cell and sat down. For the first few moments he did nothing but stare at his sister, as if trying to memorize every detail of her face.

Rachel was similarly engaged, marveling at how little his physical appearance had changed in thirteen years. Aside from being several inches taller, he looked the same as he had when she'd last seen him. If only the same could be said of her, but the years had clearly not been as kind.

"How have you been?" Sean asked, breaking the awkward silence.

"Just fine."

"And David?" he asked in reference to his nephew.

Rachel smiled in anticipation of sharing news about her family's expansion. "He's fine, too. And so are our other three children."

"Three?"

Rachel nodded. "Michael is twelve, Christian is ten and Emily is eight."

Sean smiled with the pride that only an uncle could. "Are they here with you?"

"Neal's sister, Christine, is looking after them for us at home. They have school starting in a few weeks and we didn't know how long it would take to-" Rachel caught herself before saying the words *find you*. Sean had been through enough without her reminding him of the pain his leaving had caused her. "I'm sorry," she apologized. "I shouldn't have said anything."

"No, Rachel," Sean argued. "I'm the one who's sorry. There's no excuse for the way I've treated you." He reached over and tenderly took his sister's hand. "You deserve to know the truth about why I left."

Rachel sensed how difficult it was going to be for him to dredge up old memories and tried to convey through a smile that nothing he was about to tell her would change her feelings towards him. It was a matter that she had settled in her heart long before they had ever received word of his whereabouts, and she intended to stand by it.

Sean drew strength from her smile as well as from his newly rekindled faith as a story thirteen years in the making began to unfold. "After the folks died," he began, "I know things weren't always easy for you. With Ned and me to care for and what little money Pa had left us dwindling away. But we made it together," he said with pride. "The three of us." The light behind Sean's eyes began to dim as he prepared to relate for her the next chapter in the story. "And then Neal came along. Now instead of the three of us, it was the two of you with Ned and me trying to fit in wherever we could."

Rachel sat stunned as she listened to her brother's monologue of resentments.

"He was always getting on my case about one thing or another, acting more like my pa than my brother-in-law." Sean looked away, knowing that his next admission was going to hurt her. "But I think what I resented most of all is that you never asked me how I felt. You just decided to get married and I was expected to make room for him in my life whether I wanted to or not."

Rachel realized he was right. She had never once asked him how he felt about Neal or their decision to marry. She had only been thinking about her own happiness.

Sean rose and walked to the front of the cell, gripping hold of the bars until his knuckles turned white. "I tried to make it work," he assured, wanting her to know that he hadn't taken his decision to leave lightly. "But after awhile I got to feeling like I was just in the way. Especially after David was born."

Rachel was standing now, slowly moving towards him.

"There just didn't seem to be room for me anymore." Sean turned to face her, no longer able to hold back the tears that had been building up behind his eyes. "That's when I decided to leave. I figured that no one would miss me."

"That's not true, Sean," Rachel assured him. "It was never Neal's intention to drive you away, or mine. We love you. We always have."

"I know that now." Sean reached up and wiped his eyes on the back of his sleeve. "But at sixteen…." He shook his head, contemplating the foolishness of his thinking back then. "Everything looked different. And I guess I was naïve enough to believe that leaving would somehow change all that."

"Where did you go?" Rachel asked. It was a question that had been eating at her for thirteen years. It was time to satisfy its hunger once and for all. "Neal had detectives out looking for you for months. They never turned up anything."

"Out to California."

So far, Rachel thought. *And so young.*

"But I reckon I must have tasted the dust of practically every state in the union at some point or another, Philadelphia was the first place that really felt like home since—" Sean quickly averted his gaze as his eyes began to fill with fresh tears. It took him a moment to compose himself before he could continue. "All that time, Rach," he said quietly. "All that time wandering from place to place, never knowing if...." He swallowed, turning back to face her. "Never knowing if I'd ever see you again."

Rachel gathered him into her arms, smiling joyfully through her own tears. "You don't have to wonder anymore, Sean. I'm right here. Welcome home."

* * * * *

Alec's heart nearly stopped as he came down the stairs and saw the pool of blood on the waiting room floor. He followed its trail with his gaze over to the sofa beneath the front window where Stephen sat holding an equally bloody cloth against his forehead. A young man was kneeling beside him readying what appeared to be a needle and thread. Alec could only presume this to be his alleged assistant.

"Stephen!" Alec half walked, half ran towards the scene.

Carter met him with a reassuring smile as he approached. "Don't be alarmed, Mr. Ramsey. It's not as bad as it looks. Just a lot of blood."

Alec knelt down in front of Stephen, lifting back the cloth to survey the damage for himself.

"I went boom, Papa," the youngster said with a hiccup.

"You sure did." Alec shifted his attention to Carter only after satisfying himself that Stephen's wound was not life threatening. "Thank you."

"No thanks necessary."

Neal stepped forward to make the official introductions. "Alec, this is Doctor Carter Buchanan. Carter, my brother, Doctor Alec Ramsey."

Carter offered his hand. "It's a pleasure, sir. I'm looking forward to working with you."

Alec awkwardly returned the expected pleasantries and then focused his attention back on Stephen. "Let's get you stitched up, shall we?" He reached for the needle that Carter had already prepared

"Why don't you let Carter tend to that?" Neal suggested. "You're going to be late for your own wedding as it is."

Alec was reluctant to heed his brother's suggestion, unsure if he wanted to subject Stephen to the young doctor's suturing skills. How did he know if they could be trusted?

"I'll understand if you'd rather do it yourself," Carter said, not the least bit offended by Alec's reluctance. "I'd feel the same way if it were my son."

Carter's declaration made Alec realize how foolish he was being and he quickly handed back the needle. "Just bring him over to the church when you're through. Nathan will show you the way."

Carter nodded. "I'll take good care of him."

Alec rose to his feet, gently cupping the back of Stephen's head. "You do everything Doctor Buchanan tells you, all right?"

"All right, Papa."

Alec turned and hurried out of the clinic. Neal followed, clapping him on the shoulder as they started down the front steps. "Relax, Alec. I watched Carter stitch up Sean's shoulder earlier. You've got nothing to worry about."

Alec stopped on the bottom step, turning to face his brother with a scowl. "You could have told me that sooner, you know."

Neal grinned. "I know. But you didn't ask."

CHAPTER SEVENTEEN

FOR BETTER OR FOR WORSE

"Any sign of him?" Kathleen was standing on her tiptoes, straining to see over Kirsten's shoulder as she peered out the Thompson's living room window towards the side door of the church. "The wedding was supposed to start five minutes ago."

"Not yet, Mama. No, wait…." Kirsten reached back and squeezed her mother's hand. "Here he comes now. And Uncle Neal is with him."

Kathleen breathed a sigh of relief. "Thank goodness. I'll go get Eric and Kaitlin."

"Mama…?" Kirsten dropped the curtain back into place, turning to face her. "Aunt Rachel's not here," she just realized.

"Well, perhaps she and Sean went back to the house. They probably wanted some time alone together." Kathleen smiled as she reached to cup the side of her daughter's face. "Will you do me the honor of standing up with me?"

Kirsten's heart swelled with pride. "Of course, Mama."

Kathleen's insides were doing cartwheels as they made their way over to the church. She wasn't sure if it was morning sickness or just the general nervous stomach commonly experienced by every bride on her wedding day. Or perhaps it was a combination of both. If only her mother were here. Surely she would be able to distinguish which. She had been a mother and a bride, though dare say not both at the same time.

Kathleen silenced her foolish ramblings as they mounted the church steps and came to a stop in front of the wide, open doors. Her arrival was welcomed by an overwhelming surge of love, radiating out from the crowd that had gathered inside to share in her and Alec's happiness. The beauty of the moment was marred only by her thoughts of those who were not in attendance. "Mama," she whispered with deep longing. And yes, she had to admit. That longing extended to her father, as well.

Kaitlin started down the aisle, dropping flower petals in her wake from the small wicker basket that she carried draped over her arm. Kirsten made her entrance when Kaitlin was halfway to the front. And then the organ music began to swell, signaling to Kathleen that her turn had come.

Eric entwined her arm with his. "Ready?"

Kathleen quickly banished from her mind the thought that her father should be the one asking her that question. "Ready."

The next few moments went by in a blur but Kathleen managed to store each one away in her heart to enjoy at length in the days ahead. Her walk down the aisle…Alec's beaming face as Eric transferred her hand to his…the warmth of loved ones gathered around….

"Dearly beloved…." Reverend Thompson's pleasant baritone voice filled the sanctuary. "We are gathered here this day to unite this man and this woman in holy matrimony…."

Kathleen looked up to find Alec gazing down upon her with such an enormous load of love that she felt she might collapse beneath the weight of it.

"Do you, Alec, take Kathleen to be your lawfully wedded wife? To have and to hold from this day forward? For better or for worse, for richer or for poorer, in sickness and in health, 'til death do you part?"

Kathleen's stomach flip-flopped in anticipation of his response.

"I do," Alec answered with conviction.

"And do you, Kathleen, take Alec to be your lawfully wedded husband...?"

Kathleen swayed on her feet as the room started to spin around her. *No,* she pleaded with herself. *Not now....*

"...'til death do you part?"

"I do," she managed weakly.

Alec took the ring from Neal and turned to place it on her finger. Kathleen was grateful for his steadying hand upon hers as the spinning continued in earnest.

"If there's anyone here who can show just cause why these two should not be lawfully joined together...."

I'm sorry, Alec. I tried.... Kathleen felt her knees give way right before the darkness closed in around her.

"...let him speak now —"

A wave of startled gasps accompanied Kathleen's sudden tumble to the floor.

Alec dropped to his knees beside her, gently sliding a hand beneath her head. "Kathleen?"

"Pa, what's wrong with her?" Kirsten asked on the verge of tears.

"I don't know, sweetheart." Alec looked up, searching for Eric among the pressing crowd. He finally caught his eye. "Bring the wagon around. Let's get her back to the house."

* * * * *

"Eric, go get Pa. I think she's waking up."

"I'm right here, Kirsty." Alec strode purposefully into the room and sat down on the edge of their bed where Kathleen was stretched out. He was relieved to see her stirring in preparation to reenter the realm of consciousness. "Kathleen?" he coaxed, giving her hand a gentle squeeze. "Can you hear me?"

Kathleen's dark lashes fluttered open against the backdrop of her pale complexion. It took her a few moments to focus on the face looming before her, but once she did, recognition was immediate. "Alec," she said with a wan smile.

"I'm right here," he assured, giving her hand another squeeze. "How do you feel?"

Kathleen looked from him to Eric and Kirsten at the foot of the bed, noting that all three of them shared the same concerned expression. "What's wrong?" she asked, looking back to Alec. "Did something happen?"

"You fainted, Mama," Kirsten told her. "Right during the ceremony. Don't you remember?"

Kathleen sprang up to a sitting position. "I did what!"

"Easy, now." Alec coaxed her back down onto the bed. "You've got quite a knot on the back of your head. You hit the floor pretty hard when you fell."

Kathleen slowly began to piece together the moments that had led up to her alleged fainting spell. Her flip-flopping stomach, the spinning room.... *The baby!* "Is the ba—" She paused to fold her hands protectively over her belly. "I mean, am I all right?"

"I was kind of hoping you could tell me that. Kirsten says this happened once before today."

Kathleen thought back to the incident in question. "I just got a little dizzy, is all. But I did not faint," she insisted.

"You would have, Mama, if I hadn't been there to catch you," Kirsten reminded her.

"Well, I hardly think that's any reason to get so concerned. It's not like it happens everyday."

"How often does it happen?" Alec wanted to know.

"Today was the first time. Honest."

Alec studied her for a few moments, trying to decide whether he believed her or not. "Have you been feeling poorly, Kathleen?"

Kathleen stared down at her clasped hands, biting back a smile. She knew she should just come right out and tell him that she thought she was in the family way, but for some reason the timing didn't seem right. What if it turned out that she was only experiencing the change of life? She decided it would be best to know for sure before getting his hopes up. A few more days should be all that was necessary.

"Have you?" Alec asked her again.

Kathleen shrugged. "I guess my stomach has been a little upset lately," she admitted. "But it's probably just nerves."

"Nerves, huh?" Alec looked at her suspiciously. "Kathleen Ramsey, you didn't by any chance fake this little spell of yours just to get out of marrying me, did you?"

"Of course not!" she protested. "Why would I risk the—I mean, why would I do that?"

"Pa?" Colin stuck his head in the door. "Doctor Buchanan is downstairs."

"I'll be right down, Col. And as for you, young lady...." Alec turned back to face her as he rose from the bed. "We'll finish this discussion later."

Kathleen stared once again at her clasped hands, smiling contentedly. "Whatever you say, Alec."

"Kirsty?" Alec drew her along with him as he stepped to the door. "Be sure she gets some rest. And let me know immediately if she has another fainting spell."

"I will, Pa."

Alec took his time getting downstairs, not relishing the task of breaking the news to Carter Buchanan that he had never been hired. He seemed a decent enough young man, but Kirsten had presented a good point. He should wait to see who else responded to his ad before making such an important decision. After all, he would be trusting this individual to tend to patients and make critical medical decisions in his absence. That was not to say that Carter Buchanan wouldn't fit that bill, but it was going to take more than their brief encounter at the clinic this afternoon for Alec to confidently make that determination. If nothing else, he could at least pay the young man's train fare back to Boston.

"King me!"

Alec paused in the living room entryway, smiling at the scene before him. Carter was sitting Indian style on the floor, engaged in a game of checkers with Stephen. "Who's winning?"

"Papa!" Stephen jumped up and ran to him. "I'm beating Carter at checkers!"

Carter rose to his feet with a shrug. "I'm afraid I'm not a very good checker player."

"A man can't be an expert at everything." Alec tipped Stephen's head back, studying the row of stitches across his forehead. It was the first good look that he had gotten of Carter's handiwork. Impressive was hardly the word to describe it. "Those are fine sutures."

"Thank you, sir."

"It's Alec. We might as well be on a first name basis if we're going to be—" Alec frowned as he realized he was about to make a reference to their working together. But hadn't he decided to tell the young man just the opposite?

"I really appreciate your giving me this opportunity," Carter told him sincerely. "I was planning on joining my father's practice but he passed away two weeks before I graduated."

"I'm sorry."

Carter nodded his thanks. "I tried to keep things going after that but none of his former patients were willing to trust an inexperienced physician right out of medical school."

Alec felt a nagging pang of guilt. He had been about to terminate this young man from consideration as his assistant for the very same reason. He no longer had the heart to follow through. "It's you who'll be doing me the favor," Alec told him honestly. "My patient load has more than doubled recently. You'll be plenty busy."

"I can't tell you how glad I am to hear that. I've wanted to practice medicine for as long as I can remember."

Alec smiled. "You sound like my daughter, Kirsten. She's been talking about a medical career since before she could walk. She's hoping to get accepted into the Women's Medical College of Pennsylvania in a few years."

"Really." Carter found this bit of information fascinating. "I'd be interested in talking with her sometime."

"How about tonight?" Before Alec realized it he had invited the young man to join them for supper.

"I'd be honored. But first...." Carter smiled down at Stephen. "I believe I have a game of checkers to finish."

* * * * *

Jesse had never felt more out of place than he did as he sat listening to Carter and Kirsten's on going discussion about medicine. The threesome had retired to the living room after supper and for the past two hours Jesse had heard more about surgical procedures and incurable diseases than he'd ever wanted to. But that was the least of his concerns.

He peered down the sofa at Carter, fighting to keep the green-eyed monster of jealousy from rearing its ugly head. Why couldn't Alec's new assistant have been an unattractive older man? Carter was anything but. Young, tall, handsome.... And yes, wealthy.

"So you don't think it's strange for a woman to want to pursue a career in medicine?" Kirsten was asking him.

"On the contrary." Carter turned to face her more squarely before he continued. "I admire you for following your heart."

The glow that Carter's compliment elicited from Kirsten was the final twist of the knife in Jesse's heart. He realized he was losing her. But how could he ever hope to compete with Carter? He was perfect for her. Besides sharing her love of medicine, he could provide for her in the manner that she was so deserving of, something that Jesse could only dream of doing. He knew when he was beaten. The better man had won.

"What do you do for a living, Jesse?" Carter asked with genuine interest.

"I, uh—that is, my Pa and I—we own the blacksmith shop in town."

Carter slapped a hand down across his thigh. "That reminds me. I'm going to need to purchase myself a horse. I'd appreciate any assistance you could give me."

Jesse could think of a few things that he'd like to give the upstart doctor from Boston, but none of them were probably what he had in mind. "Sure," he agreed reluctantly.

"I'll come by tomorrow and take a look at what you have, if that's all right."

"Fine."

"I can show you the way, if you'd like," Kirsten offered, adding further injury to Jesse's already wounded heart.

"I don't want you to go to any trouble."

"It's no trouble at all," Kirsten assured him. "I'd be glad to."

Carter found his gaze lingering on her far longer than he knew was proper. He quickly looked away, deciding he should leave right then before his emotions betrayed him any further. He politely announced his intentions as he rose from the sofa.

Kirsten was immediately on her feet beside him. "But it's still early. And you haven't had dessert yet."

Carter patted his stomach. "I couldn't eat another bite, really. But give your mother my thanks all the same. " He started to move towards the door but quickly found his path blocked.

"Where will you be staying?" Kirsten asked him eagerly.

"Your father has been kind enough to let me use one of the recovery rooms at the clinic until I can find other accommodations."

"Then we'll probably be seeing each other. I'm going to be helping my Pa out a couple of days a week. Sterilizing instruments, washing linens…. That sort of thing."

"I'm sure he'll be grateful for your help." Carter made another attempt to step around her.

"I'll see you to the door," she offered.

"No need. I can see myself out." Carter hurried past her, assuring himself that he was making the right decision. She was Jesse's girl, after all. The sooner he put her out of his mind the better. But as he stepped out into the brisk night air, all he could think about was the beautiful brown-eyed woman with the smile of an angel.

* * * * *

Kathleen bolted upright in bed, dumping her Bible off her lap. "Amber Lloyd!" she exclaimed.

Alec looked up from his own reading. "What about her?"

"She would be perfect for Carter."

Alec laughed. "Typical woman. The poor man hasn't even been in town for twenty-four hours and you're already playing matchmaker."

"Well, can you think of anyone more perfect for him? They have so much in common."

"Like what?" Alec was curious to know.

"They're both from Boston."

Alec smacked himself on the forehead. "What was I thinking? Based on that alone the wedding invitations should already be in the mail."

Kathleen punched him in the arm. "Alec, I'm serious. Though I dare say he already seems to be quite smitten with Kirsten. That may prove a problem."

Alec laid his book aside, interested to hear more. "Do you think so?"

"Oh, Alec, it was as plain as the nose on your face. Poor Jesse was fit to be tied."

Alec grinned. "Really."

"Now don't go getting any foolish notions. You know that Kirsten is in love with Jesse."

"I know. But a father can hope, can't he?"

Alec received another well-placed punch in the arm. "Ow!"

Kathleen rolled over with an impish smile and turned down the lamp beside their bed. "Good night, dear."

* * * * *

Sean rolled over at the sound of someone approaching his cell. He found Neal smiling in at him. "I didn't wake you, did I?"

"No." Sean swung his legs over the edge of his cot, stretching his arms over his head as he sat up. "I can't seem to sleep. Too much on my mind."

"I know what you mean. It's been quite a day."

Sean paused in the act of standing up, looking curiously between his brother-in-law and the clock on the wall behind him. It was well past eleven o'clock. "What are you doing here so late?"

"I just got word from Pinkerton. He'll be here tomorrow afternoon."

Sean quickly covered the few feet between his cot and the front of the cell. "So are you finally going to tell me what this is all about?"

"I already told you everything I know."

Sean scowled back at him. "Neal."

"All right," he conceded. "Maybe I know a little more than I let on."

"Such as?"

"Pinkerton is prepared to offer you a job."

Sean reacted with more skepticism than surprise. "A job."

"In exchange for your testimony against Liam O'Brien," Neal explained.

Sean smirked. "I knew there had to be a catch somewhere."

"Does that mean your still dead set against it?"

Sean paced back to the cot, dropping onto the well-worn mattress with a sigh. "Well, I'm not going to let myself get sent to prison for thirty years, if that answers your question. I've robbed Rachel of far too much of my life already."

Neal smiled. "She'll be glad to hear that. And so, I might add, will a certain young lady from Philadelphia."

Sean laid back on the cot with a contented smile upon his lips. "Hannah," he whispered as his eyes drooped shut.

Neal turned with a grin and quietly made his way to the door. "Sweet dreams, Casanova."

CHAPTER EIGHTEEN

NO SMALL DECISION

Eric added another log to the dying fire and then settled back to resume his silent vigil. If the nearly empty wood box was any indication, he had been there for over half the night, but sleep continued to elude him.

With less six weeks until he was scheduled to report to Fort Moultrie, his upcoming trip south was weighing heavy on his mind. And so were his grandparents. He had been thinking about them more and more lately, ever since his mother had opened up about her past. Eric treasured everything she had already shared and wouldn't trade it for anything, but it wasn't enough. Nothing short of meeting them in person was going to quench the longing that now resided in his heart. Logistically there was nothing to prevent such a meeting from taking place. He had to pass right through Charleston on his way to Fort Moultrie, anyway. It was obtaining his mother's blessing that he foresaw to be his greatest obstacle.

"Mind if I join you?"

Eric turned at the sound of his father's voice. "Hi, Pa. I didn't wake you, did I?"

"My stomach did. Do you want some company?"

Eric sensed a golden opportunity to enlist his father's support. "There is something I'd like to talk with you about."

Alec took a seat beside him in front of the fireplace. "Wouldn't be a woman, would it?"

Eric grinned. "No, sir. Actually, it's about my trip south."

Alec nodded. "That was going to be my next guess."

Eric turned to look his father directly in the eye. "I bet you didn't guess that I was going to tell you I want to meet Ma's folks."

Alec was too stunned to say anything at first, giving Eric the opportunity to further plead his case. "I figure since I'll be passing through Charleston anyway, I could stop in and visit them for a few days before I have to report to Fort Moultrie."

Alec picked up the poker and shifted one of the logs in the fireplace, sending up an array of sparks. "Meeting your grandparents, son...that's no small decision."

"I realize that, sir. But if there's a war I may never get that chance." Eric waited until his father turned back to face him before he continued. "What do you think Ma will say?"

"It won't be high on her priority list, I can guarantee you that."

Eric would settle for it being on the list at all. "Would you talk to her for me?"

Alec laid the poker aside. "Your mind's made up, then?"

"Yes, sir."

Alec smiled. "All right. No promises, but I'll do what I can."

* * * * *

Alec returned upstairs to find Kathleen curled up on his side of the bed. She looked so at peace in the realm of sleep, oblivious to all else going on around her. But how long would that peace last once she learned of Eric's desire to meet her folks? Alec dreaded the thought of telling her, dredging up painful memories from her past once again. But she had to be told. It was no longer just a matter of keeping his word to Eric. Alec sensed a divine plan at work far greater than anything the finite limitations of his human mind could ever hope to understand.

Alec slipped off his robe and climbed in beside her, drawing the quilt up around his waist. Kathleen immediately sensed his presence and wriggled her way into the crook of his arm. "I was just about to come looking for you," she said with a drowsy smile. "Where were you?"

"I was talking to Eric."

"At this hour? Couldn't it have waited until morning?" She stretched her arm out across his waist, snuggling closer against the side of his chest. "I missed you."

"It was important, Kathleen." Alec stared down at the top of her head. "Eric told me that he wants to meet your folks."

Kathleen sat up, scrambling around on her knees to face him. "Alec, you can't be serious."

Alec pushed himself back to sit against the headboard, meeting her skeptical gaze head on. "He wants to stop in and see them when he gets to Charleston."

Kathleen folded her arms across her chest, protesting like a strong-willed child. "Absolutely not. I won't allow it."

Alec leaned forward and took hold of her hands, imploring her to reconsider. "He has the right, Kathleen."

"But, Alec—"

"He has the right."

Kathleen pulled her hands free and began wringing them together in her lap. "But why now?" she wanted to know.

"He's worried about not getting the chance to know them if there's a war. Certainly you can understand that."

Kathleen stopped her nervous fidgeting. "Yes, I suppose so. But still…."

Alec reclaimed one of her hands before she could object further. "Why don't you write a letter and let them know that

Eric will be paying them a visit soon. We might even have time to get a daguerreotype taken of the children to send along with him."

Kathleen's eyes came alive. "Oh, Alec, could we?" she pleaded. "They haven't seen any of the children except for Eric, and he was only a few months old at the time."

Alec smiled at her sudden burst of enthusiasm. "Consider it done."

"Oh, Alec, thank you." Kathleen gave him a peck him on the cheek. "I'll write Mama first thing in the morning and let her know that Eric will be coming. I'm sure she'll be excited to hear that she has another grandchild on the way."

Alec stared at her bug-eyed as he realized that she wasn't talking about Eric. "You said another grandchild."

Kathleen smiled innocently. "Did I?"

Alec swallowed back his surprise. "Are you sure?"

"I will be as soon as I pay a visit to the good Doctor Ramsey in the morning. That is if he can fit me into his busy schedule."

Alec leaned back against the headboard, scratching the side of his head. "A baby. I don't know why I didn't see it before. The dizziness, the upset stomach...."

Kathleen crawled up to sit beside him, laying her head against his shoulder. "Well, it has been three-and-a-half years since we had Stephen," she reminded him. "One tends to forget little things like that. Besides, we've never talked about having another child."

"And you've been so irritable lately."

"Irritable!" she howled back. "Why, you—" Kathleen halted her burst of anger with a giggle. "I guess I have been, at that."

"A baby," Alec said again, gazing blindly across the room.

Kathleen studied his expression, trying to gauge what he was thinking. "Are you happy?" she finally asked. "About the baby, I mean."

Alec grinned as he pulled her down beside him. "I'll show you happy."

* * * * *

Eric went in search of his mother as soon as he woke the following morning. He had slept very little the remainder of the night, wondering how she was going to react to the news that he wanted to meet her folks. And he was still wondering. Had his request been granted, or would his desire to meet his grandparents remain an unfulfilled dream?

After checking for her in all the usual places, Eric stepped out onto the back porch to regroup his thoughts. He finally decided that she had probably gone into town for something and started to go back inside.

"Hey, sleepyhead!"

Eric turned to find Colin coming around the side of the house. He was carrying his fishing pole in one hand and a string of freshly caught fish in the other.

"You missed out on some great fishing," the younger man bragged. He raised the string over his head so Eric could see. "They were really biting this morning."

Eric had more important things on his mind than fishing. "Col, have you seen Ma anywhere?"

"She's out on the front porch with Aunt Rachel."

"Thanks." Eric reached to open the screen door.

"She was acting kind of strange this morning."

Eric paused with the door halfway open, looking back over his shoulder. "Aunt Rachel?"

Colin stepped up onto the porch. "I'm talking about Ma."

Eric dropped the screen shut with a bang, turning to face his brother. "Strange in what way?"

Colin shrugged. "I don't know. Just strange."

Eric tried not to read too much into Colin's assessment of their mother's behavior but couldn't help wondering if it had something to do with his request to meet her folks. "Thanks again, Col."

Eric made his way back through the house and out onto the front porch. He found his mother sitting on the swing with Rachel discussing one of her latest needlework projects. She looked up with a smile as he approached. "Good morning, dear."

"Morning, Ma. Aunt Rachel."

Rachel rose from the swing, suppressing what appeared to Eric like a chuckle. "If you two will excuse me, I promised Sean that I would come by and see him this morning." She quickly disappeared into the house with a hand clamped over her mouth. Eric found his mother employing a similar gesture when he turned back to face her. Colin's assessment of her behavior was gaining credibility by leaps and bounds.

Kathleen patted the vacated space beside her on the swing. "Join me?"

Eric studied her closely as he took the offered seat, trying to gauge her mental stability. She certainly seemed to be in good spirits, which he decided could mean only one of two things. Either she was fine with the idea of him visiting her folks...or his father hadn't gotten the chance to talk with her yet. Eric suspected the latter, realizing too late that he should have checked with his pa first.

"Did you have a good sleep?" Kathleen asked as she resumed her needlework.

"Not really," Eric admitted. "Pa wouldn't still be here by any chance, would he?"

"I'm sorry, sweetheart. He left on his rounds about twenty minutes ago. Is there something I can help you with?"

Eric wavered for a only moment before deciding to plunge right in and ask her for himself. "Actually, there is...." He paused to take a few steadying breaths before continuing. "Did Pa happen talk to you last night about—"

Kathleen shoved her needlework in front of him. "What do you think?"

Eric recognized what she was working on as a smaller version of the sampler hanging above their fireplace. A large tree graced the center, each of its branches representing a member of the Ramsey family, from his father's grandfather at the top, to Stephen at the bottom. In his fleeting appraisal Eric failed to notice that his mother was adding on another small branch just below Stephen's. "It's beautiful, Ma," he assured her. "But did Pa say anything about—"

"I'm hoping to have it finished by the time you leave so you can take it to your grandmother."

"Ma, please, I—" Eric stared back at her. "What did you say?"

"I said that I want you to take this to your grandmother when you visit. I thought it might be a fun way to let her know about the baby."

Eric's head began to swim. "Do you mean it?"

Kathleen smiled joyfully as she reached over to take his hand, "Yes, sweetheart. You're going to be a big brother again."

Eric's response was a blank stare. "What?"

Kathleen chuckled, deciding he had suffered long enough. "Yes, I meant it. You can visit your grandparents. Your father mailed off a letter just this morning to let them know that you'd be coming. *And,*" she added emphatically, "your father and I are going to have another baby."

Eric heard only the first half of what she said. His head was still swimming. "It's okay with you?"

Kathleen patted her belly. "Apparently so."

Eric smiled. "I mean about my visiting your folks. I don't want to hurt you."

"It's okay. I'm just sorry it took me so long."

Eric squeezed her hand. "Thanks, Ma."

"It's your father you need to be thanking. He's a very persuasive man."

"I will."

Eric immediately began a mental list of all the things that he wanted to ask his grandparents when he saw them, but his enthusiasm was quickly snuffed out by an unsettling thought. What if they didn't want to see him? He had failed to consider this possibility in his quest to receive his mother's blessing but it was a very real possibility, nonetheless. The son of their estranged daughter showing up out of the blue? How were they going to feel about that, and him? Would he be accepted, or shunned just as she had been some twenty years before? Eric posed that very question to his mother and received the only answer he would have expected her to give.

"You're their grandson. How could they be anything but pleased to see you."

Eric detected a degree of uncertainty in her voice but let it pass. Time alone would prove or disprove her claims.

Kathleen folded her hands together in her lap, looking at him expectantly. "So, tell me. Are you excited about the baby?"

Eric pretended to be surprised. "You're having a baby?"

Kathleen slapped his arm. "Oh, you."

Eric chuckled, leaning over to plant a kiss on her cheek. "Congratulations, Ma. Does Pa know?"

"Who do you think was his first patient this morning?"

* * * * *

"A social?"

"At the church tomorrow night." Kirsten climbed up on the side of the stall where Carter stood looking over the horse that she had picked out for him. "There'll be dancing and lots of food, including my Ma's apple pie. You haven't lived until you've tasted my Ma's apple pie."

Carter fished around for a legitimate reason not to go. "To be honest with you, Kirsten, I'm not much of a dancer." It was the only excuse he could think of that sounded even halfway believable.

Kirsten was quick to counter his objection. "Who says you have to dance? If nothing else it will give you a chance to get to know some of the folks in town. People who will be your patients."

Carter had to admit the idea appealed to him. The more he mingled with the townsfolk, the sooner he would earn their trust. But on the other hand, the less time he spent with Kirsten the better. Last night had made that uncomfortably clear.

"Oh, come on, Carter," Kirsten urged him. "It'll be fun."

Carter glanced into the next stall over where Jesse was busy pitching out the hay. "Will you be there, Jesse?"

Jesse stopped for a moment, leaning on the handle of the pitchfork. "My Pa and I have to make a trip over to Summerdale." His reply was devoid of any emotion. "Won't be back until late tomorrow night."

That was all Carter needed to hear. There was no way that he was going to spend an evening in Kirsten's company without Jesse present.

Kirsten stepped down from her perch and walked around to the opening of the stall. "Say you'll come?" she pleaded.

Carter heard himself tell her that he'd "think about it", but all the while on the inside he was screaming "no". What was the matter with him? Why couldn't he just come right out and tell her the truth?

Kirsten seemed satisfied with his reply and turned her attention to the horse. "He's a beauty, isn't he?"

"He sure is." Carter patted the geldings' sleek, muscular flank. "I think I'll take him."

Jesse said nothing as he set the pitchfork aside and went to ready a saddle.

"Where are you going to keep him?" Kirsten asked.

"Oh." Carter frowned at his poor planning. "I hadn't thought about that."

Kirsten made a grab for his arm as a thought came to her. "Why don't you keep him at our place?" she suggested. "I'm sure my Pa wouldn't mind."

Carter's inner struggle continued. He was trying to do everything he could to put as much distance between them as possible but Kirsten wasn't making it easy for him. "I don't think that would be such good idea," he told her honestly, pulling his arm free from her grasp. "I'd have to walk all the way to your place from the clinic every time I wanted to ride somewhere."

"Oh, yeah." Kirsten bit her lip. "Well, I'm sure we'll think of something."

Jesse led the gelding out of the stall and proceeded to put a bridle and saddle on him. When he was finished, Carter handed him the amount they had agreed upon. "Thanks again for your help."

Jesse bobbed his head and went back to cleaning out the stalls.

Carter was left standing alone beside Kirsten with only a hand's-breadth between them. The lilac scent of her hair launched his heart into palpitations. "I should be getting back to the clinic," he said hurriedly. "Your father and I still have a lot of work to do to get it ready for the grand opening next week."

Kirsten watched as he awkwardly gathered up the reins in preparation to mount. "Carter, have you ever ridden a horse before?" she thought to ask him.

"Actually, no," he admitted with a carefree grin as he slipped his foot into the stirrup. "But how hard could it be?"

"Carter, no! Not from that side!"

Kirsten's warning came a few seconds too late. The gelding bucked, sending Carter sprawling onto his backside with a groan. "Sorry I asked."

* * * * *

"I want you to stay off that ankle for at least a week. It's a pretty bad sprain."

Carter grimaced as he stared down the bed at his severely swollen foot, not because it was causing him discomfort, but because of the foolishness of his actions. What had caused him to think that he could ride a horse having had no previous experience? Ego, that's what. And the fact that a certain young woman had been watching. "I'm sorry, Alec," he apologized. "I don't know what I was thinking."

"Don't beat yourself up too much." Alec stuffed another pillow behind his head. "I did that same thing the first time I tried to get on a horse."

Carter followed Alec with his gaze as he stepped back to the end of the bed. "Honest?"

"Kathleen was practically raised on horseback," Alec explained as he began gathering up the unused bandages, "and I was determined to impress her with my equestrian skills. Only I ended up with a broken arm for my trouble instead of a sprained ankle." Alec paused to smile at Carter. "Downright shameless what a young man will do to puff up his ego when a young woman is present, isn't it?"

Carter swallowed nervously. Did Alec suspect that he had feelings for Kirsten?

"I'll be downstairs if you need anything. Just give a holler." Alec opened the door to find a very anxious Kirsten waiting on the other side. "Pa, how is he?"

Alec stepped aside, making a sweeping motion with his arm into the room. "See for yourself."

Kirsten hurried inside, dragging Jesse along behind her. Her gaze went immediately to Carter's bandaged ankle. "Does it hurt much?"

Carter was about to deny that he felt any pain at all but it was such prideful boasts that had gotten him in this mess in the first place. "Just a little bit."

Kirsten bit her lip, appearing on the verge of tears. "This is all my fault. If only I had—"

"No, Kirsten." Carter wasn't about to let her take the blame for his stupidity. "I had no business trying to get on that horse."

Kirsten took a seat beside him on the edge of the bed, glancing once again at his ankle. "I'm just glad that it wasn't worse."

"Bad enough. I'm afraid I won't be able to attend the social tomorrow night." Carter tried not to sound too overjoyed by this fact.

"Oh, who cares about that. There'll be other socials. All that matters is that you're all right."

Jesse smiled to himself as he looked on from the end of the bed. Though he wasn't one to wish pain and suffering on anyone, he was more than a little pleased by the sudden turn of events in his favor. Carter would be laid up for at least a week and he intended to take full advantage of that time to woo Kirsten back. If the young physician had plans to the contrary, he was in for the fight of his life.

* * * * *

Alec and Kathleen gathered the children together after supper that evening to share with them Eric's plans to visit their grandparents. "It might be nice if each of you wrote a short letter about yourself to send along," Kathleen suggested.

Kaitlin had an alternative suggestion. "Why don't we just go, too?" She was already on her feet, ready to begin packing at her mother's say so.

Stephen hopped up beside her. "I wanna go, too!"

"Not this time," Kathleen told them. "But Eric will take along a picture of all of you so they can see what you look like."

"Do you think they'll like us?" Nathan wondered.

Alec leaned forward and tousled his hair. "What's not to like?"

Kathleen's gaze traveled around the circle of faces, stopping at the two they had yet to hear from. "Colin, Kirsten? Do either of you have any questions?"

"Just one...." Kirsten pulled out what appeared to be a half knitted pair of baby booties from beneath the sofa. "About these."

Colin studied the dangling blob of knitting. "The last time I saw anything like that around here, Ma was—" His gaze swung back and forth between his mother and the booties like a pendulum. "A baby?"

Kirsten smiled, looking to her mother for confirmation. "Really, Ma? You're pregnant?"

Kathleen returned her smile with an enthusiastic nod. "Your father and I are going to have another baby."

"Oh, Ma!" Kirsten squealed and made a dash for her mother's side.

"A baby!" Kaitlin exclaimed, clapping her hands in delight. "I hope it's a girl!"

"Why not a boy?" Nathan asked.

Kaitlin planted her hands on her undeveloped hips, cocking her head to the side. "If you haven't already noticed, we have enough boys around here."

"What's wrong with boys?" Nathan snapped back.

"When's the baby due?" Kirsten was eager to know.

"The middle of April, near as I can figure," Alec was proud to tell her.

"We'll have to pick a name. Let's see…." Kirsten tapped a finger against her lips, considering the many possibilities. "How about Loren if it's a boy?"

"Lauren!" Colin made a sour face. "What kind of name is that for a boy? How about Alicia if it's a girl?" Eric tossed him a scathing look that almost knocked Colin off his chair. "Sorry, Eric."

"Well, I still like Loren for a boy," Kirsten insisted. "And Carrie if it's a girl."

"Aaron if it's a boy and Sarah if it's a girl," Colin suggested.

"Erin!" Kirsten scoffed. "What kind of name is that for a boy?"

"Well it's better than Lauren."

Alec and Kathleen slipped unnoticed out the front door to get away from the ensuing debate. Alec chuckled as they stood at the porch railing, his arms wrapped protectively around Kathleen's middle. "Can you believe those two? They're already picking out names. Do you suppose they'll raise her for us, too?"

Kathleen revolved within the circle of his embrace until they were facing one another. "You said her."

"What?"

"You called the baby a her."

"Did I?" Alec shrugged. "I didn't mean to."

Kathleen saw right through his attempt to mislead her. "Yes, you did." She grinned as she searched his eyes for further evidence to support her claim. "You want another daughter, don't you?"

Alec realized that his secret longing was no longer a secret. "I have to admit that I have been thinking about it. Kirsten will be married and gone soon. I can't deny that forever. And Kaitlin will be next."

"Alec, please don't rush her," Kathleen implored him. "She's only seven."

"You obviously haven't seen the way that little scamp, Tommy Webber, has been looking at her in Sunday school."

"Oh, Alec." Kathleen chuckled, snuggling close against his chest. "I'm just glad that the children are excited about the baby." Her head snapped back up. "A baby," she gasped, as if learning of this fact for the very first time. "Oh, Alec, are we ready for this again? And at our age?"

"Speak for yourself, old woman."

Kathleen stared up at him with a wounded look in her eyes.

"I'm sorry, sweetheart. I was only kidding."

"It's not that. I was just thinking about what's going to be facing this child when it's born. All this talk of war. What kind of world are we bringing it into?" She paused to release a worrisome sigh. "Maybe we should have been more careful."

Alec grasped her firmly by the shoulders, commanding her attention. "Now you listen here, Kathleen Ramsey. I don't think the Good Lord would have blessed us with this child if it wasn't His will. This baby is on the way and that's all there is to it. And no matter what she—"

"Or he."

Alec grinned. "Or he, may be facing in this world, they're not going to have to face it alone."

Kathleen reached up and drew the backs of her fingers down the side of his face. "You're right," she whispered. "And I love you."

"Then you won't make me go back in there." Alec bobbed his head towards the house where the heated debate was still in progress. "What would that baby say to an evening stroll through town?"

"She would be delighted." Kathleen latched onto his arm. "And so would her mother."

"You said her."

Kathleen smiled, clapping a hand to her cheek. "Did I?"

CHAPTER NINETEEN

PINKERTON'S NEW MAN

"**I** think I see him!" Nathan's alarm brought Colin and Stephen scrambling up beside him at the front door.

"Where?" Colin asked anxiously. "I don't see—"

"Right there," Nathan pointed. "Down by—ouch, Colin! You're stepping on my foot!"

"Well, move over, then!" Colin gave him a soundly placed bump with his hip.

"Hey, let me see, too!" Stephen plowed his way in between his brothers.

"There's nothing to see," Colin said dejectedly he studied the individual that had been the subject of Nathan's alarm. "That's not him, Nathan."

"Are you sure?" he asked, squinting up the road.

"I don't think Mr. Pinkerton would be wearing a dress."

"Oh." Nathan hung his head. "Sorry, Colin."

"Just keep looking. They should be here anytime."

The three boys continued to jockey for position at the door, each one eager to be the first to catch a glimpse of the famous detective, Allan Pinkerton. He had quickly become a household name since starting his own agency ten years ago, and much to the delight of the Ramsey brothers, he had chosen their household to put in an appearance.

"What if they're not coming?" Nathan asked, stating a possibility that none of them wanted to consider.

"Of course they are," Colin assured him. "Uncle Neal said they would be back here in time for breakfast."

"What are you three up to?" Kirsten asked, coming up behind them at the door.

"Waiting for Mr. Pinkerton," Nathan told her.

"He's already here."

All three boys turned to face their sister, mouths gaping. "What do you mean he's already here?" Colin asked, electing himself as spokesmen.

"He walked in the back door along with Uncle Neal and Sean about ten minutes ago."

Colin eyed her suspiciously, suspecting a prank in the works. "And I suppose right about now he's eating breakfast in our kitchen?"

"As a matter of fact, he is."

Colin still wasn't convinced. "You wouldn't be making all this up, would you?"

"Of course not. He's probably halfway through his second stack of Ma's flapjacks by now." Kirsten turned and started upstairs. "And by the way...." She looked back over her shoulder, smiling sweetly. "Fascinating man to talk to."

Nathan's eyes bugged out. "You talked to him, and everything?"

"Sure did." Kirsten bit back a chuckle, enjoying the "green with envy" expressions on their faces. "See ya, fellas."

Colin planted his hands on his hips, scowling at her back of her head as she made her way upstairs. "Well, how do you like that? Some people have all the luck."

"Colin!" Stephen whacked him repeatedly on the backside.

Colin brushed his hand away. "Not now, Stephen."

"But look!"

Colin followed Stephen's pointing finger, struck speechless at the sight of Pinkerton coming down the hallway, his father, uncle and Sean trailing along behind.

Stephen ran to greet him, not the least bit shy about making his presence known. "Hi, Mr. Pinkton!"

"Hello there, lad." Pinkerton stopped beside him, giving his dark head of hair a tousle. "And who might you be?"

"Stephen Michael Ramsey!" he belted out.

A deep chuckle rumbled through Pinkerton's chest. "One of yours, Alec?" he presumed, noting the striking resemblance between father and son.

"Yes," Alec said with pride. His gaze rose to Colin and Nathan with equal pride. "And these are two of my other sons, Colin and Nathan."

Both boys were as still as statues as their father introduced them, their eyes fixed in a perpetual look of awe upon Pinkerton.

"Two of, you say?" Pinkerton looked curiously at Alec. "Just how many arrows in your quiver are there?"

Alec smiled. "Six, all together. And one more on the way."

Pinkerton scratched the side of his head. "Seven children. "I must say you've taken the command to be fruitful and multiply quite to heart, haven't you?"

Neal grinned as he watched his brother's face turn bright red.

"Mr. Pinkton, I want to be you when I get big!" Stephen declared proudly.

"You do?"

"He means *like* you," Nathan explained, discovering at last that he had a voice. "A detective. So do I."

"Is that so?" Pinkerton pretended to be surprised, though he had heard similar declarations numerous times from young and old alike. "Well, if I'm ever in need of a few good men I'll know right where to come, won't I?"

Nathan beamed him a big smile. "Yes, sir!"

At Neal's urging the introductions were brought to a close. Colin frowned as he watched Pinkerton disappear into their father's study with Sean and their uncle for a "private discussion". It wasn't fair. They should have at least gotten the same amount of time with him as Kirsten had.

Colin moved closer to the study door, Nathan and Stephen following his lead.

"Oh, boys?" Alec called from behind them.

One by one they turned around, biggest to the smallest. Colin spoke up on behalf of the younger two. "Yes, Pa?"

"You weren't thinking about listening in on your Uncle Neal's discussion with Mr. Pinkerton, were you?"

"Who, us?"

"You are to stay away from that door until they're finished. Is that understood?"

"Ah, Pa," Nathan whined. "That could take hours."

"Then you might as well scoot upstairs and get yourself ready for school. You don't want to be late on your first day."

Nathan's eyes lit up at his father's mention of school, leaving Alec with the impression that the young man might be ill. But before he could make any official diagnosis, Nathan went careening up the stairs, spouting his plans all the way. "Wait until I tell the guys that Allan Pinkerton ate breakfast in our kitchen!"

"So much for being ill." Alec turned to Colin, noting that he had a similar gleam in his eyes. "And I suppose that you have someone to tell, as well?"

Colin couldn't get out the front door fast enough.

Alec's gaze then fell to Stephen, the only one left. "And who are you going to tell?"

Stephen held his hands up in front of him. "I don't got anyone to tell,"

"Good." Alec grinned as he scooped Stephen up and slung him over his shoulder. "Then you get to help with the breakfast dishes."

"Ah, Pa."

* * * * *

Pinkerton didn't waste anytime getting to the reason for his visit once they were all comfortably seated in Alec's study. "Over the past few months there has been a string of robberies in and around the Baltimore area, very similar to the two in Philadelphia last week."

Sean leaned forward in his chair, hanging Pinkerton's every word.

"A different group of individuals was involved every time, but we believe they're all tied to the same man."

Sean assumed that he was talking about Liam O'Brien. "Then I don't understand what you need me for. You've already got O'Brien. If you want me to testify—"

"We don't want your testimony. Not yet, anyway."

Sean exchanged a dumbfounded look with Neal before directing his confusion back to Pinkerton. "I thought that my testifying was the whole point of this meeting."

"Liam O'Brien is just a small fish in a much larger pond," Pinkerton explained. "We'd like to cast the net a little wider and see if we can catch an even bigger fish. But to do that we need someone positioned in the city. Someone who can circulate among the local establishments without raising suspicion, gathering names, information…. And then once the key players are identified, we'll move our operatives into place."

Sean began warming to the idea almost immediately. "If I agree?"

"If you agree, then all charges against you will be dropped."

"And if he doesn't?" Neal asked on Sean's behalf.

"Then he'll have to stand trial." Pinkerton's gaze fell away from Neal, settling once again on Sean. "But with your testimony against O'Brien, you should only get a few years."

A few years, Sean thought. *Long enough for Hannah to fall in love with someone else.*

"How soon do you need his decision?" Neal asked.

"I'd like to know before I leave this afternoon."

Neal frowned. "You're sure not giving him much time, Allan."

"It's enough," Sean said, looking back and forth between the two men. "I'll do it."

Neal was slow to embrace his decision. "There's no need to rush into anything, Sean. Why don't you think about it for awhile?"

"My mind's made up, Neal. I'm not going to prison."

Pinkerton sat forward on the edge of his chair, facing the young man before him. "There's one more thing I think you should know. If you accept my offer, you'll have to stay in Baltimore for as long as necessary. Could be months, could be years."

Sean took this additional information into consideration but it did nothing to alter his previous decision. All that remained was his satisfaction on the answering of one question. "Is there anything in the job description that says I can't take a wife with me?"

* * * * *

Rachel listened without interrupting as Sean told her of his plans to accept Pinkerton's offer, but all the while she was carrying on a conversation with him in her head that was full of objections. She was determined, however, that none of them would be given a voice. Sean wasn't asking for her permission, only her support. He was a grown man now and had to be free to make his own decisions, no matter how difficult it might be for her to let him go...again.

Rachel realized that he had finished and mustered the bravest smile she could. "When will you leave?" She nearly choked on the word "leave".

"I think we should leave as soon as possible."

Rachel heard only one word of what he said. "We?"

"I plan on going back to Chicago with you and Neal for a few weeks," he explained. "Spend some time with Ned, meet my new niece and nephews...." Sean clamped his lips together, trying to prevent his smile from being released prematurely. "And then ask a certain Irish baker if I can marry his daughter."

"Oh, Sean!" Rachel threw her arms around him, giddy with joy. "I've always thought of old Charlie as part of our family and now he will be."

Sean set her away from him. "It's not old Charlie that I want to marry."

Rachel laughed. "You know what I mean."

A disturbing thought snuffed out the happy glow from Sean's eyes. "What if he says no?"

"Sean, don't even think like that. You know how Charlie has always felt about you. Like you were his own son."

"That was thirteen years ago." There was no need to say more.

Rachel smiled, reaching up to cup his cheek. "Don't fret. It will work out."

Sean's worries quickly melted away beneath her touch. "What did I ever do without you for thirteen years?"

"You were never without me," Rachel assured him, making reference to the daily prayers that she had sent heavenward on his behalf. "And you never will be."

Sean pulled her back into his arms. "That goes for me, too, Rach."

* * * * *

Kathleen was sweeping the front entryway when Kaitlin arrived home from school. "How was your first day?" she asked, setting aside the broom in favor of listening to her daughters' report.

"Oh, fine," Kaitlin replied, handing over her empty lunch pail. "I stayed to help Miss Amber clean the blackboards after class. That's why I'm late."

"Not too late to help me bake cookies for the social tonight."

"Oh, boy!" Kaitlin exclaimed. "Cookies!"

"Why don't you go get changed and—" Kathleen lost her train of thought, listening instead to the commotion going on outside. "What on earth...?"

"That's probably Nathan," Kaitlin told her before turning to run upstairs.

Kathleen looked after her in hopes of more information but there was none to be forthcoming. She finally went to open the front door to investigate for herself, instantly mesmerized by the scene unfolding before her. Nathan was marching up the walkway to the house with a dozen boys in tow. The clamor they were making was loud enough to wake the dead.

"You guys wait here," he instructed, motioning for the mob to stop at the foot of the steps. "I'll be right back." Nathan turned and bounded up onto the porch, rubbing his hands together with a miserly gleam in his eyes. He stopped at the sight of his mother watching him from the doorway. "Oh, hi, Ma," he said with a nervous smile.

Kathleen stepped out onto the porch, looking over the crowd of boys. She saw not one familiar face in the bunch. "Nathan, who are all these boys?"

"Just some fellas from school," he explained. "They came to see Mr. Pinkerton."

Kathleen's gaze once again swept the crowd of faces, afraid that they were in for quite a disappointment. "Well, I'm afraid he's not here."

"What!" Nathan threw a cautionary glance over his shoulder and then crept closer to where she was standing. His voice dipped so low that she could barely hear him. "But he has to be."

"He left early this afternoon to go back to Chicago along with your aunt and uncle."

A pained expression swept across the young man's face, accompanied by a groan. "Oh, no."

"Hey, Ramsey, what's the hold up?" The comment came from a husky, blond-haired boy at the back of the group. He appeared several years older than the other boys, who were all about Nathan's age. "Is he coming out or not?"

The boys' gruff sounding voice struck a chord of fear in Nathan. "Ma, what do I do?" he whispered frantically. "I already told them that he was here."

"Then just tell them that he's not."

Nathan anxiously drummed his fingers against the bulge in his pocket. "It's not that simple."

"Nathan, you have to tell them. That's all there is to it."

"Yes, Ma." Nathan turned and painfully made his way back to the edge of the porch. He stalled for as long as could and then blurted out the bad news with one quick intake of breath. "He's not here."

"What did I tell you guys," griped the hulking blond figure in the back row. "He was probably never here at all."

"He was so," Nathan said defensively. "He just had to leave, is all."

Kathleen's heart went out to her son. It wasn't his fault that Pinkerton had left early and he shouldn't be made to suffer for it. There had to be something that she could say to help mend his reputation with his friends while at the same time keeping his fragile male ego intact. After all, no eleven-year-old boy wanted his mother to fight his battles for him.

Kathleen was mulling over what she might say when five uttered words altered her whole perspective on Nathan's plight. "I want my money back!" The demand came from a sandy-haired youth in the front row.

"Yeah, me, too!" chimed in another, sporting a mass of reddish-brown curls.

"Nathan Thomas Ramsey!" Kathleen planted her hands astride her hips, all sympathy for her son fleeing her instantly. "Am I to understand that you charged these boys to see Mr. Pinkerton?"

"He sure did, Mrs. Ramsey." It was the blond-haired boy again. He had apparently elected himself spokesman on behalf of the group. "A nickel apiece."

Nathan bit his lip, cringing as his mother stepped up behind him. She dropped a hand onto his shoulder. "I want you to apologize to these boys and then give them their money back." Her voice was stern, while still maintaining a degree of calm. "Am I understood?"

"Yes, Ma."

"Yes, Ma," snickered several of the boys. Nathan felt every ounce of blood in his body rushing its' way to his cheeks. He would never be able to hold his head up in school again.

"When you are finished," Kathleen continued, "your father will be waiting for you in his study."

Nathan scowled as he watched her turn and head back into the house. "There goes my new baseball glove."

* * * * *

"Kirsty?"

"In the kitchen, Mama!"

Kathleen greeted her eldest daughter with a smile as she entered the room. "We're about ready to leave for the social. Are you sure you won't change your mind and come with us?"

"Thanks anyway, but I'm going over to see Carter. He's been cooped up in that room all day. I'm sure he'll appreciate some company."

Kathleen's gaze dropped to the tray of food that Kirsten was preparing to take along. If it was true what was said about the way to a man's heart being through his stomach, Carter was sure to lose his tonight, if he hadn't already. Kathleen realized that it was time she had a heart-to-heart talk with her daughter about Carter Buchanan.

"Kirsten...?" Kathleen stepped up beside her at the table. "Don't you think maybe you've been spending a little too much time with Carter?"

Kirsten looked up from the slice of bread that she was slathering with apple butter. Her expression clearly advertised her confusion. "What do you mean?"

"Just that...." Kathleen fingered the tassels on her shawl. "How do I put this?" Her gaze rose to the ceiling as if the answer might be found there. "I think Carter may have feelings for you other than that of a friend."

The look of surprise on Kirsten's face told Kathleen that her daughter hadn't been aware of the affections Carter held for her. But there was still one additional matter that needed to be settled before her mother's heart would be completely at rest. "Carter is certainly a very charming young man, not to mention handsome. You don't by any chance...."

Kirsten's surprise turned to shock. "Of course not! I mean, I enjoy talking with him, about medicine and all, but it's nothing more than that." Kirsten's tone softened to match the look of love welling up in her eyes. "I love Jesse."

Kathleen couldn't put into words how good it did her heart to hear that. But there still remained the matter of

Carter's heart. Just because Kirsten didn't reciprocate his feelings for her didn't in any way nullify their existence. For Carter they were still very real.

"Just be careful that you're not giving him the wrong impression," Kathleen cautioned her.

Kirsten stared guiltily at the feast that she had prepared for him. What kind of impression was that going to give?

Kathleen read her thoughts. "I'm not saying that you shouldn't take him dinner, or even keep him company out of the goodness of your heart. Just be sure that he knows your heart belongs to Jesse."

Jesse. Kirsten hadn't even considered how he might be feeling about all of the extra attention she had been paying to Carter lately. If it bothered him, she knew he was too much of a gentleman to say so.

Kirsten turned to her mother with a smile that said "thank you" more adequately than words ever could.

Kathleen smiled in return. "You're welcome, sweetheart."

* * * * *

Kirsten pushed open the door to Carter's room with one hip while carefully balancing the tray of food on the other. "Room service!" she called out.

Carter's mouth dropped open at the sight of her.

"I brought you some of my ma's chicken soup. It's good for whatever ails you, even sprained ankles." Kirsten set the tray on the stand beneath the window and then traced her steps back to the end of the bed. "How's your ankle?" Carter blushed as she lifted the blanket that was covering him to have a look for herself. "The swelling seems to have gone down some," she noted. "That's good. Any pain?"

"Some." Carter tugged the blanket back into place, feeling suddenly naked beneath her gaze. "What are you doing here? I mean, I thought you would be at the social."

"That's where she should be."

Kirsten turned towards the voice behind her to find Jesse was standing in the doorway holding a bouquet of her favorite wildflowers. "Jesse.... What are you doing here?"

"Your Ma told me you were here." Jesse stepped further into the room. "I've come to take you to the social."

Kirsten suffered the same affliction of jawing dropping as Carter had earlier. "But I thought that you and your Pa...."

"I talked him into making the trip next week," he explained. "Being here for you is more important." Jesse handed her the flowers. "I brought you these. I know they're your favorite."

Kirsten buried her nose in the bouquet, drinking in its' sweet fragrance. "They're beautiful."

"Not half as beautiful as you." Jesse enjoyed the reaction that his compliment induced. *Even Carter can't make her glow like that,* he thought with pride. "Shall we go?"

"The social!" Kirsten gasped, suddenly remembering why he was there. "But I'm not ready. My dress, my hair—"

Jesse caught one of her flailing hands and pressed the back of it to his lips. "Please don't change a thing. I love you just the way you are."

Kirsten realized that his declaration applied to more than just her appearance. "And I love you."

Carter felt his heart shrinking as he watched Kirsten and Jesse walk out of the room. *She didn't even say good-bye,* he thought dejectedly, and then realized how foolish he was being. He should be glad that Kirsten's attentions were now focused back on Jesse where they belonged. Isn't that what he wanted?

"No," Carter confessed to himself. He knew it was wrong to pay court to his emotions but he couldn't fight the way he felt any longer. "I love you, Kirsten Ramsey."

CHAPTER TWENTY

OTHERWISE ENGAGED

The days following the night of the social had been some of the happiest that Jesse could recall. He and Kirsten had been inseparable. If she had mentioned a certain doctor by name or even said more than a few words to him during that entire time, he wasn't aware of it. For the first time since Carter had arrived in town, he could honestly say that he was secure in Kirsten's love for him. Or at least he had been until the moment came to make his intentions known.

Jesse watched anxiously as Kirsten opened the small, velvet-covered box that he had just given her. Inside was an engagement ring. It wasn't much to look at, just a plain gold band with a diamond so small that it could hardly be seen without the aid of a magnifying glass. But it was all that he could afford. And that's what worried him most. Kirsten deserved better; the best that money could buy. *Or that Carter could buy,* Jesse thought with a pang of jealousy. But that kind of money he didn't have. It had taken him months just to be able to save up enough to buy this one. Would she be disappointed?

Jesse looked up from the ring to see tears spilling down her cheeks. His hopes plummeted. She didn't like it. "I know it's not much," he rushed to say, "but I'll get you a more expensive one just as soon as I can afford it."

"No, Jesse." Kirsten turned to face him, dashing the tears from her cheeks. "I don't want a more expensive one. This is perfect." She clutched the ring box to her chest, further emphasizing how she felt about his choice. "I'll cherish it always."

Jesse breathed a sigh of relief. "I wasn't sure," he admitted to her. "He can provide so much better for you and you have so much in common."

Kirsten was puzzled by his comments. "Who are you talking about?"

"Carter."

"Jesse Cameron, did you think that Carter and I…?" Kirsten could tell from the guilty expression on his face that he had. She reached over and took his hand. "We share a love of medicine but that's all. It's you that I want. You that I love."

That was all that Jesse needed to hear. He was now ready for what he had come to do. "May I?" he asked, reaching for the ring box.

Kirsten's heart pounded in her chest as she watched Jesse remove the ring from the box and slip off the porch swing onto one knee. They had talked about getting married many times, almost as many times as she had dreamt about what it would be like to hear him utter those four special words that every young woman longs hear. And now those dreams were coming true.

Jesse took her left hand in his, holding the ring in his right. His gaze captured hers and never let go. "Kirsten Ramsey, I love you with all my heart and I want for you to be my wife…. Will you marry me?"

"Yes." Kirsten quickly dropped her gaze to watch as Jesse slid the ring onto her finger. It was a perfect fit.

Jesse rose back to his feet, smiling as he took her other hand and drew her up beside him. "I love you," he told her again.

"And I love you." Kirsten melted into his embrace, relishing in the feel of his arms around her. He had held her countless times before but this was different. He was her fiancé now. She would treasure this moment always.

"I still have to get past your father, you know."

Kirsten stepped back with a frown on her face. "Jesse Aaron Cameron, you make it sound as if you're on your way to your own execution. You know that Pa has as much as given his consent."

"I know. But I want to do this proper. I only intend on getting married once."

Kirsten smiled at him coyly. "I'm glad to hear that."

Jesse smiled back and then looked towards the front door. "Is he inside?"

Kirsten nodded, suddenly finding herself as nervous as he. But that was foolishness. Her father would never refuse Jesse's request for her hand. Or would he?

"Ready?"

Kirsten took the hand that Jesse was holding out to her. "Ready."

The young couple made their way inside and headed down the hallway towards the kitchen. Kathleen was sitting at the table enjoying an after breakfast cup of tea when they entered. She greeted them both with a smile but her attention went straight to Jesse. "You're certainly up and about early this morning, Jesse."

"Yes, ma'am."

"Where's pa?" Kirsten asked her.

Kathleen smiled as she noticed the ring box that her Kirsten was clutching in her hand. "He's outside hitching up the buggy to go into town. I'll go get him."

"Oh, that's all right, ma'am," Jesse said hurriedly. "I can come back another time."

Alec stepped in the back door, wiping his grease-soiled hands on a rag. "I'll be going now, Kathleen. Anything you need from Crowley's?"

"Alec...." Kathleen rose out of her chair to face him. "Jesse is here to see you."

"Oh?" Alec met Jesse's gaze across the room. "Something I can do for you, Jesse?"

"Well, sir...." Kirsten tightened her grip on his hand. "I'd like to speak with you if I may...in private."

Alec looked back and forth between the anxious faces of his daughter and the young man at her side. He knew what was coming. "Why don't we take a ride into town? We can talk along the way."

Kirsten released Jesse's hand, holding her breath as she watched the two men that she loved most in the world disappear out the back door. All she could do now was wait.

* * * * *

"My pa's almost done with the sign for the clinic," Jesse announced as the buggy passed by the blacksmith's shop. "Maybe by tomorrow."

"That's good to hear," Alec replied.

Jesse restlessly drummed his fingers against the side of his leg, trying to think of something else to say. "Nice weather we're having."

Alec stared ahead at the dark thunderhead that was threatening to roll through town, wondering what the young man would consider a storm. "Sure is."

Jesse continued his restless drumming. "Did I mention that my Pa's almost done with the sign for the clinic? Maybe by tomorrow."

Alec might have found the young man's nervous behavior cause to laugh under other circumstances, but knowing that he was partly to blame gave him a whole different perspective. He had done far more to discourage Jesse's relationship with Kirsten than he had ever done to encourage it and now regretted this fact deeply. Jesse was the man that had been chosen for his daughter, and no matter how much he might want to change that, he reckoned the Good Lord knew best.

Alec pulled the buggy off to the side of the road, deciding it was time to let the young man off the hook. "Jesse?"

Jesse turned anxiously to face him. "Yes, sir?"

"Wasn't there something you wanted to ask me?"

* * * * *

"What do you suppose is taking them so long?"

"Kirsten, dear, please come sit down," Kathleen implored her. "I'm sure they'll be back shortly."

Despite her mother's repeated urgings, Kirsten continued to pace back and forth between the sofa and the fireplace, wringing her hands out in front of her. She was far more nervous than she thought she'd be now that the moment to receive her father's blessing had finally arrived. What if he told Jesse no? "Oh, I couldn't bare it!" she exclaimed out loud.

"Couldn't bare what, dear?" Kathleen asked.

The sound of the back door opening brought Kirsten's pacing to a halt. She turned in the direction of the living room entryway, listening above the pounding of her heart for the sound of footsteps coming down the hall. Jesse and her father came into view a few moments later, the elder man's hand resting on the younger's shoulder.

Kirsten took a hesitant step towards them, searching her father's eyes expectantly. "Pa?"

"You're engaged, sweetheart."

"Oh, Pa!" Kirsten rushed to him. "Thank you!"

As Alec opened his arms to receive her, he realized with a great deal of sadness that his role as her protector was coming to an end. God had placed another in her life to take his place and she was more than ready for the change. Even now as he held her, he could feel her heart straining towards Jesse. He couldn't hold her back any longer. It was time to let go.

Alec took his daughter's right hand and symbolically placed it into Jesse's. The young man met his gaze with silent understanding. He knew the significance of the role that was now to be his and he accepted it without reservation.

Kathleen jumped up from the sofa to congratulate the newly engaged couple, liberally plying them both with hugs and kisses. "We'll have to have a celebration," she suggested. "Tomorrow night. We'll invite the entire town."

Alec dropped a kiss onto her cheek. "I'm afraid you three will have to plan the bash of the century without me, I've got to get to the clinic. Jesse, tell your father thanks again for the sign. He can drop it by anytime."

"I will, sir."

"And, Jesse?"

Jesse turned to face him again. "Yes, sir?"

Alec smiled, reaching out to clap the young man on the shoulder. "Don't you think it's about time you started calling me Pa?"

* * * * *

"Thank you, Lord...." Alec stood in the middle of his new exam room, wanting to pinch himself to be sure he wasn't dreaming. After twelve years of running his prac-tice out of their home, he was finally going to have his own clinic. All that remained was to put up the sign that Jesse's father was making for him and restock his supplies, both of which could be done as early as tomorrow.

Alec turned at the sound of footsteps behind him, frowning when he saw Carter appear in the doorway. "What are you doing up?"

"No offense to your bedside manner, Alec, but I have been cooped up in that room for the past five days. I can't stand it any longer."

Alec's gaze dropped to the young man's feet. "How's the ankle?"

Carter stepped forward, leaning with his full weight on the injured foot. "Still a little tender," he confessed, "but I've had worse pain from a paper cut. I thought I might take a walk and see some of the sights around town. It's got to be better than the view from my window."

Alec chuckled as he recalled that Carter's room over-looked the outhouse. "Well, just don't overdo. Doctor's orders."

"I won't."

Alec watched as he headed to the front door. "Sure you wouldn't rather ride?" he called out.

Carter tossed a scathing look over his shoulder as he went out the door.

Alec grinned. "I guess not."

* * * * *

Carter dashed across the street towards Crowley's as a loud clap of thunder rumbled overhead. He ducked inside the store just moments before the sky opened up and let loose a drenching deluge.

"Lands sakes, looks like we're in for quite a blow."

Carter turned towards the pleasant sounding voice, smiling at the woman he spied standing behind the counter off to his left. "Yes, ma'am," he agreed. "It sure does.

"Ida stepped out from behind the counter, sizing up the handsome specimen of manhood before her. "I'm Ida Crowley," she said with a becoming smile. "You must be that young doctor we've been hearing so much about."

Carter lifted a hand to the front of his shirt thinking there must be a sign on his chest. "Yes, ma'am."

"My husband Josiah and I own the store. He's out making a delivery. Probably soaked to the skin by now." She rolled her eyes with a gasp. "Lands, I hope he remembered to wear two sets of johns. Wouldn't do to have him getting sick."

Carter thought her ramblings were through but she was just picking up steam.

"Our niece Amber is the town schoolteacher. It's a shame that she's not here to meet you. About your age, she is. Wonderful girl. I'm sure you two would have lots in common, seeing as you're both from Boston, and all."

If she's anything like her aunt, Carter thought, *one could never get a word in edgewise to find out.*

"What can I get for you today?"

Carter didn't have the heart to tell her that he had only come in to wait out the storm. "How about if I just look around?"

Ida's broad shoulders lifted with a shrug. "Suit yourself."

Carter headed for the display of men's clothing in the corner, silently willing the storm to lift soon. Fifteen minutes later he was wishing that he had never left the clinic.

A rush of cold air swept in as the door opened to admit yet another soul seeking shelter. Carter's heart nearly stopped as he looked up from a stack of shirts to see Kirsten step in. It was the first time that he had seen her since the night of the social—the night that he had declared his love for her to the walls of his empty room.

"Kirsten, dear, what are you doing out in this wretched weather?" Ida chastened like a mother hen.

Carter ducked behind a stand of hats as Kirsten walked past him to the counter where Ida was stacking yard goods.

"Ma sent me in to get some more yarn," she explained. "I got caught on the way."

Carter peeked out from behind the hat stand, watching as Kirsten removed her bonnet. Long streams of shimmering, golden-brown hair tumbled down her back, leaving him hard pressed to catch his breath.

"What colors does she need?" Ida asked, turning to shelf behind her.

"Blue and yellow, she said."

Carter drew back, unable to look upon her any longer for fear his heart would burst clean out of his chest. "Kirsten," he whispered, savoring the sound of her name as it came off his tongue. "If only you knew...."

"What's that handsome beau of yours up to these days?" Ida asked as she plunked Kirsten's order down on the counter.

"Fiancé, now." Kirsten proudly thrust her left hand beneath Ida's gaze. "Jesse and I are engaged."

"Oh, bless your hearts," Ida sang out joyfully. "I always knew you two were meant to be hitched."

Kirsten started at the crash behind her. She turned just in time to see Carter scurrying out the door, leaving a barrel of apples overturned in his wake. She called for him to stop but her voice was drowned out by the sound of the pelting rain.

"Lands sakes." Ida made a tsk-tsking sound with her tongue. "What a strange young man."

* * * * *

Carter ran out of the store into the pouring rain, ignoring Kirsten's pleas for him to stop. The chilling wind that buffeted against him as he headed up the street numbed his exposed flesh but could do nothing to numb the pain in his heart upon learning of her engagement to Jesse. It had been foolish of him to ever think that he might have a chance with her. She had never been interested in him. And now she was lost to him forever.

By the time he arrived back at the clinic he was physically and emotionally drained. All he wanted to do was pack his bags and put any memory of Baxter, Pennsylvania—and Kirsten Ramsey—as far behind him as possible. There was no longer any reason for him to stay. Alec could easily find himself another assistant, but Carter doubted if he'd ever be able to recover his heart from Alec's daughter.

Alec was hanging a picture above the fireplace in the waiting room when he came through the door. "How was your walk?"

Carter strode past him without saying a word and took the stairs two at a time, not slowing his pace until he reached his room. After retrieving his bags from the closet, he tossed them onto the bed and began transferring his clothes into them from the dresser.

Alec stepped unnoticed into the doorway, watching the scene in bewilderment. "Something I should know about?"

Carter turned from the dresser, cringing inside at the look of betrayal that he saw in Alec's eyes. *He deserves better than this,* he thought to himself. *But I can't stay.*

Carter took only a few steps towards him, figuring it might be wise to keep his distance until after he had said his piece. "I don't think it's going to work out for me here," he explained. "I hate to leave you in this position, but I think under the circumstances—"

"You found out about Kirsten's engagement."

Carter nodded as he sank down onto the edge of the bed, expelling a lengthy sigh. "I'm not going to lie to you, sir...." He turned reluctantly to meet Alec's gaze. "I'm in love with your daughter."

Alec was more surprised by Carter's reversion to the use of "sir" than he was by his confession of undying love. He had known for quite some time of the feelings the young man held for Kirsten. The horse incident was only one of many that had given him away.

"I have to forget her," Carter added to lend credibility to his cause, "and I can't do that if I see her everyday."

Alec wasn't going to argue his point. He was hurting enough. "If that's what you think best."

Carter found himself disappointed, even a bit angered by Alec's response. He didn't want for him to be so understanding. What he wanted was for him to raise Cain or at the very least belt him in the jaw. It would have made him feel a little less guilty about his decision to leave.

Carter rose slowly back to his feet. "If you'll excuse me, sir, I'd like to catch the train tonight and I still have some packing to do."

"Train doesn't run past four on Friday," Alec told him. "It's after that now."

Carter sighed again, dropping back onto the bed. Even the transportation system was against him. "Tomorrow, then."

* * * * *

Carter sat down on the clinic steps, staring at the new sign that Jesse's father had just delivered. It had been beautifully crafted out of an eight by three foot rectangular slab of oak, each letter of the wording individually burned into the wood with a branding iron. *Baxter's Medical Clinic* was spelled out across the top, with Alec Ramsey, M.D. in much smaller letters beneath it. But it was seeing his own name just below Alec's that brought a lump to Carter's throat. He wished that Alec hadn't included him, but how could either of them have known how quickly things were going change? Now Jesse's father would have to make a whole new sign.

"It was Jesse's idea."

Carter turned at Kirsten's approach, commanding his heart to stay in rhythm.

"He told his Pa to put your name on the sign," she explained.

Carter found this almost most impossible to believe. Why would Jesse do something like that? "He shouldn't have."

Kirsten sat down beside him, aware of how uncomfortable it made him, but determined to hold her ground until she had said what was on her mind. "My Pa told me that you're leaving tomorrow."

Carter would have preferred that he hadn't but it wouldn't have been fair not to. "That's right."

Kirsten pressed her lips together so hard they lost all color. "It's because of me, isn't it?"

"No, Kirsten." Carter tried to look her in the eye but couldn't hold her gaze for more than a few seconds at a time. "It's me. Like I told your father, I have to forget you. And that's nearly impossible to do in a town this size."

"Can't you try?" she pleaded with him. "The town needs you. My pa needs you."

And what about you, Kirsten? Do you need me, too? "I'm sorry," he apologized, more for his private thoughts than anything else. "I can't stay."

Kirsten rose from the steps, turning her back to him as tears began streaming down her cheeks. "Have a nice trip."

Carter watched as she disappeared down the road. "And you have a nice life."

CHAPTER TWENTY-ONE

EPIDEMIC

The thunderstorms of yesterday had long since moved off to the east, but in Kirsten's heart a storm of a different nature was still raging. She knew that she shouldn't blame herself for Carter's decision to leave, but knowing and doing were two entirely different things.

"I was so sure that I would be able to get him to change his mind," she told her mother over an early morning cup of tea. "That he would realize how much the town needs him."

"That's one lesson you'll have to learn about men, Kirsty. They can be stubborn to a fault. But in this case...." Kathleen raised her cup in preparation to take a sip. "I think Carter made the right decision."

Kirsten was surprised that her mother would side with him, knowing how desperately her father needed an assistant.

Kathleen set her cup back on the table, reaching over to take her daughter's hand. "Let me ask you something.... Would you want Carter's feelings for you to interfere with his responsibilities as a physician, maybe even cost someone their life?"

Kirsten looked at her mother as if she had lost her senses. "Of course not."

"Then you have to let him go. I'm not saying that something like that might happen, but if yesterday's incident at the store is any indication of his feelings for you...."

Kirsten realized that she was right. She couldn't bare it if she was the cause of someone being unnecessarily injured, especially if it was Carter. He had already sprained his ankle on account of her. There was no telling what he might do next.

"Now cheer up," Kathleen urged, giving her hand a commanding squeeze. "We have an engagement party to plan for tonight. Let's start with the guest list." Kathleen picked up a piece of paper and began reading off the names of those they were planning to invite.

Kirsten tried hard to pay attention, but all she could think about was that a certain doctor from Boston would not be in attendance.

* * * * *

Carter peered over the top of the newspaper that he sat reading in the clinic waiting room, eyeing the clock on the wall outside the exam room door. In less than two hours he would be on his way back to Boston.

But to what, he asked himself honestly. He was fooling himself if he thought that his father's former patients were going to have a sudden change of heart and allow him to treat them. And what's more, it could take months, even years, to build up a practice of his own. At least in Baxter he would have had the opportunity to work alongside Alec, a chance to prove himself as a physician. And he was throwing it all away because he couldn't control his emotions.

It's not like you to give up that easy, he lectured himself. *If it were, you wouldn't be a doctor right now.*

But did he dare stay? Could he bury his feelings for Kirsten and work alongside her in a professional capacity?

No, he pronounced. There wasn't a hole that could be dug deep enough. He had made the right decision.

"Hello? Is anybody here?" Amber pushed open the clinic door, balancing a large package astride her hip.

Carter rose from the sofa, his gaze riveted upon the young woman before him. He tried repeatedly to issue forth some sort of greeting but found himself tongue-tied by her beauty.

"You must be Doctor Ramsey's new assistant," Amber presumed, taking it upon herself to start the conversation.

"Yes," Carter blurted, finding his tongue once again ready to cooperate. *Or rather, I use to be.* "Carter Buchanan."

Amber's gaze slid in the direction of the exam room. "Is Doctor Ramsey here?"

"Actually, no." Carter folded the newspaper and tossed it behind him on the sofa, making himself available in case she was in need of medical assistance. "He had to make a trip out to the Coulter farm. Both boys are ill."

"I was wondering why they weren't in school the last couple of days. I hope it's nothing serious."

"Me, too." Carter continued to stare, silently pleading with her to introduce herself. *Who are you?*

"Oh, I'm sorry," Amber apologized, as if having read his mind. "I'm Amber Lloyd, the town's schoolteacher."

Carter fought to keep his mouth from springing open. This was Ida Crowley's niece? She was nothing at all like her aunt. And if his memory served him correctly, she was even from Boston.

"My aunt and uncle run the general store," Amber told him needlessly.

"I know. I met your aunt yesterday."

"Yes, she mentioned….." Amber stopped herself before saying something that might embarrass him. "She said you stopped by."

Carter cheeks became unbearably warm. By now word of the scene that he had made at the store yesterday was probably the number one topic around every supper table in town. Another good reason for him to leave.

"Oh, I almost forgot why I came by." Amber patted the box that she still held propped on her hip. "This package of medical supplies arrived for Doctor Ramsey. Would you see that he gets it?"

"Of course." Carter took the package from her, realizing that he should have done so as soon as she walked through the door. It weighed a ton.

"Well, I should be going. I still have a few more deliveries to make." Amber turned towards the door, but her gaze never once left Carter. "Maybe I'll see you around sometime."

Carter was about to express how much he'd enjoy that when he remembered that his time in Baxter was quickly ebbing away. "I'm going back to Boston on this afternoon's train," he told her reluctantly.

"Oh." The light dwindled from Amber's eyes. "I'm sorry to hear that."

Not half as sorry as I am, Carter thought, realizing for the first time that he had gone more than two minutes without thinking about Kirsten Ramsey.

"Well…." Amber offered him a parting smile. "Have a nice trip."

"Thank you."

Carter closed the door behind her, aware of a stirring in his heart that he had never experienced in Kirsten's presence before. Could it be that what he thought he was feeling for her wasn't love at all? He had to admit that it was a very real possibility. But how was he going to know for sure?

Carter pondered the dilemma before him as he carried the box of medical supplies into the exam room. He was no closer to discovering an answer when Alec walked in twenty minutes later. Carter gathered from the pained look on his face that the news from the Coulter farm wasn't good but decided to wait for Alec's official report before jumping to any conclusions. "Amber Lloyd dropped off some supplies earlier," he said instead, indicating the box sitting on the exam table. "I hope you don't mind but I took the liberty of putting them away."

Alec cast only a brief glance at the fully stocked medicine cabinet before sinking down onto the chair next to it. He leaned forward with his face buried in his hands, releasing a sigh that sounded as if it originated from the very depths of his soul. "The oldest Coulter boy just died."

"I'm sorry, Alec." Carter wished that he could offer a more appropriate form of condolence but he couldn't honestly say that he knew what Alec was feeling. He had never been in the position of losing a patient before. "Do you know what it was?"

Alec lifted his head, staring aimlessly at the wall across the room. "Influenza."

A tremor of fear rippled through Carter, starting at his feet and moving upwards. "How's the other boy?"

"He's holding his own." Alec didn't sound too confident that this would remain the case, however. "I just pray that we don't have an epidemic on our hands. But where there's one, there's usually more."

Carter silently echoed his concern. His father had battled an influenza epidemic in Boston several years ago. More than a hundred people had perished before the illness had finally run its course.

"I'm going to take a ride out to some of the outlying farms later. Hopefully the Coulter boys are just an isolated—"

"Doc Ramsey!"

Alec rushed out of the exam room with Carter close on his heels. A young man that he recognized as a new settler to the area came bolting through the clinic door. "Doc, it's my

Megan," Jeb Walker sputtered on the verge of tears. "She's terrible sick."

Alec looked past the young man to the bundled figure lying prone in the back of the wagon outside the clinic. *Where there's one, there's usually more....* His own words had just come back to haunt him.

"I didn't know what else to do so I brought her here."

"Easy, Jeb." Alec laid a hand on the distraught man's shoulder, trying to lend what comfort he could. "You did right. We'll handle things from here."

Carter helped Alec carry Megan Walker to one of the rooms upstairs and then returned downstairs to sit with her husband while Alec made his examination. The young man was in no condition to be waiting alone.

"How long have you two been married?" Carter asked, hoping to distract him from his worry.

"Just two months," he replied with a newlywed gleam in his eyes. "But we're already thinking about starting a family. My Megan, she only wants a couple of young'uns. But me, I want a whole passel." His eyes began to fill with tears as he realized that his dream might never become a reality. "Oh, God, please!" he cried out. "Don't take my Megan!"

Carter swallowed to rid himself of the lump in his throat but it wouldn't budge. He was at a loss to know how to comfort this grieving man. It was not something that he had been taught how to do in medical school.

The two men sat silently for another ten minutes before they heard Alec's tread upon the stairs. Carter's heart sank as he turned watch his descent. He was wearing the same expression as he had been after returning from the Coulter farm. Jeb Walker's dreams of having children would go unfulfilled.

The young man got to his feet, moving ever so slowly towards Alec. "Doc?" His voice rose expectantly with each step. "Megan?"

"I'm sorry, Jeb. There was nothing I could do."

Carter was expecting the young man to break down but he appeared too numb to even shed tears.

"Can I sit with her for awhile?" he requested.

"Of course."

Alec escorted the young man to his wife's side and then rejoined Carter downstairs. Carter started as he smacked the palm of his hand against the staircase banister. "Influenza," he seethed, pronouncing the word as if it left a bad taste in his mouth.

Carter met his gaze without flinching. He knew what was coming.

"I know that you've got your heart set on leaving this afternoon but I could really use your help."

Carter placed a hand firmly upon Alec's shoulder. "Where do we start?"

* * * * *

Alec returned home just long enough to break the tragic news of Jordan Coulter and Megan Walker's deaths, as well as to pick up a few changes of clothes. He instructed Kathleen to leave them for him in the barn. He wasn't about to risk going into the house.

After securing the bag behind the saddle of his horse, he turned to address his family huddled on the back porch. "I don't know how long I might be gone!" he hollered across the yard. "I'll try to come by as often as I can! Don't try to come by the clinic! Keep everyone as close to home as possible!"

"I will, Alec!" Kathleen called back. "You'll be in our prayers! You and Carter both!"

Kirsten watched solemnly as her father rode away. Any relief she felt upon learning that Carter had decided to stay was overshadowed by the reality of what she knew they would be facing in the days and weeks ahead. As much as she wanted to be there to help, she knew that her father would never allow it. She would be forced to wait for word along with the rest of the family.

Kathleen slipped an arm around her shoulders. "Your Pa will be fine. They both will."

Kirsten could only pray she was right.

* * * * *

Alec stopped by Crowley's on his way back to the clinic and dropped off a list of supplies that they would be needing—everything from cots and blankets...to shovels for burying the dead. He instructed Josiah to deliver them as soon as possible and then headed on to the clinic.

Carter was waiting anxiously on the front steps when he rode up. "Thank goodness your back. A Mr. Randall just brought in his son, Tad, along with an elderly couple, the Peterson's."

Alec more stumbled than stepped down from his horse. The Randall's and the Peterson's both lived in town. The illness was no longer content to remain on the outlying farms. It had moved into the heart of where they lived and worked, where their children went to school, where they worshiped their God. There would be no stopping its' savagery now.

"Oh, and...." Carter swallowed. "Miles Coulter sent word."

Alec didn't need for him to say more. Six-year-old Matthew had followed his older brother to be with Jesus.

"I put the Randall boy in the room where Megan Walker was—"

Alec quickly shook off his grief for the dead and turned his energy to the cause of the living.

"—and the Peterson's right next door," Carter told him.

"Fine." Alec turned to untie his bag from the back of the saddle. "Josiah will be by later with some cots and other supplies. We're going to need them."

As Alec followed Carter back inside, his gaze came to rest upon the sign that Jesse's father had made for him, still leaning against the steps where it had been all night. He hadn't even had time to put it up and already the clinic was undergoing a fiery trial that would severely test his skills as a physician…as well as his faith in the One who had entrusted those skills to him. Alec could only hope that when all was said and done he would not be found lacking in either.

* * * * *

"Amber!" Carter ran to her side as she came through the clinic door, fearing she might be ill, but his concern for her well-being quickly changed to outrage at the carelessness of her actions. "What are you doing here? Don't you realize you could get sick?"

"I might ask the same of you, Carter Buchanan." There was no animosity in her tone, merely curiosity. Hadn't he told her that he was leaving on the afternoon train?

"I decided to stay and help Alec," he explained.

Amber began stripping off her gloves. "That's exactly why I'm here—to help. I've had the influenza before and I don't intend on getting it again. So if you would kindly tell me what needs to be done…."

Carter could only stare.

"Oh, Alec!" Amber signaled for him to join them as he stepped out of the exam room. "I brought the supplies you wanted. They're outside in the wagon."

"Then we best get to unloading." Alec walked past Carter, giving him a thump on the back. "Coming?"

Carter could only stare.

* * * * *

"Jesse, are you feeling all right?" Kathleen's concern for the young man had been mounting all evening. He didn't look well at all.

"Yes, ma'am," Jesse assured her as they stepped to the front door. "It's just been a long day. I'm real sorry about the engagement party having to be cancelled."

"I know. But in light of what's happened, I don't think any of us would have felt much like celebrating tonight." Kathleen leaned over and gave him a motherly peck on the cheek. "Thanks again for coming by. I know Alec will appreciate your concern."

"Your welcome. I just wanted to make sure that everything was all right." Jesse turned to Kirsten, taking both her hands. "Are you coming in for church tomorrow?"

"Ma?" Kirsten looked to her mother for permission, recalling what her father had said about keeping everyone close to home.

"I'm sure it will be all right," she decided. "The Walker's and Coulter's live way outside of town."

Jesse smiled, pleased that her decision had gone in his favor. He turned again to Kirsten. "I'll be by for you in the morning, then."

"I'll be ready."

* * * * *

By day's end Alec was no longer reluctant about calling it an epidemic. Seven more individuals had been brought in to the clinic, three of which died within minutes of their arrival. The course before him was unmistakably clear. He had no choice but to call for a quarantine.

"I'll make the official announcement tomorrow," he shared with Carter and Amber as they gathered for a short break before returning to the care of their patients. "We'll have to cancel all church services, and school," he added, looking to Amber. "Any gathering where there might be large numbers of people. It's imperative that we keep it from spreading."

"What about the train?" Amber asked.

"All in bound and out bound trains will have to be held up until we're sure there are no new cases, which could take weeks." Alec turned to open the glass doors of the medicine cabinet, taking a visual inventory of the supplies they had on hand. "Fortunately, I got in a fresh shipment of just about everything yesterday, including quinine."

"But will it be enough?" Carter wondered. He knew that quinine was the only defense they had against the fever once an individual became infected with influenza.

Alec honestly didn't have an answer for him. "God only knows."

CHAPTER TWENTY-TWO

NO GREATER LOVE

A steady stream of hot coffee and assorted baked goods arrived at the clinic throughout the night, left on the front steps by anonymous donors. The offerings were greatly appreciated by the trio working inside, fueling their physical need for sustenance as well as lifting their spirits.

But where food was plentiful, sleep was not.

Amber rose wearily from the bedside of Tad Randall and plodded downstairs to get a fresh pitcher of water. She stumbled on the next to the last step and would have fallen had Carter not been there to catch her. Their eyes locked for a moment as she righted herself. Carter was shocked by how depleted she looked. "You can't keep going on like this. You've got to get some rest."

"I'm fine," Amber insisted, knowing it was the last thing that he wanted to hear.

"Amber."

She gritted her teeth, repeating her statement a second time with more force. "I said, I'm fine."

"Would you stop being so stub—" Carter cut short his rebuke at the sound of a wagon pulling up out front. It was a sound they had all come to dread. The sound of sickness arriving...and all too often death.

Alec walked soberly to the door, hastening his pace only at the urgent call of his name. Zack was just climbing down over the side of the wagon as he stepped outside. Alec was relieved to see that he appeared to be in good health. "Morning, Zack."

Zack bobbed his head towards the back of the wagon. "I came across him lying by the side of the road halfway between here and his place."

Alec strode to the back of the wagon, wondering which of his neighbors had succumbed to the illness. Nothing could have prepared him for the identity of the young man lying inside. "Jesse...."

Alec climbed up into the wagon, kneeling down beside the motionless form of his future son-in-law. He pressed the back of his hand against the young man's forehead and then quickly snapped it back as if he had been burnt, shocked by how hot his skin was to the touch.

"He mumbled something about his Pa being sick right before he passed out," Zack thought to mention. "I'll help you get him inside and then go by their place to check on him."

"Thanks, Zack."

All six rooms upstairs were already occupied, as well as the two downstairs, so Carter set up a cot in the exam room for Jesse.

Alec administered a dose of quinine first thing and then turned his attention to lowering the young man's dangerously high body temperature.

Jesse regained consciousness for a few moments as Alec began applying cool cloths to his chest. "My pa," he croaked, staring up at Alec through fever-glazed eyes. "Please...help my pa."

"Your pa's going to be fine, Jesse. You just rest easy."

Jesse's eyes slowly closed, his mouth forming the word "Kirsten" just before he slipped back into unconsciousness.

Alec rose from beside the cot, turning to Carter who stood watching the scene from the doorway. "Keep a close eye on him. I'll be back in half an hour."

* * * * *

"Alec...." Kathleen ran out onto the back porch in her bare feet when she saw him ride into the yard. For a moment she did nothing but stare at the mounted figure before her, drinking in the sight of him. "How are you?" she asked eagerly, hungry for news of his well-being.

Alec decided to dispense with the pleasantries. He didn't even bother to dismount. "Where's Kirsten?"

"She's upstairs getting ready for church. Jesse is coming by for her. I hope it was all right to tell her that she could go. I didn't think that—" Kathleen was struck silent by the pained expression on his face. "What's wrong?"

"Zack brought him to the clinic a little while ago. He's got the influenza. He and his father, both."

Kathleen pressed her hands over her mouth. "Oh, no."

Alec drew the reins taught as his horse began to dance restlessly beneath him. "You'll have to tell her for me." He despised himself for pawning off such an ugly task on her but it couldn't be helped.

Kathleen nodded, hugging herself tight against a sudden chill. She knew that the news would not be easy for Kirsten to bear.

"I'll try to come by again tomorrow." Alec turned his mount to leave, stopping only at the sound of her terrified gasp. "What is it?"

"Jesse.... He was by the house yesterday evening." Kathleen now recalled how poorly he had looked even then.

"Was he inside at all?" Alec asked.

"Yes. He ate supper with us." Kathleen covered her mouth again, fighting back tears. "Oh, Alec, I didn't know."

"You couldn't have," he was quick to tell her. The last thing he wanted was for her to start blaming herself. "It's no one's fault."

Kathleen looked up at him with a fragile smile.

"Everything's going to be all right." Alec longed to take her in his arms and express the same assurance through touch, but words would have to suffice for now. "I've got to get back."

"Alec...." Kathleen stepped to the edge of the porch, moving as close to him as she dare. "You know that when Kirsten finds out she's not going to be able to stay away."

Alec had already prepared himself for that inevitability. "Tell her I'll be waiting."

* * * * *

Kirsten arrived at the clinic a short time later with the blessings of both her parents. Alec led her into the exam room, drawing a chair over beside the cot so she could sit next to Jesse.

Kirsten took his hand, bringing it up to the side of her face. "Jesse...can you hear me?" She leaned closer when there was no response, brushing back the sweat dampened curls from his forehead. "Jesse, it's me. I'm here now."

Still no response.

Kirsten's gaze moved further down his body, watching the shallow rise and fall of his chest. "Pa...is he going to die?"

Alec stepped up behind her, laying a hand on her shoulder. He wanted nothing more than to tell her that he was going to pull through but it wouldn't be fair to give her false hope. "He's strong, sweetheart. He has a good chance."

Kirsten's eyes filled with tears, blurring her vision of the ring that Jesse had placed on her finger only two days before. "I can't lose him, Pa. I can't."

Alec did what little more he could to comfort her and then rejoined Carter in the other room. "I don't think there's anything harder than watching your children suffer. Except maybe having to tell another parent that theirs didn't make it."

Carter's mouth went dry. "I know this is lousy timing, Alec, but Emily Bennett just passed away. Her folks are waiting outside and...." He shook his head. "I didn't know what to say to them."

"It's all right." Alec clapped him on the shoulder. "I'll go talk to them. Why don't you see to Jesse's father."

"Thanks." It hardly seemed like an adequate response but it was all that Carter could offer.

As Alec walked to the door to break the news to the Bennett girls' parents, the names of others they had also lost ran through his head like a roll call of death. Jordan Coulter...Matthew Coulter...Megan Walker...Edward Peterson.... The list went on and on. Was the suffering never going to end?

"Please, Lord," Alec prayed earnestly, "for Kirsten's sake...don't let Jesse be added to that list."

* * * * *

Twenty-four hours passed with only three new cases reported, but Alec didn't draw much comfort from this fact. He knew there could still be many individuals, too weak to have made it into the clinic, suffering alone in their homes. Zack was right now checking on some of the older folks who lived out of town and might not have been able to send word if they needed assistance. In the meantime, there remained plenty to do.

Alec wandered into the kitchen and joined Amber beside the large tub of water where she was washing out some linens. "How are you feeling?"

"I'm fine."

Alec said nothing in reply, giving her the impression that he didn't believe her. She turned on him with a heated look on her face. "I said I was fine!"

Alec took a step back, fearing she was about to slug him. "I believe you."

Amber offered him a contrite smile. "I'm sorry, Alec. I'm just so use to having Carter contradict me all the time." Her right hand flew out of the tub, flinging soapy water across the room. "Honestly, that man would try the patience of a saint."

"Could just be that he likes you."

Carter? Me? Amber turned to argue Alec's claim but he had already left the room. A feather-light smile brushed her lips. Could Alec be right?

Carter stepped away from the front window as Alec walked out of the kitchen. "Zack's back."

Alec followed Carter outside, relieved to see that Zack had returned from his rounds with an empty wagon. But then he noticed the small, dark haired figure that Zack was reaching for on the seat beside him. Alec's heart stopped cold. *Stephen....*

"Eric flagged me down as I was passing by your place," he explained. "He said to tell you that everyone else is fine."

But not Stephen. Alec stood paralyzed, staring at the motionless form of his youngest son.

Zack lowered Stephen halfway over the side of the wagon, expecting Alec to step forward and take him. "Alec?"

"Give him to me." Carter brushed past Alec, reaching to take Stephen for himself.

Zack then handed down a bundle of extra clothing. "Kathleen sent these for him."

Alec finally came to his senses, grabbing blindly for the bundle. "Let's put him in with Jesse."

While Alec and Kirsten readied another cot, Carter continued to cradle Stephen in his arms. He looked down at one point and was surprised to find the youngster gazing up at him.

"Do you want to play checkers?" he asked.

The innocence of his request caused Carter to choke up. "Sure, pal. Just as soon as you're feeling better."

That was all Stephen wanted to hear. He drifted back to sleep with a contented smile upon his face.

"We're ready for him."

Carter ignored Alec's prompting to bring Stephen over to the cot. "Do you mind if I hold him for a while longer?"

Alec exchanged a glance with Kirsten, finding her as equally touched by Carter's concern for Stephen as he was. "Of course not."

Carter sat down on the chair that Alec placed behind him, gently lifting Stephen's sleeping form up to his shoulder.

Amber watched the tender scene unnoticed from the doorway, viewing a side to Carter Buchanan that she had never seen before.

* * * * *

Kirsten finally convinced Carter to lie Stephen down on the cot several hours later, but not without first promising to come get him the moment he showed any sign of regaining consciousness.

Amber met him with a smile and a steaming cup of coffee as he came out of the exam room. "Let's sit and talk for awhile."

Carter gladly accepted the coffee and her invitation, following her over to the sofa by the front window. He laid down with his head at one end, propping his feet up on the arm at the other. Amber settled into the chair facing him. "How are you holding up?" she asked.

Carter laced his hands behind his head, allowing his eyes to drop closed. "I'm fine."

Amber started to laugh. "Now where have I heard that before?"

Carter joined her, marveling at her ability to find humor even in the darkest of circumstances. *She's truly a remarkable woman,* he thought to himself. She had lost four of her students in almost as many days and yet she was still able to find a reason to smile. Where did she draw her strength from?

A thud against the front door brought Carter leaping up off the sofa. Amber remained at a distance as he went to investigate. "Carter, be careful," she implored as he reached to open the door. She issued a startled gasp as a man slumped inside at his feet.

Carter knelt down, checking the individual for a pulse and then for the presence of a fever. He had both. "Do you know him?"

Amber wagged her head, inching closer to the scene. "No. I don't believe I've ever seen him before."

Carter glanced behind her, searching for Alec.

"He's not here," Amber said, anticipating his next question. "He went home to check on his family and then to send a wire to the pharmacy in Harrisburg. He's worried about how low our supply of quinine is getting."

Carter understood his concern. They had used far more than either of them could have anticipated since the start of the epidemic. And with the quarantine still in effect, there wouldn't be any new shipments by train for quite some time to come.

Carter looked up at Amber, gauging her physical strength based on the size of her frame. "Do you think you can help me lift him?"

Amber planted her hands on her hips with a willful cock of her head. "I'm not as frail as I look, Carter Buchanan."

Carter grinned, enjoying her fiery spirit. "Yes, ma'am."

* * * * *

Kaitlin pushed open the door to her mother and father's room, drawn by the sound of crying from inside. Kathleen was on her knees beside the bed, clutching onto her Bible.

Kaitlin padded over and began stroking the back of her head, just as her mother had done for her so many times before. "Please don't cry, Mama," she begged. "Stephen will be all right."

"Oh, Kaitlin." Kathleen pulled her down onto her lap, hugging her close. "You don't know how much your Mama needed to hear that just now."

Alec had been by only a short while ago with a similar report but the effects of his repeated assurances were already wearing off. It was tearing Kathleen up inside to not be able to look after Stephen herself, but she couldn't risk the baby, or leaving the rest of the children motherless. She was comforted some knowing that at least Kirsten was there to fulfill that motherly role for her. And from Alec's telling, Carter was more than making up for her absence as well.

"Can we have a party when Papa, Kirsten and Stephen come home?" Kaitlin asked.

Kathleen hugged her tighter. "You bet we can, sweetheart. The biggest, bestest party you've ever seen."

* * * * *

"Well, I'll be." That was Alec's reaction when he walked into the room where Carter and Amber had placed what they were calling their "mystery patient". "I would have thought he'd be too ornery to get sick."

"Who is he?" Amber asked, burning with curiosity.

"Isaac P. Jameson the third, the town banker."

Carter gazed down at what had probably been an impressive looking individual before the illness had taken hold. "I take it you two have met before."

"Just once," Alec told him, recalling Jameson's attempt to purchase the clinic. "But it was enough."

"What did you find out from the pharmacy?" Carter asked, turning the conversation to more pressing matters.

"I've got their reply right here." Alec removed a telegram from his pocket and handed it to Carter. "They have more than enough quinine to meet our need but will only agree to transport it halfway, to Maytown. Someone will have to pick it up from there."

Amber blinked in surprise. "Break quarantine?"

"We have no choice. We can't take the risk that the quinine we have left will be enough. So…." Alec looked back and forth between Carter and Amber. "Any volunteers?"

Carter's stomach twisted in knots but he knew what he had to do. "I'll go."

Alec and Amber both stared at him; Alec as if he was out of his mind, and Amber as if he was the most remarkable man she had ever met.

"Do you have someone better in mind?" Carter asked in response to Alec's silent objection.

"Me," he stated plainly. It had been his intention all along.

"No, Alec. You have your family to consider. I've got no one." Carter was keenly aware of Amber's gaze boring into him. "I'm the one with the least to lose."

"Except for your life. Or have you forgotten what happened the last time you tried to get on a horse?"

Carter had indeed not forgotten, but he wasn't going to let a simple thing like never having ridden a horse before stop him. "I can do it. Maytown couldn't be more than what, one or two miles?"

"Try five. And most of it over very rough terrain," Alec thought to add.

"All right then, five miles. If I leave tonight I can be there and back by morning, easy. You've got more than enough quinine to last you until then."

"If you make it back," Alec warned, making one final attempt to dissuade him.

Carter refused to even entertain such a thought. "We don't have time to stand around arguing about this. I'm going."

* * * * *

"Greater love hath no man than this, that a man lay down his life for his friends."

Carter turned from saddling his horse as Amber appeared beside him out of the darkness. "Did you write that?"

"Of course not." Amber smiled at his sense of humor. "It's from the fifteenth chapter of John, verse thirteen. As if you didn't know."

Carter finished cinching up the saddle and then turned to face her. "John who?"

Amber retracted her smile, realizing that he wasn't joking. "Haven't you ever read the Bible before? Or even the gospel of John?"

Carter shrugged. "Can't say as I have."

Amber was suddenly at a loss for words. She had never considered the possibility that he wasn't a believer. She had just assumed, and she had assumed incorrectly.

Amber slipped a hand into the pocket of her apron and took out a small New Testament. She then reached for his hand, turned it palm up and pressed the small volume into it. "I want you to have this."

Carter stared down at the book, recognizing it as the same one that he had often seen her reading out of to their patients, though he had to admit he had never stopped long enough to listen to its contents. He slid it into his coat pocket, offering her a simple, "Thanks." It was all he could think to say.

Amber drew her shawl more securely around her shoulders as the wind suddenly picked up. "Do you have everything?" she asked, sensing he was uncomfortable with her gift and anxious to be on his way.

Carter patted the canvas bag hanging off the horn of his saddle. "I've got a map, a compass and the moonlight to guide me. Plus food and water enough for two days."

"There's one more thing I want you to take with you...." Amber stretched up to give him a kiss on the cheek.

Carter was taken aback by her show of affection. "Was that for luck?"

Amber pressed her hand against the Bible in his pocket. "I don't believe in luck."

Carter respected her conviction but failed to grasp the significance behind it. "I'd better be going."

Amber took a step back as he awkwardly hoisted himself up into the saddle. "Carter...are you absolutely sure about this?" Neither she nor Alec would fault him one bit if he changed his mind.

Carter gathered up the reins as best he knew how and eased the horse forward with a gentle nudge. "I'll see you in the morning."

Amber watched as he rode away, urgently pleading with her Heavenly Father for his physical safety, but even more so for his eternal soul. "Go with God, Carter Buchanan."

CHAPTER TWENTY-THREE

THE MIDNIGHT RIDE OF CARTER BUCHANAN

Carter had the weather in his favor for the first couple of miles and then rode straight into a downpour that left him soaked to the skin within minutes. He had brought along an extra change of clothes for just such an occasion but there was little sense in donning them until after the storm had passed. So he pressed on.

For his first time in the saddle, Carter thought that he was fairing remarkably well. Every so often his horse would challenge him in a way that he wasn't expecting but he handled each incident with the poise and skill of a seasoned horseman.

If only Kirsten could see me now, he thought with pride, then quickly realized that it was no longer Kirsten he wanted to impress. Whatever feelings he once had for her began to fade the moment he met Amber Lloyd.

Carter felt his skin growing hot despite his damp clothing as he thought about the kiss that she had given him right before he left. He hoped that it meant she shared the same feelings for him as he did for her. Not infatuation like he had felt for Kirsten, but something much deeper. Something that fueled a desire within him to take care of her for the rest of her life.

Carter arrived at the agreed upon drop off point a few hours later. It was a densely wooded area less than a mile outside of Maytown. He decided that it would be safer to dismount rather than try to ride through the trees, so he set off on foot, leading his horse behind him. He hadn't gone more than twenty feet when he located the hollowed out log where the supply of quinine was suppose to be waiting for him.

Suppose to be....

Without even realizing that he was doing so, Carter tossed up a makeshift prayer just before reaching inside the log. He smiled in relief as his hand closed around the mouth of a large drawstring bag. Inside he found eight glass bottles filled with the precious white powder, more than enough to meet their current need and then some. "Thank goodness," he uttered into the night sky.

After securing the bag onto his saddle, he located a relatively dry patch of ground and began changing into the extra clothing that he had brought along. The storm had finally let up and he was becoming extremely chilled. It wouldn't do to collapse from hypothermia when he was so close to completing his mission. Some hero he would be, then.

When he was finished, he walked his horse back through the trees to an open area where he could safely remount. "Let's get home, boy," he urged, giving the animal an affectionate pat on the neck as they started forward.

The hours seemed to fly by and Carter gauged that he was making even better time on the return trip. He had to be well over halfway back.

But then something went terribly wrong....

Carter lost his grip on the reins as his horse reared suddenly and sent him flying through the air. The last thing he heard as he hit the ground was the sound of breaking glass. And then everything went dark.

* * * * *

Baxter

"Where are you, Carter Buchanan?" Amber's plea went unanswered, just like all the others that she had already made on his behalf. He had said he would be back by morning. Well, the sun had been up for hours...but still no Carter.

Amber drew her feet up under her as she continued her vigil from the sofa by the front window. The hours since his departure had given her plenty of time to evaluate her feelings for him. What she had discovered surprised and even frightened her. She was in love with him, just as sure as she knew that the sun would rise again tomorrow. But she also knew that even if Carter felt the same, she could never encourage their relationship, not without breaking the promise she had made to herself long ago to never become romantically involved with an unbeliever. It saddened her deeply to think that Carter was not the man God intended for her, but unless something happened to change his views....

"Please, Lord. Please help him find—" Amber caught herself just before saying "You". There was certainly nothing wrong with praying for Carter's salvation, but she feared she would be doing so for purely selfish reasons.

"Please, Lord," she began again. "Just bring him back safe."

* * * * *

When Carter regained consciousness he found himself lying on a raised pallet in one of the homeliest looking cabins he had ever seen. Every inch of his body was screaming out in pain but he didn't have a clue why. He reached up with unsteady hands and explored the makeshift bandage that adorned his head. What surface wounds he could see on his hands, arms and chest had also been bandaged. But beyond that, he couldn't tell what other injuries he might have sustained. The lower half of his body was buried beneath a layer of warm quilts. Someone had clearly gone to great lengths to see to his comfort and well-being. Now if only he could figure out how he had gotten in such a wretched condition in the first place.

Carter sensed that he wasn't alone and turned to find a middle-aged woman, more round than she was tall, watching his return to consciousness from across the room. Was this his Good Samaritan?

"My name's Lottie," she said with a friendly smile, approaching the pallet where he was lying with a wobble in her step. "That there's my man, Earl." Her flabby arm swung around to point at the hulking figure sitting at a corner table. He acknowledged the fact that he was being introduced with a guttural grunt and then returned to his meal. "He come acrost ya whiles out huntin' this mornin'," she explained. "Horse musta thrown ya. Figured ya fer dead but 'pears the Good Lord has other plans."

Carter sifted everything she had said through his jumbled thoughts but nothing made any sense to him. What would he have been doing on a horse? He didn't even know how to ride. "You must be mistaken, ma'am," he told his benefactress. "I don't even own a horse, let alone know how to—" Carter's eyes flared open as the cobwebs finally began to clear. He bolted straight up, ignoring the searing pain that tore through his head upon his rapid ascent. "The medicine!" His gaze swerved all around the cabin in search of the bag that contained the precious cargo. "Where's the medicine!"

"Easy there, young feller." Lottie eased him back down onto the pallet and then stepped back with her hands planted where her hips should have been. "You mean that's what all that there white powder in them fancy jars was? Medicine?"

Carter stared up at her. "Was. You said was."

"They's broke, every single one. Musta happened when ya fell."

"Oh, no." Carter's eyes slid closed but only for a second. "I've got to get back. They're expecting me...." He struggled to sit up again but lost his battle as the room began to spin. He collapsed back on the pallet, grasping the sides of his head.

"You're not goin' anywhere. Least not 'til that head of yours clears."

Carter knew she was right. In his condition he wouldn't make it more than two feet out the cabin door, let alone be able to sit a horse. But that still didn't erase the urgent problem at hand. How to get more quinine and it get it back to the clinic in time.

Carter reached over and grabbed Lottie's wrist. His fingers barely wrapped all the way around. "Please," he implored her. "You've got to send word to a Doctor Alec Ramsey in Baxter. Tell him what's happened. Tell him he needs to get more...." That was all he got out before the darkness returned.

Lottie bent over him, drawing the layer of quilts up under his chin. "You jest rest easy now, young feller," she crooned, smiling to reveal a mouth lacking more than a few teeth. "Lottie will take care of everythin'."

* * * * *

Alec's gaze went back and forth between the occupants of the two cots in the exam room. "You two are certainly looking better."

"That's because we're feeling better." Jesse smiled over at Stephen before turning back to Alec. "How's my Pa?"

"His fever broke about a half hour before yours did," Alec was pleased to report. "If you'd like, we can move your cot into his room upstairs."

"Mine, too!" Stephen begged.

Alec chuckled. "All right, yours, too."

Stephen bounced up onto his knees, trying to see around his father into the other room. "Papa, where's Carter? He said he'd play checkers with me."

Alec exchanged an awkward glance with Kirsten. "He had to go somewhere, son. But I'm sure he'll play checkers with you as soon as he gets back." *If he gets back,* Alec added for his thoughts alone. "I'll go get your room ready."

Kirsten followed him a few moments later, reaching his side just before he started upstairs. "You're worried about him, aren't you, Pa?"

Alec turned to face her, letting the expression on his face speak for him.

"You're not the only one." Kirsten directed his gaze to Amber. "I don't think she's left that window all day."

"He should have been back by now. She knows it and so do I." Alec whacked the palm of his hand against the wall behind him. "I should have never let him go. I should have gone myself."

"Then it's you we'd be worrying about." Kirsten stepped into his arms, tilting her head back to look up at him. "It's not your fault, Pa," she assured him. "Besides, I don't think you could have stopped him, anyway."

Alec smiled down at her. "You're probably right."

"I know I'm right. Men can be stubborn to a fault sometimes."

"Now where did you get an idea like that?"

"From Ma."

Alec smiled again, leaning down to kiss her forehead. "Why don't you go and see what you can do to lift Amber's spirits while I get Jesse and Stephen settled upstairs."

"I was thinking the exact same thing."

Kirsten left her father's side and made her way over to the sofa. "Do you mind if I join you?"

Amber turned from the window, acknowledging her request with a smile. "How's Jesse?" she asked.

"He's going to be fine." Kirsten settled down beside her. "Stephen, too."

"I'm glad to hear that." Amber's gaze drifted to Kirsten's engagement ring, conjuring up forbidden images of Carter placing such a ring on her finger.

"You're in love with him, aren't you?"

Kirsten's query caught Amber off guard. She quickly ducked her head, hoping to hide the blush that was in full bloom on her cheeks. "Is it that obvious?"

"It's not hard for a woman in love to spot another of her kind."

Kirsten's reference to her relationship with Jesse stirred feelings of jealousy in Amber's heart. *I wonder if she knows how lucky she is.*

"Are you worried that he doesn't feel the same?" Kirsten asked.

"On the contrary," Amber told her. "I'm worried that he does."

Kirsten blinked in surprise. "I don't understand."

"Carter...he, uh...." Amber nearly choked on her reply. "He's not a believer."

That Kirsten understood. She was so blessed that Jesse loved the Lord as much as she did, perhaps to the point of taking such a blessing for granted sometimes. "Just because he isn't a believer now doesn't mean he won't be someday," Kirsten told her. "If you two are meant to be together, God will change his heart."

Someday, Amber thought. *But I love him now.* It was then that she remembered the gift she had given him right before he left. Her eyes brightened as she turned to tell Kirsten. "I gave him my Bible."

Kirsten smiled, reaching over to take her hand. "Then we'll be praying that he reads it."

* * * * *

Carter woke a few hours later, wrinkling his nose at the pungent aroma that was flooding the cabin. He slowly walked himself up onto his elbows, looking around for the cause. What in the world could it be?

"Would you like some vittles?" Lottie called from beside the fire. She indicated the big black pot that she was tending. "I got a whole mess of possum stew on to cook."

Possum? Was that what he was smelling? Carter wrinkled his nose again. "No thank you, ma'am. I'm not very hungry."

"Just let me know iffen ya change your mind."

Carter assured her that he would and then pushed himself all the way up to a sitting position so he could take a more thorough look around his new surroundings. As he did so, he noticed that his coat was draped over the back of a chair a few feet away. If his memory served him correctly, he still had a sandwich in one of the pockets. No offense to Lottie's possum stew, but he preferred ham and cheese.

Carter leaned over as far as he could to his left and managed to yank it free. After checking one of the pockets and finding it empty, he reached into the other. All he found for his effort was the Bible that Amber had given him before he left. "Can't eat that," he said with a scowl.

He was about to dismiss the small black book entirely when he recalled how surprised Amber had been that he had never read it before. But why, he wondered. Why was this book so important to her?

Carter thumbed aimlessly through the well-worn pages for a moment and then turned back to the table of contents. The name *John* leapt out at him almost immediately. Amber had mentioned something about John.

Spurred on by curiosity, Carter located the first page of the chapter and began reading silently to himself.

In the beginning was the Word, and the Word was with God, and the Word was God....

* * * * *

Alec continued to do what he could to tend to those in need of his care but the supply of quinine was running danger-ously low. If Carter was not back by morning, he would have no choice but to ride to Maytown himself, leaving Kirsten and Amber with the full responsibility of running things at the clinic during his absence.

Alec took his daughter by the shoulders, looking from her to Amber. "Do you two think you can handle things while I'm gone?"

"Of course we can, Pa," Kirsten assured him. She turned to Amber who quickly nodded the same assurance.

Alec smiled at them both. "I never should have doubted it for a second."

"Kirsten...?" Stephen appeared at the top of the stairs. "Will you tell me a story?"

Kirsten saluted her father, smiling as she headed for the stairs. "Duty calls, sir."

* * * * *

"It does my heart glad to see that you're a God fearin' man."

Carter looked up from his reading as Lottie approached, tracing her smiling gaze back to Amber's Bible. "Oh, no, ma'am," he blurted, anxious to refute her claim. "I was just—"

Lottie didn't give him the chance to complete his thought. "I took Him as my Savior when I was only six, and I never regretted it none since." She pulled up a chair beside the pallet, settling in for what appeared to be a long stay. "I can remember back when I was about your age...."

Carter smiled politely as she continued to share the testimonial of her faith, but all the while he was thinking to himself that it was going to be a very long night.

CHAPTER TWENTY-FOUR

SEEK AND YE SHALL FIND

"...and God bless Mama, and God bless Papa, and God bless Eric, and God bless Colin, and God bless Nathan, and God bless Kaitlin, and God bless Miss Amber, and God bless Carter, and God bless Jesse, and—"

"Stephen, that's enough God bless you's," Kirsten implored him. "Just say, amen."

"And God bless Kirsten. Amen." Stephen's big brown eyes popped open, which he proceeded to fix directly upon his sister. "Will you tell me another story?"

"No," Kirsten told him firmly, becoming wise to his antics. "I already told you three. It's time to sleep."

"But I'm not tired."

Kirsten ignored his protests and tucked a blanket up under his chin. "Good night, Stephen." She rose to her feet from beside his cot, shaking her head in awe of her mother's patience. "Honestly, I don't see how she does it. I'm worn out just putting one to bed."

Kirsten slipped across the hallway to check on Tad Randall, and by the time she returned, Stephen was fast asleep. Seeing that Mr. Cameron was also asleep, Kirsten took advantage of this rare opportunity to curl up beside

Jesse and just be lazy for a while. Her father would call for her if he needed help.

"This is nice," she said with a contented smile, snuggling her head against the side of his chest. "We've hardly had any time alone together since we got engaged. It's kind of romantic."

"I wouldn't call snuggling on a cot with my father snoring a few feet away romantic, but...."

Kirsten giggled quietly. "You know what I mean. I wouldn't care if we were in a whole room full of people. When I think about how close I came to losing you...." She bit the inside of her cheek to keep from crying out. "I've never been so scared in all my life," she confessed.

Jesse curled his arm tighter around her. "You didn't lose me. You are going to be my wife, Kirsten Ramsey. And we are going to have a whole passel of kids for you to put to bed every night."

Kirsten giggled again. "Oh, please."

"Kirsty...?"

Kirsten sat up beside Jesse as her father appeared in the doorway. The tone of his voice sent an unwelcome shiver down her spine.

"Zack just brought in the Thompson's. Their both sick."

"Oh, no." Kirsten turned to look back at Jesse, conveying her apologies.

"You go on," he urged her. "Your pa's going to need your help."

Kirsten reluctantly left Jesse's side and followed her father downstairs. Romance and influenza did not mix.

* * * * *

Lottie came to the end of her thought with a gasp. "Lands sakes, I've been babbling on for hours. My apologies to ya."

"No, don't apologize. I've really enjoyed listening to you." Carter was surprised to hear himself say that.

"Well, that's right kind of ya, but my man's been sawing a log for near an hour now and I best be joinin' him." She hefted her bulk out of the chair and began maneuvering towards the sound of snoring in the opposite corner of the cabin.

"If the lamp won't bother you," Carter called after her, "I'd like to read for awhile longer."

Lottie smiled to herself. "Ya go right ahead." She watched as the young man in her care picked up the small Bible to resume his reading. "Lord," she whispered on his behalf, "he be a seekin' tonight. Please let him find ya."

The hours ticked by but Carter was hardly aware of their passing. He couldn't explain what was driving him to keep reading, but he did know one thing—the Bible was no ordinary book, and Jesus had been no ordinary man. Carter recalled the joyful glow that had lit up Lottie's face as she had talked about Him, as if he were as near to her as her next breath, a friend that she could always turn to. He had seen that same glow in Amber's eyes many a time.

Carter stared hard at the book that he held in his hands, struck by a revelation that would forever change the course of his life. This book...this was where Amber drew her strength from.

In the beginning was the Word, and the Word was with God, and the Word was God....

This was the reason that she could look the death of her students in the face and not be shaken, because she knew that this life was not the end.

I want that, Carter realized with a longing that would only be quenched by the complete surrender of his heart. *I want what Amber and Lottie have.*

And yes, he now realized, what Alec and Kirsten and Jesse had. The list could go on and on.

Carter closed the Bible for a moment and pondered what he should say. There didn't seem to be adequate words enough. "God," he began uncertainly, "I don't know what I'm supposed to say, but I do know that I need you in my life. I accept the free gift of salvation that you offer through your son, Jesus Christ. Forgive me of my sins and make me whole in You.... Amen."

* * * * *

"Just a little bit more.... That's it." Kirsten supported Naomi Thompson's head as she drank down the dose of quinine that her father had prescribed.

"Bless you, dear," she murmured shakily as Kirsten lowered her back down onto the cot. Her head turned in search of her husband lying on the next cot over. His eyes were closed in sleep, his brow glistening with fever. "That man would do anything to get out of celebrating our wedding anniversary."

Kirsten smiled. "Today's your anniversary?"

"Forty-five years. And I love him more now than on the day I said 'I do'."

"Forty-five years...." A dreamy look appeared in Kirsten's eyes, as if she were trying to see that far into the future. "And Jesse and I are just starting out."

"You'll get there," Naomi said with unwavering confidence. "You've picked yourself a fine young man."

Kirsten smiled fondly at the older woman. "That means a lot coming from you."

"Kirsty, can I speak with you for a moment?"

"I'll be right back," she assured Naomi before rising from the cot to join her father in the doorway. He was holding a clear glass bottle with only a trace of white powder visible at the bottom. She knew immediately what his concern was.

Alec turned his back on the room, shielding their conversation from the occupants inside. "We only have enough quinine for them each to have one more full dose. Then we'll have to cut it in half after that."

"You make sure my Naomi gets a full dose every time, Kirsten."

Alec scowled at the owner of the comment. "Lands, Clive, you've got ears like a hawk. You weren't supposed to have heard any of that."

Clive reached over and tenderly grasped his wife's hand. "Just promise me that you'll take care of her first."

Alec looked helplessly at Kirsten. What else could he do? The reverend had spoken. "All right," he told the elder gentleman reluctantly. "Ladies first."

* * * * *

When Carter woke the next morning there was a fullness in his heart that he had never known before. His gaze came to rest reverently upon the Bible lying beside him as the events of last night came flooding back. *Amazing grace,* he thought to himself. There was no other way to describe it.

"Hungry?" Lottie called from beside the fire.

Carter thumped the sides of his stomach. "I feel like I could eat a horse."

"You'll have to settle for bacon and eggs. We're fresh outta horse."

Carter smiled. "Well, if that's all you have...."

Lottie placed a tray on his lap with enough food to satisfy his hunger three times over. Carter paused for a moment before beginning his meal to offer a word of thanks. He had always taken such things like food and clothing for granted in the past, but now it seemed so natural to say "thank you" to the One who had provided it all.

Halfway through his meal a nagging thought snaked its way into his mind and refused to leave. Why hadn't anyone come for him yet? Or at least sent word that they were aware of his situation? "Lottie…?" Carter paused in between bites of his eggs. "How long have I been here?"

"Let's see…." She pursed her lips as she bent over to remove a pot of coffee off the fire. "Been a day since my Earl found ya, I reckon."

A day. Almost two since he'd left Baxter. Something wasn't right. "Are you sure no one has come by asking about me?"

Lottie seemed reluctant to discuss the matter further. "Would ya be wantin' some coffee?" She pointed to the pot now sitting on the table. "It's fresh."

Carter's face paled as the unthinkable crossed his mind. "You did send that telegram, didn't you?"

Lottie walked slowly towards him, dry washing her hands out in front of her. "Neither me nor my Earl has the power to write none," she finally confessed. "But I can read some." She picked up his small Bible and began to demonstrate her ability with pride.

Carter tossed back the quilts that were covering him, ignoring the fact that he was only half dressed. Now was not the time to be concerned with modesty. "I've got to go." He rose unsteadily to his feet, searching for the remainder of his things. "I appreciate all that you've done for me," he said, reaching around her to pluck his shirt off a nail on the wall, "but there's an influenza epidemic in Baxter and they were running short of quinine when I left."

Lottie flashed him a big, toothless grin. "Influenzer, ya say. Shucks, all ya be needin' for that is willow bark tea. Takes the fever right down."

Carter froze in place with his shirt only halfway on. "Willow bark?"

Lottie nodded her head, setting her jowls to bobbing. "I've used it on my Earl many a time."

Do I dare trust her? Something told Carter that he had no choice. "Do you have any to spare?"

Another toothless grin. "How much do ya reckon ya be needin'?"

* * * * *

"Now let's go over everything one more time just to be sure."

"Pa." Kirsten's gaze told him that he was treating her like a two-year-old. "I couldn't be any more prepared than I am right now."

"All right." Alec leaned down and kissed her on the forehead. "I should be back by dark. But if I'm not—" The clinic door opened, distracting Alec from completing his thought. Carter stepped in looking as if he had just gone ten rounds with a grizzly bear. "Anybody looking for me?"

"Carter!" Kirsten ran to his side, taking first honors in welcoming him back.

Carter grinned as she threw her arms around him. "I ought to go away more often."

"Let's first clear the air about where you've been this time." Alec walked towards him, looking with concern at the bandage around his head.

"My horse threw me about a mile and a half from here." Carter explained. "But I'm all right. Some folks took real good care of me."

Alec didn't bother to ask him why he hadn't sent word of his whereabouts. He was back safe and sound and that's all that mattered. That, and one other thing. "What about the quinine?"

"I'm afraid it didn't fair as well I did. But...." Carter reached into his bag and took out a jar with a strange looking plant-like substance in it. "I have it on good authority that this will work just as well."

Alec took the jar from him, examining its' contents from all possible angles. "What is it?"

"Willow bark. You brew it into a tea."

Alec looked from Carter to the jar and then back to Carter again, wondering if his head injury was more serious than he claimed.

Carter sensed his skepticism. "Trust me, Alec."

Kirsten took the jar from her father, not at all shy about trying the new remedy. "I'll go boil some water."

Alec became aware that Amber was standing a few feet behind him, eagerly awaiting her own turn to welcome Carter back. "And I'll go...." He couldn't think of anything that needed doing. "I'll just go," he said with an awkward smile.

Carter's gaze went straight to Amber as Alec stepped out of the way. He had so much to tell her. Where to start? "Did you miss me?"

Amber wanted nothing more than to throw her arms around him as Kirsten had done earlier and declare her love, but for some reason all that came out of her mouth were words of rebuke. "Carter Buchanan, I don't know what you were thinking about riding out of here the way you did the other night! You're lucky you didn't break your neck!"

Carter reached into his coat pocket and took out the Bible that she had given him. He pressed it back into her hand. "I don't believe in luck."

Amber stood speechless, gazing up into his eyes as the meaning of his words became clear. A smile appeared on her lips, which Carter quickly covered with his own. Amber found herself responding back to his kiss, her hands moving up to lace together behind his head. When they finally moved apart, she was aware of nothing but the indescribable joy welling up inside her. He had come home, first to God, and then to her heart. And Amber knew that was where he would always stay.

* * * * *

Despite Alec's earlier skepticism, the Thompson's began showing signs of improvement after only a few doses of the willow bark tea. And Stephen…? Alec could no longer keep him in bed.

He chuckled as he stood watching the youngster jump back and forth between Jesse's cot and his own. "I think it's about time to send you home, young man. This clinic is for sick folks." Alec stepped forward and caught him in the middle of a jump. "What do you say? Should we go see your Ma?"

Kathleen was sweeping the back porch when Alec rode into the yard. He was startled by how exhausted she looked. *She shouldn't be working so hard,* he thought to himself. *Not in her condition.* Hopefully he would be able to remedy that real soon. Jesse, his father and Tad Randall were all well enough to go home. And Isaac Jameson and the Thompson's would be following in a day or so. Then barring any further outbreaks, he would be home to stay.

Kathleen stopped sweeping as he reined in alongside the porch steps. She leaned forward, resting on the handle of the broom. It was all that appeared to be holding her up. "Alec…I wasn't expecting you to come by today."

"I had a little delivery to make."

Kathleen followed his gaze to the side of the house just Stephen came running around the corner. "Mama!"

"Stephen!" Kathleen couldn't get down the porch steps fast enough. She swept him up into her arms, suddenly imbued with energy she didn't know she had. "Thank God you're all right." Her gaze quickly went back to Alec. "Kirsten and Jesse?"

"They're both fine, too. Kirsten is going to stay on at the clinic and help for the next few days but the immediate danger has passed."

Kathleen looked at him expectantly. "Does that mean...?"

Alec swung down off his horse, reaching her side in two lengthy strides. Kathleen tumbled into his arms. "Oh, Alec...if it had gone on one day longer...."

Alec put his chin down on top of her head, pulling her closer against him. "I know."

"Hey!" Stephen squawked. "You're squashin' me!"

The happy couple separated just enough to give the youngster some breathing room. Stephen looked back and forth between them. "I think I'm hungry."

Alec tossed him up in the air, eliciting a string of giggles. "What else is new?"

CHAPTER TWENTY-FIVE

I DO, TIMES TWO

September 1860

Alec watched from the doorway as Clive Thompson assisted his wife up into their buggy. It was hard to believe looking at them now that this was the same couple he had watched being carried into the clinic on the brink of death just five days before. They had both made a remarkable recovery. "Surely God was in this place."

"Amen to that."

Alec smiled over at Carter as he joined him at the door to see the Thompson's off. *What would I have done without him these last couple of weeks,* he wondered to himself. The young man had more than proven himself a capable physician, going above and beyond the call of duty during the recent epidemic. But what were his plans now that the crisis had passed?

Alec didn't even want to entertain the thought that he might still decide to return to Boston. It was solely Carter's decision to make, of course, but he intended to do everything he could to persuade him to stay. The town needed him. *I need him,* he admitted to himself. *And I'm not going to let him go without a fight.*

"Good-bye, Reverend!" Carter lifted his hand in a parting wave as the buggy pulled away. "See you in church on Sunday!"

Carter's reference to attending church on Sunday caused Alec to smile once again. The young man's conversion experience had been nothing short of miraculous, like Saul on the road to Damascus. Alec couldn't have orchestrated the circumstances any more perfectly if he had tried. Amber's Bible...Carter's fall from his horse.... Even Lottie and her possum stew. God had planned it all to draw Carter Buchanan to Himself and accomplish His perfect will. But did God's will for Carter also include him staying in Baxter? Alec knew that if it didn't he had to let the young man go, but it wasn't going to be easy.

Carter closed the door and turned to find Alec deep in thought. He knew exactly what was on his mind; the burning question that was begging to receive an answer. Carter decided not to keep him waiting for one any longer. His mind was made up. He knew where God wanted him to be. "We made a pretty good team, didn't we?" he started by saying.

Alec met Carter's gaze, sensing an opportunity to make a plug for his own cause to keep him in Baxter. "Yes, we did. It sure would be a shame to break things up now."

"I agree."

Alec felt the scale tipping slightly in his favor.

"I also think it's about time we put that sign up out front," Carter suggested. "Jesse's father was kind enough to make it for us. Be a shame not to display his handiwork."

"Us?" Alec wanted to pinch himself. "Does that mean you're going to stay?"

"I don't see how you could get along without me, Doc."

Alec smiled, clapping the younger man on the shoulder. "That's one thing I'm sure of."

The sound of a door closing somewhere on the second floor drew the attention of both men to the stairway. Isaac

Jameson appeared at the top a few moments later. He was the last of their patients to leave.

Alec watched his descent, mustering the closest thing to a smile as he could. "It's good to see you up and around, Mr. Jameson." He offered his hand, hoping to mend a few fences in the process. "I know we got off on the wrong foot that first day—"

Jameson pressed a wad of bills into Alec's open palm and then strolled out the door without uttering a word.

Carter was dumbfounded by his lack of gratitude. "Can you believe that? He didn't even say thank you."

Alec held up the wad of bills. "I think Mr. Jameson speaks in a different language."

Carter whistled as he studied the sizeable contribution the banker had made. "I'm not going to argue with what he said."

"Nor am I. This will more than cover all of the supplies we need to replace." Alec stuffed the money into his pocket for safekeeping. "Well, now that the fun is over, we've got some cleaning up to do. Do you want dishes or laundry?"

"Actually, neither. I was kind of hoping to go by the store this afternoon to see Amber." Carter hunched his shoulders. "You know."

Alec waved him on. "Go. And consider yourselves both invited to supper tonight."

"Thanks, Alec." Carter bolted for the door.

Alec looked around him at the now empty clinic. "So, Alec," he said to himself. "Do you want laundry or dishes?"

* * * * *

"Amber, dearest, are you quite certain about this?" Ida pinned her niece to the back wall of the store with a concerned gaze. "You hardly know this man."

"I know everything I need to know, aunty," the younger woman insisted. "And if he intends on going back to Boston, I'm going with him." A look of utter bliss lit up Amber's eyes as she began to enumerate Carter's many admirable qualities. "Carter Buchanan is the most gentle, loving, considerate—"

"Coming in the door!" Ida grabbed Amber's arm and jerked her attention around to the front of the store just as Carter walked in. "Well, if it isn't our young doctor from Boston." Her emphasis on the word Boston elicited a glare from Amber. "What brings you to our establishment this fine day?"

Carter saw no reason to keep secret the purpose for his visit. Everyone, including Amber, would know of his intentions soon enough. "I came to see, Amber." His gaze caressed her lovingly. "How are you?"

"Fine," she replied.

Ida jumped in before any further pleasantries could be exchanged. "Amber mentioned that you were thinking about returning to Boston."

Amber glared at her once again. "Aunt Ida."

"I was only repeating what I was told."

"Actually, ma'am, that was my original plan," Carter admitted in the elder woman's defense. "But things have—" He cut himself short as his gaze came to rest upon the notice tacked up on the bulletin board behind Amber's head. *Room For Rent* (inquire Crowley's General Store). "Excuse me, ma'am, but is that room still available?"

Ida squeezed her way in front of Amber, intrigued by his request. "You're interested?"

"Yes, ma'am. Alec has been kind to let me stay at the clinic but I'd like to have a place of my own."

Amber traded places with her aunt, coming within in inches of Carter. "Then you're not going back to Boston?"

"That's what I came by to tell you. I've decided to stay."

Amber wanted to hear him say that it was because of her, but it didn't really matter what his reasons were. He was staying. "I'm so glad," she said quietly, not wanting to appear too forward.

Ida took a far different view of his decision. She didn't know if she liked the idea of having this strange young man living under their roof, hanging around Amber till all hours of the night. What if anything did they really know about him? Yet if his staying kept her from traipsing off to Boston with him, then perhaps it was all for the best. At least with him here she could keep an eye on him.

"Would you like to see the room now?" she asked cordially.

"If it wouldn't be too much trouble, ma'am."

"I'll show it to him, Aunt Ida," Amber volunteered eagerly. "Didn't you say that you had something to do in the storeroom?"

Ida decided to humor her niece, though it went against her better judgment to leave them alone together. There was no telling what might happen. "Yes, I did. If you two will excuse me."

Amber waited until she was in the storeroom before leading Carter upstairs. "This is the room right here," she said, stopping at the first door they came to.

Carter followed her inside, taking only a brief look around before making his decision. "I'll take it," he announced, enjoying the look of surprise on her face.

"But you've hardly even looked around."

"I've seen all I need to see. It's exactly what I've been looking for."

Amber didn't know what to make of his comment. Was he talking about the room...or her?

Carter took a more thorough look around but it was a mere formality. His mind was made up. "It's plenty big enough. That is...." His gaze came back around, stopping directly upon her. "Until we need something bigger."

Amber's knees almost buckled beneath her. Had she heard him correctly? "We?"

Carter moved slowly towards her, gathering courage with each step. "I'll let you know right up front. I don't believe in long engagements."

Amber smiled in understanding. "How does next week sound?"

* * * * *

"You're not!"

"We are." Amber brushed past her aunt and took a seat on the stool at her dressing table.

Ida scurried up behind her. "But why so soon?"

"Carter says that he doesn't believe in long engagements. And frankly...." Amber vigorously took a brush to her hair. "I don't want to wait."

"But you hardly know one another," Ida argued further.

"I believe that's what the honeymoon is for."

Ida suppressed a gasp, shocked by her nieces' brazen tongue. "Amber, dearest, you've got to reconsider. What will your parents say?"

"Mama and Papa will offer us their blessing," she said confidently, "not try to discourage us."

"I'm not doing anything of the sort. I'm only trying to protect you."

Amber rose abruptly from the stool, coming face to face with her aunt. "I am twenty-two years old, a grown woman. Carter loves me and I love him. And we *are* going to be married. The sooner you accept that the better. Now if you will excuse me...." Amber plunked the brush firmly back down on the table. "Carter and I are expected at the Ramsey's for supper."

Ida watched with her mouth gaping as Amber strolled quickly from the room, stopping only to give Josiah a peck on the cheek before disappearing out the door. "I don't know what has gotten into that niece of yours."

Josiah gazed at her over the top of his newspaper. "My niece. And I suppose if she had taken your advice she'd be your niece."

"Exactly."

* * * * *

Alec's heart overflowed with thankfulness as he looked at each one present around their table that evening. For the first time in weeks they were all together as a family. And as if that weren't reason enough to celebrate, Carter and Amber had just announced their plans to wed. For once Kathleen's matchmaking instincts had proven her right.

"Will any of your family be able to attend the wedding?" Kathleen asked the bride-to-be.

"I'm afraid not. My father has been ill for some time and my mother won't travel alone." Amber's shoulders rose and fell with a shrug. "I don't have any brothers or sisters."

"That's a shame. But at least your aunt and uncle are here."

Amber shrunk back at the mention of her aunt. Their conversation earlier had upset her more than she realized. She knew that she didn't need it, but she wanted her aunt's approval of her and Carter's decision to wed just the same, especially if they were all going to be living under the same roof together. But would that be such a wise decision in light of their recent falling out? Amber was beginning to have her doubts. But where else could they go?

"Will you two be living at the store?" Alec wondered, fueling Amber's discomfort further.

"We were thinking about it," Carter told him. "But now...." He turned to Amber, pausing to search her eyes. "I'm thinking that it might be better if we get a place of our own."

Amber was surprised to hear him make such a declaration. She had never said one word to him about her conversation with her aunt, or her own uncertainties about their living at the store. How could he have known?

"In the meantime," Carter continued, turning back to Alec, "I'd like to keep my room at the clinic, if that's all right. Just until after the wedding. I'm sure I'll be able to find us a place by then."

"There's a nice two-story up for sale about a half mile out of town," Jesse told him. "I've had an eye on it myself but I'm no where near ready to make an offer. I'd be happy to drive you out there tomorrow if you'd like."

"Thank you, Jesse. I'd appreciate that." Carter turned again to Amber and was relieved to find a smile on her face. He had made the right decision.

"While we're on the subject of weddings...." Kirsten looked back and forth between her parents. "When are you two going to set a new date?"

Alec leaned back in his chair, exchanging a glance with Kathleen. "I guess we haven't given it much thought."

"How about next week?" Carter suggested. "We can make it a double ceremony."

Amber was instantly in favor of the idea.

Alec wasn't. "That wouldn't be fair to either of you. It's your special day."

"We wouldn't mind," Amber assured him. "Honestly."

Alec withdrew himself from the conversation in favor of having Kathleen make the decision. "All right," she consented. "But on one condition...." Her gaze came to rest upon the young woman seated to her right. "Amber has to agree to wear my wedding dress."

Amber's hands flew up to her mouth. "Oh, Kathleen."

"Heaven knows that I won't be able to fit into it by next week," Kathleen confessed, alluding to her ever-thickening waistline. "And I'd really like for you to wear it."

Amber whisked away a few tears, overwhelmed by her offer. "I'd be honored."

"Now that that's settled...." Carter slid an arm around Amber's shoulders. "All we have to do is plan our honeymoons."

Alec placed a hand on Kathleen's belly. "I'd think we've already had ours, but you two go right ahead."

"Alec!" Kathleen swatted his hand away.

Carter turned to his bride-to-be. "Any suggestions?"

Amber didn't need to think twice about where she wanted to go. "I've always wanted to see Niagara Falls."

"Then Niagara Falls, it is."

Stephen tapped Carter on the arm, looking up at him curiously. "Who's Niagara? And why'd she fall?"

* * * * *

Chicago

"Tell me another story, Uncle Sean. Please?"

Sean couldn't help cracking a smile as eight-year-old Emily trained her big green eyes on him. She was in top form tonight, and as usual, he didn't have the heart to tell her no. "What will it be? Goldilocks or Cinderella?"

Emily pondered her choices for a moment. "Cinderella'" she decided. "It's longer."

"Cinderella, it is. Once upon a time, in a land far, far away—"

"Are you really leaving tomorrow?"

319

Emily's query caught Sean off guard. He hadn't even been aware that she knew of his travel plans. "Yes, sweetie, I am. I have a very important job to do in Baltimore."

Emily sat up, throwing her slender arms around his neck. "I don't want you to go."

I don't want to go, either, Sean admitted to himself. But as much as he had enjoyed spending time with Rachel and her family, he had given Pinkerton his word and he wasn't about to go back on it now. Baltimore was waiting...and so was Hannah.

Emily turned her big green eyes on him once again. This time they were moist with tears. "Will you come back and visit us?"

Sean lifted a hand to the back of her head, gently stroking her long, auburn hair. "Every chance I get," he promised.

Emily gave him a final hug and then snuggled back down under the covers. "You don't have to tell me another story if you don't want to."

Sean smiled, picking up right where he had left off. "Once upon a time, in a land far, far away...."

Emily drifted off to sleep somewhere between Cinderella's arrival at the ball and the stroke of midnight. Sean dropped a kiss onto her forehead, blew out the lamp beside the bed and headed downstairs. He found Neal and Rachel enjoying their nightly chat by the fire. "Emily's finally asleep," he told them.

"How many stories did she wring out of you tonight?" Neal asked.

Sean grinned sheepishly. "Only four."

Neal chuckled. "You're worse than I am."

Rachel patted the empty space beside her on the sofa. "Come join us."

"Not tonight. I'm going to turn in. I've got a long day tomorrow."

"Speaking of which…." Neal leaned forward and gathered up a folder off the coffee table. "Pinkerton dropped this by for you. A little reading material for your trip."

Sean moved forward to take the folder. "What is it?"

"Your new identity."

Sean stared hard at his brother-in-law. "My what?"

"Pinkerton doesn't want to take the chance that someone might connect you back to Liam O'Brien and the robberies in Philadelphia, so he has taken the liberty of giving you a new identity. Name, background, that sort of thing. It's standard procedure."

Standard for who, Sean wondered. He opened to the first page of the file, curious to find out what his new name was going to be. "Shane Donavan?"

"At least you're still Irish," Neal joked.

Sean found nothing about the matter laughable. It was all finally beginning to sink in, the enormity of what he had agreed to do. He wasn't concerned for himself. After thirteen years of wandering from town to town, he reckoned he could put down roots just about anywhere. And as for changing his name, it wouldn't be the first time. But what about Hannah? Would she be happy leaving her life in Philadelphia to start over again in Baltimore, assuming a new identity? Was it fair of him to even ask that of her?

Maybe it would be better to wait until after he completed his obligation to Pinkerton before even thinking about asking her to marry him. He didn't like the idea of waiting, but it wasn't about what he wanted. It was about what was best for Hannah. Either way, he would have to make a decision soon. She was expecting him in Philadelphia in a few days and he had already alluded to her in a recent letter that he had something important to speak with her about. She was a smart woman. He was sure that she had probably figured it out by now.

Neal rose to answer an unexpected knock at front the door, leaving Rachel to sort out the troubled look on her brother's face. "Are you all right?"

Sean closed the file, fixing her with a tremulous smile. "Just tired, I guess."

Rachel may have missed out on a lot in her brother's life, but she still knew him well enough to know when he wasn't being straight with her. "It's Hannah, isn't it?"

Sean's guilty expression gave him away.

"Are you worried that she won't accept your proposal?"

"Actually…." Sean sat down on the arm of the sofa. "I'm worried about what might happen if she does."

Rachel moved closer to him. "What do you mean?"

"What if something should happen to me?" he cited for example. "She would be all alone in a strange city, no family, no friends." Sean shook his head. "How can I ask her to marry me now?"

Rachel reached out and closed her hand over his. "As hard as it may be, that's something you're going to have to let Hannah decide for herself."

Sean knew she was right. Hannah would have to make up her own mind. But the decision to propose or not was still up to him, and he wasn't so sure anymore that now was the right time. "I just wish I had a sign."

"Hey, you two, look who's here?"

Sean and Rachel turned curiously to see who Neal had with him. "Charlie!" Rachel rounded the sofa and ran straight into his arms. "Oh, Charlie, it's so good to see you."

"I apologize for coming by so late but I be needin' to speak with Sean."

Sean moved towards him, recalling the last time they had spoken. The older man had been overjoyed to the point of shedding tears when he had asked for Hannah's hand in marriage. Sean didn't have the heart to tell him that he was now having second thoughts. "Is something wrong, Charlie?"

Charlie looked his future son-in-law straight in the eye, his voice strong and steady. "I sold me bakery today and I be going with ya ta Baltimore."

The room became so quiet that Sean could almost hear the beating of his own heart. "You sold the bakery?"

"Aye," he said with a nod of his head. "And I be going with ya ta Baltimore."

Sean could hardly believe what he was hearing. Hannah's father was not talking about visiting them for a week or two and then returning to Chicago. He was talking about moving to Baltimore permanently.

Charlie laid a hand against the breast pocket of his overcoat. "I already got me ticket for tomorrow's train so it won't do ya any good ta try and talk me out of it."

"Does Hannah know?"

Charlie's eyes welled with love at the mention of his daughter. "I want ta surprise her."

She'll certainly be that, Sean thought. *But no less than I am.* "I don't know what to say." At least that was one thing he could be completely honest about.

"Good. Then I won't be hearing any objections."

Neal clapped the elder man on the back. "How about some coffee, Charlie?"

"That would be much appreciated, Neal."

Rachel smiled up at her brother as Charlie followed Neal into the kitchen. "Is that a clear enough sign for you?"

* * * * *

Amber had been hoping to avoid any further confrontation with her aunt that night but Ida was waiting for her as she walked through the door. The younger woman immediately went on the defensive. "You didn't have to wait up for me," she spat, tossing her shawl onto the arm of the sofa. "I'm not a child."

"I know," Ida said calmly. She was as anxious to avoid another confrontation as Amber, but there were still a few things that she felt had to be said, starting with an apology. "Did you have a nice time at the Ramsey's?"

"Very nice." Amber settled onto the sofa, drawing her feet up under her.

Ida fished around for something more to say. "I suppose that Carter will be moving his things in tomorrow."

"No, he won't," Amber said bluntly.

Ida stared at her niece, puzzled by this sudden turn of events. The young doctor had seemed so set on renting the room above the store. What had changed his mind? Was the wedding off as well?

"He's decided to stay at the clinic until after we're married," Amber explained. "He doesn't think it would be proper for us to be living under the same roof before then. And besides...." She hesitated, unsure how to break the news to her aunt that she and Carter would not be living above the store even after they were married. Why was it so difficult for her? Isn't it what she wanted? "Carter thinks that it would be best if we get a place of our own. He'll be looking at a house for sale tomorrow."

Amber's announcement took Ida by surprise but she knew that it shouldn't have. Josiah had warned her that something like this might happen if she persisted in opposing Amber and Carter's desire to marry. She had no one to blame but herself. Not only had she hurt her niece deeply, but now she had driven her away as well.

Amber got up from the sofa. "I'm going to bed."

"Amber, wait."

"Aunt Ida, I already know how you feel about my marrying Carter and there's nothing more you can say to change my mind."

"Please," Ida urged her. "Just hear me out."

Amber wavered for a moment and then retook her seat on the sofa. "I'm listening."

Ida plowed straight ahead, trusting that the words would come. "When we received word that you were coming out here to live with us, it was one of the happiest days of my life. As you know, your uncle and I were never able to have children of our own. And I guess over time...." The elder woman grew misty-eyed. "Well, I've come to think on you as if you were my own daughter."

Amber felt her defenses beginning to crumble. She had never known how painful not being able to have children had been for her aunt.

"I suppose that's why I've been so reluctant to give you and Carter my blessing," she confessed. "I didn't want to lose you."

"Oh, Aunt Ida." Amber jumped up and grabbed hold of her hands. "You're not going to lose me. And if you want us to live here for awhile after we're married, we will."

"No, sweetheart. That wouldn't be fair to either of you. Newlyweds need a place of their own."

Amber pulled her close. "Will you stand up with me? With Mama and Papa not able to come, you're the only family I have."

Amber's request set Ida to bawling. Amber quickly joined her.

Josiah stumbled out of their bedroom, half asleep. "What's going on out here?"

Ida turned to him with a toothy grin. "Shake the dust off your good suit, Josiah. You've got a bride to give away."

CHAPTER TWENTY-SIX

THE SIN OF GREED

Carter met Jesse outside the blacksmith's shop early the next morning. He was eager to begin his search for a place that he and Amber could call home. She had given him a detailed "it must have" list, and from Jesse's description of the property they were going to look at, it sounded like a perfect match.

"How long has it been up for sale?" Carter asked as the two men set off in Jesse's buckboard.

"Only a couple of weeks. The current owners are moving west. California, I think. I'm really surprised that it hasn't sold yet. You'll understand why when you see it."

"You mentioned that you were interested in it yourself."

"Yeah," Jesse said with a wistful smile. "But I could never afford it, not now. Besides,

Kirsten and I aren't getting married until next spring. I figure that we've got plenty of time to find something else by then."

Carter was surprised to hear they were planning a spring wedding. Why were they waiting so long? Or were he and Amber moving too fast? "Do you think Amber and I are rushing things?" he asked the younger man.

Jesse turned the tables on him. "Do you think you are?"

"I didn't at first. But when you mentioned that you and Kirsten were waiting until spring…it made me wonder. We have only known each other a few weeks."

"So did Alec and Kathleen before they were married, and that was twenty-three years ago."

"So in other words, you think I'm worrying for nothing."

"I think you should do what's right for you and Amber. I personally believe in long engagements. That's why Kirsten and I decided to wait. But that doesn't mean you two should."

Carter smiled, clapping him on the shoulder. "Thanks, Jesse."

"You can thank me later. Right now let's find you two a place to live."

Jesse pulled the wagon off the main road five minutes later and followed the winding drive that led up to a beautifully whitewashed two-story house. Carter was immediately impressed by what he saw. It was exactly as Jesse had described it, something right out of a fairy tale, picket fence and all.

Amber would love this, Carter thought as he stepped down from the buckboard to get a better view. It wasn't an overly large house, he noted, but what it lacked in size, it more than made up for in charm and character. If the inside was anything like the outside, his search was over. He had found their new home.

"So what do you think?" Jesse asked needlessly.

"It's perfect," Carter pronounced.

"Now you know why I've had my eye on it. Come on. I'll introduce you to the owners."

Jesse led the way up the cobbled walkway to the front door. He knocked twice and then waited for what seemed a reasonable length of time before knocking again. "Mr. Caldwell?"

Several minutes passed with no reply from inside. "It doesn't look like they're home."

Carter's spirits sank. He had been hoping to at least see the inside, and perhaps even make an offer if everything checked out.

"We could wait awhile if you want," Jesse offered. "Maybe they just went into town."

Carter moved a few steps to his right and shielded his eyes as he peered through one of the front windows. "I think we might have a long wait. It's empty."

Jesse took a look for himself and then swung his gaze around to the buckboard. "Come to think of it, I didn't see the for sale sign when we drove up."

"There's a good explanation for that, gentlemen. The property has already been sold."

Carter's expression soured as Isaac Jameson appeared around the side of the house.

"I wonder what he's doing here?" Jesse whispered.

"I think I know."

Jameson entered the yard through a side gate, swinging a gold knobbed walking stick beside him. He came to a stop directly in front of Carter, looking quite pleased with himself. "As I previously stated, gentlemen, the property has already been sold. I took possession just this morning."

Carter's spirits sank even lower. There went Amber's dream home. "Any chance you're ready to sell?" he asked in a purely joking manner.

"Perhaps.... If the price is right."

Carter wasn't sure what game Jameson was playing but he was willing to ante up just to find out. "How much?"

Jameson quoted him an amount that set Carter to laughing. "You've got to be kidding."

"That's twice what it's worth," Jesse threw in.

"Maybe so, but that's what I'm asking."

Carter knew there was little hope of changing Jameson's mind. He had obviously

Purchased the property solely for the purpose of making a quick buck and had no intention of occupying it himself. Carter, however, refused to play into his hand. The stakes were much too high.

"So...." Jameson's left brow arched ever so slightly. "Do we have a deal?"

"Forget it. I'll find something else."

"I wouldn't count on it. I'm in the process of buying up all the available property in the area. By the time I'm through—"

"Then I'll build," Carter asserted.

"On what?"

It took all the restraint that Carter could muster to keep himself from landing the arrogant banker on his backside. "You'll never get away with this."

"I already have," Jameson said smugly. "Now, if there is nothing further I can assist you gentlemen with, I will kindly ask you to vacate my property."

"Gladly," Carter sneered back.

Jesse grabbed Carter's arm before any more words could be exchanged and steered him back to the buckboard.

"I have never met a more self-serving, pompous—" Carter took a deep breath to calm himself down. "Now I know why he was so anxious to buy the clinic."

"What are you going to do?"

"I'll tell you what I'm not going to do. I'm not going to let that man rob Amber and me of the chance to have a home of our own." Carter climbed up onto the seat of the buckboard. "He's got to have a chink in his armor somewhere. But until I figure out what it is, we'll just have to live at the store with her aunt and uncle."

Jesse climbed up beside him and unwound the reins from the brake handle. He understood Carter's frustration and wanted to do whatever he could to help. After all, the same thing could happen to them when he and Kirsten were ready to buy their first house.

Jameson had to be stopped. But how?

"If you've got any ideas, just sing out," Carter told him.

Jesse turned to face him. "I think I might."

"What?"

"Does Jameson know that you and Amber are engaged?"

"I don't see how he could. We only announced it last night."

"That's it, then."

"What is?"

Jesse smiled. "A way to give Isaac Jameson a taste of his own medicine. I'll explain

on the way back to town."

* * * * *

Amber caught her breath when she saw herself in Kathleen's wedding dress. "Oh, Kathleen. It's so beautiful."

"I think you might have a little something to do with that." Kathleen swept up Amber's hair and fanned it out evenly around her shoulders. "Carter Buchanan is a very lucky man."

Amber pivoted from side to side in front of the mirror, taking in every angle of her reflection. "Are you absolutely sure about this, Kathleen? I'll understand if you change your mind."

"I'm sure. Besides, what else are you going to wear? Your Aunt Ida's dress?"

Amber giggled at the reference to her aunt's full figure. "I think the wedding would be over by the time we finished all the alterations. But this...." She pivoted again, admiring the perfect fit of Kathleen's dress. "It's like it was made for me."

"It does suit you," Kathleen had to agree.

Amber turned to her. "By the way, what are you going to where?"

Kathleen rested a hand on her thickening waistline. "Your Aunt Ida's dress?"

The two women erupted into laughter just as Kirsten slipped into the room. "I hate to break up the party, ladies, but the bridegroom is downstairs and he wants to see bride."

Amber let out an excited squeal. "He must have news about the house." She was halfway out the door before Kathleen could catch her.

"Amber, the dress! You can't let Carter see you in it."

Amber stamped her foot. "Oh, drat. I'm sorry, Kathleen. I don't know where my head has been lately."

Kathleen smiled as she reached up to unbutton the back of the dress. "I think I know.

Now you go ahead and change. I'll go keep the groom company."

Carter was already being thoroughly entertained by the time Kathleen made her way downstairs. Stephen had just returned home from his fishing trip with Eric and was excitedly sharing the story of his catch. "It was this big!"

Carter exchanged a smile with Kathleen as Stephen's hands kept moving further and further apart with the telling.

"Lands sakes, Stephen. I'm not sure if Mama has a frying pan big enough."

The youngster stared at his hands for a moment and then moved them closer together.

"Do you have one this big, Mama?"

"That I can do."

Stephen faced Carter again. "It was this big!"

"That's quite a catch."

"I'll say it was. Now you run along and get cleaned up for lunch." Kathleen shooed him upstairs and then turned to greet Carter. "Amber will be right down."

"There's no rush."

Kathleen read a different story in his eyes. "I gather the house hunting didn't go too well."

"Not exactly." Carter shared with her what had happened during his visit to the Caldwell property with Jesse.

Kathleen was shocked. "I can't believe that he would do that. And after everything you did for him during the epidemic."

"Well, he did."

"If you don't mind me asking, what are you going to do?"

"Jesse has this idea to—" Carter cut short his explanation as Amber came hurrying down the stairs. She planted a kiss on his cheek and then began firing off questions about the house.

How many rooms did it have? How big was the kitchen? Did it have a separate dining room? He didn't have the heart to tell her that he had never even seen the inside, unless you count the few seconds he had spent peeking in the front window. When he was finally able to get a word in edgewise it wasn't at all what Amber had been expecting to hear. "Kathleen, is there someplace that Amber and I can talk in private?"

"Certainly."

Amber never once took her eyes off Carter as Kathleen showed them into Alec's study.

Why was he being so secretive about the house? The news couldn't be that bad, could it? "Carter, what's going on?" she demanded to know as soon as they were alone.

Carter did his best to explain for her what had happened, just as he had for Kathleen. Her initial reaction was much the same. "Why would he do that?"

"I don't know," Carter admitted, mentally scratching his head for answers. "But for some reason he has it in for me."

Amber reached to take his hands. "Don't worry. There'll be other houses. And in the meantime, I don't mind living at the store."

Carter tightened his grip on her hands. "What if I told you there still might be a way for us to get this house?"

Amber questioned him silently with her eyes. *How?*

"You could buy it," he told her.

Amber had the urge to look behind her to see if he was speaking to someone else. "Me?"

"It was Jesse's idea. He figures that since Jameson doesn't know we're engaged...."

"But what makes you think he'll be any more likely to sell it to me?"

"I don't know that he will," Carter told her honestly. "But at least it's worth a try."

Amber's first reaction was that the house must be something pretty special to have Carter so fired up about it. But then she realized that it wasn't about the house at all. It was about standing up to people like Isaac Jameson who used their power and position at the expense of others to satisfy their own greedy desires. She was proud of Carter for wanting to take that stand. And if he was willing to do so, then the least she could do was to stand with him.

"I'll understand if you don't want to do it," Carter assured her. He was prepared to let the whole matter drop at her say so, no questions asked. "Like you said, there'll be other houses."

Amber reached up and needlessly began straightening his tie. "Do you think that Jameson is back in his office by now?"

Carter swallowed anxiously. "I saw his buggy outside the bank on my way here."

"Then I'd better be going."

Carter took her by the shoulders, looking long and hard into her eyes. "Are you sure about this?"

Amber's smile erased any doubts about her intentions. "Just leave him to me."

* * * * *

Amber found herself walking through the front door of the bank twenty minutes later.

She was relieved to see that there were no other customers inside at the time, only a mousy looking young man behind the counter that she assumed to be the teller. "Thank you, Lord," she whispered. The last thing that she wanted for her acting debut was an audience. She was nervous enough as it was.

"Can I help you, ma'am?"

"Yes." Amber went forward to the counter, smiling politely through the row of bars that separated her from the gentleman on the other side. "I'm here to see Mr. Jameson."

"Do you have an appointment, ma'am?"

Amber's smile slipped away. "I wasn't aware that I needed one."

"Well, Mr. Jameson is, uh…." The young man cleared his throat "Indisposed at the moment. But if you'd care to take a seat, I'm sure he'll be with you shortly."

"Thank you." Amber turned and made her way to one of the padded chairs in the corner.

As she sat waiting for Jameson, she began having second thoughts about what she was there to do. She knew it was wrong of her to mislead him into believing that she wanted to buy the house for herself when it was really for her and Carter both, but what else was she to do? She had already told Carter that she'd do it. And if she didn't, Jameson would continue his scheming ways and eventually put a stranglehold on the entire town. She could never live with herself if that happened. He needed to understand that they were not going to abide anything but fair and honest dealing, and she was now in a position to deliver that message to him personally.

Amber released a lengthy sigh. "Just relax," she told herself. "You're fretting for nothing."

"Amber, dear."

Amber looked up with a gasp at the sound of the all too familiar voice. Out of all the people who could have walked through the door at that moment, why did it have to be Eliza Tate?

The woman had the distinct reputation of being a busybody, and Amber for one didn't want to be the next hot topic of conversation around her supper table that evening.

"My heartiest congratulations, young lady."

Amber tried to play dumb. "For what?"

"For what." Eliza Tate made a tsk-tsking sound with her tongue. "There's no need to be so modest with me, dear. I was just in the store earlier—"

Please don't mention Carter, Amber pleaded with her.

"—and your aunt told me all about your engagement to that fine young doctor from Boston."

Amber stole a glance at the door behind the counter, which she assumed led into Jameson's office. He could come walking out at any moment and hear everything. If he hadn't, already.

Eliza Tate was yapping loud enough to wake the dead. *I've got to get her out of here! She's going to ruin everything!*

"She also told me that you're looking to buy a—"

"Mrs. Tate!" Amber jumped up and whispered something in the elder woman's ear. She proceeded to gasp, turn several shades of red and go scurrying back out the door. Amber breathed a sigh of relief as she retraced her steps back to her chair. She was certain that word of her inappropriate tongue would eventually make its way back to her aunt, but it was better than having Jameson learn of her engagement to Carter.

The banker emerged from his office a few minutes later. "Ah, Mr. Jameson." The teller directed his attention towards Amber. "There is a young woman here to see you. She doesn't have an appointment—"

Jameson silenced him with an upraised hand as his gaze fell upon Amber. "Thank you, Jason. That will be all for now. Why don't you take an hour for lunch."

The young teller's face lit up as if he had just been offered free access to the vault.

"Yes, sir. Thank you, sir."

Amber's stomach churned nervously as Jameson stepped out from behind the counter and strode towards her. "Miss Lloyd, isn't it?"

"Yes." Amber rose and took his extended hand with a smile. "Thank you for seeing me."

"The pleasure is all mine, I assure you. Why don't we step into my office where we can talk more freely."

Amber didn't like the idea of being alone with him in his office, or anywhere else for that matter, it couldn't he helped. "That will be fine."

Jameson put an "OUT TO LUNCH" sign in the window and then locked the front door before escorting Amber back to his office.

"I'm quite flattered that you remembered my name, Mr. Jameson."

"On the contrary. It's I who am flattered. And grateful. I never got to properly thank you for the exceptional care you gave me during the recent unpleasantness."

"Thanks are hardly necessary. Besides, it's Doctor Ramsey and Doctor Buchanan who deserve all the credit." Amber hoped that her casual mention of Carter hadn't tipped her hand. If Jameson suspected anything, however, he didn't let on.

"So, what can I help you with today?"

"Well...." Amber settled onto the chair that he was holding out for her. "I'd like to buy a house. More specifically...." Her gaze followed him as he stepped behind the massive desk that occupied nearly a third of his office space "I'd like to buy the Caldwell property."

Jameson paused midway to his chair and then slowly sank the rest of the way. "The Caldwell property."

"Yes. I've admired it ever since I moved here three months ago. And then when I learned that it was for sale.... Well, I can't tell you how delighted I am at the thought of being able to own it myself."

Jameson leaned forward with his hands folded in front of him on the desk. "You aren't aware then that I took possession of the property just this morning?"

"You—" Amber brought a hand up to her mouth. "Oh, I'm so embarrassed. If I had known I never would have—" She rose abruptly to her feet, pulling out a lace hanky which she used to dab at the pretend tears in her eyes. "I'm sorry to have taken your time. Please do excuse me."

"Miss, Lloyd, wait." Jameson rushed out from behind his desk, grabbing for her arm.

"I can see how much this property means to you. I'm sure we can come to some agreement that will be mutually beneficial for both of us. That is, if you're still interested."

"Of course I am, but...." Amber sniffed, dabbing once again at her eyes. "I'm sure that I could never afford it, not now."

"What if I could guarantee you that you could?"

Amber lowered the hanky from her eyes, staring at him intently.

"I'll sell it to you for what I paid for it," Jameson explained. "Plus my fees, of course.

But they're modest, I assure you."

Amber was stunned by his offer. It was more than she could have hoped for. "Oh, but...that hardly seems fair to you," she told him, taking her role as the damsel in distress to the next level.

"I think it's fair." Jameson inched closer to her. "That house was made for you. I want you to have it."

Amber didn't have to act the part of being excited. Jesse's plan was working perfectly.

"Oh, Mr. Jameson. I can't tell you how much this means to me. If you only knew...."

"Then perhaps you'd care to further express your gratitude." Jameson reached up and

caressed her cheek with the backs of his fingers. "Over supper tonight...at my place."

Amber recoiled from his touch, shuddering at the suggestive nature of his invitation.

"Another time, perhaps," she said politely. "How soon can you have the papers drawn up?"

"Give me two hours."

"Fine. I'll be back."

After seeing Amber to the front door, Jameson returned to his office to celebrate his latest conquest. He knew that he was sacrificing the potential for a sizeable profit by letting her have the house at cost, but he didn't mind. He could easily get it back if and when he should choose to do so. "And I'll have Amber Lloyd as well."

* * * * *

After learning of Jameson's inappropriate advances, Carter insisted that Amber take her uncle along with her when she returned to sign the papers. Amber didn't argue with him. Jameson made her extremely uncomfortable and she had not been looking forward to setting foot back in his office. But with her uncle there to keep him in line, she would be able to relax some and actually enjoy the experience ahead of her. She was about to become a homeowner.

"What do you think, Uncle Josiah?" Amber watched anxiously as he looked over the papers that Jameson had prepared for her to sign. If there were anything out of the ordinary he would be sure to find it. That was another reason that Amber was thankful he had come along.

She knew nothing about such matters and it would have been easy for Jameson to take advantage of her. Besides, it had been worth it just to see the look on the banker's face when her uncle had followed her into his office. He had not been at all pleased.

"I think Mr. Jameson is a very generous man to be letting the house go at this price."

Jameson leaned back in his chair, basking in Josiah's flattery. "Well, when I saw how much your niece admired it, how could I refuse."

Josiah laid the papers on the desk in front of Amber. "Everything seems to be in order, darlin'. Whenever you're ready."

Amber took a deep breath as she picked up the quill pen that had been provided for her use. As she began to sign, she couldn't help but think about Carter. He should be the one here closing the deal on their first home, not her. But all of the documents would have to remain solely in her name until after the wedding next week. Then they could add his. That is, if Jameson allowed them to. Amber was a little nervous about how he was going to react to the news that Carter was her fiancé. She had already decided that she would tell him herself rather than have him hear it somewhere else, but only after she had the keys to the Caldwell property firmly in hand.

Amber finished signing the last of the papers and then slid them across the desk. "All finished."

Jameson briefly reviewed each one before handing her back her copies. "Congratulations,

Miss Lloyd. You are now a homeowner."

"Oh, thank you, Mr. Jameson." Amber crushed the papers against her chest. "I can hardly believe that it's really ours. My fiancé will be so surprised. He has no idea."

Jameson's face lost all expression. "Your fiancé?"

"Yes. Doctor Buchanan. Didn't you know? We're to be married next week. The house is going to be my wedding gift to him."

Jameson was furious with himself for not seeing this coming sooner. After his heated confrontation with Carter Buchanan earlier that morning, he should have realized the young man would try something deceptive to gain possession of the house. But he never would have expected that deception to come in the form of Amber Lloyd. He had to hand it to her. She had played her role flawlessly.

"I'll have to ask you not to say anything about the house to him until then," Amber requested. "I want it to be a surprise."

Jameson forced a smile to his lips. "I wouldn't dream of it."

"I appreciate that. Now...." Amber held out her hand, palm up. "I believe there's still the matter of the keys?"

Jameson retrieved them from the top drawer of his desk and dropped them reluctantly into her hand. "The keys."

"Thank you again." Amber rose to her feet with a parting smile. "We really must be going now. I have so many things to do before the wedding next week. Don't bother seeing us out."

Jameson sat unmoving at his desk after they left. He wasn't aware of anything but the ticking of the clock above his head until Jason knocked a half hour later.

"Mr. Jameson?" The young teller took the liberty of poking his head in the door when there was no response from inside. "I'm sorry to disturb you, sir, but your three o'clock appointment is here."

"Cancel it."

"Sir?"

"Cancel all of my appointments. I'm not feeling well."

"Yes, sir."

Jameson sequestered himself in his office for the remainder of the day, refusing to speak with anyone. He was embarrassed enough to admit to himself that he had been taken by a woman, but he didn't dare let word of it get outside the walls of the bank. He would never be taken seriously as a businessman again. For now, he would have to let Amber Lloyd enjoy her little victory, but only until he could figure out a way to regain possession of the house. Sooner or later an opportunity would present itself.

"You may have won this round, Buchanan," he seethed, "but I can guarantee you the fight's not over."

* * * * *

Amber giggled as Carter picked her up and carried her through the front door of their new home. "Carter Buchanan, you put me down!" she insisted. "We're not even married yet."

"I was just practicing for next week." Carter set her back on her feet and then swung his arms out to his sides. "So what do you think?"

Amber's gaze swept the room they were standing in, drinking in every detail from moldings to windowpanes. "Oh, Carter, it's absolutely perfect. Better than anything I could have ever imagined. All we need now is some furniture. A sofa by the window, some chairs by the fireplace—" Amber fell silent when she saw what she mistook for regret in Carter's eyes. How could she have been so insensitive, prattling on about buying furniture when he had barely even gotten his practice up and running? And she certainly couldn't afford much on her teacher's salary. Furniture was a luxury they would have to do without. "I'm sorry if I got carried away," she apologized. "I realize that it will be awhile before we can afford such things. But I don't mind," she hurried to add, hoping to alleviate any pressure he may be feeling about providing for her. "Who needs furniture, anyway?"

Carter stepped forward and took her hands. "We may not have to wait as long as you think. I wasn't going to say anything until after the wedding, but my father left me a sizeable inheritance when he passed on. I want you to go into your uncle's store and order anything you want for the house."

Amber shook her head in protest. "No, Carter, I couldn't. That money is yours."

"It's *ours*," he argued. "And since you bought the house...." A smile appeared on his lips. "I figure the least I can do is furnish it."

Amber pulled away from him, turning to gaze into the empty fireplace. Ever since leaving Jameson's office earlier she had been wrestling with her conscience about what she'd done. Carter's reminder only fueled her guilt all the more. "I'm still not sure we did the right thing," she confessed, putting a voice to her concerns. "Maybe we should have just looked for another house."

Carter stepped up behind her, slipping his arms around her waist. "The man needed to be taught a lesson, Amber. And besides, he didn't have to sell you the house if he didn't want to. It was his decision. You've done nothing wrong."

"Deep down in my heart I know that. But I still feel...." Amber turned back to face him.

"What if he makes trouble for us?"

"He won't. He's too proud to let on to anyone about what happened." Carter smiled down into her eyes. "And

I'm proud of you. You handled everything perfectly. Even Eliza Tate."

"I have to admit I was a little nervous when she walked in. I thought for sure she was going to spoil everything."

"Speaking of Eliza Tate...." Carter looked at her curiously. "Just what was it you said to her?"

Amber suppressed a chuckle as she leaned forward to whisper it in his ear.

Carter grinned at her as she stepped back. "Amber Lloyd. Just what sort of brazen vixen am I about to marry?"

CHAPTER TWENTY-SEVEN

TIL DEATH DO US PART

Philadelphia

S ean's heart began pounding in his chest as the hack that he and Charlie were riding in came to a stop in front of the boardinghouse. It had been nearly a month since he had seen Hannah and he was aching to hold her in his arms again. But would she still feel the same about him? There had been nothing in her letters to suggest otherwise, but sometimes there were things that just couldn't be said in a letter.

"Nervous, lad?" Charlie asked him as they stepped down.

"Now what ever gave you an idea like that?"

After paying the driver and retrieving their bags, the two men walked slowly up to the front door. Sean was about to knock when Charlie reached out to stop him. "Not just yet, lad. There's something I be wantin' ya ta know before we go in."

"Sure, Charlie." Sean leaned back against the porch railing, facing the elder man. "What's on your mind?"

"Me daughter."

Sean smiled. "That makes two of us."

Charlie stared at the young man before him, overcome with emotion. "I never told ya this before, but I've always had a secret hope in me heart that ya were the one for me Hannah, ever since that first day ya wandered into me shop."

Sean had no trouble recalling the day in question. He remembered it well. "I couldn't have been more than ten years old."

"That ya were. And me Hannah was smitten with ya even then."

Sean pushed himself away from the railing. "She was there that day?"

"Hiding behind the counter, she was. Ya didn't know that, did ya?"

"No," Sean admitted. "But that does explain why she started following me home from school everyday."

"Aye. Like a lovesick pup, she was. Nearly broke her heart the day ya—" Charlie quickly dismissed the remainder of his thought. "But that's in the past now. Ya two have a second chance, which is more than most ever get."

"If she'll have me."

"Ya two were meant to be together, lad," Charlie assured him. "Don't ever be doubtin' that. Besides, if she turns ya down, she'll be havin' her Pa ta answer to."

Sean smiled. "I may have to take you up on that." He turned again to knock but found his attempt blocked for a second time.

"There's one more thing I be needin' ta tell ya...."

As Sean stood waiting for the elder man to continue, he was struck by how tired he appeared to be. "Charlie, are you all right?"

Both men started as the door opened behind them. Sean turned to face a smiling Mrs. Tyler. "I thought I heard voices out here."

"Good morning, Mrs. Tyler."

"Sean, my boy. I can't tell you how good it does my heart to see you again. And Mr. Cavanaugh...." Her gaze settled affectionately upon Charlie. "Hannah didn't mention that you were coming."

"I wanted ta surprise her."

"Well, come on in here, both of you. You must be chilled to the bone."

Sean followed Charlie inside, setting their bags down in the entryway. He took a quick look around but didn't see any sign of Hannah. It would be his own fault if she had already made other plans. He had failed to let her know they would be arriving a day early.

"She just stepped out back to bring in the wash," Mrs. Tyler told him. "And none too soon by the look of that sky. I think we're in for a real downpour. Shall I tell her that you're here?"

"No, thank you, ma'am. I'll tell her."

Hannah was just gathering the last of the laundry off the line when Sean stepped out the back door. He slowly began moving up behind her, grateful for the rumble of thunder overhead to drown out the sound of his approach.

Hannah scowled as a single drop of rain pelted her cheek, foretelling of things to come. "Don't you dare," she warned, casting a scathing glare at the darkening sky overhead.

After quickly taking down the last of the sheets, she turned to pick up the large wicker basket sitting on the ground behind her. A startled gasp escaped her lips when she found another set of hands already gripping the handles. "Might I be of some assistance, ma'am?"

"Sean!" Hannah catapulted himself into his arms, causing him to drop the basket. "Oh, Sean, you're really here! Why didn't you tell me you were coming a day early? I wasn't expecting you until tomorrow."

"It's my fault. I should have wired ahead to let you know that we were able to catch an earlier train."

Hannah stepped back, blinking at him. "We?"

Sean realized that he had almost given away her father's surprise. "I meant me. Or rather, I. I was able to catch an earlier train."

Hannah peered at him closer. "Are you feeling all right?"

Before Sean could reply, the sky above them released a drenching downpour, just as Mrs. Tyler had predicted.

Sean grabbed Hannah's hand as they both ran laughing to the house. "What about the laundry?" he asked as they ducked in the back door. "Should I go back and get it"

"Forget the laundry." Hannah quickly closed the door and then turned to face him. "I want to talk about us...." She reached out and took hold of his hands, her eyes probing his expectantly. "You mentioned in your last letter that there was something important you wanted to talk with me about."

Sean swallowed nervously. "There is."

"The answer is yes."

"What?"

"Yes, Sean Donnelly. Yes, I will marry you."

Sean was overjoyed that her feelings for him hadn't changed during their month long separation, but she needed to know the whole truth before making her decision. He proceeded to explain his need to change his identity while in Baltimore, and that if they were to marry, she would have to change hers as well. "That being said, I'll understand if you don't want to marry me right now."

"Sean Donnelly." Hannah released his hands, planting her own astride her hips. "It's you I want to marry, not your name."

Sean smiled. "Then you really—"

"When?" Hannah asked eagerly.

"Is today too soon? Pinkerton wants me—us—in Baltimore as soon as possible."

"Then today it is."

Hannah giggled as Sean swept her into his arms, but her mood quickly sobered as her thoughts turned elsewhere. "I wish that my father could be here."

"Did I hear someone askin' for her pa?"

Hannah whispered the word "Papa" as her father appeared in the kitchen doorway.

"You'll have to speak up a might louder than that when ya say 'I do', darlin'."

Hannah ran into his arms, expelling a torrent of joyful tears. "Oh, Papa, I never dreamed you'd be able to come. How long can you stay?"

"Until I wear out me welcome, lassie. I'm moving with ya to Baltimore."

"You're what?" Hannah looked from her father to her husband-to-be. "Did you know about this?"

"Not until a few days ago. Your father's a good one for keeping secrets. Which reminds me...." Sean turned to his soon to be father-in-law. "You said there was something you wanted to tell me."

Charlie seemed reluctant to discuss the matter while Hannah was present. "It can keep, lad. Right now we've got ourselves a wedding ta prepare for."

* * * * *

With the help of a few of Hannah's closest friends and the women from Mrs. Tyler's sewing circle, the boardinghouse sitting room had been transformed into a beautiful wedding chapel. Sean would have been content with a quick trip to the Justice of the Peace, but Hannah wanted the ceremony to be performed by a real minister, with all the appropriate trimmings. Sean had readily agreed to her wishes. He wasn't about to disappoint his bride.

Charlie slipped into the room where he and Sean would be hiding out until their cue from Mrs. Tyler. He stood for a moment watching the younger man's anxious pacing before closing the door. "Everythin's just about ready," he announced.

Sean stopped just long enough to acknowledge his report with a nervous smile before continuing his pacing. "How's Hannah?" he asked a few moments later.

"A sight better than you, lad."

Sean sank down onto the chair that Charlie placed in front of him, reaching up with a trembling hand to wipe the perspiration from his forehead. "I've never been so nervous in all my life," he admitted,

"That will pass the moment ya set eyes on your bride," the elder man assured him. "Ya should have seen me Ellen on the day we wed. What a vision she was."

"I don't believe I ever met her."

"She passed on when Hannah was only four."

"I'm sorry."

"No need ta be, lad." A peaceful smile settled upon his lips. "I'll be seeing her again real soon."

Sean looked up to find the elder man's eyes closed. "Are you all right, Charlie?"

"Aye, lad." His eyes slowly opened again. "Just a might tired, is all."

Sean quickly stood up, motioning for him to take the chair. "I think you need this more than I do."

Charlie dismissed his concern. "I'll be fine."

Sean stepped towards him, sensing there was something the elder man wasn't telling him. "Charlie, if there's ever anything you want to talk about...."

A grinning Mrs. Tyler poked her head in the door. "The bride is ready, gentleman."

Sean caught hold of Charlie's arm as he headed for the door. "About what I was saying...."

"Not now, lad. The bride is a waitin'."

* * * * *

Chicago

"...And they lived happily ever after." Rachel closed the book that she had been reading from and laid it on the stand beside Emily's bed. When she turned back to her daughter she was surprised to find a frown upon her face. "Now what's that look all about? I thought that Cinderella was your favorite."

"I miss Uncle Sean."

"Why's that?" Rachel tucked the covers up under her chin. "Because he reads you more than one bedtime story?"

"No. I just miss him, is all. Read his telegram again, Mama," she pleaded. "Please?"

Rachel smiled, surrendering at once to her daughter's wishes. "All right. But just once more."

Emily climbed from beneath the covers and settled onto her mother's lap as she unfolded the telegram they had received from Sean only a few hours earlier. "Greetings from Philadelphia," she read. "Hannah and I were married this afternoon! I wish that all of you could have been here but it is enough just knowing that we are in your prayers. I will let you know when we get settled in Baltimore. I miss you...I love you. Sean."

Emily stared at the telegram for a moment and then looked up at her mother. "Can I sleep with it under my pillow?"

"Of course you can."

Emily wiggled her way out her mother's lap and slipped the telegram beneath her pillow before snuggling back down under the covers. "He promised to come back and visit us."

"I'm sure he will as soon as he can, sweetheart," Rachel assured her. "He and Hannah, both. Now you get some sleep."

"Yes, Mama."

After checking in on the boys across the hall, Rachel headed back downstairs. She stopped just short of the bottom step when she heard voices at the front door. One of them was Neal's but the other she didn't recognize.

"Thanks for coming by," Neal was saying.

"I wasn't going to at first," the other voice said, "but under the circumstances I thought that you and Rachel should know."

Rachel caught her breath as she finally realized who the other voice belonged to. She inched her way down a few more steps, hoping to overhear more of their conversation, but Neal had already closed the door. He turned to find her watching him from the stairway. "How long have you been standing there?"

"I just came down." Rachel moved slowly towards him, glancing at the front door to let him know that she was aware they'd had a visitor. "Was that Doc Johnson I heard at the door?"

"Yeah."

Rachel waited for him to expound further about the reason for his visit and then finally took it upon herself to restart the conversation. "What was he doing here this time of night?"

Neal turned and headed into the living room. "He was looking for Charlie."

"Charlie?" Rachel tagged along behind him.

"The doc got worried when he didn't show up for his appointment yesterday." Neal settled onto the sofa. "Apparently Charlie never bothered to tell him that he was moving to Baltimore."

"That doesn't sound like Charlie. Maybe he just forgot about the appointment."

"Rach...." Neal reached over and took her hand as she sat down beside him. "Doc Johnson told me that Charlie is very ill. He has been for some time."

"Ill?" Rachel blinked, trying to make sense of what he was telling her. "He never said anything."

"He didn't want anyone to know, not even Hannah. He made doc swear not to tell her."

"But why? If he was ill...." Rachel pressed a hand over her mouth, nearly choking on the next words that came out. "He's dying, isn't he?"

Neal gripped her hand tighter. "Yes."

Rachel swallowed the lump in her throat that often accompanied the onset of tears. "How long does he have?"

"Doc says it could be anytime now. That's probably why he wanted to move to Baltimore with Hannah and Sean."

"Hannah," Rachel whispered. "Oh, Neal, that poor girl. Sean was so concerned that she wouldn't have any family or friends in Baltimore. And then we found out that Charlie was going with them. And now...."

Neal gathered her into his arms as she succumbed to her grief, bringing his chin down to rest on the top of her head. "She's going to be fine, Rach," he assured her. "Sean's her family now, and so are we. She's going to be just fine."

* * * * *

Philadelphia

Sean closed the front door after saying good-bye to the last of the their guests and turned with a smile to face his wife. "They're gone. Now I have you all to myself."

"Not just yet." Hannah planted both of her hands against his chest as he prepared to kiss her. "I think we should see what we can do to help Mrs. Tyler clean up first."

Sean looked around the room, coming quickly to the same conclusion. "Where do we start?"

After straightening up the best they could in the sitting room, the newlyweds went in search of Mrs. Tyler to see what else needed to be done. They found her standing at the kitchen sink up to her elbows

in soapy water. The stacks of unwashed dishes beside her on the counter spoke of many more hours of work ahead.

"We've come to help, Mrs. Tyler. I'll wash and Sean can dry."

Esther Tyler turned with a gasp to find Hannah rolling up the sleeves of her dress. "Oh, no you won't!" she protested. "Not on your wedding night."

"But, Mrs. Tyler—"

"Don't you 'but Mrs. Tyler' me. There is a beautiful room all ready for you upstairs. Now away with you," she demanded with a flick of her wrist. "Both of you!"

Hannah knew better than to argue with her landlady and allowed Sean to lead her upstairs. As they stopped outside the room that Mrs. Tyler had prepared for them, Hannah's gaze continued down the hallway to the room that her father was occupying. He had disappeared from the reception hours ago and she was concerned that he might not be feeling well. "Would you mind if I check on Papa before we turn in?"

"Not at all." Sean leaned down and pressed a kiss to her the forehead. "Take as long as you need."

Hannah thanked him with a smile and then proceeded to the room at the end of the hall. There was no response from inside the first time she knocked so she tried again. "Papa?"

The door opened a few moments later. Hannah was shocked by how tired her father looked. "I'm sorry, Pa. Did I wake you?"

"No, lass," he said wearily. "I was just restin'."

Hannah couldn't shake the feeling that something more was wrong. "Are you all right, Pa?"

Charlie Cavanaugh had never lied to his daughter about anything before and he didn't want to start now, but he couldn't tell her that his time had come, not on her wedding night. "I'm fine, lass."

"Well...." Hannah wrung her hands. "Is there anything I can get you? A glass of water? Some tea, perhaps?"

"No, child. Ya go on," he urged her. "Your husband's a waitin'."

Hannah's eyes filled with tears as she wrapped her arms around his frail body, clinging to him for a moment as if sensing she would never do so again. "I love you, Papa."

"I love ya, too, lass. Now off ya go."

Charlie watched as she made her way back to her own room and then walked over to lie down on the bed. His eyes closed for the last time just moments before his earthly life slipped away. "Good-bye, lass...."

CHAPTER TWENTY-EIGHT

A NEW BEGINNING

Hannah woke early the following morning and headed straight downstairs to begin what was going to be a very busy day. She thought she was the first one up until she entered the kitchen and found Mrs. Tyler with breakfast preparations well underway.

The elder woman turned from the stove with a clearly defined frown. "Didn't anyone ever tell you that new brides are supposed to sleep until noon?"

"That does sound tempting, but I've got a lot to do if we're going to leave on the afternoon train."

Mrs. Tyler tempered her frown with a wistful smile. "I'm going to miss you two around here."

Hannah returned her smile with equal affection. "And we're going to miss you. But Baltimore isn't that far. We'll come and visit."

"You'd better," the elder woman teased.

Hannah joined her at the stove, watching as she transferred one perfectly formed pancake after another from the frying pan to the plate that she was holding. "I was going to try my hand at cooking breakfast for my husband but I see that you've already beaten me to it."

"Well, when you've been cooking as long as I have...." She paused to add one final pancake to the stack. "It just becomes a habit. But if you'd like to finish things up, I'm sure that Sean will never know the difference. All that's left to do is the eggs."

"He'll know. Unless you plan on moving to Baltimore with us to cook all of his meals. I'm afraid my culinary skills leave little to be desired." Hannah looked with regret upon the stack of pancakes as Mrs. Tyler set them on the counter. "I should have taken you up on your offer to teach me months ago."

"It's never too late."

"Yes it is. We're leaving today, remember?"

Mrs. Tyler turned to face her. "The best way to learn anything is just to dive right in." She handed Hannah a bowl full of eggs. "I've got laundry to tend to."

"But, Mrs. Tyler—" Hannah's plea fell on deaf ears. She was about to get her first cooking lesson whether she wanted it or not. "Here goes nothing...."

Hannah managed to get all of the eggs cracked open and into the pan without incident, but it was the actual cooking process that she was most concerned about. How did Sean like his eggs, anyway? Scrambled? Over easy? She so wanted their first breakfast together as husband and wife to be perfect and now wished that she had paid closer attention to the way that Mrs. Tyler always prepared them for him. "Oh, well," she said with a lingering sigh. "It's not the first thing that I'm going to have to learn about my new husband and it certainly won't be the last."

Hannah finally decided to scramble them all just to be safe and then added what she felt was the appropriate balance between salt and pepper. They were almost done when Sean walked in. "Something sure smells good in here."

Hannah knew she should be comforted by the fact that he wasn't holding his nose but she wasn't. Smell was one thing; taste was quite another. She smiled nervously as Sean came to stand beside her at the stove. "What's on the menu, Mrs. Donnelly?" he asked with a thump to his stomach. "I'm starved."

"Pancakes, eggs and bacon."

Sean eyed the stack of pancakes beside her on the counter. "What more can a man ask for? She's beautiful and she can cook, too."

"Mrs. Tyler made the pancakes," Hannah confessed. "I'm only in charge of the eggs."

"Like I said, she's beautiful and she can cook."

Hannah giggled as he nuzzled the side of her neck. "Sean, stop that! You're going to make me burn the eggs. Why don't you go and set the table?"

"Yes, ma'am." Sean opened the cupboard next to the sink and took out two plates, hesitating a moment before removing a third. "Is you're father joining us?"

"I'm not sure. I don't even think he's awake yet." Hannah thought back to the conversation that she'd had with her father last night and how tired he had been. "I hope he's feeling all right."

Sean set the plates around the table. "It's probably just all the excitement of the past few days. The wedding, moving to Baltimore...."

"But even when he was here visiting last month I sensed that something was wrong," Hannah now recalled. "Like he was keeping something from me."

Sean had gotten that same impression from him yesterday but he didn't want Hannah to worry. "I'm sure he'll be fine."

Hannah smiled, wanting to believe he was right. "Would you go up and check on him for me? Breakfast is almost ready."

Sean returned a few minutes later, but he came back alone.

Hannah ignored the secret fears welling up inside her and continued to bustle around the table making the last minute preparations for their meal. "Isn't Pa hungry?" she asked as Sean came to stand beside her. "Lands sakes, that man hasn't been eating enough lately to keep a bird alive."

"Hannah...."

"The milk. I forgot the milk."

Sean caught hold of her arm as she was about to turn away. Hannah avoided his gaze, her lower lip trembling as tears found their way to her eyes. "He's gone, isn't he?"

Sean swallowed, wrestling with his own emotions. "Yes."

"Oh, Papa," she cried out.

Sean held her tight as she poured out her grief for the next few minutes. When she finally stepped back, her eyes were dry and she was demanding answers. "Why didn't he tell me? He must have known."

"I think he tried to tell me yesterday," Sean admitted.

Hannah thought for a moment about her father's sudden decision to come with them to Baltimore. She now understood why.

Sean was thinking about Baltimore as well, but his thoughts were of Hannah, not her father. How could he possibly think of asking her to go with him now? The only sensible thing to do would be to send her back to stay with his family until he completed his obligations in Baltimore. Lord willing, it wouldn't be for long.

Hannah stood a little straighter, refusing to be ruled by her emotions. "We'll have to make arrangements for the funeral right away," she said bravely.

"You let me handle that," Sean insisted as he gently took hold of her upper arms. "And then I'm sending you back to Chicago to stay with my family."

"What?"

"I think it would be for the best under the circumstances."

"No," she protested.

"Hannah—"

"No, Sean. I'm not going anywhere without you, and that's final."

Sean knew that it was pointless to argue with her any further. She was her father's daughter, Irish stubborn to the core. But so was he. "Well, if you won't go without me... then I'll just have to go with you. I'll wire Pinkerton and tell him to forget about Baltimore."

"But you can't. You'll be sent to prison."

Sean closed his eyes, lowering his head like a beaten dog. "I'm sorry. I don't know what I was thinking."

"I do." Hannah waited for him to raise his head again before she continued. "You were thinking about me and I love you for it. But we have to go on with our lives. It's what my Pa would want." She enlisted a smile to assure him that she was going to be just fine. "We are going to Baltimore, Sean Donnelly—you and me—together."

Sean reached up and tenderly caressed her cheek. "That's right...together."

* * * * *

Baxter

"Amber Buchanan. *Mrs*. Buchanan. Mrs. *Carter* Buchanan. Oh, what's the use?" Amber scowled as she crumpled up the paper in front of her and tossed it over her shoulder. "None of them sound right."

"I'm sorry but that's the only name I have to give you."

Amber smiled at the figure standing in the doorway. "What are you doing here?"

"I missed you." Carter wound his way through the rows of desks to the front of the schoolroom. "What's this all about?" he asked, reaching behind her chair to pick up the paper that she had discarded on the floor.

"I was just trying to decide what to have the children call me after we're married."

Carter took a seat on the edge of her desk. "What do they call you now?"

"Miss Amber."

"So why change it?"

"Miss is a title for an unmarried woman."

"I don't mind as long as you remember that you're married before you come home every night."

"Very funny." Amber rose and began gathering up the books that she needed to leave with Naomi Thompson. The elder woman had graciously volunteered to take over her class for the next two weeks while she and Carter were on their honeymoon. "What are you *really* doing here?"

"I told you." Carter dropped the wad of paper into the small metal trashcan beside her desk. "I missed you."

"Carter Buchanan...." Amber hefted the stack of books up to her hip. "Now that you are a homeowner, there are a few things you need to know. For starters, there's a little thing called a mortgage payment that's due the first of every month. You can't just leave work every time you miss me."

"True enough." Carter relieved her of the stack of books. "But I saw my last patient for the afternoon, it's pouring down rain, and I thought I would be a gentleman and drive you home."

"Oh." Amber smiled up at him. "Well, that's different." She linked her arm with his as they started back through the rows of desks. "Since I have you here, there is something that we need to discuss."

"Sounds serious."

"It is. I just can't seem to decide what color our living room drapes should be."

Carter stopped abruptly, turning to face her. "Drapes?"

"Yes. Kathleen is going to help me sew them but I'm having a terrible time trying to pick out just the right color of fabric."

Carter continued to stare. "That's the big crisis?"

"I didn't say it was a crisis but it is important. If I choose the wrong color—"

Carter started to laugh.

"Carter Buchanan!" Amber slugged him in the arm. "It's not funny."

"Forgive me. I flunked interior design in medical school."

Amber was certain that he was still mocking her but she was willing to let it pass. "Would you mind taking a look at some material with me when we get back to the store?"

"For you, my dear, I would swing from the chandelier."

Amber giggled. "Lucky for you we don't have one."

* * * * *

"Mail call for Lieutenant Eric Ramsey."

Eric looked up from his desk as his mother walked in carrying an oblong shaped package about four inches thick. "Who's it from, Ma?"

"Uncle Sam."

Eric came off his chair as if those two simple words had lit a fire beneath him. "I bet I know what that is."

Kathleen set the package down at the foot of his bed. "I'm sorry that I can't stay for the fashion show but I have a cake in the oven."

"Thanks, Ma. I'll come down later and model it for you."

Colin sat up on his bed, watching curiously as Eric tore into the package. "What is it?"

"Well, if my hunch is correct...." Eric took the lid off the box and folded back the protective paper inside. "It's my new uniform. I was worried that it wasn't going to get here before I had to leave."

Colin watched dejectedly as Eric tried on the jacket, fastening up the row of shiny buttons that ran down the front.

"What do you think, Col?" Eric turned around in a circle, holding his arms out to his sides. "Do I look like a lieutenant?"

Colin shrugged. "How should I know?"

Eric dropped his arms back to his sides. "I expected a little more enthusiasm than that, especially from you. Won't be long until you're wearing a uniform like this yourself."

"Five years," Colin reminded him. "And that's *if* I pass the exam next year."

"Are you still worried about that?" Eric sat down beside him on the bed. "Look, I know that I'm leaving in a couple of days and I won't be able to tutor you anymore, but you're more than ready to take that exam."

"It's not the exam," Colin admitted, but that was all he was willing to admit. The young man clammed up, refusing to say anything further on the subject.

"Oh, come on," Eric urged him. "It can't be that bad."

Colin finally gave in to him. "I don't know if I want to wait that long to wear a uniform," he confessed. "One year until I can take the exam, and then four more until I graduate."

"And I'm supposed to take that to mean what?"

Colin got up and walked the short distance over to the window, staring aimlessly into the pouring rain. "I'll be eighteen in a little less than a year," he tried to explain. "And even if I get into West Point there's no guarantee that I'll graduate."

Eric came up behind him. "What are you getting at, Col?"

Colin turned to face him. "I'm thinking about joining up next year instead of going to West Point."

Eric took a moment to digest what his brother was telling him. "So let me see if I've got this straight. You're going to give up your dream of going to West Point just because you don't want to wait another five years to wear a uniform."

Colin scowled at himself. "I didn't realize how stupid it sounded until you said it."

"It's not stupid, Col." Eric took him firmly by the shoulders. "If joining up is what you want to do…. Well, then that's what you should do."

Colin was surprised to hear Eric express his support. He had been expecting just the opposite. "You're not going to try and talk me out of it?"

"You're old enough to make that decision for yourself."

"What about Ma and Pa? Do you think I should tell them?"

"Not if you actually want to make it to your eighteenth birthday."

Colin smiled. "Thanks, Eric."

"Hey…." Eric stripped off the jacket and handed it to him. "Want to try it on?"

Colin's eyes gleamed. "Can I?"

"Just don't tell Uncle Sam."

* * * * *

"What about this color? Do you like this one?"

Carter studied the sample of material that Amber was holding up for his approval. "Yes. But I also like the other dozen or so you've already shown me."

"Well, you can only pick one. Now which is it going to be?"

"I personally like the blue."

Amber turned with a start towards the voice behind her. It was the first time that she had set eyes on Isaac Jameson since signing the papers on the house four days ago. He still made her skin crawl.

Carter sensed how uncomfortable she was and took a protective half step in front of her.

"I'm sorry if I startled you," Jameson apologized, looking directly past Carter as if he wasn't even there. "But I really do like the blue."

Carter bore down on him, making sure that his presence was clearly felt. "I don't recall anyone asking for your opinion."

Jameson's hands came up protectively in front of him. "I was just trying to be neighborly."

Amber reached for Carter's arm, coaxing him back to her side. "Carter, please."

Jameson slowly relaxed his defensive stance. "I trust that you're all settled into the house?"

The last thing that Carter wanted to do was give Jameson a decorating update, but for Amber's sake he would humor the man. "I've moved my things in," he said with mock politeness. "And the rest of the furniture we've ordered should be here by the time we return from our honeymoon."

"That's right. You're getting married soon."

"Tomorrow," Amber told him.

"Well…." Jameson looked back and forth between them, his gaze lingering on Amber. "I wish you nothing but the best." He tipped his hat with a smile. "If you'll excuse me."

Amber took a step away from Carter, watching as Jameson crossed the store and engaged her aunt and uncle in conversation. "He was actually civil. Maybe we've been all wrong about him."

"Don't forget the Garden of Eden," Carter warned her as he stood glaring at the back of Jameson's head. "Even snakes look harmless sometimes."

"Mrs. Crowley!" Everything in the store came to a stand still as Colin tore through the door.

"Lands sakes, young man, what's the matter?"

"Have you seen my—" Colin's plea ground to a halt when he saw Carter. "Oh, Carter. Am I glad to see you." Colin rushed to his side. "I'm looking for my pa. Have you seen him?"

"He was out on a call when I left the clinic earlier. What's wrong?"

"It's my ma. She took a bad fall."

Carter waved the younger man back towards the door. "Let's go."

* * * * *

Philadelphia

Hannah listened numbly as the same minister who had married her and Sean less than twenty-four hours earlier now presided over her father's funeral. They had chosen a small cemetery near the boardinghouse so that it would be easy for Mrs. Tyler to tend the grave sight from time to time. Hannah assured her that it wasn't necessary, but the elder woman had insisted all the same.

"Earth to earth, ashes to ashes, dust to dust. In sure and certain hope of the resurrection to eternal life through our Lord and Savior Jesus Christ...."

Hannah shuddered, prompting Sean to remove his coat and drape it around her shoulders. But it wasn't the damp chill in the air that caused her to do so. She was struck by how quickly things had changed. A few hours ago she had been making plans for their trip to Baltimore, the three of them together. And now she and Sean would be making that trip alone. It was a humbling reminder that their lives were not their own.

"...Amen."

Hannah stepped forward at the close of the invocation and picked up a handful of loose dirt. With trembling hands she tossed it on top of her father's casket, symbolizing the return of his mortal body to the ground. Tears flooded her eyes, momentarily blurring her vision of the earthly scene before her, but in her mind's eye she could see her father at her mother's side, peaceful and happy, no longer suffering within the constraints of his humanity. He was home at last. "Good-bye, Papa...."

Back at the boardinghouse, Hannah threw herself into preparing for their departure later that afternoon. Sean had suggested that they postpone their trip a day or two to allow her some time to rest but she wanted to put Philadelphia and all the painful memories of the day behind her as soon as possible. Sean had finally consented to her wishes and headed off to the station to make the final arrangements. He returned just an hour later.

"Were you able to get our tickets?" Hannah asked as he came into their room.

"Yeah." Sean joined her beside the bed where she was busy packing their bags. "The train is scheduled to leave at four o'clock."

"That's good." Hannah picked up the daguerreotype of her father that she kept on the stand beside the bed and tucked it safely into her bag. It had been taken several years ago before the ravages of old age had taken their toll. It was how she always wanted to remember him.

Sean sat down on the bed facing her. "I also wired Pinkerton to let him know that we'll be in Baltimore some-time tomorrow night. That is, unless...."

Hannah stopped what she was doing. "Unless what?"

Sean cleared his throat. "Unless you change your mind about going to Chicago. It's still not too late," he rushed to add. "If I trade in your ticket right now—"

"Sean." Hannah threw the pair of socks she was holding down on the bed with an exasperated sigh. "I've already told you. I'm not going to Chicago." She turned and sat down beside him, grasping his hands imploringly. "Please don't worry about me. I'm actually excited about the idea of moving. New city, new friends.... A whole new beginning, for both of us."

Sean could do nothing but stare at her. "You are an amazing woman, Hannah Donnelly."

"I know," she said, smiling back at him. "And don't you ever forget it."

* * * * *

Baxter

Alec leapt out of the buggy and ran across the yard towards the house. In his right hand he was clutching the note that Colin had left for him at the clinic. The younger man had offered very few details about what had happened, only that Kathleen had fallen and he was needed home immediately. Alec was naturally fearing the worst. "Please, Lord. Please let them be all right."

Kirsten was waiting for him as he burst through the back-door. "Kirsty—"

"She's fine, Pa. Just a few bumps and bruises and a sprained ankle. Carter is upstairs with her right now."

"And the baby?"

"The baby's fine, too."

"Oh, thank God." Alec leaned back against the door, still clutching Colin's note in his hand. "How did it happen?"

"She was standing on a chair trying to reach something off the top shelf in the pantry and lost her balance."

"Standing on a...." Alec gritted his teeth as he crumpled up the note and tossed it on the table. "How many times have I told her to ask for help when she can't reach something? She could've broken her neck."

"But she didn't," Kirsten reminded him.

A smile started at the center of Alec's lips and slowly spread outward. "You're right, and I'm over reacting as usual."

"Don't be too hard on her, Pa," Kirsten appealed to him. "She's already feeling bad enough as it is about what happened. Especially now that she won't be able to walk down the aisle tomorrow."

"The aisle?"

"You're getting married, remember?"

"Oh, right. The wedding." Alec scrubbed a hand back and forth across his forehead. "I guess we'll have to set a new date—again."

"No you won't," Kirsten said with a secretive smile, reaching to take her father's arm. "Come with me."

"To where?"

"Your wedding."

Carter had just finished bandaging Kathleen's left ankle when Alec and Kirsten entered the room. "It's about time you got here, Doc," the younger man teased.

"I would have been here sooner but Mrs. Johnston decided at the last minute to have twins. What's the diagnosis in here?"

"It's not a bad sprain...." Kathleen winced as Carter lifted her foot to slip a pillow beneath it. "But she's not going to be walking on it any time soon."

Alec approached the end of the bed, shaking his head at her as one would a disobedient child. "Kathleen Elizabeth Ramsey. What am I going to do with you?" His gaze dropped to her swollen ankle. "First you faint, and now this. I think you would do just about anything to get out of marrying me."

Kathleen wanted to shrink beneath the covers and never come out again. "I'm sorry. I've ruined everything."

"No you haven't," Carter assured, coming to her defense. "We'll just postpone our wedding until your ankle is better."

"No, Carter. I couldn't let you do that. You and Amber go on with your plans tomorrow. Alec and I can get married anytime."

"She's right." Alec stepped around the side of the bed. "And there's no time like the present."

Kathleen gaped at him. "What?"

"Carter and Kirsten are here. They can be our witnesses. And if you decide to faint again, at least you're already lying down."

Kathleen put a hand up to her mouth, chuckling quietly to herself.

"I guess what it comes right down to is…can you think of one good reason why we shouldn't get married right here and now?"

Kathleen dropped her hand back to her side, smiling happily. "Not a one."

"All right, then…." Alec sat down on the edge of the bed and took her hands as Carter and Kirsten drew up beside him. "I, Alec, take you, Kathleen, to be my lawfully wedded wife. For better or for worse, for richer or for poorer, in sprained ankles and in health," he said with a smile, "'til death do us part."

Kathleen smiled back, eagerly following his lead. "And I, Kathleen, take you, Alec, to be my lawfully wedded husband. For better or for worse, for richer or for poorer, in sickness and in health, 'til death do us part. Now what?" she asked.

Alec grinned as he leaned over her. "You may now kiss the groom."

CHAPTER TWENTY-NINE

HERE COMES THE BRIDE... WHERE WENT THE GROOM?

A mber was awake well before dawn on the morning of her wedding. After spending some quiet time in prayer, she turned her attention to packing for her honeymoon. "I wonder how cold it is at Niagara Falls this time of year...?"

Amber sorted through the clothes that were lying on her bed and picked out the things that she felt would be most appropriate. As she began putting them into her bags, she found her enthusiasm for the whole experience waning but she didn't know why. Weren't new brides supposed to be excited about going on their honeymoons? Yet she wasn't. It certainly had nothing to do with not loving Carter or wanting to spend time alone with him. It was something else. Perhaps she was feeling guilty about leaving her students so soon after the school year had started. Or maybe it was the thought of all the work that she knew would be waiting for her at the house when they got back. "Or maybe you're just being a silly goose," she chided herself.

"Knock, knock."

Amber stepped across the room to open the door, thankful for the diversion. "Come in, Aunt Ida."

Ida entered carrying a tray with a small teapot and two cups. "I heard you up and thought you might like some tea."

"You thought right." Amber cleared a space on the bed for her to set the tray. "Sorry about all the mess."

"Is there anything I can do to help, dear?"

Amber took a quick look around the room before sitting down to enjoy her tea. "I think most everything is taken care of. The boxes in the corner can be dropped at the house whenever you have the time."

"Which reminds me...." Ida handed her a cup of tea. "Be sure to give us the keys before you leave today."

Before you leave.... Her aunt's reference to their planned departure on this afternoon's train refueled Amber's reservations about leaving town.

Ida was quick to pick up on her mood change. "Is there something wrong, dear? You're not getting cold feet, are you?"

"No, nothing like that." Amber struggled with how to explain her concerns. "I just have the strangest feeling that Carter and I shouldn't leave town today. Like something terrible is going to happen if we do. It's been bothering me all morning but I don't know why. I know it sounds foolish...."

"You're right, it is foolish. Mrs. Thompson is more than capable of handling your class while you're gone, and your uncle and I will look after the house. All you need to concern yourself with is having a wonderful time on your honeymoon with that handsome new husband of yours."

Amber wanted to do just that but the nagging feeling refused to be so easily dismissed. She didn't want for her aunt to worry, however. "Thank you, Aunt Ida. You always have a way of making me feel better."

The two women settled in for a leisurely chat, enjoying what Amber realized would be the last time they would be taking their morning tea together. "I'm really going to miss these little chats of ours."

"Who says they have to end? You're welcome to come by anytime." Ida gasped, nearly spilling her tea. "Time. What time is it?"

"I don't know. Almost nine, I guess."

Ida quickly set her cup back on the tray. "Lands sakes, I've got to get over to the parsonage."

Amber failed to see the need to cut short their time together. "But the wedding's not for hours."

"I know, but...." Ida bit her lower lip, fearing she may have already said too much.

"But what?" Amber asked, looking at her suspiciously. "Aunt Ida, is there something going on that I'm not supposed to know about?"

"No," Ida chuckled. "Of course not. I just promised Naomi that I would come by early and help set up for the reception, is all. I thought you might like to join me."

"I'd love to...." Amber rose to finish packing her bags. "But as soon as I'm through here I'm going out to the house to fix breakfast for Carter."

"You can't do that," Ida objected. "It's bad luck for the bride and groom to see one another on their wedding day."

"Oh, Aunt Ida, you don't believe that superstitious nonsense anymore than I do."

"No, but I do think it's more romantic that way. Besides, Carter isn't home. He stopped by here a half hour ago on his way over to the Ramsey's. So you have no excuse not to come with me to the parsonage."

Amber planted her hands on her hips, scowling at her aunt. "There is something going on."

"There is nothing going on," Ida insisted.

Amber laughed, tossing her hands in the air. "All right, you win. I'll go with you to the parsonage. But first I need to decide what to wear on the train this afternoon." She selected two dresses, holding them up side by side in front of her. "Which one do you like the best, the blue or the green?"

"I personally like the blue."

Amber's face momentarily lost all color. Those were the exact words that Isaac Jameson had used at the store the other day when relating his color preference for their living room drapes. Amber felt a heightened sense of uneasiness about leaving town. Was Jameson the cause of it?

"I think I'll wear the green," she decided, tossing the blue dress back on the bed as if it were contaminated. If blue was Jameson's color of preference, she wanted nothing to do with it.

"Blue, green.... I don't expect that Carter will care one way or the other," Ida told her honestly. "New grooms tend to be color blind about everything except their bride's eyes. On the other hand...." She stepped out the door and returned carrying a rectangular box. "He might want for you to wear this."

Amber snatched the box from her. "Carter?"

"Who else?"

Amber set the box on the bed and tore back the lid. Inside was a beautiful rose-colored dress. "Oh, Carter...." Amber lifted the dress from the box and held it up in front of her. "It's absolutely gorgeous."

"It certainly is."

"I've got to try it on. You don't mind, do you? It will only take a minute."

Ida wasn't about to deny her. It would be worth being a few minutes late to the parsonage just to see the smile back on her niece's face. "You go right ahead, dear. Take all the time you need."

* * * * *

"Thanks for breakfast, Alec." Carter wiped his mouth and then tossed his napkin atop his now empty plate. "After burning a dozen eggs I gave up trying to fix anything for myself. I guess I'm a bit nervous."

"Don't think anything of it. It's the least a best man can do."

Kirsten turned from the stove with an annoyed look on her face. "Excuse me?"

Alec smiled back at her. "And the daughter of the best man, of course."

"That's more like it."

"My thanks to you both. It was wonderful." Carter relaxed back in his chair, enjoying a few sips of his coffee. "How's Kathleen this morning?"

"Kathleen." Alec exchanged another smile with Kirsten as she began clearing the table. "Well, she should be in bed resting her ankle, but trying to keep her away from anything to do with this wedding is like asking her to stop breathing. She had Eric drop her off at the parsonage a couple hours ago to help Naomi set up for the reception."

"Did she tell you about the surprise party for Amber?"

"How'd you find out about that?" Alec was curious to know. "She swore me to secrecy."

"Ida told me when I stopped by the store earlier."

Kirsten gasped, almost dropping the stack of dishes she was holding. "You didn't see Amber, did you?"

"Relax. There was no way I was getting anywhere near her with Ida on guard."

Alec chuckled. "Dear, Ida."

Carter handed Kirsten his plate and then downed the last of his coffee before handing her the cup as well. "I hate to eat and run but I told the reverend we'd meet him at the clinic around nine to go over the ceremony."

"I'm ready. Do you want a lift into town, Kirsty?"

"No thanks, Pa. Jesse is coming by for me."

Alec glanced out the window as a wagon pulled up out back. "There he is now."

"Pa, come quick!" Nathan ran into the room, wriggling like a worm on a hook. "Stephen locked himself in the water closet and I gotta go!"

"Not again." Alec pushed his chair back from the table. "Carter, help your self to another cup of coffee. This shouldn't take long."

Carter stared after him. "I'm almost afraid to ask, but do things like that happen around here often?"

"I don't know if I should answer that." Kirsten reached across in front of him to gather up the last of the breakfast dishes. "You may change your mind about wanting to have children."

"Not a chance. I want at least—" Carter fell silent as his gaze came to rest upon Kirsten's ring. "Oh, no."

"What's wrong?"

"The ring." Carter stood up, patting down his jacket pockets. "I forgot the ring at the house. Tell your father that I went back to get it and I'll meet him at the clinic later, all right?"

Jesse stumbled backwards as Carter raced past him out the door. "Where's he going in such a hurry?"

"He forgot the ring at home."

Jesse grinned, taking her by the shoulders. "Speaking of homes, I may have found us one."

"Oh, Jesse, really?" Kirsten quickly turned and set the dishes back on the table, fearing she might break them in her excited state. "What's it like?"

"Well, it's a little run down…." Jesse rethought what he was going to say. "Actually, it's a lot run down. That's probably why Jameson hasn't snatched it up yet. But if I do all of the repair work on it myself…."

"When can I see it?" Kirsten asked, feeding off his enthusiasm.

"I can take you over there right now if you'd like."

"Oh, I'd love—" The fire in Kirsten's eyes petered out. "I almost forgot. I'm suppose to go to Amber's surprise party at the parsonage."

"Couldn't you be a little late?" Jesse suggested.

Kirsten smiled at the expectant gleam in his eyes. "I suppose so."

Jesse smiled back. "Good. I can't wait for you to see it."

Kirsten ran to tell her father that she was leaving but in her excitement forgot to mention to him that Carter had ridden back home to get the ring. It was a mistake that would later prove to save a young boy's life.

* * * * *

Amber stood to her feet, craning her neck around to watch the horse and rider that went streaking past her uncle's wagon. "That was Carter!"

"Amber, dear, sit down before you fall." Ida yanked her back down onto the seat. "Now what was that you were saying about Carter?"

"He just rode past." Amber turned to look over her shoulder, gripping onto the back of the seat as her uncle brought the wagon to a stop in front of the parsonage. "You don't suppose there's anything wrong, do you?"

"No, I don't." Ida climbed down leaving Amber sitting alone on the seat.

"But the church is in the opposite direction. Why would he—"

"The ceremony isn't for hours yet. Perhaps he's just going home for awhile."

Her aunt's explanation seemed reasonable enough but Amber still couldn't shake the feeling that something was wrong. Had Carter suddenly gotten cold feet about marrying her? "Maybe I should try to find out where he went."

"You will do no such thing. You are coming with me."

Amber reluctantly climbed down and followed Ida up to the front door of the parsonage. She still didn't understand why it was so important for her to be there, but if it meant that much to her aunt....

Ida knocked several times but there was no response from inside.

"It doesn't appear that anyone's home, Aunt Ida."

"But that can't be. Naomi specifically said...." Ida opened the door to a thunderous, "Surprise!"

Amber's mouth dropped open at the sight of all the women who were gathered inside. She turned to her aunt, mouth still gaping. "Did you know about this?"

Ida hunched her shoulders "Surprise."

* * * * *

Carter was halfway back to town with the ring safely tucked in his jacket pocket when a disturbing sight caused him to rein in. A young girl of about eight years of age was running towards him, her face streaked with tears. He recognized her as one of the students in Amber's class but couldn't remember her name.

Carter swung down from his horse and rushed to the girls' side. "What's wrong, sweetheart?"

"My brother," the girl sobbed. "We were playing behind the house. He fell down a hill. I called to him but he wouldn't answer. I think he's hurt bad."

"What's your name?"

"Mary. Mary Webster."

"Are your folks home, Mary?"

"No. They went into town." Her eyes once again became pools of tears. "I'm scared."

"It's okay. You did the right thing going for help. Come with me." Carter walked her back to his horse and lifted her up into the saddle. He then climbed up behind her and gathered the reins. "Which way?"

Carter was relieved that the girl's home was only a few minutes ride from where he had found her. As soon as he slowed the horse to a walk, Mary slid off and ran towards the wooded area behind the house. Carter followed quickly behind her, praying they would be in time.

Mary stopped at the edge of a steep slope, pointing down. "That's where he fell."

Carter leaned out as far as he could without slipping over the edge himself. He could see the boy lying at the bottom of the slope. He had fallen at least twenty feet or more and didn't appear to be moving. There was no telling how severe his injuries might be...or if he was even still alive. "What's his name?" he asked Mary.

"Jacob."

Carter cupped his hands around his mouth and called the boy's name. He heard nothing the first few times he tried, but then finally the faint sound of crying reached his ears. The boy was alive. "Jacob, listen to me!" Carter called to him. "My name is Doctor Buchanan! Try not to move, son! I'm coming down to get you!" He turned back to Mary. "Do you know where there's some rope?"

"In the barn. I'll get it."

The girl returned shortly with a forty-foot length of rope. Carter proceeded to tie one end securely around a tree and the other around himself. "Okay, Jacob, I'm coming down! Just hang on!"

Carter worked his way slowly down through the thick underbrush that covered the slope, sidestepping rocks and fallen tree branches as best he could. It took him nearly three minutes to reach the place where the boy was lying.

After untying the rope from around his waist, Carter knelt down to assess the boy's injuries. The first thing he noticed was a large knot on his forehead. A more thorough examination revealed a broken leg and some minor cuts and bruises on both arms. There was also some tenderness on the boy's left side just below his rib cage. Carter feared the possibility of internal injuries, but without the aid of a stethoscope, he had no way of knowing for sure.

Carter removed his jacket and draped it over the boy to keep him warm He then turned his attention to figuring out how to get him back up the slope without further aggravating his injuries. One thing was for sure, he wasn't going to be able to do it alone. Mary was going to have to go for help.

"Mary, listen to me!" Carter hollered up to her. "Your brother is hurt too bad for me to leave him. I'm going to have to stay here while you ride to town and get help! Do you think you can do that?"

Carter saw the girl nod her head. "Good girl! Try to find your parents or Doctor Ramsey! He should be at the medical clinic!"

And so should you, Carter thought, just now remembering his meeting with Reverend Thompson. Maybe Alec was already out looking for him. But then why would he be? Kirsten would have told him that he had ridden home to get the ring. It could be hours before anyone even missed him. All he could do now was wait and hope that Mary returned with help in time. The last thing he wanted to do was leave his bride waiting at the altar.

"That's not going to happen," Carter told himself. "Mary will be back in plenty of time. You have nothing to worry about." Except for Jacob....

Carter turned his attention back to his young patient. Of all the boy's injuries, it was the knot on his forehead that he was the most concerned about. It could be nothing more than a minor concussion but he wasn't going to take any chances. He would have to keep the boy conscious or risk the possibility of him lapsing into a coma.

"How old are you, Jacob?"

"Five," the youngster replied shakily.

"Do you go to school?"

"Uh, huh."

Carter smiled down at him. "I know your teacher. She's real pretty, isn't she?"

* * * * *

Alec was growing more and more concerned as the hours ticked by and there was still no word from Carter. He had never thought to question the younger man's whereabouts until he failed to show up for their scheduled meeting at the clinic with Reverend Thompson. Even then he had no reason to suspect that anything was wrong. But now the wedding was less than an hour away. The time for remaining calm had passed.

Kathleen was sitting at a small table in the kitchen putting the finishing touches on the wedding cake when Alec slipped in the back door of the parsonage. She smiled as he came to stand beside her chair. "Alec, didn't the cake turn out beautiful?"

"Have you seen Carter?"

Kathleen stared up at him, licking a dab of icing off her finger. "What do you mean have I seen Carter? Isn't he with you?"

"I haven't seen him since he came by the house for breakfast this morning." Alec stepped to the doorway behind her, searching among the faces in the next room. "Is Kirsten here?"

"No. When she didn't come by for the party I just figured she changed her mind. She's probably off with Jesse somewhere."

Alec struck his fist gently against the doorjamb. "I was hoping she might know where he is."

Kathleen was just now grasping the seriousness of the situation. "Alec...the wedding is in less than an hour."

He turned back to face her. "I know. I'm going to ride through town and then head towards his place. Maybe somebody has seen him. In the meantime, if Kirsten shows up, try to find out whatever you can from her. I'll check back in a little while."

"What about Amber?"

Alec glanced once again into the next room. Amber was sitting on the sofa, laughing as several of the ladies fought over how to style her hair. "Don't say anything to her just yet. There's no sense in upsetting her until we know something for sure."

Jesse was just bringing the wagon to a stop in front of the parsonage when Alec came back around the side of the house. Kirsten was bubbling over with excitement as he approached. "Oh, Pa, you should have seen the—"

"Where have you been?"

Kirsten was taken aback by the urgency in her father's voice. "Jesse took me to look at the house that he's thinking about buying. What's wrong, Pa?"

"Have either of you seen Carter?"

"Not since—" Kirsten gasped, just now realizing her mistake. "I was supposed to tell you."

"Tell me what?"

"Carter remembered that he left the ring at home. He was going to ride back and get it."

Alec heard nothing in Kirsten's account to suppress his concern. Carter's place was only a half-mile out of town. He should have been back long before now.

Kirsten read his mind. "He's not back yet?"

"No. I'm going out to look for him right now." He bobbed his head to Jesse. "I may need your help."

"You've got it. We can take my wagon."

Alec helped Kirsten down and then climbed up beside Jesse. "Tell your Ma where we've gone."

"I will, Pa. We'll be praying."

Jesse turned the wagon around and headed back out of town. They had traveled only a short distance when a horse came cantering towards them down the middle of the road. The young girl in the saddle appeared to be crying.

"Alec...." Jesse brought the wagon to a quick stop, recognizing the horse as the one he had sold to Carter. "That's Carter's horse."

Alec jumped down and grabbed hold of the horse's bridle as the girl rode up beside him. "What's happened, sweetheart?"

"My brother...." Mary poured out the entire story in between her sobs and then tumbled into Alec's outstretched arms. "It's all right," he assured her. "We're going to help your brother."

Alec lifted Mary up onto the seat beside Jesse and then quickly tied Carter's horse to the back of the wagon. If her brother was hurt as bad as she said, they didn't have a moment to spare.

* * * * *

Amber turned her back to hide her tears as she stood listening to Kathleen's report of Carter's disappearance. She knew that he would never leave her waiting at the altar unless something terrible had happened to him.

"I'm sure that Alec and Jesse will find him," Kathleen said in an attempt to console her. "They're probably on their way back right now."

"That's right," Ida agreed, moving up to stand behind her. "In the meantime, why don't we go on back to the store? We can wait for news there."

"No." Amber turned back to face them, whisking the tears from her eyes. "I'm going over to the church and I'm going to stay there until Carter gets back...no matter how long it takes."

CHAPTER THIRTY

THE SERPENT STRIKES

Carter could tell from the position of the sun overhead that his worst fear had been realized. He had left Amber waiting at the altar. For all she knew he could be lying by the side of the road somewhere seriously injured...or worse. If only he hadn't forgotten the ring then none of this would have happened.

Carter glanced down at Jacob, suddenly realizing how wrong he was. Even if he had remembered the ring, Jacob would still have fallen and Mary would still have gone looking for help. Only he wouldn't have been there when she needed to find him. The more he now thought about it, the more Carter realized that forgetting that ring had probably saved the boy's life.

"I just hope that Amber will be as understanding," he said aloud.

"Who are you talking to?" Jacob asked.

Carter smiled down at him. "No one, kiddo. How are you feeling?"

"Not so good," the boy replied weakly. "When's my sister coming back?"

Carter wished that he knew the answer to that question himself. It had been nearly two hours since Mary had left for town and Jacob's condition was continuing to deteriorate. If help didn't arrive soon....

"Carter!"

Carter rose to his feet, shielding his eyes as he stared up the slope. "Alec?"

"And I thought Kathleen had a good excuse for getting out of our wedding!"

Carter laughed in relief. "Am I glad to see you!"

"How's the boy?"

"He'll be a lot better once we get him back to the clinic!"

"Jesse and I will rig up a stretcher! We'll have you out of there in no time!"

"Hey, did you hear that, Jacob?" Carter's heart nearly stopped when he looked down and saw that the boy's eyes were now closed. "Jacob?" Carter dropped to his knees and gently shook him by the shoulders. "Jacob!"

The boy's eyes slowly opened again, followed by a lengthy yawn.

Carter rocked back on his heels, smiling in relief. "The next time you decide to take a nap, will you warn me first?"

* * * * *

Amber watched soberly as the church emptied out one pew at a time. Word had quickly spread that there wasn't going to be a wedding and before long only a handful of well-wishers remained to console her, including the parents of two of her students. This wasn't at all how she had envisioned her wedding day.

"I wish we could stay longer, dear," Rebecca Webster was saying, "but we left Mary at home to look after Jacob. We really should be getting back."

Amber smiled through her pain. "I understand. Thank you so much for—"

"Papa!" Stephen leapt off Kathleen's lap and ran up the aisle as his father came through the back door of the church.

Amber stood numbly as Alec approached her, bracing herself for the news. The first words out of his mouth told her all that she wanted to know. "He's all right."

Amber squeezed her eyes shut, releasing the tears that she had been so bravely holding back. Her prayers had been answered. "Thank you, Lord."

Rebecca Webster gave her a congratulatory embrace. "I just knew everything would work out."

"Thank you, Mrs. Webster."

"Webster...." Alec studied the woman's face, then that of the man at her side. "Alan and Rebecca Webster?"

Alan Webster stepped towards him. "That's right."

"I'm afraid there's been an accident involving your son...."

* * * * *

Carter had just finished putting a splint on Jacob's leg when Alec returned to the clinic with the boy's parents. "Look who I found?"

"Mama, Papa!" Jacob smiled as they followed Alec into the exam room. "I fell down."

"You certainly did," Rebecca Webster crooned as she rushed to her son's side. "Are you all right?"

"I'm fine, Mama."

Alan Webster shook his head as he looked over the extent of his son's injuries. "Well, that settles it. Come tomorrow morning I start building a fence out back. It should have been done the day we moved in."

"Can I help, Papa?" the boy pleaded.

"Of course you can, son. Just as soon as Doctor Buchanan says you're well enough."

Rebecca Webster looked with concern at the lump on her son's forehead. "He is going to be all right, isn't he, doctor?"

"He'll be fine," Carter assured her. "But I would like to keep him here for a few days just to monitor his condition. One of you, of course, is welcome to stay with him. We can set up a cot in his room."

"Thank you, doc, for everything." Alan Webster pumped Carter's hand. "I don't even want to think about what might have happened if you hadn't come along when you did. I'm just sorry it had to happen on your wedding day."

"Speaking of which...." Alec smiled over at Carter. "Amber is on her way over from the church."

"I think that's my cue." Carter stepped to the edge of the exam table, resting a hand on Jacob's splinted leg. "I've got to go now but Miss Amber and I will come by and see you later, all right?"

"All right."

Carter offered a few parting words to the boy's parents before hurrying out onto the front steps to watch for Amber. It wasn't long before he saw a procession of wagons coming up the road. Amber was riding in the first wagon, along with her aunt and uncle. The Thompson's, Kirsten and Jesse and the rest of the Ramsey's weren't too far behind. Carter would have preferred their reunion to be a bit more private but he wasn't going to let that deter him from finishing what he had started.

Amber scrambled down just as soon as her uncle brought the wagon to a stop. "Carter!"

"Sorry I'm late," he said with a contrite smile as he stepped forward to meet her.

Amber threw her arms around his neck, willing herself not to start crying again. "You're here now. That's all that matters."

Kirsten found it difficult to watch the couples' emotional reunion. They would have been married by now if it hadn't been for her.

"I know what you're thinking, Kirsten…." Jesse slipped his arm around her shoulders. "But it's not your fault. If you hadn't forgotten to tell your pa where Carter went, he never would have had a reason to go looking for him. We might not have gotten to Jacob in time."

"You're just saying that."

"No, Kirsten." Carter approached the side of the wagon where she was sitting. He had overheard Jesse's comments to her and wasn't about to let her take the blame for what had happened. "Jesse's right. Jacob might have ended up permanently lame if I hadn't gotten that leg of his set properly when I did. Another few minutes and it might have been too late."

Kirsten searched is eyes and saw nothing to cause her to think that he wasn't being anything but truthful with her. "Do you really mean it?"

"I mean it. Now…." Carter pulled the ring from his pocket as he turned back to face Amber. "What do you say we pick up where we left off?"

"But there's no one over at the church. Everyone got tired of waiting and went home."

Carter looked at all the smiling faces gathered around them. "Not everyone. How about it, reverend?"

Clive Thompson grinned, getting right into the spirit of things. "I say let's have ourselves a wedding!"

* * * * *

After exchanging their vows in a small ceremony at the clinic, Carter and Amber spent some time with Jacob before heading home to change and get ready for their departure on the afternoon train.

Carter was as proud as any man had the right to be as he carried his bride across the threshold into their new home. "Welcome home, Mrs. Buchanan."

Amber took a slow walk around the living room as soon as he set her down, looking at everything as if she had never seen it before.

"Something wrong?" Carter asked her.

"No." Amber retraced her steps to his side. "It's just the first time that I've been in here as your wife. I want to remember this moment forever."

Carter pulled her into his arms. "I've got a few memories I want to make myself."

Amber smiled demurely as she pushed him away. "I think I'd better go and get changed. We don't want to miss our train."

"There'll be another train tomorrow," Carter reminded her as his arms found their way back around her waist. "Who says we have to leave today?"

Amber was more than a little tempted to give in to his wishes. They had both been through so much today and she was still plagued by the strange feeling that they shouldn't be leaving town at all. But after thinking about it further, she decided that getting away might be just what she needed to put these ridiculous fears of hers to rest once and for all.

Carter stood patiently waiting for her decision. "Well?"

"Today, Carter Buchanan." Amber brushed his lips with a feather-light kiss before turning to head upstairs. "Today."

While Amber was upstairs changing, Carter carried their bags outside and put them in the back of the wagon that Alec had been kind enough to let them borrow for the afternoon. He was on his way inside when the sound of an approaching buggy drew his attention back to the yard. Nothing could have prepared him for the sight of Isaac Jameson at the reins. "What on earth is he doing here?"

"Whoa, there." Jameson brought his buggy to a stop alongside the wagon. "Afternoon, Buchanan."

Carter walked reluctantly back to the front gate. "Something I can do for you?"   Jameson removed his hat as he stepped down. "I just came by to offer my congratulations to you and your lovely bride. I'm sorry that I was unable to attend the ceremony but I had pressing matters to attend to at the bank."

"You weren't invited."

Jameson reacted to Carter's rebuff as if it were a slap in the face. It took him a moment to compose himself before he could continue. "Actually, I came by on another matter, as well. If you have a few moments I'd like to discuss it with you. It's most urgent."

"We have a train to catch," Carter told him, making no apology for the curtness of his tone.

Jameson glanced at the bags in the back of the wagon. "Well, perhaps when you get back, then. As I said, it's most urgent." He settled his hat back on his head as he turned to climb into the buggy. "Have a nice trip."

"We intend to."

Carter made his way back to the house, deciding not to mention Jameson's visit to Amber. But his good intentions were short-lived. He found her waiting for him as soon as he walked through the door. She had seen Jameson's arrival from their bedroom window upstairs.

"What was he doing here?" she asked, clearly shaken by his presence.

Carter smiled in an attempt to calm her. "He just came by to offer his congratulations. Are you all ready?"

Amber nodded, handing him the bag she was holding.

"Then let's go, shall we?" Carter placed a hand against the small of her back as he steered her out the door. "Niagara Falls is waiting."

* * * * *

The newlyweds were greeted by a throng of well-wishers when they arrived at the station a short while later. After a quick round of good-byes, they boarded the train to begin their trip to New York.

Amber began to relax almost as soon as they were underway. She was now grateful that she hadn't allowed her fears rob her of this special time with her new husband.

"Promise not to laugh if I tell you something?" she asked him.

"You wish you hadn't married me."

Amber giggled. "No, of course not. I've had this feeling that something horrible was going to happen if we left town today."

"Let's see...." Carter took out his watch. "We've been gone for five minutes and the worst thing that's happened so far is that I have to share you with a train full of strangers all the way to New York."

Amber smiled. "So you think I'm worrying for nothing."

"I think that everything that could possibly go wrong today already has. We're due for a little good luck."

"I don't believe in luck, remember?"

"Mr. Buchanan?"

Carter looked up as the conductor appeared beside their seat. "Yes?"

"A gentleman asked me to give this to you as soon as we were under way."

Carter reached for the envelope that was being held out to him. "Thank you."

Amber snuggled over beside him. "I wonder who it's from."

"Let's find out." Carter opened the envelope and took out the single sheet of stationary from inside. The letterhead at the top erased any doubt about the identity of its sender. "Jameson...."

Amber slowly pulled away from him, almost afraid to ask what was going through her mind. "What does he want?"

Carter's eyes slid closed as he dropped his head back against the seat. "I don't believe it."

"Carter, what is it?"

"He's calling in our loan."

Amber wasn't exactly sure what that meant but it didn't sound good. "Can he do that?"

"He can and he did. It says right here...." Carter pointed out the section in the letter to her. "If we don't have the balance of the loan paid in full by the end of the month, the house reverts back to him."

"By the end of the.... But we won't even be back from our honeymoon by then."

"I think that's what he's counting on. He's probably had this planned all along and has just been waiting for the right time to strike."

Amber finally understood why she had been so uneasy about their leaving town. She was also now convinced that Jameson's so called congratulatory visit to the house earlier had simply been a ruse to check up on their travel plans. "What are we going to do? Should we go back?"

"We're not going back." Carter refolded the letter and stuffed it back into the envelope. "That's exactly what he wants us to do."

"But the money. There's no way we can come up with that much by the end of the month."

"There's still some left from the inheritance."

"But not enough."

"No," Carter admitted.

Amber looked away to hide the pain in her eyes. She realized what was about to happen. "We're going to lose the house."

Carter grabbed her shoulders, turning her back to face him. "We are not going to lose the house. I won't allow it."

"But Jameson—"

Carter put a finger against her lips. "I'll wire Alec at our next stop and let him know what's going on. Maybe there's something he can do on his end to buy us some time. But for now...." Carter reached up and cupped the side of her face. "I don't want you to worry about it. Promise me?"

Amber didn't feel right about making a promise that she knew she couldn't keep but she didn't want to spoil their trip. "All right," she agreed. "I promise."

* * * * *

"Pardon me, but is Lieutenant Ramsey receiving this evening?"

Eric smiled as his father appeared in the doorway of his room, standing at full attention. "Hi, Pa."

"Your ma sent me up to tell you that supper will be ready in ten minutes."

"I'll be finished by then. Just doing some packing." Eric emptied out the two dresser drawers that he had been using for his clothes and transferred everything to the trunk at the foot of his bed.

Alec stepped up beside him. "Is it that time already?"

"Yeah." Eric paused, staring down into the trunk. "It's hard to believe it's been three months. It went by so fast."

"Too fast," Alec agreed. "We're going to miss you around here."

"I'm not so sure about Colin. He'll probably be glad to have the room all to himself again. And the dresser." Eric put the last of his things in the trunk and closed the lid.

"What about you?" Alec sat down on the end bed, facing him. "Are you excited about your assignment to Fort Moultrie?"

Eric rocked back on his heels, giving his father's question some thought. "I have admit that I was disappointed at first about not going to Washington, but I suppose that pushing paper around could get old pretty fast. At least at Fort Moultrie there'll be plenty to do."

"On that note...." Alec pulled a rolled up newspaper from his back pocket. "I thought you might be interested to see this."

"What is it?"

"Take a look."

Eric unrolled the paper and was surprised to find an article about Fort Moultrie right on the front page. His excitement only escalated from there. "It says here that Captain John Foster has been assigned to make repairs at Moultrie and two other forts in Charleston Harbor, Sumter and Castle Pickney." Eric smiled as he continued reading silently to himself. "How about that. John Foster."

"Do you know him?"

"He was my engineering instructor at West Point the first two years I was there. He's considered the most brilliant engineering mind in the army."

"Then he'll be in good company, won't he?"

Eric grinned at the compliment. "Do you mind if I take this with me?"

"Consider it yours."

Eric tucked the paper inside the satchel that he would be taking with him on the train. His thoughts then turned elsewhere. "How's Ma?"

"Her ankle's still a little tender but it doesn't seem to be slowing her down any."

"I don't mean about her ankle." Eric sat down beside his father on the bed. "I mean about my leaving tomorrow. Has she said anything to you?"

"Not that I can recall. But I'm sure she has her share of concerns. It's not like when we sent you off to West Point. At least then we knew when you were coming home."

Eric hated the thought of boarding that train tomorrow morning knowing how difficult it was going to be for his mother. Maybe he should have pushed harder for the assignment in Washington.

"I know what you're thinking," Alec said in response to his silence. "And I'm sure that you're mother would rest a whole lot easier knowing that you were safely tucked away in Washington. But do you honestly believe that's where God wants you to be?"

Eric knew exactly how to answer his father. Because of his reassignment to Fort Moultrie, his mother had reconciled with her past and agreed to let him meet his grandparents. He wouldn't trade that opportunity for anything, Washington included. "No, sir," Eric told him honestly. "And I don't believe that Ma would either."

Alec smiled as he rose back to his feet. "That's exactly what I was waiting to hear. Now let's go eat."

CHAPTER THIRTY-ONE

OLD FRIENDS,
NEW ENEMIES

Near Baltimore

Hannah had fallen asleep shortly after their departure from Philadelphia yesterday afternoon, and with the exception of breakfast that morning, had yet to waken for more than a few minutes at a time. Under other circumstances Sean might have thought her to be ill, but he knew that the events of the past few days had left her emotionally and physically drained. Sleep was what she needed right now above anything else.

He, on the other hand, had slept very little, electing to pass the time reading through the file that Pinkerton had given him before he'd left Chicago. He now realized that he had made a grave mistake by not doing so sooner. Nowhere was there any mention that he was going to be compensated for the information that he gathered, leading him to only one conclusion. It would be solely up to him to provide for their needs while in Baltimore. To have assumed otherwise was his own fault. And now Hannah would be made to suffer for his carelessness.

Sean glanced down as she stirred on the seat beside him, wishing now that he had insisted she return to Chicago to stay with his family. At least there she would have been guaranteed a roof over her head. But what could he offer her in Baltimore?

"Is there something I can get you, sir?"

Sean looked up as the butcher boy stopped beside their seat with a basket of sandwiches and fruit for sale. He was about to decline but then realized that it might be the last opportunity they had to get something to eat until he found work.

Sean paid the young man for two sandwiches and four apples, tucking two of the apples in his bag for later. If worse came to worse they would at least have something for breakfast tomorrow morning.

Hannah woke up as he was unwrapping one of the sandwiches. "Hungry?" he asked her.

"Famished." Hannah pushed herself up on the seat, taking the sandwich he was holding out to her.

Sean unwrapped the second sandwich for himself, deciding to eat only half of it now.

"Where are we?" Hannah turned to the window beside her, searching the passing landscape for clues. Nothing looked familiar. But then why should it? She had never been east of Philadelphia before in her life. "Are we almost there?" she finally asked.

"It'll probably be another half hour."

Hannah detected something in his tone that she didn't understand. "Is something wrong?"

"Why do you ask that?" Sean took another chomp out of his sandwich, avoiding her gaze.

"Because yesterday when we boarded the train you seemed so excited about getting to Baltimore. And now...."

"I'm excited."

"Sean Donnelly." Hannah scolded him first with her tongue and then her eyes. "We may have only been married for two days but I know when something is bothering you. Now what is it?"

Sean decided there was no reason to keep his concerns from her any longer. She would find out the truth soon enough. "I don't know where we're going to stay tonight, for starters."

Hannah almost laughed, finding his concern rather trivial. "I'm that sure Baltimore has hotels. And then tomorrow we can start looking for a small room to rent. Until we need something bigger, of course." Her eyes gleamed at the thought of starting a family.

"No, you don't understand...." Sean attempted again to explain the situation, alluding to the fact that he had no way to support them. "It's my own fault for not checking things out sooner."

Hannah found herself more confused than ever. "But why wouldn't you be paid just like any of Pinkerton's other agents?"

"Because I'm not an agent," he reminded her. "I agreed to this deal to keep myself from going to prison, nothing more."

"But he's got to pay you something."

"Does he?"

Hannah realized his point. Just because she wanted it to be so didn't mean that it was so. "Then you'll just have to get a job," she decided. "And I can help out by taking in laundry and sewing...." Hannah reached over and took his hand, further emphasizing her resolve not to let this one little setback back spoil the start of their new life together. "We'll be fine."

Sean was continually amazed by her ability to take life just as it came. It made him love her all the more. "Well, I guess if you're not complaining then I shouldn't be either."

Hannah laid her head against his shoulder. "The Lord will provide for us, Sean. He always has."

Sean smiled, thinking how very right she was. "I can't argue with you there."

* * * * *

Baltimore

Blake Harris took one final look around his room to be sure he hadn't forgotten anything and then headed down the long hallway that led to the second story landing. He stopped at the top of the winding staircase, taking a firmer grasp upon the handles of his bags as he started down. His mother stood waiting for him at the bottom, her cheeks glistening with freshly shed tears.

"Blake, dear." Abigail Harris reached up and tenderly caressed the side of her eldest son's face. "I wish that things didn't have to be this way, but your father—" She started as the study door slammed shut behind her. "He refuses to change his mind."

"It's all right, Mother," the young man assured her. "I think we both knew this was coming. It's best that I go."

Abigail pressed a lace handkerchief against her mouth, fighting back her grief. "Promise me that you won't leave the city. I couldn't bare it."

"I won't." Blake leaned over and kissed her goodbye. "I'll write you as soon as I get settled. And tell Andrew that I wish him luck at Harvard. Maybe father will finally have a son he can be proud of."

"Blake, you mustn't think that way. Your father loves you!"

Blake ignored his mother's final pleas as he strode out the front door. He didn't stop until he reached the massive iron gate at the end of the walkway, deciding only at the last moment to turn back for one final glimpse of the only home he'd ever known. He caught his father's eye as the elder man stood watching his departure from the window of his study. The look of disappointment on his face was like a hot poker in the young man's heart.

Blake took a deep breath as he turned away, setting his sights down the road ahead of him. "I'll give you a reason to be proud of me one day, Father," he whispered into the descending night sky. "I promise you I will."

* * * * *

Sean took a firm grip on Hannah's hand as they stepped off the train at Baltimore's Calvert Street Depot just before eight o'clock that night. Neither of them uttered a word as they stood looking around at their new surroundings, unsure what to do next. Sean had been hoping there would be someone waiting to meet them when they arrived, but it appeared that for now they were on their own.

"It's going to be dark soon," he finally said. "We best find a hotel."

"Shane Donavan? Is that you?"

Hannah took a firmer grip on Sean's hand as a tall man in a dark overcoat came running towards them.

"It's all right," Sean whispered to her. "He's probably one of Pinkerton's contacts."

The man stopped in front of them, smiling as wide as his mouth would allow. "I couldn't believe it when I saw you. Why didn't you let me know you were coming?" His voice lowered considerably as he continued but the smile remained in place. "Jared Neeley. I work for Mr. Pinkerton. I apologize for the impromptu greeting but you can never tell who might be watching." His voice rose again. "So how long are you in town for?"

"Well, I…." Sean wasn't sure how to respond.

"That's great. I think you're really going to like Baltimore." Neeley tipped the brim of his hat towards Hannah. "And this must be the lovely Mrs. Donavan." His voice lowered again. "I realize this is short notice but there have been some new developments in the case that I need to discuss with you right away. Perhaps after you get your wife settled."

Sean exchanged an awkward glance with Hannah. "We don't actually have a place to stay yet."

"That's all been taken care of by Mr. Pinkerton. He secured a room for you at a boardinghouse just a few blocks from here. You and your wife should be quite comfortable there."

Sean turned again to Hannah and found her smiling for the first time since they stepped off the train.

"I'll walk you over and introduce you to the landlady, if you'd like," Neeley offered. "Then we can talk."

"That's very kind of you."

"Anything for an old friend." Neeley thumped Sean on the back. "Gosh, it's good to see you."

* * * * *

Hannah was quite taken with the accommodations that Pinkerton had arranged for their stay. The furnishings were modest at best, but the room possessed a certain charm that made her feel right at home from the moment she set foot inside. Sean's only concern was that it might not fit their budget. He probably had enough for a night or two, but if they wanted to remain any longer than that, he would have to begin looking for work first thing in the morning.

"How much do I owe you, Mrs. Morgan?"

The elderly landlady waved her hands back and forth as Sean reached for his billfold. "Not a cent, young man. The room has been paid for in advance for the next six months, and that includes meals."

Sean's mouth gaped open. "Six months?"

"That's right. Now if there's anything you young folks need you just let me know. I'll be downstairs in the kitchen."

Hannah walked with her to the door. "Thank you, Mrs. Morgan."

"My pleasure, dear."

Hannah closed the door and then turned to face her husband. His mouth was still gaping. "Well, don't look so surprised. Didn't I tell you that the Lord would provide?"

"Yes, you did. I just wasn't expecting free room and board for six months. Now all I need is a job."

"You'll get one." Hannah moved over to the bed to begin unpacking their bags.

Sean slipped up behind her, looping his arms around her waist. "Neeley asked me to meet him at the restaurant across the street. Will you be all right here alone for awhile?"

Hannah turned to face him. "I'm not exactly alone, you know. Mrs. Morgan did say there were three other boarders. I'm sure I can find someone to converse with should the need for human companionship arise. But thanks for caring," she added with an appreciative smile.

Sean returned her smile before planting a good-bye kiss on her forehead. "I don't know how long I'll be so don't wait up."

After Sean left, Hannah finished putting their things away and then decided to go and explore their new home. As she stepped from the room, she collided with a young man carrying a stack of books tucked up under his chin. The books ended up on the floor in a jumbled heap. "I'm so sorry," she apologized, stooping down at once to pick them up. "I wasn't looking where I was going."

"No harm done. Here, let me take those." The young man knelt beside her, reaching for the books that she had already gathered up. "It's my own fault for trying to carry so many at one time."

"That's very understanding of you." Hannah handed him the last book, taking note that it was on the subject of criminal law. "Oh. Are you a lawyer?"

"Not a practicing one, but yes, I have studied law. I'm hoping to start my own—" The young man froze as he met Hannah's gaze over the stack of books. "Hannah...? Hannah Cavanaugh?"

* * * * *

Sean looked curiously at the envelope that Neeley had just slipped him under the table. "What's this?"

"For any expenses that you might have while you're here. If it's not enough just let me know."

Sean looked inside the envelope and was shocked by the amount of money inside. "Is Mr. Pinkerton always this generous? First the room at the boardinghouse and now this?"

"He's being paid quite handsomely by the railroad to find whoever is responsible for the robberies. And he figures that the less time you have to spend working somewhere else to put food on your table the more time you can spend working on the case."

"I won't argue with him there." Sean tucked the envelope inside his coat for safe keeping until he could turn it over to Hannah. She would know best what their current needs might be. But first things first. "You mentioned that there was a new development in the case."

Neeley passed him a handbill with the words *The Son's of Secession* printed in bold letters across the top. "I take it this isn't an invitation to choir practice," Sean jested.

"Hardly. The leader of that charming little group is a man by the name of Mason Alexander. He recruits well-educated young men from wealthy families and force-feeds them his anti-government rhetoric. Last week a handbill just like the one you're holding was sent to the president of the railroad, Samuel Felton. On the back was a handwritten letter from Alexander allegedly claiming responsibility for the robberies. Felton, of course, wanted every member of the group rounded up and branded by sundown, but without more evidence we never would have gotten a conviction." Neeley locked eyes with Sean across the table. "And that's where you come in."

"What do you want me to do?"

"Infiltrate the group."

Sean leaned forward in his chair, curious to hear more. "How do you propose I do that? I don't exactly fit the profile."

"With a little help from a new friend. His name is Blake Harris. He's twenty-three, a graduate of Harvard Law School and a known member of the Son's of Secession. A couple of weeks ago Harris and another young man in the group by the name of Theodore Johnson were caught trying to steal the flag outside the capital building. Johnson's father waved a bit of green under all the right noses and young Teddy was back out on the street a few hours later. Harris spent two weeks in jail and was just released today. We're hoping that his little brush with the law didn't sour him too much and he'll settle right back into his old pattern of behavior. In the meantime, we want you to befriend him. Do whatever's necessary to gain his trust. If we're lucky, you just might get yourself an invite to choir practice."

Sean was overwhelmed by the thought of what he was being asked to do, but he knew that the sooner he uncovered the evidence that Pinkerton needed, the sooner he and Hannah could be on their way back to Chicago. "Any idea where I might find young Mr. Harris?"

"Try across the street," Neeley suggested. "He moved into the boardinghouse two hours before you did."

* * * * *

Despite Neeley's repeated assurances that Blake Harris had never exhibited any violent tendencies, Sean was unsettled at the thought of having him living under the same roof. It would make his assignment to befriend the young man that much easier, but at what cost to Hannah's safety?

Sean made his way back across the street to the boardinghouse, noting that the upstairs window of their room was still aglow with lamplight. He was glad that Hannah had decided to wait up for him. It would give him the chance to talk with her before making contact with Harris. But just how much should he reveal to her about their fellow boarder? Neeley had suggested that the less she knew the better, but Sean didn't feel right about withholding things from her. She had the right to know what he was being asked to do, especially if his life might be in danger because of it.

Hannah ran to greet him as soon as he walked through the front door. "There you are. We were just talking about you."

"We?" Sean stepped further into the room, only then noticing the young man sitting on the sofa off to his right. He didn't need a formal introduction to know who this was.

"Shane…." Hannah took his hand as she led the way back over to the sofa, "I'd like for you to meet, Blake Harris. Blake, this is my husband, Shane."

Sean silently praised her for remembering not to use his real name. Now was not the time to blow his cover.

Blake was immediately on his feet, ready with all the appropriate pleasantries. "It's good to meet you, sir."

"Likewise." Sean shook the younger man's extended hand.

"You can't imagine how surprised I was when I ran into your wife upstairs earlier," Blake told him. "We haven't seen each other in years."

Sean felt as if he had just been kicked in the stomach. "You two know each other?"

"Blake use to date my friend Charlotte's younger sister, Doreen, back in Philadelphia," Hannah explained. "We met while he was visiting her over Christmas break from Harvard three years ago. Small world, isn't it?"

Too small, Sean was thinking. No one, not even Neeley, could have foreseen that Hannah and Blake Harris were former acquaintances. The rules of the game had just gotten a lot more complicated.

Sean felt a hand on his arm and looked down into Hannah's concerned gaze. "Are you all right?"

Sean forced a smile past his lips. "Just a bit tired. Do you mind if we turn in?" He was anxious to put as much distance between her and Harris as possible.

Hannah was visibly disappointed. "I was hoping we could all visit for awhile. Mrs. Morgan just put some water on for tea."

"Actually, I have another engagement, anyway," Blake said suddenly. "Perhaps we can talk more tomorrow." His smile flowed from Hannah over to Sean. "Again, it was nice meeting you. Have a good night."

Sean watched as Harris disappeared out the front door. Where could he be going at this time of night? To steal another flag? Or something more sinister. Sean was itching to follow him but didn't know how he would explain his absence to Hannah.

"Sean, are you coming?" Hannah was already halfway up the stairs.

Sean cast a final glance at the front door before turning to join her. He would have to begin his investigation of Blake Harris another time.

"How was your meeting with Mr. Neeley?" Hannah asked as they entered their room.

"Fine." Sean closed the door and walked over to sit down on the end of the bed.

"What about that new development he was talking about? Did they find out who is responsible for the robberies?"

Sean removed one of his shoes and let it drop to the floor with a thud. "They have pretty good idea," he admitted. Should he tell her that Harris might be involved? Would she even believe him if he did?

"I still can't get over running into Blake after all these years." Hannah sat down at the small vanity beside the bed and began taking the pins out of her hair. "I'll have to write Charlotte and let her know."

Sean dropped his other shoe to the floor. *You have to tell her before this goes any further*, he decided. *She needs to know the truth.*

Hannah picked up her brush, tapping the end of it against her chin. "I wonder if her sister Doreen ever got married."

"Hannah...." Sean reached into his coat pocket and took out the handbill that Neeley had given him. "There's something that I think you should know about Blake Harris...."

Sean proceeded to tell her everything that Neeley had shared with him about the Son's of Secession, including Harris's recent release from jail.

Hannah got up from where she was sitting and moved to sit beside him on the bed, her gaze riveted upon the handbill. "I can't believe that Blake would be involved in a group like that."

"I'm afraid he is."

Hannah swallowed uneasily, unsure she wanted to know the answer to her next question. "Do you think that he was involved in the robberies, too?"

"I don't know. That's what Neeley's hoping I can find out."

"By pretending to be Blake's friend?"

Sean could tell by the tone of her voice that she didn't approve. "I don't like the thought of deceiving him any more than you do," he assured her. "But if he knows something that can help us…."

Hannah took the handbill from him, studying it at further length. "Then I guess you don't have any choice, do you?"

Sean slipped an arm around her shoulders. "I think we've talked enough about this for tonight. Why don't we try and get some sleep?"

Hannah agreed and proceeded to ready herself for bed. Yet despite her best efforts to put Blake Harris from her mind, she found herself thinking about him all the more. Sean awoke almost two hours later to find her still up. "Are you all right?" he asked.

"I just can't sleep." Hannah slid from beneath the covers and reached for her robe. "I think I'll go downstairs and get some warm milk. Would you like some?"

"That sounds like a fine idea."

Hannah walked to the door, smiling feebly at him over her shoulder. "I won't be long."

"Do you want me to come with you?"

"I'll be fine."

Hannah headed down the hall to the staircase, using the soft glow from the sconces that were spaced intermittently along the wall to light her way. She stopped suddenly when a figure appeared just a few feet in front of her. "Who—who's there?" she stammered nervously.

"Hannah…." The figure staggered closer, reaching a trembling hand towards her through the darkness.

"Blake?"

"Please…help me…."

Hannah stepped back with a startled gasp as the young man collapsed to the floor in front of her. She called his name again but there was no response. "Sean!"

Sean came bolting out of their room. "Hannah—" His plea ground to a halt when he saw Harris's lifeless form lying at her feet. "What happened?"

"I don't know." Hannah backed up a few more steps, visibly shaken by the scene before her. "He just collapsed."

Sean knelt beside Blake, noting that the young man's face was a swollen mass of cuts and bruises. "He's been beaten up pretty bad."

Hannah slowly inched her way back, peering over Sean's shoulder. "Is he…?"

Sean felt for a pulse at the hollow of his neck. "He's alive."

Hannah squeezed her eyes shut. "Oh, thank God."

"Do you know which room is his?"

Hannah looked back up the hallway, trying to remember which room she had seen Blake go into earlier. "I'm not sure."

"Let's put him in ours." Sean slipped his hands beneath the young man's shoulders, instructing Hannah to grab his feet. Together they managed to carry him back to their bed where Hannah set right to work washing away the matted blood from his face with a damp cloth. "Who do you suppose did this to him?"

Sean picked up the handbill from off the nightstand beside the bed. "This would be my guess."

Hannah stared for a moment at the slip of paper and then quickly turned her attention back to Blake. "Some of these cuts are pretty deep. And there's no telling what might be busted up inside. Maybe we should call a doctor."

"I'll go get Mrs.—" Sean stopped as Blake began to stir. His eyes opened slowly, coming to rest upon Hannah. "Where…." He strained to lift his head.

"You're in our room at the boardinghouse," Hannah told him. "You collapsed out in the hallway."

Blake expelled a sigh as he relaxed his head back against the pillow. "I was hoping it was all a bad dream."

Sean stepped to the edge of the bed. "Do you want to tell us what happened?"

The young man shook his head. "I can't."

"Blake...." Hannah gently laid a hand against his shoulder. "We want to help you. Please let us."

"No." Blake grimaced, grasping the side of his rib cage. "I can't take the chance that you might get hurt, too."

Sean held the handbill up where he could see it. "Does it have anything to do with this?"

Blake stared back at it like a frightened child. "Where did you get that?"

Sean pulled a chair over beside the bed and sat down. "Before I answer that, there's something you need to know.... My name isn't Shane Donovan. It's Sean Donnelly." Sean realized that he was be taking a huge risk by revealing his true identity, but something about Blake Harris reminded him of himself only a few months ago. Where would he be now if Neal hadn't taken a similar risk?

The young man's confusion was obvious. "I don't understand."

"I was hired by Allan Pinkerton to find out who's behind all the robberies."

Blake looked up at Hannah, realizing what she must be thinking about him. "You don't believe that I...."

"No, Blake. No, of course we don't." Hannah stole a glance at Sean before she continued. "But if you know who did...?"

Blake turned away, reluctant to carry the conversation any further.

Sean wasn't about to let him off that easy. "Was it Mason Alexander?"

The young man kept to himself for a few moments longer and then slowly turned back to face Sean. "Yes. He never did any of the dirty work himself but he was behind it all the same."

Sean scooted his chair closer to the bed. "Do you know what he's planning?"

"No. He never talked about what the money was going to be used for and most knew better than to ask. Those who didn't...?" Blake left the rest to their imaginations.

"How did you get mixed up with a man like that?" Hannah wanted to know.

Blake fell silent again, trying to find the words to explain. "All of my life I've always done everything that my father wanted me to, including going to law school and ending my relationship with Doreen. He said that she wasn't on the same rung of the social ladder as we were and he threatened to cut me out of his will if I didn't stop seeing her."

Hannah could tell from his expression how deeply he regretted his decision to do so. "Blake, I'm so sorry."

"It's all right. It probably wouldn't have worked out between us anyway."

Sean cleared his throat, trying to steer the conversation back to the matter at hand. "You still haven't explained how you came to be involved with The Son's of Secession."

"Right." Blake took a moment to gather his thoughts. "I joined the group a couple of months ago because they stood against everything that my father believed in. It was my way of letting him know that he wasn't going to run my life anymore. But the truth is...I never felt too good about my decision after that. Especially when people started getting hurt."

"Including you?" Sean asked, alluding to the beating the young man had taken.

Blake nodded. "I went to tell Alexander that I wanted out of the group. This was his reply."

Sean was surprised by how closely Blake's experience with Mason Alexander mirrored his own with Liam O'Brien.

He was now more determined than ever to do all that he could to help this young man before it was too late.

Hannah was thinking the very same thing. "We can't just let him get away with this," she said in reference to Alexander. "There has to be something we can do."

"There is," Sean assured her, already devising a plan in his mind. He turned back to Blake. "When's the next meeting?"

"Tomorrow night. But why?"

"I want you to take me with you."

CHAPTER THIRTY-TWO

THE SON'S OF SECESSION

Baxter, Pennsylvania

Kathleen struggled to control her emotions as the family gathered to see Eric off on the train the following morning. She had made a promise to herself that she wasn't going to cry and was determined to hold herself to it no matter what. The last thing she wanted was for his final moments with them to be marred by her tears.

"Are you sure you have everything?" she asked him. "The daguerreotype and the needlework for your grandmother? And the cigars for your grandfather?"

Eric nudged the bag at his feet. "I've got everything right here, Ma."

"Not everything." Kirsten handed him the package that she had been hiding behind her back. "It's from Jesse and me. I hope you like it."

"If it's from you I'm sure I'll—" A lump rose in Eric's throat as he tore back the brown paper to reveal a black, leather-bound journal with his initials stamped in gold on the front cover. "It's beautiful, Kirsten."

"We thought you might like to write about all of your adventures down South," she explained. "Do you like it?"

"I love it. Thank you." Eric placed a kiss on her fore-head. "Thank Jesse for me, too."

"I will. He wanted to be here himself but—"

"You-hoo! Eric!"

"Oh, no." Eric groaned when he saw Alicia mounting the platform steps behind him. "How did she find out what time I was leaving? I purposely didn't tell her."

Colin took a nervous step away from him. "Oops. I think that was me."

Eric glared at him but that was all he had time for. Alicia was closing in fast.

"Oh, thank heavens I got here in time," she panted, scrambling to Eric's side. "I was afraid I might have missed you."

"It really wasn't necessary for you to come all the way down here, Alicia."

"Nonsense. I couldn't let you leave without giving you a proper good-bye." Alicia's gaze swept him from head to toe. "My, how handsome you look in that uniform. It gives me chills the way it brings out the blue in your eyes."

"They're brown," Eric reminded her.

Alicia peered at him closer. "Oh, so they are. Silly me."

"Last call! All aboard!"

Eric silently thanked the conductor for his timing. "Excuse me, Alicia, but I only have a few moments left and I'd like to spend them with my family."

"Oh, of course. How inconsiderate of me. Good-bye, Eric." Alicia closed her eyes as she puckered her lips in anticipation of his kiss.

Eric opted for a firm handshake instead. "Good-bye, Alicia."

Alicia's eyes flew open. "Eric Lee Ramsey!" she fumed. "You are the most infuriating man I have ever met! If you think I am going to wait around here for you while you're off playing soldier then you are sorely mistaken! It is over between us, and this time for good!"

Eric tried not to snicker as he watched her stomp away in a huff. "I think those are the nicest words she's ever said to me."

Colin moved back to his side. "Does that mean I'm forgiven?"

Eric started to glare at him again but quickly replaced it with a smile. "You're forgiven."

"Eric...." Alec clapped him on the back. "You'd best get on board that train before it leaves without you. Be a mighty long walk to South Carolina."

"It sure would be, Pa." Eric picked up his bag, releasing a sigh as he stood back to his feet. "I guess this is it."

"Be sure to write as soon as you get there," Kathleen implored him.

"I will, Ma." Eric hugged her and then moved on to all the others, ending with his father.

"You'll be in our prayers," Alec told him.

"And you, mine." Eric hugged him close and then made a dash for the train. He barely made it on board before it pulled away.

"Good-bye, Eric," Kathleen whispered bravely.

Alec slipped an arm around her waist, watching her as she watched the train. "Are you going to be all right?"

Kathleen let her gaze linger for a few moments longer on the departing train and then turned to smile up at him. "I'll be fine, Alec," she assured. "I just have to keep reminding myself that God must have a purpose for sending Eric to South Carolina."

"I know He does. Now let's get you home and off that ankle."

Alec helped her up onto the wagon seat and then plunked Stephen down beside her while the other children piled into the back. He was readying to climb up himself when someone hailed him from behind. The telegraph operator, John Russell, was quickly approaching the wagon.

"I'm glad I caught you before you left, Alec," the young man panted. "This just came for you."

"Thanks, John."

"Who's it from, Pa?" Nathan asked.

"Maybe Eric," Stephen said.

"No, silly. He just left." Nathan turned back to his father, waiting for his reply.

"It's from Carter."

Kathleen smiled. "Oh, what a nice surprise. Are they enjoying Niagara Falls?"

Alec frowned as he began reading the message the young man had sent. "I don't believe it."

"What's wrong?"

"Jameson has called in their loan."

"What?"

Alec handed her the telegram. "If they don't pay off the balance by the end of the month they lose the house."

Kathleen shook her head as she read the disturbing news for herself. "But they won't even be back from their honeymoon by then."

"I'm sure he's well aware of that." Alec took the telegram from her and tucked it in his pocket. "I think it's time that I had a little chat with Isaac P. Jameson, the third. Colin, will you take your ma and the others on home?"

"Sure, Pa." Colin stepped over the back of the wagon seat and took hold of the reins.

Alec reached up and laid a hand on Kathleen's knee. "I'll see you at home later."

"Alec...." Kathleen grabbed his hand before he could pull it away. "Please be careful."

"It's Jameson you should be worrying about."

* * * * *

"Sir?" Jason rose from the stool he was sitting on behind the counter, following Alec with his gaze. "Excuse me, sir, but you can't go back there!"

Alec ignored the teller's repeated protests as he stormed through the bank on his way to Jameson's office. He burst through the door a few moments later with Jason hot on his heels.

"Mr. Jameson," the young man sputtered, "I apologize, sir. I tried to stop him."

Jameson rose from his chair, resting his palms in front of him on the edge of his desk. "That's quite all right, Jason. I have a few moments before my next appointment."

"Yes, sir." Jason scowled at Alec before sulking out of the office. The door clicked shut behind him.

Jameson swept his hand towards the chair on the opposite side of his desk. "Please, have a seat."

Alec chose to remain standing.

Jameson settled back into his own chair, folding his hands in front of him. "To what do I owe the pleasure of this visit?"

Alec took Carter's telegram from his pocket and tossed it on Jameson's desk. "You called in the Buchanan's loan."

Jameson stared smugly at the slip of paper. "So I did."

"Why?"

Jameson focused his gaze back on Alec. "An investment opportunity came up and I needed to liquidate some assets. It was purely a business decision."

"You call threatening to take away a man's home a business decision? What have you got against Carter Buchanan?"

Jameson rose back to his feet, his jaw clenched. "Nothing, and I resent the implication. Now if you're quite through...."

"I'm through." Alec stepped towards the door, turning back at the last moment. "Oh, and by the way. The next time you're in need of medical attention, I'm afraid I won't be able to treat you. It's nothing personal, you understand. Purely a business decision."

* * * * *

"Are you absolutely sure about this, Josiah?" Alec watched uneasily as the elder man counted out every cent that he and Ida had saved over the past twenty years. "That's an awful lot of money."

"I'm sure that I'm not going to let my niece lose that house, Alec." Josiah slipped the money inside his coat. "Now would you care to accompany me back to the bank?"

Alec grinned. "I wouldn't miss it for the world."

* * * * *

Jameson smirked as Alec walked into his office for the second time in less than an hour. "Well, doctor. Have you come to apologize for the little scene you created earlier? Or do I have to—" Jameson's smile petered out as Josiah appeared at Alec's side. "Mr. Crowley."

"Mr. Jameson." Josiah stepped forward and plunked down a stack of bills in the center of his desk. "I believe that should cover it."

Jameson recoiled from the money as if it were about to bite him. "What's this?"

"I'm here to pay off my niece's loan."

Jameson swallowed back his discomfort before eliciting a nervous chuckle. "Indeed. Well, isn't this a pleasant surprise?" He reached reluctantly to gather up the money. "I suppose you'll be wanting a receipt."

"If you don't mind."

Jameson's demeanor remained cordial as he readied the paperwork, but inside Alec could tell that he was seething. The serpent had been beaten at his own game.

"Here you are." Jameson handed over the deed to the property along with a receipt. "I believe you'll find everything in order."

Josiah looked over the papers before slipping them inside his coat. "Thank you, Mr. Jameson. And don't bother getting up. We'll see ourselves out."

* * * * *

Baltimore

Jared Neeley listened closely as Sean outlined his intentions of accompanying Blake Harris to a *Son's of Secession* meeting that night, but he was less than enthusiastic about giving the young man his approval. "I don't like it," he said when Sean was finished. "It's too risky."

Sean was both confused and disappointed by his lack of support. "I thought that infiltrating the Son's of Secession is what you wanted me to do."

Neeley transferred his gaze over to Blake, "That was before I saw Alexander's handiwork up close."

Sean refused to let a few cuts and bruises deter him. "I'm willing to take that risk."

"I'm not." Neeley's tone left little room for negotiation. "You're a civilian. You haven't been trained in undercover procedures."

"You knew that when I stepped off the train last night," Sean reminded him. "Or would you prefer to wait for another opportunity to get close to Alexander?"

Neeley realized the younger man had him backed into a corner. It could take months, even years, to get another such opportunity. They had to act now. "All right," he agreed.

"It's still against my better judgment…but I don't see as where we have much choice. Just be careful—both of you," he urged the two young men seated before him. "If something doesn't feel right, and I mean anything, I want you to—" Neeley turned to look over his shoulder at the door to Blake's room.

"What is it?" Sean asked.

Neeley pressed a finger against his lips. "There's someone listening at the door."

Sean was quickly out of his chair. "I think I know who it is."

Hannah started as the door opened, turning to make a hasty retreat down the hallway.

"Hannah, wait!" Sean caught up with her just as she was about to enter their room. He wasn't prepared for the tears he saw in her eyes as she turned to face him. "Hannah…." Sean reached up to wipe her cheeks, but for every tear he whisked away, there were two more ready to take its place.

"I'm sorry," she said through trembling lips. "I know I shouldn't be carrying on so. It's just…. Oh, Sean, I'm so scared. I don't want to lose you."

Sean gathered her into his arms as her sobs continued. "You're not going to lose me," he assured her. "I'm going to be fine."

Blake reluctantly approached the couple from behind, feeling as if were intruding upon a private moment. "We should be going."

Sean waved him on. "Wait for me downstairs."

Hannah turned her head as Blake filed past with Neeley close behind him. She couldn't bear to look at him. The bruises on his face were a painful reminder of the danger that her husband was walking into.

Sean gently turned her back to face him. "I have to go now. But no matter what happens, remember that I love you."

Hannah nodded bravely, closing her eyes as she received his kiss to her forehead. When she opened them again a few moments later, he was gone.

Hannah slipped quickly into their room and made her way over to the bed, weeping uncontrollably. "Please, Lord," she implored fervently as she sank to her knees. "Please protect him. I need him. Our baby needs him."

Hannah gasped through her tears, realizing what she had just said. A baby? But how was that possible? They had only been married a few days. It was too soon to know if she was with child.

"But I do know," she realized. *For with God all things are possible....*

Hannah smiled as she pressed a hand against her midsection, marveling at the beautiful gift that she had been given. She knew it was God's promise to her that Sean would be coming back to her—to them both. "Thank you, Lord." Hannah raised her eyes to the ceiling as tears of joy streamed down her face. "Thank you."

A sudden knock at the door interrupted her private celebration. "Hannah, dear?"

Hannah quickly composed herself. "Yes, Mrs. Morgan?"

"I was just about to have some tea, dear, and I thought you might like to join me."

"I'd love to, Mrs. Morgan. I'll be right down."

Hannah rose and went to the basin beside the bed to splash some water on her face and reinsert several pins in her hair that had come loose. When she headed downstairs a few minutes later, her face was beaming. "You're going to be a father, Sean."

* * * * *

"Is this where all the meetings are held?" Sean asked as he and Blake approached an old abandoned barn about a half-mile out of town.

"No. It's a different location every time. That's probably how Alexander has been able to stay one step ahead of the law."

Sean stopped suddenly as they were about to go inside, causing Blake to stumble in an attempt to avoid running into him. A smile spread slowly across his face. "A baby?"

Blake looked at him as if he had lost his senses. "A what?"

Sean shook his head, eliciting an abbreviated chuckle as he reached to open the barn door. "It's nothing."

Blake immediately drew the attention of a tall man in a stylish black suit as soon as they entered. Sean watched as the man excused himself from the group that he was talking with and began walking towards them. "Is that him?" he asked, sensing Blake's sudden uneasiness.

"Yeah," Blake whispered back.

"Harris...." Mason Alexander approached with a beguiling smile, his gaze securely fastened upon Blake. "I'm delighted to see that you decided to join us after all." He reached up and lightly touched one of the many bruises still visible on the young man's face. "No hard feelings?"

"No, sir," Blake said calmly, trying not to flinch beneath his touch.

"Good." Alexander's piercing blue eyes bore into Sean next. "And who do I have the pleasure of meeting this fine evening?"

Blake turned to make the introduction. "This is a friend of mine, Shane Donavan. He's interested in joining our cause."

"Well, Mr. Donavan...." Alexander took a moment to size up the young man standing before him. "Did Mr. Harris inform you of the price of admission?"

"Yes, sir." Sean slipped an envelope from under his coat and handed it to Alexander. "One thousand dollars."

Alexander thumbed through the contents of the envelope. "Fine. Welcome to the Son's of Secession."

Sean reluctantly grasped the man's offered hand. "Thank you, sir."

"Why don't you gentlemen find a seat. We're about to get started."

An immediate hush fell over the gathering as soon as Alexander stepped behind a makeshift podium at the front of the barn. "I want to thank all of you for coming here tonight," he began. "You're unswerving devotion to our cause is commendable." He paused to take a few steps to his right, standing with his hands laced behind his back as he turned once again to address the gathering. "It's been a hard road, but now after eight long months we are at last nearing the end of our journey. And this, gentlemen...." Alexander swept his arm out to his side, directing their attention to the large tarp that was draped over a bed of hay bales off to his right. "This is what all of your hard work has brought us."

A round of excited murmurs circulated through the onlookers as Alexander pulled back the tarp to reveal a large stockpile of weapons.

Sean exchanged a nervous glance with Blake, shuddering to think what Alexander was planning with such an arsenal at his disposal. There was enough firepower to start a small war.

"It's a good start, gentlemen...." Alexander's gaze swung back to the captive audience before him. "But it's not enough. Therefore, I am in need of three volunteers to accompany me tomorrow night on one final mission." His gaze traveled from one anxious face to the next, stopping directly upon Sean. "Perhaps out newest member. Donavan, wasn't it?"

Sean felt every eye suddenly trained upon him. He knew that if he refused Alexander's request he ran the risk of inviting suspicion upon himself. That left only one clear path before him.

Sean rose to his feet, taking a bold step forward. "Count me in."

* * * * *

Sean and Blake met up with Neeley at a prearranged location after leaving the meeting. He was pleased to learn that Alexander would be personally leading the so- called "mission" tomorrow night. It was the break they had been waiting for. "It can't be this easy."

"I wouldn't exactly call it easy," Sean argued. "We still don't know what the target is."

"He didn't give you any clue at all?"

"No. Just that I'm supposed to meet him tomorrow night at seven o'clock, same place we were at tonight."

Neeley directed his next question to Blake. "What about the other two men he handpicked to accompany him on this little escapade?"

Blake shrugged. "I've seen them at a few meetings before but I don't know who they are."

"I'm surprised he didn't volunteer you," Sean told him.

"I get the feeling he doesn't trust me after what happened the other night. Besides, I don't think I have the stomach for it."

All three men fell silent, interrupted a few moments later by a suggestion from Sean. "Why don't you just arrest him when he shows up tomorrow night? Being in possession of all those weapons must constitute the breaking of some law."

"That's a fine idea in theory," Neeley told him, "but he's probably already moved them to another location. And unless we catch him with weapons in hand, there's little chance of getting a conviction that will stick. I'm afraid our only hope is to find out what the intended target is for tomorrow night and then be there waiting for him when he shows up."

"I can find out," Blake said, surprising even himself by the boldness of his proposal. "I can follow them."

"That's out of the question."

Blake turned on Neeley. "Do you have a better idea?"

"Nope," Neeley admitted with a grin. "So I'll just have to join you."

CHAPTER THIRTY-THREE

END OF THE ROAD

Niagara Falls, New York

Carter looked on with concern as Amber aimlessly pushed the food around on her plate. They had been served their meal over twenty minutes ago but he had yet to see her take a single bite.

Ever since learning of Isaac Jameson's plans to call in the loan on their house two days ago, her mood had been on a downward spiral. He had been hoping that a nice lunch in the hotel dining room followed by a day of sight-seeing at the falls might help to lift her spirits, but it seems he had been wrong.

"You really should eat something," he urged, for all the good he knew it would do.

Amber let her fork clatter to the plate. "I'm just not hungry." She stared at him imploringly across the table. "Do you mind if we just go back to the room? I don't feel much like sight-seeing today."

"If that's what you want."

Carter escorted her from the hotel dining room into the lobby, making a stop at the front desk on their way to the elevator. "Buchanan, room two thirty-two."

"Two thirty-two...." The clerk turned to the wall of small cubbyholes behind him. "Ah, yes, Mr. Buchanan." He plucked an envelope from the box that corresponded to their room number. "This telegram arrived for you a short while ago, sir."

"Thank you." Carter stepped down to the end of the counter, slipping a finger beneath the flap of the envelope to break the seal.

Amber rested her head against his shoulder, watching as he read its contents. "Who's it from?"

"Your uncle."

Amber forgot all about her own misery at the thought of trouble back home. "Is something wrong?"

Carter found just the opposite to be true. "They've paid off our loan."

"What?" Amber grabbed the telegram from him, wanting to read it for herself. "Carter...that must be every cent they have. We can't let them do it."

"They've already done it. Besides, do you want to be the one to tell your aunt no?"

Amber failed to see the humor in his attempt to lighten her mood.

Carter took her by the shoulders. "We'll pay them back every cent, with interest if you like. I promise."

Amber seemed satisfied with that and even managed to coax forth a smile. It was promptly followed by a sudden burst of laughter, drawing curious stares from several of the lobby's other patrons, as well as from Carter. "What's so funny?" he wondered.

"I was just thinking about how much I would have loved to have seen the look on Jameson's face when Uncle Josiah marched in and paid off the loan."

Carter smiled down at her. "And I was just thinking about how wonderful it is to see a smile back on your face."

He took her hand and slipped it through his arm. "Shall we go and enjoy the rest of our honeymoon, Mrs. Buchanan?"

"Only if we can start in the dining room," she requested. "I'm starving."

* * * * *

Baltimore

Sean looked up from his plate to find Hannah staring at him from across the kitchen table. He took a self-conscious swipe at his mouth. "Do I have something on my face?"

Hannah smiled back at him. "No."

Sean returned to his meal but remained curious about her odd behavior. "You've been awful quiet all day. Are you feeling all right?"

"Fine," she assured him.

Sean watched as Mrs. Morgan disappeared into the pantry. Now that they were alone, maybe Hannah would feel more comfortable opening up to him about what was bothering her. He began with the obvious. "Are you worried about tonight?"

Hannah's smile became even more pronounced. "Not at all."

"Well, is there something you want to talk to me about?"

Hannah couldn't deny that there was, but she didn't feel that now was the right time to tell him about the baby. He needed his head to be clear tonight, free of distractions. "We'll talk when you get back."

"Are you sure? I have a few minutes."

"I'm sure."

"All right." Sean rose and leaned across the table to kiss her good-bye. "I'll see you later."

Mrs. Morgan stepped out of the pantry after Sean had left and slipped up behind Hannah's chair. Her hands came to rest on the younger woman's shoulders. "Sooner or later you're going to have to tell that young man that he's going to be a father."

"I will, Mrs. Morgan," Hannah assured her. "Just as soon as he gets home tonight."

* * * * *

Blake shifted on the balls of his feet, eliciting an uncomfortable groan in the process.

Neeley shot him a look of concern. "Are you all right?"

"Yeah. My foot just went to sleep."

The two men had taken up position in the wooded area across the road from the barn almost an hour ago but there was still no sign of Alexander. Either he was running late, or they had all been led on a wild goose chase. Neeley was beginning to suspect the latter.

Blake was thinking the same. "It's way past seven. How long are we going to—"

Neeley silenced him with an upraised hand as two men walked out of the woods not thirty feet from where they were and began approaching the barn. "Do you recognize either of them?" he whispered.

Blake strained to see through the quickly descending darkness. "The tall one is Alexander...but I don't recognize the other man."

Neeley took a firm grip on the handle of his revolver when only Alexander entered the barn, leaving the unidentified individual waiting outside. "Something doesn't feel right."

* * * * *

Sean was beginning to think that no one was going to show when he heard the barn door creak open behind him. He was surprised to see Alexander walk in alone. "Where are the others?"

"They won't be joining us." Alexander approached him, grinning as if he had a secret that he had no intention of sharing. "But don't worry. For what I have planned tonight I don't need an army. You'll do just fine, Donavan." His grin turned into a menacing scowl. "Or should I say…Donnelly."

Sean took a startled step backwards as Alexander pulled a gun. "Did you really think you were going to get away with it?"

Sean swallowed nervously. "Get away with what?"

"I believe you're acquainted with my associate." Alexander directed his attention back to the door.

Sean knees almost gave way beneath him as Liam O'Brien stepped in. "Hello again, lad." The Irishman's deep brogue was steeped in hatred. "Are ya surprised ta see me?"

Surprised is understatement, Sean thought to himself. The last time he had seen Liam O'Brien he was being handcuffed and shoved into the back of a prison wagon in Philadelphia. What was he doing in Baltimore?

Alexander yanked the watch from his vest pocket, flipping open the cover. "I hate to break up a happy reunion, gentlemen, but I have a schedule to keep." He handed O'Brien his gun. "Take him out back. Make sure you bury him deep."

O'Brien tucked the gun in the waistband of his trousers, leering at Sean like a cat about to devour a mouse. "It will be me pleasure."

Sean didn't struggle as O'Brien roughly took hold of his arm and shoved him in the direction of the small door at the back of the barn. He was too stunned to do anything but ponder his impending fate. They were going to kill him. And what of Neeley and Blake? Were they already dead?

O'Brien gave him a final shove through the door, sending him sprawling to the ground. "It's pay back time, Donnelly."

Sean rolled over onto his back, finding himself once again staring up at the barrel of a gun. *Father,* he prayed, *please take care of Hannah and the baby.*

O'Brien sneered down at him, bringing the gun to bear on his head. "Say good-bye...."

Sean calmly closed his eyes, bracing himself for the anticipated burst of pain...but it never came.

"Did you see that? I actually did it."

Sean opened his eyes to find Blake standing over O'Brien's unconscious form, still holding the tree branch that he had used to whack him upside the head. "Blake...." Sean's shoulders slumped in relief. "I thought for a second I was—"

The sound of a shot from inside the barn brought their revelry to a premature end. Sean scrambled up to his feet, fearing the worst. "Neeley...."

"Did someone call my name?" Neeley appeared in the doorway with a disgruntled looking Alexander in tow.

Sean smiled at the scene before him, expressing relief enough for he and Blake both. "Thank God you're all right."

"I'm fine." Neeley took note of O'Brien's motionless form on the ground. "But that's more than I can say for him. Did you do that, Harris?"

"Yes, sir."

"We might make a Pinkerton agent out of you yet."

Blake beamed at the compliment. "Thank you, sir."

Neeley tossed him a length of rope. "Tie him up. And as for you...." He turned back to Alexander.

"You don't have anything on me," Alexander snarled at him.

"Conspiracy to murder one Sean Donnelly, and that's just for starters." Neeley shoved him back into the barn. "Let's go, fancy pants."

Sean stepped over beside Blake, watching as the young man secured O'Brien's hands behind his back. A myriad of emotions welled up inside him, thankfulness being chief among them. "You saved my life, Blake. I don't know how I can ever repay you."

Blake rose to his feet, humbled by the unwarranted praise. "You don't owe me anything. There's no debt between friends."

* * * * *

Sean stood as Mrs. Morgan entered the sitting room carrying a tray with four steaming cups of coffee. He assisted her in placing it on the table in front of the sofa where he had been sitting with Hannah and Blake. "I'm sorry that I've no champagne for your celebration," she apologized, "but I'll allow nothing stronger than rubbing alcohol in this house."

"No apologies necessary, ma'am," Neeley assured her. "I'm not much one for spirits anyway." He leaned forward and picked up one of the cups, raising it in a mock salute to Sean and Blake. "Here's to a job well done, gentlemen."

"Amen to that," Hannah chimed in.

Sean retook his seat beside her on the sofa, directing his thoughts in Neeley's direction. "What I still don't understand is how O'Brien got out of prison."

Neeley relaxed back in his chair, taking a sip of his coffee. "Well, from what I've heard through the grapevine, O'Brien lured one of his guards into his cell by pretending to be ill. He then killed him, changed into his uniform and walked out a free man."

"But how did he know that Sean was in Baltimore?" Hannah asked.

"That remains a mystery."

"And so does what Alexander was planning to do with all those guns," Sean added. "We may never know that now. But at least they're off the streets." A thorough search of the barn following Alexander's arrest had uncovered the stash of weapons hidden beneath some loose floorboards. "That's one less headache that Pinkerton will have to deal with."

Neeley once again raised his cup. "I'll drink to that."

Mrs. Morgan bustled back into the room to answer a sudden knock at the front door. "May I help you?" she asked cordially of the gentlemen on the stoop.

"I'm here to see my son."

Blake shot to his feet, craning his head for a clear view of the individual at the door. "Father?"

Edward Harris stepped inside, removing the hat perched on his head. "Hello, Blake."

Mrs. Morgan closed the door behind him. "May I offer you a cup of coffee, Mr. Harris?"

"No, thank you, ma'am." His gaze returned to his son. "Is there someplace we can talk?"

Blake led the way upstairs to his room, conscious with every step of his father's presence only a few feet behind him. He remembered all too well the emotional chasm between them when they had parted ways several days ago and couldn't fathom what his father was doing here now.

Blake offered him a chair as soon as they entered the room but chose to remain standing. An awkward silence settled in almost immediately.

The elder man made the first attempt to break it, but for all his effort, he couldn't bring himself to look his son in the eye. "How have you been?"

"Fine, sir. And yourself?"

Edward Harris swallowed uncomfortably. "Just fine."

Blake stared hard at his father, unsure what to make of his strange behavior. Wasn't this the same man who had ordered him out of the house just two days ago? And yet here he was acting as if all of the emotional fences between them had been mended.

"Your mother...." Edward Harris paused a moment to clear his throat. "She misses you."

"And I, her," Blake assured him. "Father, what's going on? Two days ago you could hardly stand the sight of me. What are you doing here?"

Edward Harris focused his gaze on his clasped hands. "I heard about what you did tonight."

Blake was stunned. He opened his mouth to ask "how" but his voice failed him.

"I've been wrong about you, son," the elder man confessed, swallowing around the guilt induced lump in his throat. "I've been wrong about a lot of things...including Doreen."

Blake backed up and sat down at the end of his bed, no longer trusting his legs to support him. These were words that he had never expected to hear fall from his father's lips. And he wasn't through yet.

"I'm sorry for the way I've treated you." Edward Harris managed with great difficulty to finally look his son in the eye. His own were now moist with tears. "I'm proud of you, son."

Blake broke down as he recalled the promise he had made to one day make his father proud of him. He no longer had to wonder if that day would ever come.

Edward Harris rose and began walking towards his son, narrowing the emotional chasm between them with each step. "I love you, Blake," he said with great emotion as he came to a stop in front of him. "I always have."

Blake rose to stand before his father as tears began streaming down his face. "I love you, too, sir."

Edward Harris smiled as he quickly gathered the young man into his arms. "Welcome home, son. Welcome home."

* * * * *

Hannah laid her brush on the nightstand and turned towards the bed where Sean was already settled in for the night. "Isn't it wonderful about Blake and his father?"

"Yeah," Sean agreed. "He's been through so much. It's good to see a smile on his face for a change."

"And do you know what he told me?" Hannah's voice rose with her excitement. "He's going to Philadelphia next week to see Doreen. Oh, I hope things work out between them."

"Me, too."

Hannah slipped off her robe and crawled in beside him, relaxing into the crook of his arm. "So what now, Mr. Donnelly? You've done everything that Pinkerton asked of you and then some. Any immediate plans?"

Sean hadn't given much thought to their plans beyond that night but realized that it was time he did so. After he testified, there was nothing preventing them from boarding a train back to Chicago or anywhere else they might choose to go. And yet something was telling him that God wasn't finished with him in Baltimore.

"It wasn't a trick question?" Hannah teased, confused by his lengthy silence.

Sean tilted his head so they were looking eye to eye. "What would you think about staying here in Baltimore?"

Hannah was a little surprised that he would make such a suggestion knowing how much he missed his family in Chicago, but her heart was open. "If that's what you want."

Sean turned onto his side, propping himself up on his elbow. "I want to know what you want."

Hannah reached out and placed a finger in the middle of his chest. "I want to be with you. And whether that's in Baltimore, or Chicago, or Timbuktu, so be it."

Sean smiled. "I guess that settles it, then. Baltimore, it is." He dropped a kiss onto her forehead and then rolled onto his back, settling in to sleep.

Hannah joined him but found herself unable to relax. There was one final matter that needed to be addressed. "Sean...? Do you remember before you left tonight when you asked me if there was something I wanted to talk to you about?"

"Yeah."

"Well, there was. Or rather, there is."

Sean slid a hand beneath the covers and placed it over her belly. "You mean about the baby?"

Hannah sat up, turning around to face him. "You already know?"

"Yeah. I can't explain it but somehow I do."

Hannah smiled as she recalled her own moment of revelation the other night. There could be only one explanation that she knew of. *With God all things are possible.*

* * * * *

Baxter, Pennsylvania

Alec stepped out onto the back porch, easing the screen door shut behind him. He stood for a moment watching Kathleen as she sat gazing up at the brilliant array of stars that dotted the clear night sky. "Can't sleep?"

Kathleen turned at his approach. "It's the heat. I can't remember a September this hot."

"It is that." Alec sat down beside her on the steps. "Maybe we should take the kids swimming tomorrow."

All but Eric, Kathleen thought. She laid her head against Alec's shoulder, returning her gaze to the sky. "Where do you suppose he is right now?"

Alec slipped an arm around her waist. "Probably New York. Gazing up at the same stars we are."

Kathleen lifted her head, turning to face him. "When you put it that way he doesn't seem so far away."

Alec smiled as he laid the palm of his hand over her heart. "He's not."

EPILOGUE

New York City
Eric's Journal

September 17, 1860

 I have decided to heed my sister Kirsten's suggestion to keep a detailed accounting of my travels, but even though I left home two days ago, I feel in a sense that my journey really began today when I stepped off the train in New York. Never before has the growing threat of war been so tangible. In a town the size of Baxter it is easy to overlook such signs, but here they are as numerous as the stars in the night sky— on the front page of every paper, on the lips of every politician and in the eyes of every passerby.

 Tomorrow I will board another train and begin the next leg of my journey. Should any or all of the Southern states decide to sever their ties from the union in the coming months, I shall find myself at the very heart of the conflict. Were it not for my unwavering faith in the sovereignty of Almighty God there would be much to fear. But I know whom I have believed, and am persuaded that He is able to keep that which I have committed unto Him against that day.

Printed in the United States
200031BV00003B/286-321/A